She's the bad boy's bait... whether she likes it or not.

RAVEN
Kindred Book One

SCARLETT FINN

Copyright © 2016, 2022 Scarlett Finn
Published by Moriona Press 2016, 2022

All rights reserved.

The moral right of the author has been asserted.

First published in 2016

No part of this book may be reproduced in any form or by an electronic or mechanical means, including information storage and retrieval systems, without permission in writing from the publisher, except by a reviewer who may quote brief passages in a review. It may not be used to train AI software or for the creation of AI works.

All characters in this publication are fictitious and any resemblance to real persons, living or dead, is purely coincidental.

Original cover by Najla Qamber Designs
www.najlaqamberdesigns.com

ISBN: 9781914517303

www.scarlettfinn.com

Also by Scarlett Finn

NOTHING TO...
NOTHING TO HIDE
NOTHING TO LOSE
NOTHING IN BETWEEN: ONE
NOTHING TO DECLARE
NOTHING TO US
NOTHING IN BETWEEN: TWO
NOTHING TO SAY
NOTHING TO GAIN
NOTHING IN BETWEEN: THREE
NOTHING TO YOU
NOTHING TO THIS PREQUEL: ONE WILD NIGHT
NOTHING TO THIS
NOTHING IN BETWEEN: FOUR
NOTHING TO DO
NOTHING TO FEAR
NOTHING IN BETWEEN: FIVE
NOTHING TO DENY

GO NOVELS
GO WITH IT
GO IT ALONE
GO ALL OUT
GO ALL IN
GO FULL CIRCLE

EXILE
HIDE & SEEK
KISS CHASE

WRECK & RUIN
RUIN ME
RUIN HIM

THE BRANDED SERIES
BRANDED
SCARRED
MARKED

FORBIDDEN PREQUEL DUET
ALL. ONLY.
ONLY YOURS

THE FORBIDDEN NOVELS
FORBIDDEN DESIRE
FORBIDDEN WANT
FORBIDDEN WISH
FORBIDDEN NEED
FORBIDDEN BOND

TO DIE FOR...
TO DIE FOR TRUTH
TO DIE FOR HONOR
TO DIE FOR VIRTUE
TO DIE FOR DUTY
TO DIE FOR LOVE

LOVE AGAINST THE ODDS STANDALONE COLLECTION
SWEET SEAS
HEIR'S AFFAIR
RESCUED
MAESTRO'S MUSE
GETTING TRICKY
THIRTEEN
REMEMBER WHEN...
RELUCTANT SUSPICION
XY FACTOR

KINDRED SERIES
RAVEN
SWALLOW
CUCKOO
SWIFT
FALCON
FINCH

THE EXPLICIT SERIES
EXPLICIT INSTRUCTION
EXPLICIT DETAIL
EXPLICIT MEMORY

MISTAKE DUET
MISTAKE ME NOT
SLEIGHT MISTAKE

RISQUÉ & HARROW INTERTWINED
TAKE A RISK
FIGHTING FATE
RISK IT ALL
FIGHTING BACK
GAME OF RISK

LOST & FOUND
LOST
FOUND

ONE

FOR AS LONG AS she could remember, Zara Bandini had been enthralled by the idea of adventure. While other kids wanted to be rock stars and actors, all her childhood games featured Indiana Jones or James Bond. Imagining herself as a Lara Croft type kick-ass hero fighting battles and saving the world took up most of her time.

Those fantasies all came before puberty when innocence was her constant companion. After hitting her teens, her life changed dramatically. At the age of fourteen, she lost her mother to cancer and found herself thrust into the role of 'woman of the house', looking after her father and brother.

Her childish dreams were replaced by a determination to escape her hometown and make it in the big city. Against her father's wishes, she blew out of his farm in a beat-up truck and headed northeast to get herself a college education.

Now, a decade beyond that dramatic day, she had cultivated a routine to remind herself of how far she'd come. Every Friday night Zara went to Purdy's, a corner bar on the same block as her place of employment, Cormack Industries, CI. She sat alone, sipped a glass of dry white wine, and reflected on her achievements.

At first, she'd just been grateful to be free of oppressive

small-town life. College had been an eye-opening experience that made her proud of her independence. After college, she had almost fallen victim to the suck of the shallow corporate world. It would have been so easy to fall into the role of trophy wife or to get haughty about her achievements. Setting this routine of coming to Purdy's was Zara's way of ensuring she didn't take the privilege of her life for granted.

It was after ten p.m. by the time she got to Purdy's on that particular Friday night. Zara was exhausted and needed sleep, but she would never flout tradition and miss an appointment with herself. In the warm interior of Purdy's, she enjoyed the solid mahogany of the stocked bar and the gold pinstripe of the wallpaper that glowed under muted lighting.

Catering to an affluent clientele, Purdy's held single malts and champagne to fulfill the expensive tastes of those who frequented it. It was a far cry from her father's smoke filled kitchen where a layer of grease covered everything.

After seating herself on a brown leather stool, the bartender brought over her usual drink. She sipped the cool liquid and exhaled.

"That's some glass of wine."

Turning to her left, Zara saw a striking blond man come up beside her. One of the reasons she loved this bar was its patrons. In the center of the city's business district, this classy joint was overflowing with rich, influential people and the wannabes who listed "networking" as a hobby on their resumes.

Designer suits and smiling faces charmed each other until hands were shaken and deals made. This was a place for the elite to gather and praise each other for being so filthy rich and successful. Given where she'd come from, there were often times she fazed out of the moment, edges became blurred, until everything seemed dream-like.

For her, the meaning of success had morphed through the years and frivolous adventure was long forgotten. The most effective way she could make a positive difference in the world was through careful use of her position as Premium Personnel Coordinator to Grant McCormack, CEO of Cormack Industries.

The clean-shaven man beside her flashed a row of straight white teeth that gleamed almost as much as his shirt under his tailored gray blazer that matched his slacks. All the men she interacted with on a daily basis were assured and this guy's arrogance was proven when he took up occupancy on the stool next to hers and leaned in close.

"Can I get you another glass?" he asked.

"I just started this one," she said, taking another sip of wine while not allowing herself to smile. When dealing with intelligent men who usually enjoyed a puzzle, she'd learned it was best not to give too much away about her own mood. "Did I ask you to sit down?"

"No need," he said, undeterred, his smirk remained in situ. "It's a public bar, anyone can sit anywhere."

Leaving him guessing, she didn't give any physical hint of her interest. "And you chose the stool right next to mine?" she asked. The establishment was busy, but there were a half a dozen free stools at the bar, so he didn't have to choose the seat right next to hers. "Didn't your mother teach you manners? It's polite to be invited to join a person."

His confidence remained in place, and he twisted his body to face hers, trapping her crossed legs between him and the bar. The flirtation in his countenance matched his positioning and his gaze danced over her figure. "Women like a man to take charge."

"Do they?" she asked, keeping her expression loose as she examined the bottles displayed behind the bar. Remaining aloof didn't mean she didn't notice how impeccable he was and how good his expensive cologne smelled. It wasn't too overpowering and merged with the scent of the hair gel that kept his locks in check. But she had to portray herself as a challenge, to match his confidence with sass if she wanted to intrigue him.

"Yes," he said. "Women want an alpha, a guy who is strong enough to look out for her."

This conversation was going to happen whether she coveted it or not, so she rotated to accept him into her company. "To look out for her?" she asked, dragging her fingertips over the bulge of her glass to settle them on the rim.

"Why is that? In case of wolf attacks?"

Observing her body, her expression, and her glass, he was taking in all the details and his interest wasn't platonic or professional. "Forward of you to ask me to go camping with you, but I'm game if you are."

Dreams of travel and adventure had been put on the back burner so many times that she had given up all realistic hope of achieving either in deference to living a responsible life, but she could play along.

Tensing her cheeks, she teased a vague smile and relaxed into wry indifference to test his acuity. "A guy who can pick up and leave at a moment's notice," she said. "I sense a red flag."

He wasn't discouraged, being quick-witted was definitely a point in his favor as far as she was concerned. "Do you now?"

Raising her hand higher until only the very tip of her finger remained on the top edge of her glass, she drew a short crescent around it. "That tells me you have no responsibilities."

"None that would override a weekend away with a beautiful woman like you."

His grin came closer, and his upper arm brushed hers. Mischief lit his eyes, tapering them, yet they remained aware. A guy like this with charm and looks could take his pick. It could be perceived as an insult or a compliment that he'd chosen her and that he thought such cheesy lines might work to woo her.

Maybe he thought she looked easy or maybe he thought she was the top prize in the room, though that was unlikely given she was still wearing the black suit dress she'd had on at the office all day. Her makeup was faded, and her hair was beginning to escape the confines of her chignon. Being only five feet seven inches tall, she wasn't as leggy as some of the other trophies surrounding them.

Betraying that he was a physical guy by his need to get close, she chose not to relent to his advances just yet. "And where would we go on this impulsive getaway?" she asked.

With a short shrug, he watched her lips move as she

spoke. "Anywhere you wanted. Manaus?"

Taken aback by such an unusual response, Zara tried to maintain her poise, but didn't like to reveal how untraveled she was. Exuding sophistication and eloquence were her ways of hiding the truth of her origins. A direct question like this could compromise her camouflage. "I don't even know where that is."

"A city on the Amazon."

Insecurities retreated to be replaced by a smile because there was little chance of that location being the first on her list of travel destinations. "Bugs and snakes? You know how to sweep a girl off her feet. Are you just hoping to get the chance to suck the poison from a snake bite?"

"If there was a chance of sucking, I know where I'd like to get bit."

That sort of brazenness was very uncharacteristic of his type, and she had to work to stop herself from releasing a reflexive laugh. The smart suit and dashing smirk were an excellent disguise. She drew back. There was more to this guy than there was to the usual conservative yuppies who would hit on her at Purdy's. That type didn't tempt her, she preferred her men to be more casual, rawer. It was possible this guy fit that bill.

"Your mother would be ashamed of that mouth," she said, feeling the first curl of instinctive attraction in her diaphragm.

As though he'd sensed her budding intrigue, he pushed the boundary of what was proper and leaned in until he was almost against her. "A man needs to know that his woman is strong too," he said.

She needed a minute to get herself together. Taking a mouthful of her wine, Zara hid her smile. A man who was this bold and authentic touched her primitive desires. Being on the periphery of luxury, the men who usually made a move on her were polished to the point of garish. Finding a guy who had any sort of a rough edge was unheard of, even guys who came from modest roots tried to hide any natural coarseness.

Returning her glass to the bar, she turned into his semi-embrace and translated for him. "You want a woman who isn't easily offended?"

"A woman who isn't too squeamish."

"Or too hard to please?"

Slowing their banter, his shrewd expression tantalized her. "Oh, I'm happy to take the time to please my woman," he said, reducing his voice to a purr and again watching her lips as she talked.

"Are you?" she asked. Knowing how a man liked the chase, she returned to her wine and after finishing it, she rested a hand on his forearm.

"You're a man who knows what he wants."

"Yes, I am," he said, taking his time over each word.

"I wish you luck in finding it."

Twisting on her stool, she had to brush her legs across his to get onto her feet. Testing the strength of his interest in her, she reached back to snag her purse from the bar, locking her gaze onto his. He might stop her. He might let her go. The answer came when his hand landed on the padded backrest of her stool, blocking her exit.

"Why do you come in here every week?" he murmured.

Zara had expected him to provoke her with a joke, in an attempt to keep her here and fire her curiosity. The revelation that he knew her habits made her frown and the excitement of this encounter faded. She couldn't remember seeing this man ever before and he was attractive enough that she would have remembered if Grant had dealings with him in CI.

Conscious of what his question could imply, her mouth dried, and the prospect of being stalked flitted into her mind. "How do you—"

His broad smile indicated that he wasn't concerned with the possibility of scaring her. But Zara wasn't going to let his easy manner mollify her. Any future partner would have to be strong and assured, but she wouldn't be taken advantage of or marginalized. Standing up to her father and brother had taught her a lot about fighting to maintain her identity.

Zara cleared her expression and held herself rigid until she got an explanation for his disturbing comment. "I asked the bartender about you after I noticed you a couple of weeks ago."

Caught off-guard by this reply, her façade of indifference slipped. "You noticed me two weeks ago?" she asked, and his humble shrug endeared her.

His confidence had gotten him over here and had piqued her interest, now she sensed a depth beneath it. That he had spotted her was flattering and it amazed her how a man who epitomized everything she would ask for in a fantasy partner had picked her out of a crowd.

"I've been psyching myself up," he said. "And I wanted to check if I had competition. No boyfriend, right?"

The boyish hope gleaming through his features made her smile. "No boyfriend," she confirmed, relaxing, though her purse remained in both hands against her chest.

His brows came up and she read swagger in his teasing. "Fuck buddies?"

Squinting, she returned to their previous game. "Is that your way of asking if I'm a slut?"

"Let me lay it out for you. I travel a lot for business and don't have time for your usual sort of prolonged courtship. So when I see a girl that I want I like to get the contracts signed up front."

Backing up into her stool, she put her purse back on the bar and awaited an explanation. "I'm not even sure what that means."

His hand left the bar and he spread his fingers around her knee. "It means I don't mess around with games. I make my intentions clear."

"What are your intentions?"

Beckoning over the bartender, he ordered drinks for both of them. "This is where I'm starting," he said, pushing her wine glass toward her. "I'm Timothy Sutcliffe, and if you want me to leave you alone say so now or forever hold your peace."

Zara didn't usually pick up guys in bars after work, but there was just enough intrigue around this one to keep her in her stool. Wrapping her fingers around the stem of the glass, she brought it up to her lips in a signal of acceptance.

***

THREE GLASSES OF WINE later, they left the bar at closing time, which was later than she'd been out for anything other than work in a long time. Although she'd been at Cormack Industries before seven a.m. that morning, her conversation with Timothy had been worth forgoing sleep.

Caught in the crush of Purdy's patrons who were all trying to get through the same narrow door, Tim snagged her hand so they wouldn't lose each other. She was surprised to feel how rough his palm was. The last few men she'd dated were metrosexual types who had no qualms about admitting their dependence on the mani-pedi.

Their discussion featured her as the central focus. Tim listened and asked questions, he made jokes and flirted with her. Nothing after he admitted having noticed her a couple of weeks ago was strange or awkward. Talk flowed and he made her laugh. Until she actually relaxed into the current of their conversation and let it sweep her along, she hadn't realized how much she had missed social, romantic contact.

Tim guided her away from the crowd outside the bar, most of whom were waiting for cabs at the taxi stand opposite the door. If they waited their turn for a ride behind the other Purdy's customers, they could be there all night. Her date must have been of a similar mind because he led her down the block to the next street and stopped on the corner.

"I can get you a car," he said. Most of the men who'd picked up women at Purdy's were probably making similar declarations.

Staying close to him, she basked in the fresh autumn air, the susurration of the city streets, and the strength of the hand locked in hers. It was an incredible feeling to relax and just exist in time and space with her new friend.

Acknowledging that she was probably tipsy, her coy veneer was gone, and she didn't mind showing her amusement. "Displays of wealth won't get you into my underwear, Tim."

His shining teeth and glittering blue eyes looked as gleeful as she felt. "Any tips on what will?" he asked.

Twisting herself into his body, she began to walk him

backward into the shadow of the building beside them. When it came to men and sex, she had never been shy, but the alcohol certainly gave her confidence a boost. Urging Tim's substantial form against the concrete, she got her first real feel of what was beneath the expensive fabric of his suit. She was impressed.

Taking hold of his tie in one hand, she slid the other upward. "Strong women turn you on?" she whispered.

"You turn me on, Zara."

"Good," she said. "Just one more thing we have to check."

Pulling on his tie, he put up no opposition when she joined their mouths. Fatigue fled in the face of arousal and intoxication. Although she was the one in front, the strength of his kiss erased any hint that he was a reluctant participant in this exchange.

Reminding herself to unwind and bask in the rush of hormones that had been dormant in her for too long, she was further emboldened when Tim flipped their positions to press her back into the wall. By taking control of the kiss, he had fueled her arousal. Her private fantasies always featured a rough, powerful man who exerted authority over her.

But Zara had no chance to surrender to the moment because an instant later, her companion's mouth left hers and the shelter of his form vanished too. In sync with her eyes opening, she heard the thud of a body hitting the pavement.

Blinking into the empty space Tim had occupied, she dropped her focus to see the man she'd been kissing seconds before sprawled face down on the concrete at her feet. The dry sidewalk was stained with the sticky ooze spilling from a hole in his head. There was no way that the fluid discoloring his hair could be anything except blood.

Her reactive scream was so loud that it echoed through the cavern of this deserted street and even her hands over her mouth didn't muffle it. Alone, she gasped for air, and tried not to shriek again because she had to be smart, to keep her wits about her. Dropping down to her knees, she fumbled for a pulse, but found none. Her heart was beating hard enough for two bodies, but she couldn't share her pulse with Tim's prone form.

He was dead, shot, and with that clarity came the realization that she might not be as alone as she thought. Glancing around for signs of an assailant, she scrambled into the nearby alley and hunkered down behind the dumpster to hunt for her phone in her bag.

She had never seen a person shot before and certainly never murdered. Tears blurred her vision and keeping her head was difficult. Panic, screaming, and wailing wouldn't bring Tim back and her survival instinct seemed to suck the alcohol and exhaustion from her system.

Replaying their walk from Purdy's, Zara tried to visualize any possible attackers. She couldn't remember seeing another soul, but that knowledge didn't reassure her. While standing on the sidewalk before Tim was killed, Zara would've said that they were by themselves. Given that she'd been wrong then, there was a good chance she was wrong now. The murderer could be closing in on her.

Phoning the police, she begged them to hurry because she was too scared to venture out into the open until they arrived. She was given assurances that they would be quick, but it wouldn't be quick enough. Hoping she'd be safe if she just stayed hidden, Zara remained where she was, alone and crouched, until the cavalry arrived.

***

"AND YOU'D NEVER seen him before?"

Zara had already answered all Officer Kraft's questions. The whole area was roped off and the scene was swarming with cops and other relevant professionals. Timothy was dead and there wasn't any amount of talking that would change that.

Her thoughts were meandering around in her mind in their own haunted bubbles. Floating and sinking, they tried to arrange themselves in some sort of order that made sense. But she was struggling to remember what she'd said a few seconds ago, so it was unlikely she'd be able to remember the course of the night with any kind of clarity, certainly not while her fatigue was making it harder to think.

"No, he approached me at Purdy's," she said, and her head moved in a haphazard shake. "We talked and when the bar closed, he walked me down here. We were just standing here. We kissed and then, boom, he was gone."

The cop's lip twitched. "You were very lucky. This professional had his target in sight. You could easily have been hurt."

"A professional?" she asked, letting her gaze fall to Tim's sheet covered form.

While hiding in the alley she had been in fear for her life. But it hadn't occurred to her that this was any kind of professional hit. Her fear had been for a mugger, an opportunistic robber who had seen them on the corner and hoped to steal himself a few bucks after eliminating Tim who might have been a threat to the criminal's safety.

If it was a professional job, then Tim was something more than he'd portrayed himself as. She could've been caught in the crossfire, been collateral damage in a battle she hadn't even known was going on. Considering this made some of her melancholy give way to anger and confusion. Those emotions were easier to get a handle on than grief.

"You're certain you didn't hear anything?" the detective asked. "Or see anything?"

"No," she said, still languishing in the near miss and the idea that she could have lost her life tonight. In a single instant, she could've been snuffed out and suddenly her work at CI didn't seem quite so significant. "I didn't see anything. There was no one on the street. Aren't there security cameras on any of the buildings around here?"

CI was on the perpendicular street. It was a couple of blocks over, too far away to reveal anything about this crime, which frustrated her because it was the only video footage she'd have direct access to or the authority to release to the cops.

"We'll be checking that out, Miss Bandini. Would you like an officer to take you home?"

Snapping out of her semi-daze, she made eye contact with the detective. "Are we finished?"

"Yes, we're finished," Kraft said and retrieved a card from his breast pocket to hand her. "If you think of anything else…"

"I'll call you," Zara said, snatching the business card and slipping it into the front of her purse.

Glad to be dismissed, Zara was escorted away from the scene and past the barricades. She refused the offer of a ride from the cops and instead hailed a passing cab. Shock was still vibrating through her, so it took her a couple of tries to give the driver her address. When they were on the way, she relaxed and told herself that the safety of her apartment and her uneventful life was just one car ride away and that when she got there everything would go back to normal.

TWO

ZARA'S FOURTH FLOOR APARTMENT had beautiful arched windows with wide window seats. On purchasing the place, she'd had visions of sitting in them to read her fiction books. It hadn't worked out that way. Most of her time at home was spent holed up in the second bedroom turned office, rather than in the fifty-foot-long studio space of her living room, kitchen, and dining area with its twelve-foot columns holding up the ceiling.

Working for Grant McCormack might take up all her time and eat into her social life, but it paid well, as her apartment evidenced. Though no amount of money or space could comfort Zara after what she'd gone through with Tim and the police tonight.

Without turning on any lights, she dragged her exhausted body into her bedroom. Looping the strap of her purse up over her head, she removed it from across her body and laid it on the end of the bed, before slipping her feet out of her shoes.

She would give anything to discover a twenty-four-hour pedicure service that would come to her home in the middle of the night. She doubted she would sleep much, despite her tiredness, and her feet could use the relief.

There was no requirement for her to be at CI this weekend because Grant was in New York. But that didn't mean she wouldn't be going into work tomorrow. There was plenty to do even when the boss was out of town. Life would carry on as normal, giving her no time to stop and think about Tim and his demise, which would probably be a blessing. She was trying to convince herself that she could slip into her professional skin, adopt her office persona, and that somehow that would save her from reality.

A man she had been attracted to and known for such a short period was dead in a possible professional hit. At times like this, she regretted not spending more time cultivating friendships. CI was her shield. She didn't have to think about her horrible relationship with her father when she was there. Didn't have to spend time on romances that never went anywhere. She could just sit at her desk and work. At CI she was useful, and she loved to feel useful, it made her feel important.

After watching Tim die, she didn't feel useful or important. She could use a strong shoulder to cry on tonight, one that might hold her close and promise to protect her from the evils of the world. But men didn't like how outspoken she could be, and women seemed to be threatened by her independence. Zara had gotten where she was through hard work and dedication to her goal. No one handed her anything for free and she was proud of her ability to fight through adversity.

Trying to quiet her thoughts, because she knew they wouldn't help her sleep, she unzipped her dress and hung it in a dry-cleaning bag. Going through the motions, she propped her foot on the bed to unroll her stocking.

"Leave them on."

The bassy male voice came from the corner of her bedroom and it made her leap back onto her feet in time to see her floor lamp switch on. The identity of the speaker remained a mystery because whoever this intruder was, he had angled the light toward his legs so that his face was shrouded in shadow. He wore black cargo pants, and one boot was resting on its side on his opposite knee showing how relaxed this stranger was in her home.

The sight made her gasp in for a scream, but her throat gave out under the strain. Her body had no doubt lost its ability to produce hormones. After the night she'd had her well of anxiety was bone dry and she floundered in her attempts to identify how to react to this development. Her river of panic had evaporated and her nerve-endings fizzled to a smoldering, smoking death leaving her unable to conjure anger.

He spoke before she'd had a chance to make sense of anything. "The phone is disconnected, and by my calculations there isn't enough juice left in your cellphone for a second emergency call tonight," he said with ease, like a man here for leisure and not harassment.

Twitchy and bewildered, she struggled to cope with a new injection of concentrated adrenaline. "Who are you? What are you doing in my home?" Zara demanded, trying her best to sound authoritative, which was tough for a woman wearing only her underwear. In the name of modesty, she backed up to retrieve her kimono from the hook on the door and pulled it on before edging in the direction of her nightstand where she knew there was a weapon.

"Don't bother," he said, sounding more fed up than concerned. "The only thing left in there is your vibrator, and I'm not afraid of that. But feel free to use it yourself if you need the stress relief."

Ceasing her journey, she wasn't sure how to act and had no idea if he was armed or intended to harm her. But he'd obviously removed the knife she kept in her drawer for protection, meaning she was defenseless.

"Who are you?" she asked again. Unsure if she should be terrified or start looking for a candid camera, Zara was having the most surreal night of her life bar none. The fatigue caused by these adrenaline spikes made her space out a bit.

"That doesn't matter," he said.

Indignation overtook her confusion and starched her spine. It was bad enough that he'd taken the liberty of letting himself into her house and into her bedroom. Now he was telling her what mattered and what didn't. Her father was a bully, her brother too, so she knew what it was to be pushed around. As a grown woman, she didn't have to tolerate that kind of behavior.

"It matters to me," she asserted, finding her grounding in outrage. "How dare you come in here like this! I can plug in my cell and call the cops, you know? So if I was you, I'd get out of here now!"

Her threat didn't concern him and neither did her tantrum because his tone remained unchanged. "I'm much faster than you, Ms. Bandini," he exhaled in more of a growl. "You're gonna listen to me. If you don't, I'll take extreme measures and you really don't want me to do that. I'm supposed to protect you. I'd hate to have to mess you up just to make you behave."

Calling the cops for a second time tonight wasn't on her agenda, and it was obvious that this person could hurt her before she got near her charger. Either he'd kill her or he'd bolt, and the cops couldn't do anything about a phantom who left no trace of himself. Rolling with it, Zara hoped listening to him might get her answers or would at least get him out of here faster.

"Protect me from what?" she asked.

"Many of your dates end up dead at the end of the evening?"

Somehow finding out that the events were related rather than this being the mother of all coincidences reassured her. Statistics would suggest that two such bizarre events occurring on the same night were astronomical. She didn't want to face the possibility that she was having some sort of aneurysm and this was all a psychotic delusion.

"How do you know about that?" she asked, tightening the belt on her robe, which just grazed the top of her thighs.

"I know everything about you, Zara. And you're gonna know everything about me…you just don't know it yet."

His cryptic confidence served to frustrate her and her hold on her patience began to slip. "I don't have a clue who you are. You're trespassing until you identify yourself and I grant you permission to be here, so I ask again: who are you?"

Nothing she said or did seemed to faze him. "I'm not ready to answer that yet," he murmured.

His audacity kept her off kilter. Breaking into women's apartments must be a norm for this guy because there was no urgency to his words. He wasn't at all concerned with her threats about the cops or her assertion that he was going to get in trouble for this infringement. "You're not ready to—"

"I don't trust you, and if you mentioned my name to anyone, there could be trouble for both of us," he said. "You're not ready to hear the full story or prepared to deal with the consequences of our association."

Feeling like she'd walked onto a movie set as opposed to into her own apartment, Zara tried to remain calm. This man in her bedroom was a person, just the same as her, so she chose to treat him like one rather than a threat. Making friends with the hostage taker was the best way to stay alive.

"So if you're not here to hurt me or rob me and you don't want to talk, why are you here?" she asked.

He didn't move. Nothing about what she could see of him suggested he was even talking, but his words were throaty and certain. "I'm here to tell you that you've stepped into the middle of a war. Now that they know who you are, they're gonna try to get to you. Timothy was just the beginning."

"You know why they killed Tim?" she asked, taking a step in his direction. Her hope vanished as clarity slapped her. "Wait, who is they?"

"You're not ready to know that yet either." This person was so frustrating that her hands balled into fists. Screaming at him might provoke him into hurting her and she didn't want that. But she did want to know if Tim would get any justice and who might be interested in her now that she was associated with a murder victim. "What you need to know is that anybody new in your life is a potential threat. Keep your secrets. Reveal nothing."

"Does that include you?" she asked, bothered by his nonchalance.

"Especially me."

Disbelieving any altruistic motive, Zara hoped to get a straight answer as to the motivation for this intrusion. The stranger had broken into her bedroom for a reason, and she didn't like the idea that he, or someone else, might choose to invade her privacy again.

"So you came here to warn me out of the goodness of your heart?" she asked. By being indirect she hoped to provoke him into giving details beyond what she'd get with a closed question.

"No," he said. "I'm a player in the war and I want your trust. You're vital and that makes you vulnerable. I've been watching you and I'm not the only one."

If he wanted to hurt her, he could have done it before she knew he was present. Taking him at his word that he was here to protect her, she softened because if what happened to Tim was anything to go by, she might need an ally. And the truth was, she was too tired to think of a cunning way out of this situation. Asking for help, might encourage him into helping her form a plan. "What do I do? Should I go to the cops or—"

"You do nothing. You carry on with your life as you normally do. Keep note of anything strange or suspicious. If there's any danger, don't play the hero. Stay away from it and don't answer questions."

That was the sum total of his advice? Do nothing. Zara had never been great at sitting on her hands when a task had to be accomplished and after what had happened to Tim, she felt like a sitting duck.

"Why is this so important to you?" she asked. "You said that you want my trust, but why?"

"I'm not the only one. Tim wanted your trust too. He thought fucking you was the way to get it."

He swore with the same ease as he spoke every other word. Kraft's assertion that Tim had been killed by a professional seemed certain now. Embarrassed by her willingness to believe Tim had been genuinely interested in her, she couldn't believe how quickly she'd been drawn in by the man who seemed too good to be true.

All she'd done was go to a bar for a drink, she hadn't asked for any of this. "Tim was involved, how?"

The stranger was great at staying completely still and at ignoring the obvious emotion in her words. He didn't attempt to soothe her, he was aloof, here for a reason, and not interested in deviating from his mission. She might not be concerned for her life at this exact moment, but he would have a hard time winning her trust if he kept up the mysterious veil and refused to answer direct questions.

"You'll figure it all out," he said. "I had to show myself tonight to give you a piece of advice. Don't tell Grant about what happened tonight. He'll be out of town until Monday night and Kraft won't be back in touch. You can keep this quiet if you keep your mouth shut."

She didn't know what she would do about this, but she wasn't wild about him crossing off options from her list. "Why would I do that?"

"It's the only way you'll live through this." It was an answer, a useful one, but she didn't like it.

"How do you know Grant?" she asked.

"That one I can answer," he said, rising to his feet and switching off the lamp. In the darkness, she could make out movement, but the ink of night concealed his features. The musky scent of intoxicating cologne came to her side and the heat of wet breath ruffled her hair. "I'm an old friend of the family."

His form carried on out of the bedroom and she remained perfectly still. Listening to the silence that followed his departure from the bedroom, she strained to hear if he was still in her apartment. It was only when the front door closed that Zara exhaled her tension and ran through the apartment to pounce onto the window seat on her knees.

With her face and palms pressed to the glass, she sought the stranger out. But she didn't see him exit the building, and the street below was empty. Giving up hope of seeing the intruder, she sank down to sit on her heels and reflect on her night.

This afternoon she had been a normal, boring executive assistant. Now she had witnessed a murder and been hijacked in her own bedroom. She could try to hope that she'd experienced all the oddities she ever would, but after what her apparent guardian angel had said, she doubted the veracity of that.

Embracing the abandon of a flirtation with a stranger in a bar was an invigoration that she hadn't experienced for a long time and after how the night had ended, Zara doubted she would be throwing caution to the wind again anytime soon.

Dedicating all her hours to Cormack Industries had meant fast promotion and she was respected in the firm but didn't have any associates who could make sense of this night for her. The stranger in her bedroom had given her advice meant to save her life, and at least for now, she couldn't risk defying it.

THREE

ZARA DIDN'T NEED to worry about telling anyone what had happened on Friday because she didn't see anyone for the rest of the weekend. This wasn't unusual as her life was dedicated to doing a good job and that meant she spent more time with paperwork than with people. Immersing herself in work kept her from thinking too much about Tim or the stranger who'd intruded upon her private space.

Because she felt jumpy alone at home, she'd come into the office knowing she'd be protected in the towering black glass and steel building that was covered by twenty-four-hour security. No one could get to her here. Every time she pressed her fingerprint to one of the glowing pads on each internal door, her paranoia lessened.

The cocoon of modern décor and strict operating procedures gave her a reprieve from watching the walls of her home, which no longer felt safe. So she'd spent her weekend at CI catching up and giving herself a head start for the following week.

Grant McCormack was supposed to return first thing on Monday. Mid-morning she got the call to say that he'd been delayed. When her bedroom stranger commented on Grant's itinerary, she hadn't given it much thought. But his words rushed back to her after Grant's call. The stranger had known before her, and maybe before Grant, that her boss' timetable would change.

That unsettled her further. Being Grant's chief assistant, Zara knew everything there was to know about Grant's professional life. She couldn't figure out how an apparent stranger could've known that Grant would stay in New York later than originally planned. Either Grant had known it too and hadn't clued her in, or the stranger had somehow sabotaged Grant's itinerary to delay him. Neither possibility appealed to her.

But she couldn't ask her boss too many questions, especially not ones that might be personal. They had an informal rapport, but their relationship had always remained professional. Grant McCormack was fair and direct, though he didn't like to have too many people buzzing around him, so Zara—being the most senior—was the only assistant allowed in his office, which gave her sway. But even she wouldn't test the limits of his patience.

Now that she was thinking about it, Grant's behavior over the previous week had been odd. He usually took an assistant with him on business, this time he hadn't. Grant made his own travel plans, which was another first. He reserved the hotel and requested his jet be prepared without any assistant support. She'd thought it was weird, but guessed the trip included some kind of romantic interest, and so didn't ask questions.

While sitting at her desk throughout that Monday the stranger's assertions pounded against the inside of her eardrums. She found herself wondering if Grant could be a part of this war the stranger had referenced. There was something sinister about the whole affair, which made her second-guess her and Grant's inadvertent involvement.

By the time Grant walked onto the executive floor it was after six p.m., and most of the rest of the building had gone home. Coming out of her own office, she greeted her boss with a smile and followed him into his office after he passed her. "I've got a long list of calls for you to return," she said.

His short, clipped hair and tailored suit betrayed the efficient executive that he was. He was only a few years older than she was, yet he was much more accomplished. He came from a privileged family and had the best education money could buy. His etiquette was polished and his manners impeccable. But with all she'd learned recently, she speculated there could be more to him than his genteel exterior suggested.

"Hold on to the business messages," he said, pulling himself in at his desk and opening his laptop. "Did anything come through on the second line?"

That was a shock and a question he'd never asked her before. Already her mind was buzzing with the confusion of the last few days, and he'd just thrown her a curve ball.

Taking her eyes off the stack of notes on her notepad, she paused and was speechless for a couple of seconds. "The...the second line?" she stuttered.

The second phone line was so top secret that she wasn't sure anyone else knew it existed. Grant used the line to contact her, bypassing the gauntlet of hold music and neophyte assistants. Since telling her of its existence, he had never actually brought it up in conversation.

"Yes" he said, logging into the CI network. "You do keep it active?"

Quick to reassure, she nodded. "Always," she said. "But there have been no calls."

"Okay, don't slip," he said, opening up some programs on his computer. "This is important."

She worked so hard for Grant and for CI because she believed he was a good man and that their work in medical and scientific technology was important. The products that CI built helped people and although she was only a small cog in a massive machine, she liked playing her part in a company that eased suffering and contributed to medical breakthroughs.

Crossing to stand opposite him at the desk, Zara tucked her notebook into her palm and attempted to broach the sensitive topic. "Sir, is there something going on that I should be aware of?"

Before the weekend, Zara wouldn't have considered disrupting the status quo. Her normal behavior was to follow instructions, not to pry. But too many things had occurred in such a short space of time for her to consider them coincidences.

"No," he said, disregarding his computer to hunt through his desk drawers. "But if a man named Sutcliffe calls it's important that you take his message carefully and get in touch with me right away. And don't tell anyone about him or repeat anything he says."

Sutcliffe. That was Tim's name. For a second, she forgot to breathe, another coincidence? It was unlikely. Grant had never mentioned that name before, yet here he was talking about Tim three days after she'd watched him die. Much as she didn't like to admit it, it seemed that the stranger in her bedroom was telling the truth. But he'd told her not to tell Grant about what happened to Tim on Friday night and had claimed to be protecting her, so she clammed up.

She and Grant didn't talk about personal matters. It wasn't her natural state to gossip about her private life at work or with her boss. This revelation confirmed that Tim happening upon her in Purdy's was not motivated by attraction and she would be embarrassed to admit she'd been so gullible as to drool over the seemingly perfect man. If she did try to bring up Tim it would no doubt be awkward for her and Grant.

Zara made the split-second decision not to tell Grant about her encounter with Tim in case the bedroom intruder was right about the war. She realized that Grant couldn't know about Tim's murder if he was expecting a phone call from the dead man.

Retreating from her feelings of confusion and shame, Zara chose to rely on their professionalism instead of revealing her own naivety. "We have confidentiality," she said.

That was true. She'd signed an NDA when she started at CI and since that day, she'd followed Grant McCormack with blind loyalty. Given his association with Tim and the bedroom stranger's misgivings, she was beginning to question if her gullibility extended to her conclusions about Grant.

"His name is Albert Sutcliffe," Grant said, shuffling papers in his drawer aside to look beneath them.

So Grant wasn't expecting Tim to call, but an Albert who had to be related to Tim. The surname couldn't be a coincidence. "Sir..." she started, curious about why he was late back from New York. "Was there a problem today?"

Just because she wasn't going to offer information about what she'd gone through, didn't mean she wasn't going to try and extract some information from the CEO. If the trip had been motivated by CI business, then there was no reason he should hide what happened from her.

Taking a stack of documents from his drawer, he squared them on the desk next to his laptop. "Nothing you have to concern yourself with, Zar," he said, glancing over the top sheet.

Now she was on full alert and couldn't deny the truth. Whether the bedroom stranger was right or not, something was definitely going on. Trying to peek at the document Grant was reading, she edged closer. "Was it...? Personal? Maybe family related?"

His distraction dissolved into an acute awareness that made him stop reading to glower up at her. She quickly stepped back to hide her attempts to read what was on the desk. "My parents died a long time ago, you know that. I don't do family."

Everyone knew Grant McCormack's tragic backstory, about how his parents had been killed in a boating accident when he was just fifteen. With no other close family to take the reins, he had inherited the multi-billion-dollar family company, Cormack Industries. Following that, Frank Mitchell, his father's best friend and CFO, had raised him.

Over time, Grant grew into the perceptive professional he was today. He finished school and went to college, all while monitoring the company, under the guardianship of Frank, who had died just last year.

Feeling guilty about hitting a nerve, she knew Grant wasn't going to offer any useful explanations. "Okay," she said, spreading a non-threatening smile across her lips. "I just... if there are any situations going on, work or personal, I can help."

His scowl was uncharacteristic, and she worried he might be angry. "You concentrate on answering the phones, Zara, and leave my business to me. You don't need to think about my life."

Grant wasn't usually brusque, and he didn't condescend her position in the firm either. Known as a serious man, he was stern and private, but she'd always believed he was honest with her. After five years at his side, she could read his moods and nuances, and could tell he was hiding something from her.

Tim hadn't been honest about his interest and Grant was being cagey. So far, the only person being straight with her was the stranger in her bedroom and even he wasn't disclosing everything. If she was in the middle of something as he'd said, then she already wanted out of it.

***

THE REST OF THE WEEK passed and when Friday night arrived, Zara made herself go into Purdy's for a glass of wine. For fear of repeating last Friday's events, she avoided anyone who made eye contact with her and downed her drink in a quick succession of sips that meant she was out of the bar within thirty minutes.

Having a date drop dead wasn't something anyone would get over in a week. She was still shaken up by the memory of Tim's body falling to the asphalt. His attraction to her might not have been real, but his death was. She didn't want to repeat the experience by associating with new people who might try to wheedle their way into her life, especially when those new people might have a dishonest agenda.

Unsure if she was being paranoid or vigilant, Zara logged incidences when Grant had been distant at work. He'd been secretive about a couple of particular meetings. With her interest piqued, she took special notice of a lunch meeting he'd gone to alone that she found out was taking place in a private hotel suite.

Without the interference of the stranger in her

bedroom, she might have assumed Grant was in the midst of a fling, except Grant showed no other indications of being in the throes of early love. The stark truth was that the stranger knew more about her life than she did. He had known these oddities would arise before she had discerned that anything unusual was going on.

Waiting in the doorway of Purdy's until a cab pulled into the taxi stand opposite the bar, Zara ran into the first vehicle that arrived and recited her apartment address. Closing her eyes, she rested her head back against the seat.

The car started moving and as it lurched around the first corner, the cab driver spoke. "Rough night?"

Sapped of energy, she was ready for this week to be over and didn't really want to engage in small talk. She wanted to numb out, to get home and get to bed where she could sleep and all these inconsistencies in her life would cease to bother her.

"No, completely uneventful," she said, feeling her body relax into the cradle of her seat. "Thank God."

She was too polite not to reply. Having worked beside so many well-educated people, she always did her best to mind her manners and elocution, so it had become habit. At all costs, she wanted to avoid admitting her farm girl heritage. Once people found out she came from lowly roots they often got this look in their eye like she was either charity or had slept her way up through the ranks to reach Grant's side.

The cab driver didn't take the hint that with her eyes closed and her words heavy, she didn't want to talk, because he carried right on. "You look tired. You ran in here like you were trying to escape something."

Letting the rocking motion of the car console her, she anticipated getting home and switching off. "Escaping nothing," she said. "I am just avoiding trouble."

"When trouble wants you, it finds you."

Zara wasn't worried about trouble finding her. She just didn't want it finding anymore of her dates. If the person who killed Tim wanted her dead, they could've shot her on the street. Logic didn't always win the day and sometimes she was twitchy about who could be watching her. But she'd had a long week and had learned that worrying about something often didn't affect the outcome.

The swaying of the car was soothing, and after a few minutes, she began to feel herself drift toward slumber. To prevent herself from falling asleep, she sat up straight to look out the window. Except the view she got wasn't the one she was expecting. Picking out the landmarks, she realized they'd driven north out of the city limits.

Concern and disbelief made her curl her fingers around her purse in her lap. Was this person a criminal with evil intentions or an opportunistic cab driver looking to earn a few extra bucks? "Where are we going?" she asked.

"I'm gonna show you something."

"Show me something?" she gaped, pissed that she'd gotten a cab driver who wanted to overcharge her for a ride. It seemed that she just couldn't catch a break these days. "Are you kidding me? Is this the scenic route? I'm a local and I want you to take me home. Straight home."

Unaffected by her irritation, his words were slow. "Did anything odd happen this week?"

Perplexed, she didn't understand how he could be so aloof when she was so angry. "Odd? What do you care about my—"

"Are you wearing those stockings again?" he asked. "Are they a Friday special?"

The question and that husky tone stole her breath. The revelation of his identity slapped her with shock and Zara remained dumbfounded for a good thirty seconds. This was the man from her bedroom. Instead of breaking into her apartment, he'd apparently decided to kidnap her instead.

With an increased heart rate, she tightened her grip on her purse that was slung over her body and resting in her lap. "How…?" she asked. "I… It's you?"

"Yes."

He had to have been waiting for her to exit Purdy's in order to pick her up when he did. "But how did you…?"

"I told you, I know everything about you."

At least she didn't have new bad luck. This was just the old bad luck coming around for a second pass at screwing her up, except she still couldn't figure out what this stranger wanted. "You...you..."

She had spent a large part of this week thinking about the outsider who had appeared in her bedroom, about his husky voice and musky scent. There hadn't been a man in her bedroom for a long time and a man of his illicit skill and conceit had never been a feature in her life. But being enclosed in this space with him, on the road to an unknown location, her romantic notions about his intentions became suspicion.

"You can call me Raven," he said.

Having his name was somewhat reassuring, but she needed more. "Are you here to hurt me? Where are you taking me?"

"I'm gonna take you home," he said. "After I show you something."

He didn't answer the question about hurting her, but he'd claimed before that he wanted to protect her. When she glanced around, she saw no signs of a weapon, and there was a screen between her and the front seats too, so neither party could get to the other.

Calming her fears, she wanted to probe deeper into who this person was and why he might be helping her. "Why do you trust me with your name now?"

Ravens were an omen of death, so this new detail didn't exactly settle her reservations about his character. She considered the idea that he only trusted her with his moniker because she wouldn't have a chance to utter it to anyone else. That implied he was driving her to a secluded location in order to kill her, so she didn't linger too long on that thought.

"It's not my name. It's an alias," he said, as cool as he had been before. "And you get it because you did as I said, you told no one about our meeting or about what happened with Tim."

Wondering how he could be sure of that, she didn't refute his assumption and went with honesty. "I thought about telling Grant. He trusts me. But when I brought up his family, he shut down. He doesn't have family. He lost his family when he was a teenager."

With what might have been a smirk in his tone, he

ridiculed her statement. "I know what Grant's public story is."

"His public story?"

Making that distinction suggested that the story the world knew wasn't the whole truth. Grant's history was another thing about her boss that she hadn't thought to question. The weight of contradiction was beginning to crush her. Nothing made sense anymore. She didn't even know who to trust because she still didn't know exactly what was going on or what her role was.

"It's not the truth. But that doesn't matter now," Raven said, maintaining his focus on the road up ahead.

Intent on the job at hand, he didn't waste any movement and exerted only as much energy as was required. In addition to that noted efficiency, she also observed how he conversed with her as though nothing else was going on, like driving was not a task worth concentrating on.

"Why do you keep doing this? Showing up with the cloak and dagger theme?" she asked, seeing a chance, given that they were alone and he was unable to run away.

"I'm not ready to give you the whole truth, not yet."

An unsatisfying response, yes, but a truthful one all the same. "So what's the point of tonight?" she asked.

"Just sit back and enjoy the drive."

The car was dark and although the screen between her and the front blocked most of her view of him, she observed his broad shoulders clad in a black shirt that came above the shoulders of the seat. His dark hair was shorter on the sides than on the top, and she detected that same musky masculine scent that he'd left in her bedroom.

Peering up at the rearview mirror, she tried to get a better look through the dim light of the car. All she saw was the clear skin of his strong forehead and temple, with the occasional glimpse of the roots of his dark hair.

She continued to gawk and he had to have somehow noticed because he leaned back and one long-lashed brown eye came into her view. The intensity in that half-stare pinned her to her own seat. The disapproving eye went away and they kept on driving.

Her gumption had left her, meaning conversation

stalled. This journey had a purpose and until she knew what it was, she didn't want to ask more questions. Approaching the coast, they were a good twenty or thirty miles away from her apartment. They got to the cliffs at White Falls, the highest point of the coastline closest to the city, which was now just twinkling lights in their wake.

He parked on the isolated cliff and pointed out to sea. "You see the blue light?"

The shining blue light out in the dark swell of the invisible sea appeared to be adrift on the water. The blue glowed bright, comparable to a reflection of the brilliant shining moonlight, except it was too vivid and too close to the water to be a natural phenomenon. At the same moment that he pointed a broad finger out of the windshield, the light grew larger then dimmed.

Intrigued at the sight he pointed out, all emotions gave way to intrigue. "What is that?" she asked, shifting forward to look through the screen between the headrests of the front seats.

"It's the manor."

"What manor?" she asked, fixated on the illumination. "Is the light coming from an island?"

"It's connected to the mainland, set out on a narrow peninsula. It's all private land. Twenty miles south of the city. It's McCormack Manor."

"What?" she asked, astonished by this admission. "I thought that was a myth. It's abandoned. It has to be, doesn't it? If Grant owned that land—"

"He doesn't own it, but it's definitely there."

Transfixed by the blue light that glowed and dimmed in a rhythm suggesting a lighthouse or something similar, the motion was hypnotizing. "And why are you showing me? Have you been there?"

He took a breath and his shoulders rippled. "I brought you here to prove to you that you don't know everything there is to know about Grant McCormack. He's a liar. His parents died in the stretch of water you're looking at now. He was standing right here on this cliff and saw it happen with his own eyes."

"How do you know that?" she asked, trying to measure his sincerity, but he kept his eyes facing forward, meaning she wouldn't be reading any of his expressions.

Long fingered hands appeared on the steering wheel. Stretching his fingers around the leather cover, he seemed to enjoy tightening his fists around it. "I do my research. Grant hasn't told you any of this, has he?"

She and Grant didn't have that kind of a relationship, not one that involved long intimate discussions about their families and their pasts. What she knew of him beyond their day-to-day encounters at work came from the media and corporate materials.

"No, that's so personal," she said, watching the blue light on the black expanse of sea swell and ebb until it vanished then returned. "I would never dream of asking about something like that."

"If your relationship with him isn't personal, why should you tell him about a date you went on last week?" he asked. "Don't give him all your trust until he gives you his."

Confused by these new facts while fighting to marry them with the old ones, she closed her eyes and shook her head. "Do you think I need it?" she said. "I'm his assistant. He's my boss."

So the point of this exercise was to break her trust in Grant and to make her question her loyalty to him. Zara had concluded herself that there was more to Grant than she'd considered. But Raven still hadn't given her any reason to trust him.

"Has he given you anything?" Raven asked. "Any new or unusual instructions?"

She thought about what Grant had said about the second line and the man, Albert Sutcliffe, whom he expected to call. Raven's abrupt question proved that he wasn't interested in making sense of this for her, or even guiding her through it. He wanted information. Last week he'd told her he wanted her trust and this was an example of how he was going to obtain it.

Shaking the foundations of her relationship with Grant wasn't enough for her to turn on him. She still wanted to believe that her boss was a good man. He would have his reasons for getting involved in whatever was going on and she wanted to believe that those reasons were just.

Raven was hard to the point of insensitive. His manner betrayed that he didn't have much patience or tact. Where he was from and his own motivations were difficult to decipher when he was so detached. Whatever he was doing here, he wasn't happy about it, or maybe he just wasn't happy about having to deal with her.

"Maybe," she said. "But I don't trust you enough to reveal confidential corporate information."

"You don't need to reveal it, not yet," he said.

Seeing a chance, she questioned him on something that had been plaguing her all week. "How did you know that Grant would be late back from New York on Monday?"

"Because I knew he had a meeting… one that you knew nothing about."

Raven hadn't been the one to sabotage her boss, so from that she'd guess it wasn't his intention to hurt Grant. But this mysterious man had more knowledge than he was sharing.

Being excluded from CI business, where Grant was concerned, was an experience she hadn't had since her early years with the firm and she didn't like it. "What meeting?" she asked.

"What's important is that you're on guard."

She still didn't understand why he wanted to protect her. "Why do you care if I'm on guard?"

"Because if you get dead, Grant is gonna work harder to conceal his actions," he said. "Before I bring you inside, I need to know if you're capable of handling the pressure. This is gonna get complicated."

Protecting her was obviously only a byproduct of his need for information. He didn't give her a heartfelt answer, just a matter of fact one, and one that suggested she was on a deadline. Once he had the information he wanted, he would no longer be interested in protecting her.

"I still don't know what's going on," she said, frustrated by all these half-answers and ambiguity. Putting the pieces together when you only had a few disparate parts of the jigsaw made seeing the whole picture impossible.

"I have to go away for a few days," he said. "When I get back, if you do as I've said and you're still alive, then we can talk about what I need from you."

It took some amount of skill to be completely unaffected by a person so completely adrift. Any hope that he might extend her some compassion and reassure her was lessened every time he spoke.

"I don't understand any of this," she murmured.

"You will, Zara. You are capable of staying alive through this, as long as you trust me. I'm the only one who can keep you safe."

"Safe from what?" she asked, resting her fists on the Perspex screen.

"If I was to tell you that, you'd jump in the ocean and never come back."

Pursing her lips, she prevented herself from growling at him and considered that keeping her in the dark about the details might actually be his way of protecting her emotions, or at least protecting her from saying something to someone that might get her hurt.

"Will I ever get a straight answer out of you or do you enjoy screwing with people's heads?" she asked.

His only response was to start the car and reverse in a curve to bring them back onto the road toward the city. As if this was a normal taxi ride, he drove in silence, ignoring his passenger. But he wasn't being polite and giving her privacy, he was doing the mysterious thing again.

If he was going out of town, then he wouldn't be dropping in on her soon, so she decided to probe for more answers while she had the opportunity.

"What do you do for a living?" she asked but received no response. "Do you live around here? Have a girlfriend?" He just kept on driving without answering her. Yapping out these questions, without receiving a reply from him, made her feel like an inconvenience. Yet it was him who had picked her up, him who needed her. She only wanted answers because she'd feel better if she knew something about him and he'd have no chance of coaxing information out of her if she didn't understand him. "You know, you'd have an easier job of gaining my trust if you told me something about yourself."

His inhale was silent, but the rushed exhale was loud enough to signal his irritation. "Yes, I live around here and no, I don't have a girlfriend."

"And a job? What's your job?"

He paused before replying. "That's a more complicated question. Now sit there and shut up. I'm just gonna ignore your fucking questions, which will piss you off again. Save yourself the hassle."

Accepting that she wasn't going to get any more information out of him tonight, Zara spent the rest of the journey enjoying the ride because at least while she was with Raven, she was safe. She didn't know much about him yet, but at least she could say nothing bad had happened to her while she'd been in his presence and these days that meant something.

When he pulled up outside her apartment, he switched off the headlights but kept the engine running. "Record anything that you believe to be significant," he said over his shoulder. "When I get back it will be useful to know Grant's schedule, his routine."

For a shady character, she noted how he slipped from cursing and clipping his words to enunciating without missing a beat.

Ensuring he knew her stance, she didn't leave him with any illusions. "You don't have my trust yet," she said. "I appreciate the ride, Raven. But you're still a party of one."

Departing the cab, she knew it was important to portray confidence, because if he thought she was afraid of him, he would own her and may resort to harming her if he didn't get what he wanted. So she didn't look back.

Questions consumed her. She didn't know anything about who this Raven guy was. Grant was anxious, which was out of character, and she was ignorant to the details. Figuring this out was going to be a frustrating process, but at least she had a name for Raven now. She was wiser this Friday than she had been last week and she speculated on what new revelations might be coming over the next week.

FOUR

EIGHT NIGHTS LATER, on a Saturday, she had to talk herself into going on a date with Julian Scanlon, one of the firm lawyers. He'd been pursuing her for a while and Zara didn't feel much electricity with him, so she'd been doing her best to deflect his advances.

But her encounter with Timothy still haunted her thoughts and taking the plunge with Julian was her attempt to get back to normality before she developed a complex about dating and was spooked for life. After their dinner, her opinion about Julian and their chemistry hadn't improved, but she did feel a lot more relaxed about the general dating experience.

"I had a great night," Julian said upon exiting the restaurant, which wasn't far from Purdy's. His moist hand was sticky and uncomfortable in hers, but when Zara tried to withdraw, he tightened his hold. He was the epitome of tall, dark, and handsome. Very well educated, his only flaw was an awkwardness that followed him in social situations.

"Yes, it was a good night. The food was excellent," she said, reaching for something positive to say.

His brief laugh didn't seem genuine. "Maybe next time we should try somewhere further from work," he said.

Julian's idea of a date was not eating in a restaurant on the same avenue as their place of employment and he'd said as much when she suggested the eatery. He hadn't voiced displeasure at her choice of apparel, but from the way his lip had curled as he looked her up and down, he made it clear he was unimpressed by her casual workwear of a loose short skirt and cowl neck top.

Zara wasn't in the habit of making herself out to be more than she was, but Julian was rich and successful, so he was probably used to women making more of an effort to impress him. But with Zara, what you saw was what you got and if he disliked her dedication to hard work then there was no chance of any relationship between them.

That being said, he had been nothing but gracious and attentive all night, she couldn't fault his manners. It wasn't his fault that she wasn't excited by him. "Yes," she said, showing remorse in the smile she flashed in his direction as they walked down the block. "Sorry, I had some work to finish this afternoon. Thanks for meeting me at the office."

A major bonus of dating a colleague was that he had security clearance to meet her at her desk. It also meant he'd have been background checked before taking his position, giving Zara some reassurance that he wasn't deceiving her about his romantic interest.

Julian drew them to a stop at the corner of the block. "Should we get a cab?" he asked.

That implication prompted her to be more forceful in retrieving her hand, she wasn't going to be rude, but she also didn't owe him anything. "Actually, I still have some work to do."

Surprised, and probably offended, his mouth dropped open. "Work? It's almost ten at night."

"Yeah, I'm a workaholic," she joked, trying out a self-deprecating laugh. There were no pressing assignments, but Zara needed an excuse to refuse his request because returning to either his place or hers for a drink was the last thing she wanted to do when she wouldn't be agreeing to see him again.

"Is there anything I can help you with?" he asked, still unhappy with her declaration while not getting the subtle hint.

"I'd like to continue our evening."

"Maybe another time," she said, hoping the gentle letdown would work because she didn't want an enemy at work.

"You are a workaholic," Julian said, agreeing with her earlier statement. "Grant works you too hard. I should talk to him about it."

Julian had no influence over Grant. In all honesty, her boss didn't have many friends who did. He had associates and contemporaries, who he socialized with when the occasion called for it. Julian was not one of those men. He wasn't in Grant's inner circle at all. But it was nice of the conservative lawyer to imply that he cared enough to stand up for her if need be.

"Thanks for dinner," she said, removing herself from him when he tried to get up close. "I'll see you at work."

Walking away from him before he had the chance to say anything else, Zara traveled the familiar route to the CI building. Staying on the edge of the pavement near the streetlights, she made a point of smiling at everyone she passed in hopes they would remember her if something unthinkable happened to her and they found themselves making a statement to police. Zara knew she was being paranoid, but with Grant's odd behavior and everything Raven had said, the possibility that something bad could happen was a recurring theme in her thoughts.

Using her security codes, she got into the CI complex and assumed that the night guard was on his rounds when she didn't see him at his desk. This was a nice time of night to be in CI. Usually it was a bustling hive of activity on the lower floors. Now it was quiet, still, and safe—the subdued emergency lighting was her only companion. The motion sensors, which activated the main lights, took a few seconds to register her movement. Once they did, the lights flickered on in her wake after she'd passed through each section.

The executive floor was cool because the usual ambient heat from lights and bodies had been abating since quitting time yesterday when the full staff departed. The lights on this floor were off because she deactivated the motion sensors at night before she left.

Heading in the direction of her own modest office, she passed the executive reception desk, and went behind the silver screen that blocked Grant's office from passing eyes. Her office was small but located adjacent to Grant's in a testament to how impatient he was when he needed her.

Zara slowed when she noticed that the blinds over the internal glass wall of Grant's corner office were closed. They'd been open when she left a couple of hours ago. The four walls of his office were smoked glass, so she should have a broad view over the buildings surrounding CI. Instead, she only saw the outside of his blinds.

Trying to decipher who could have closed them, she came up with only one candidate: Grant. Her fingerprint was one of two that opened his door. Even the cleaning staff was only allowed in when either she or her superior were present. Confusion and intrigue only grew the nearer she got because the door was actually open, which was another oddity. Either they were being robbed, or Grant was here.

She couldn't think of what could be so important to bring her boss into work at this time of night, especially on a weekend. But Grant didn't scare her, so her paranoia eased. Her boss didn't even kill the spiders that snuck onto the top floor despite their lack of security clearance, so he'd never hurt her. The prickle of panic that had heated the back of her neck began to subside.

Heading toward the door, she planned to find out why he was here and to offer assistance with whatever he was working on. But when she heard the rumble of an unfamiliar male voice, she slowed, and came to a stop beside the vacant outer assistant's desk. The woman who sat out here during daylight hours was tasked with wrangling those waiting to see Grant, a job that Zara didn't envy.

Her suspicion about Grant being here was confirmed when his voice followed the stranger's. The warmth of her panic began to rise again. Craning to hear more, she narrowed her eyes and concentrated.

"No deal," Grant said.

"I want both," the unfamiliar voice said. She knew

her job and who Grant was working with and that voice didn't belong to any of their clients or colleagues.

The men weren't exactly arguing because no one's voice was raised, but their conflict leached from their hostile inflections. "Kahlil, I told you not to come here," Grant said with the air of a man who had better things to do. "You interrupted my night for a meeting that should not be taking place. If your boss thinks he can threaten or intimidate me then he's underestimated who he's dealing with."

"No, Mr. McCormack," Kahlil said, speaking with ominous urgency. "We know exactly who we're dealing with. Don't forget who started this."

Zara didn't want to miss any hints about what they were talking about. Silencing her own thoughts and emotions, she absorbed their words.

Grant became stern. "You weren't the only one who got the offer, and until I'm satisfied there won't be a deal."

"What you're offering will change the course of the future," Kahlil said, ambitious and declarative. "Don't pretend you're naïve to that. You don't want to upset your buyer."

"Don't threaten me," Grant sneered. "It's been considered, you buy from me, and the contracts will be ironclad. If you try to come after me, I'll blow the whistle and ruin you."

"Ruining yourself too."

"Better that than dead," Grant said. "You think I'll do business with a man I can't trust?"

"You said you perfected the kill switch," Kahlil said.

"Yeah," Grant said. "Don't forget that."

"You can trust us. Just don't think that you can disrespect us. We protect ourselves too."

Their grandstanding betrayed how unintimidated they were by each other. But without knowing exactly what they were talking about, or who Kahlil was, Zara had no way to know if she herself should be scared or if their composed aplomb was genuine.

Grant cleared his throat. "You called this meeting. If you're losing your nerve—"

"We want to bring negotiations to a close. Name your

price."

Holding her breath, Zara almost couldn't believe what she was hearing. CI had no official business with this Kahlil, of that, she was sure. Raven had been right; there was some sort of deal going down. Kahlil wanted what she assumed Grant was selling. Grant had told her Albert Sutcliffe would be calling. With him and Kahlil in the running, there were at least two parties going head-to-head over this elusive product.

"You're impatient," Grant said in a superior drawl. "That concerns me."

A bang made her jump and she guessed someone had hit the desk. "What do you expect to happen while you're dicking around? You have a product and we want to buy it. I foresee no issues with the transaction."

"I like a man who can hold his wad," Grant said. "Take that back to your boss, Kahlil."

This clandestine meeting was not meant for her ears and if Grant caught her out here eavesdropping then he may question her loyalty. Despite this suspicious behavior, the Grant she knew was rational and moral. Storming in to make accusations could embarrass him in front of this Kahlil, and she didn't want a confrontation.

Zara had no memory of a client named Kahlil ever being associated with CI and Grant always called her before unexpected or last-minute meetings, even the private ones. Clueing her in on all meetings meant he wouldn't forget anything and could call on her for information he hadn't retained.

When Grant and Kahlil's conversation tailed off, she began to back away. Remaining as quiet as she could, Zara got around the screen and went straight to the elevator. The night guard would be finished with his rounds by now, so if she went out the main entrance, he would recognize her, meaning he could identify her to Grant. Zara didn't want her boss questioning her ethics when he found out she'd eavesdropped on his meeting. Determined not to reveal her presence, she selected the parking garage floor and began to descend.

The elevator doors whooshed open and she strode

onto the dark parking floor, which was deserted at this time of night. Rounding the pillars flanking the executive parking area, she was heading for the pedestrian exit on the far side of the space where she could input a security code to release herself from the building unseen.

What she didn't expect to see was a vehicle parked in the executive area that didn't belong to Grant. The dark car didn't belong to the person whose spot it was in either, and the nearer to it she got, the more uneasy she became. Up and down, she was riding the adrenaline rollercoaster again—the building she'd previously considered a sanctuary had become unsafe.

Carrying on through the echoing concrete cavern, Zara fixed the glowing exit sign in her sights and kept on walking. Dull emergency lighting glowed as her only means of illumination and she just kept on going, trying to get to the exit as quickly as she could while ignoring the car she hoped was vacant.

The click of a car door opening quickened her pulse and revealed to her that she wasn't alone. The beat of her heels on the floor sped up. The thump of her heart vibrated her limbs until her fingers throbbed. A figure rose from the far side of the anonymous vehicle and her vision began to blur. Hopes of an easy escape dwindled when the car door closest to her opened as well and a second male appeared.

"What are you doing here so late?" the man furthest from her asked as he rounded the car to meet his buddy by the trunk. Both of them had tanned skin and dark hair, suggesting Middle Eastern ancestry, but his accent was American without any foreign nuance.

Neither of the men was familiar to her, so she doubted they knew who she was. Except she couldn't pretend not to hear them or feign ignorance that they were talking to her, because there was no one else around.

"I'm just leaving," she called. Keeping her focus ahead, she continued on her trek, determined to reach her freedom. Her destination shrank into the distance. None of her strides seemed to bring her closer to the door, which had never appeared so far away.

"Didn't answer the question," one of them said as both closed in on her.

No, she didn't and she wouldn't because she had no explanation. "Why are you here?" she asked. Turning the tables on them, she prayed that her direct question would prompt them to retreat. It was doubtful they wanted to reveal why they were here.

But they weren't that easily deterred and kept on coming toward her. When they blocked her route, she was forced to stop. Zara tried to side step, but the men moved in time with her attempts to dodge them.

"Don't run away," the one on the left said, while the other circled to cut off a rear escape. "We're here with our boss. He'll want to know who saw us."

She didn't want to panic; it was obvious that these assailants enjoyed seeing her squirm. If she screamed out or cried, they would get a kick out of her torment, which might trigger them into doing God knew what with her.

Suppressing her fear didn't mean she was looking to provoke them, so she tried to allay their supposed concerns. "I don't know who you are," she said, but it was obvious they were some kind of security for Kahlil. Both were muscular and had a keenness about them that made her cautious. Bodyguards who had not gone with their protectee had to be edgy. Their decision to descend on her proved that they were itching to start trouble.

"What matters is that you've seen us," the guy in front of her said. "And that poses a problem for our boss. We don't like to be seen. That's why we operate in the cloak of night."

The guy behind her laughed. "The cloak of night, I like that," he said. He was so close that his breath moved her hair at the crown of her head. She held her breath, with little choice except to remain in this sandwiched position.

Reminding herself of where she was, she found some of her gumption because it was ridiculous to suggest she'd done anything wrong when they were the ones here for some dark purpose. "If you'd stayed in your car, I wouldn't have known you were here," Zara said. At CI she was respected and dealt with awkward clients all the time, she couldn't let them push her around here on home turf. "I'm important in this institution, so whatever you're thinking about doing—"

A thick forearm came around her throat, forcing her to swallow her words as she was pinned to the man behind her. The one in front pulled out a switchblade and grazed the tip from the groove of her throat down to her cleavage.

Whispering his words, he was so close that he had to feel her trembling. "We're going to make sure you stay quiet," he said.

"How do you plan to do that?" she asked, the fog of each quivering pant moistened the air, but she held eye contact, determined not to be overcome by fear.

Resting a hand on his cohort's shoulder, the man in front leaned in. "I'm going to show you what we can do. When we're through with you, you won't think about ratting us out. Your pretty head will be filled with so much horror that you'll be scared to open those sugar lips ever again. Hope your boyfriend doesn't come after me when you stop sucking his dick."

Grabbing the back of her neck, he kept the knife in her cleavage and wrenched her forward, trying to force his mouth over hers. Adrenaline surged and Zara pursed her lips as she tried to twist away from the disgusting advance. Her attempts to shove him away only made him struggle to keep her close, using his partner as the wall to restrain her against. But she wouldn't give in to this violation without a fight, she'd been standing up to strong, bullying men all her life.

If she couldn't get rid of the guy in front then a rear departure was needed. Knowing that they weren't expecting her to, she reversed her fortune by reversing their roles. Using the man in front as her wall, she pushed, causing the one at her back to give out.

He recovered quickly, but their brief second of confusion gave her enough space to duck down and twist, to squeeze her body out from between them.

On her hands and knees, she tried to scramble away. One of them kicked her thigh then her ankle in a half-kick gone awry. Curling to protect herself, she fell onto her side in a roll, and tried to think.

Getting out of this wouldn't be easy, she could go to the rear exit and maybe find a friend, or she could be running into a deserted alley, giving these men the perfect opportunity to do what they wanted with her. Going back upstairs would mean facing Grant and Kahlil, but that relied on the elevator arriving before these men caught up with her, which was unlikely.

The sound of a punch, then a thump put a stop to further assault. As her frightened thoughts sharpened, she unfurled her body to seek out the cause of her reprieve.

One of her attackers was flat on the ground. The second was engaged in hand-to-hand combat with a tall man, dressed in black wearing a hooded leather jacket.

They punched and kicked, but she was mesmerized by the slick movements of the man in the hood. Both were trained, that much was obvious from the way they blocked blows and weaved around each other. In comparison, there was something so easy about the way the hooded man moved, about the deftness of his maneuvers. The other guy seemed frazzled and overwhelmed, but the guy in the black hood was calculated, moving only just as much as he needed to.

After blocking a punch, the hooded man landed his own hit. When his opponent staggered sideways, he curved a strong leg around to take his victim off his feet onto his back on the concrete with such force that he didn't get back up.

Both of her attackers were on the ground, groaning or twitching, so she knew they were alive, but they weren't in any hurry to fight again. The hooded man stalked over to her and held out a hand.

Bewildered, she just gawped at the hand as she tried to get her thoughts straight. "Get up," he said. All she could see was the stubble on his defined chin and jaw. She didn't know who this crusader was and taking the hand of a man so capable could be a transformative decision.

Being vigilant instead of hasty, she stayed on the ground. Her weight-supporting hands and ass were getting cold on the asphalt because her skirt had ridden up during the tussle, but she couldn't throw her lot in with a stranger who could be as dangerous as the men who had just attacked her.

Her hesitation was noted by the stranger. He raised his hand to the back of his head to tug his hood back a couple of inches, just enough that the shadow lifted from his eyes and she recognized the man from the taxi rearview mirror staring back at her. Shock made her mouth drop open, she'd been in trouble and Raven had materialized to rescue her.

"Zara, come on," he said.

The edge of impatience in his voice was probably attributable to the residual adrenaline in his bloodstream from the confrontation, except he displayed no indication that he was harried. Raven, it turned out was true to his word. He'd said he was going to protect her and he'd just saved her from a situation she'd never have been able to get out of on her own. Nothing bad had ever happened to her when Raven was around and he'd proved he was capable of keeping her safe.

Gratitude made her snatch his hand, even though he was no longer offering it, and Zara scrambled up in preparation to run away with him. But when her weight landed on her feet, her legs gave way causing her to fall into his unyielding form.

His arm came around her ribs, beneath her arms, to hold her up. "What's the problem?" he asked, keeping an eye on the men who were beginning to show signs of getting up.

"My ankle," she said, keeping the weight off her injured leg. "I think I sprained it or—"

"We've got to get out of here," he said, displaying no concern for her pain or interest in her explanation. Dipping to hook his arm under her legs, her feet didn't touch the ground when he swept her out of the parking garage and into the dark lane outside.

This was a pedestrian access, so there weren't meant to be vehicles parked here, there never had been before. But he dropped her onto the back of a monstrous black motorcycle that was standing up in the narrow space.

"Hold on to me," he said, taking his seat up front and kicking the bike into gear.

Resting her hands on his waist, there was no time to tell him that she hadn't done this before. He grabbed her wrists and forced them all the way around his torso, merging their bodies. Her instinct to withdraw was quashed when he revved the engine and roared forward. The momentum made her clamp her elbows and her knees into him and all thoughts of polite decorum went out the window.

The vibrations of the vehicle, and the heat that began to permeate, stimulated her. With the tumultuous emotions caused by this eventful night, she struggled to pinpoint the source of her blood pressure increase. It could come from fear, arousal, or maybe something else. The rush of wind as they wound through the streets loosened her hair but she didn't let go of him, she didn't decrease her grip for a second.

After becoming accustomed to the motion and the noise, she let her rigid muscles relax. Still holding on to him, she let herself breathe and rested her cheek on the leather at his back while trying to recall a time when she had felt so free. She came up blank. Given what she'd just been through, her exhilarated mood was quite a pronounced turnaround and it was all down to Raven and the security he provided her.

The streets whizzed by and although she recognized that their route would take them back to her apartment, she was almost sorry about the brevity of their trip. She'd never been on a motorcycle or had a man so solid and formidable between her thighs. For the first time in her life, she wondered what it would be to live a life free of all responsibility and throw caution to the wind, as Raven did.

He drove straight into the service alley at the rear of the building and pulled into a space between the dumpsters, then switched off the engine. In his same move of getting off the bike, he swept her up off her feet.

He didn't blink, just carried her in his arms to the back door, and keyed in the private code to the security pad. She didn't know how he knew it, but he didn't hide his knowledge. Now that she thought about it, he hadn't used a security code to get out of CI, divulging he had expertise beyond the physical.

Carrying her up the stairs to her apartment, she unlocked the door while still in his embrace. He took her inside, kicked the door shut, and carried her across the room, past the first column, to lie her on the couch.

Elevating her right leg, he seated himself perpendicular to her body, between her legs, and made no apology for squashing her left leg between his ass and the back of the couch or his presumption. He slipped off her shoe and touched her injured ankle.

The contact made her recoil. Without invitation, he strengthened his grip around her heel and tested her range of movement with his opposite hand. His thumb pushed into the delicate bones beneath her skin to move her ankle as he wanted it to move.

He was so sure, so unapologetic, so entitled. Such a show of brutish control proved his power; he could contort her any way he chose to and all she could do was comply. Yet, by assessing her injury, he was demonstrating some level of care about her wellbeing.

Each time they came into contact, she learned a little more about who he was. She might not have specifics, but his deeds spoke for him. He had never hurt her, despite his superior strength. Had never put her down, despite the hints of class behind his gruff exterior. He had a mission to protect her and tonight he'd proved he was a man of his word.

The firm hold of his rough fingers rasped her smooth skin and her gratitude bloomed. Her feminine awareness was awakening too. Raven had saved her life and then taken her on an exhilarating ride through the city streets. Adrenaline, endorphins, hormones, they were all chemical and they were combining in her head, slinking down her spine, through her organs to tickle her enlivened skin.

It was dark, but she could see the line of his jaw and how his hair was mussed suggesting he never did more than finger comb it. The musky scent of him made her pelvis grow heavy and the whisper of butterflies in her stomach began to gain speed and mass.

He was touching her, exploring her injury, and didn't reveal any signs he was as raw as she felt. With every second of contact, she grew more sensitive to his actions and her hips began to squirm.

Fearing he would sense her interest or that she might do something embarrassing like whimper, she sighed. "Stop it," she said, tugging her foot away from him.

He caught her limb, pulled it back, and laid it on his lap. "You'll have to elevate it and ice it," he said. "Nothing's broken, but it will probably swell, so take it easy for a few days."

"I have to go to work. I can't just sit on my ass doing nothing."

With his focus still on her leg, he addressed it rather than her. His frown made her speculate. Was he pissed that he was here tending to her? Or was he a man with more on his mind than he was letting on?

"Grant will understand," he said. "You haven't taken a fucking sick day for three years."

By now, she was getting used to him knowing everything about her and her life. Other, more relevant, questions plagued her, like why he had come to her aid and how he got into CI. She wanted to know if he knew Kahlil and what he and Grant were doing having a clandestine meeting, but at the same time, she didn't want to betray Grant.

"I'm not taking a sick day," she said, sitting up without removing her legs from around him. Taking time off might help her sore ankle but sitting in her apartment alone would only exasperate her confusion and there would be no answers here after Raven left her. "I need to know, Raven, why were you at CI tonight? How did you know that I needed help?"

Still inspecting her leg, he sounded tired when he replied. "Both have the same answer… I'm watching."

"You're still watching me? You said you were going away."

He circled her foot in his grip. There was no reason for him to be examining her still, except if he needed the distraction from establishing eye contact. "How'd you get mixed up with those guys?" he mumbled.

"Kahlil and his men?"

His whole demeanor changed. He grew tense, and his awareness became acute as his eyes slid up to hers in time with the whisper of his hands skimming up her shin. If she'd been vulnerable to him before, now that susceptibility intensified until her throat began to parch and her muscles ceased. Inching closer, he forced her to lean back when he propped a fist on the couch cushion by her hip.

Intimidating her with the intensity of his mysterious brown eyes, his fixation tested the limits of her rapid heart rate. Doing her best, though it probably wasn't enough, she tried not to reveal how affected she was by having his body within a few centimeters of hers, but her insides were beginning to feel like simmering soup.

"How do you know his name?" he growled.

The accusation laced through his question didn't provoke distress as such, but she did feel small caged here beneath him at his mercy. "I went to the executive suite after my date with Julian," she admitted. "Grant was there talking to a man he called Kahlil."

"What were they talking about?" he asked, using his size to ease her back further until she was in a submissive reclining position against the arm of the couch.

His physical authority meant he didn't have to ask her to lie down. He leaned forward and made her bend to his will. With the seal of eye contact and proximity broken, he took advantage of the opportunity and examined every nuance of her expression. The way his gaze gobbled up her features made her feel like prey being dominated and toyed with by a starving predator.

While she had been slowed by her own hormones, she hadn't thought his were on alert. But nothing else could explain why his eyelids grew heavy over his sharp eyes. Off-kilter in the swamp of his unanticipated amorous attention, she tried to focus. "I don't know exactly," she stuttered. "A deal, I think. Kahlil wanted to buy something that Grant was selling."

"Did they talk about what it was?" he asked, keeping his volume low. Curling a finger around a tendril of her hair, he let it slip free, then curled it around his digit again. The repetition of this private, personal contact calmed her.

"No," she said, taking the liberty of sliding her hands up his chest because she wanted to feel the heart that beat beneath his clothes. But his solid breadth made her catch her breath. She stroked up and down then up again until her hands floated around to the nape of his neck. "Do you know what it was?"

The murmurs of her words were small gasping exhales that made her mouth water. Maybe it was the lack of light, the terror of the night, or the weight of him resting against her side, but this moment was intimate and somehow familiar, and she found herself transfixed by the proximity of his mouth. Lying in the cage of his arms, her next inhale made her shoulders slip back, causing her to arch into him.

"Did they see you?" he asked, letting her hair fall from his grip for a last time.

"Does it matter if they did?" she murmured, curious about the tinge of concern she deciphered in his tone.

When he tipped his chin a fraction higher, her mouth was tempted to ease closer. "If they did, I'll need to alter my strategy."

Still trying to maintain the thread of conversation, while not being distracted by their fascination for each other, she made herself look into his eyes. "Your strategy?"

"You'll be in danger," he said, moving his hand onto her face.

Moving her head, she stroked her cheek against his palm, encouraging him to widen his fingers. "And your strategy is to keep me safe?"

"Part of it."

Dazed by his considerate words, her eyes closed as she smiled. "That's very sweet," she whispered.

"Sweet's got nothing to fucking do with it," he said.

Seizing the back of her head, he tugged her forward to close his mouth over hers. Opening for him, Zara welcomed the mass of his tongue that plunged against her own, cool and delicious. She opened her hands on the leather of his jacket and tilted her chin to signal her own compliance. This was new. This man was dangerous. Yet her body was alive with sensation and eager to explore every facet of him. Questions outweighed answers, but all she cared about was pressing her body up to his.

He kissed her deep then sucked her lower lip as he

withdrew and cast his eyes down. The tension in him made her stroke the width of his shoulders in solace and encouragement because she wasn't finished, she wanted more, but her bubble was burst when he spoke.

"I wasn't supposed to do that," he exhaled.

Catching her breath, she barely recognized her raspy tone. "Not in your timetable?" she asked.

"You've been through a trauma and you're still in danger."

Scooping her hands up over his jaw, she made him look at her while she confessed. "The last man who kissed me ended up with a bullet in his head. I think you're the one in danger."

Because he had returned to examining her mouth, Zara wondered and hoped that he might kiss her again. It seemed somehow right in this night of madness that she should embrace her desire to be reckless.

"He didn't die because he kissed you."

She smiled and loosened. "One day you'll tell me what you mean by all these cryptic half statements you make."

"One day, I might," he said, though she didn't assume it was probable. A man who wouldn't even give out his real name was unlikely to hand out his secrets without imminent cause.

Clutching the open edges of his jacket, she inhaled the scent of this man and this moment. She wanted it to be real because she hadn't felt an attraction this strong in her life. But she had to ask, "Is this your way of gaining my trust? Like you said Tim was trying to do?"

"You don't trust the men you sleep with, not in the way I need you to trust me."

Again, he revealed how well he knew her, though she couldn't imagine how he knew something so personal. Especially being that she hadn't had a long-term boyfriend for a couple of years. Zara was accustomed to holding herself back in relationships. It was what came with being disappointed by men one too many times.

"Then kissing me was probably not a good idea."

"No, it wasn't," he said. Sweeping his arm around

behind him, he trailed his fingertips down the length of her leg and elevated her foot onto the cushions stacked at the end of the couch. "Tell me what happened upstairs at CI."

He didn't kiss her again, although she got the sense that he wanted to by the way his interest flicked to her mouth and over her body. Flattered by his attention, Zara's arousal didn't cool, but it was obvious he had returned to business, insinuating that they probably weren't going to explore their attraction further, at least for tonight.

"Nothing," she said. "They didn't see me. I listened for a while and then I left."

"Grant didn't see you?"

Now that they'd acknowledged the want of their bodies, it was easier to maintain her senses. "No."

"And you overheard their conversation?"

Measuring his gaze, she anticipated his next question with suspicion. She wanted answers and didn't want to reveal too much because despite his odd behavior this week, Grant had never given her cause to betray him.

"Some of it," she said.

"What did they say? Give me specifics."

Releasing all her weight onto the scroll arm of her couch, she told the truth. "Grant has been good to me. I'm not going to sell him out just because you kissed me."

When he sat upright, their trance of familiarity was broken. "How about because I saved your life tonight? Or because I've been looking out for you for weeks?"

Wondering about what he might have protected her from without her knowledge, she asked, "Have you seen any danger?"

He propped a hand on the back of the couch. "Danger like your boyfriend being shot dead in the street? Or thugs jumping you in an underground parking garage?"

His point was valid. She didn't need to know about unseen danger when the seen danger was scary enough. "I don't want harm to come to anyone," she said. "But I don't believe that Grant would endanger people. He's a good man and CI's remit is to help people with what we create."

Switching position, he removed himself from her

couch and sat on the edge of the coffee table. Resting his elbows on his knees, he joined his hands. "Why didn't you show yourself to Grant tonight?"

Driving her fists into the cushion beneath her, Zara tried to get upright while keeping her leg elevated because somehow it seemed more civilized to talk while sitting up. But the position was awkward and strained her abdominals because there was nothing substantial at her back to support her.

"I wasn't expecting him to be at the office and when I heard that he wasn't alone, I didn't want to interrupt." Simple as that, yet Raven wasn't buying it.

His sneer betrayed that he didn't believe the excuse and called her on it. "I'd guess that a woman with your credentials has interrupted meetings before. Does he usually have late night meetings that you don't know about?"

Averse to being brow beaten, she returned his derision. "How would I know?" she asked, willing to match his icy tone with her own. She worked late often and got enough late-night calls from Grant to know tonight's events weren't the norm, but she wasn't going to reveal that to Raven yet. She had to give Grant the benefit of the doubt.

Some of Raven's frost dispersed and he seemed to be trying to appeal to her better sense. "Because you're astute and conscientious, Zara. You know that something else is going on here."

"I do because you've drawn my attention to it. You've made me so paranoid that I'm preoccupied by every suspicious detail." Falling back onto the arm of the couch, she ran her hands through her hair and exhaled. "You're making me crazy." With the danger and now with the kissing too.

"No, I'm preparing you for what's coming," he said and didn't sound as flummoxed as she felt. In fact, he was positively cool and collected. "I'm proud that your blinders are coming off. If you don't want to trust me, then don't. Others will approach you and they won't be as gentle as I've been."

And because she truly believed in her boss, she knew she could turn to him for help. "Grant won't let anything happen to me."

Raven rose. "Then you've picked your side. You go to him and you tell him everything. Ask him for the truth… If he's the man you think he is, then he'll give you the full story and order round the clock protection for you."

"Protection?" By standing up for Grant, she'd managed to lose Raven's goodwill. Without him, she'd be unguarded leaving her at the mercy of any other attackers intent on causing her harm.

It seemed he was severing their association, but he did relax for a second. "I'll give you one last warning for free," he said. "What Grant plans, what he's about to do, it will test your loyalty to him and once you're on the inside of the secret, there's no getting back out."

He began to walk away. "Raven," she said before he could leave her. Seeking him out, she had to tip her head all the way back to locate him beyond the couch. "I won't tell him about you."

"You owe me nothing, Ms. Bandini, and you don't know enough about me to give me up to anyone. Take care of yourself because no one else will."

The tattoo of his heavy steps receded. The door opened and closed. He was gone. Her life at CI had kept her busy and she'd never assumed Grant was capable of dubious dealings, but there was definitely something unpleasant about what had happened tonight.

Steadfast in her loyalty to Grant McCormack, she was almost disappointed by the truth that she would never see Raven again. Reaching over her head, she groped for her cordless phone and speed-dialed her boss. It was late, but she knew he was awake because he'd been at the office. Except the line rang out until it went to voicemail.

Grant might be busy now, but she'd clear a space for them to talk on Monday because she was tired of the questions and she wouldn't deceive him anymore.

FIVE

GRANT DIDN'T RETURN the missed call and he was late to the office on Monday. He said nothing about his Saturday night meeting with Kahlil and not a word about the men in the parking garage. Either he hadn't been told about what had happened or he hadn't put the pieces together and identified her as the woman who was attacked. If she had to, Zara would put money on the former because the Grant McCormack she knew would be outraged by any woman being intimidated, especially on his property and as such would no doubt have brought up the incident with her as a prelude to strengthening security.

Executive parking was one of the few areas in the building without video surveillance. A directive had been issued to remove all cameras from there a couple of months ago. At the time, it hadn't made much sense, but no one questioned it. Now she had an inkling that Grant's motive was to conceal these secret meetings with shady characters.

After lunch, he was alone in the office with the blinds open, as they were when he was present. With no imminent meetings, Zara decided that now was her chance to speak to him. She hurried away from her desk, ignoring the pain in her ankle, which had slowed her down throughout the day. At that moment, her injury was secondary to talking to her boss.

Having walk-in privileges meant the front desk assistant didn't blink when Zara entered Grant's office. Because she sometimes came into Grant's office just to leave a document or pick one up without them exchanging a word, he didn't acknowledge her entry, even after she closed the door.

Creeping forward, she was nervous about bringing up what she knew because she didn't want this man she revered to believe she'd been snooping. They had never had an outright confrontation before, but she'd witnessed him arguing with others and it was obvious that he didn't like to be challenged.

But there was no backing out of this, she had to take a risk. "Sir, do you have a minute?" she asked.

While he was still writing, a smile quirked his lips. "Oh, she pulled out the sir, it must be serious." Grant pushed aside the document he'd been working on and opened his hand toward the chair beside his desk.

As per his silent invitation, she crossed to seat herself while considering how to broach the subject. "It is serious," she said, and his smile fell away in light of his new interest.

"You know I'll help you out of any jam," he said, swiveling his chair in her direction.

She took a breath. "It's you that I'm worried about," she admitted, trying to judge the subtle changes in his expression to figure out if he was angry or just confused by her statement.

"Me?"

Their professional relationship was integral to both of their lives. They saw each other every day and were often informal, but neither had attempted to intrude on the personal life of the other. But from what she'd heard of Grant's meeting with Kahlil they were doing some sort of business together, so as far as Zara was concerned, she was well within her rights to bring it up. Especially if Kahlil was the same caliber of man as she'd met in the parking garage, because she couldn't believe Grant would do business with them if he knew the truth.

Except his shoulders straightened and the groove between his dark brows deepened, and for the first time she thought she might be crossing the line into inappropriate and was terrified that she might offend or disrespect him.

But she couldn't retreat, not after being assaulted. Raven indicated that all her recent experiences were linked to something that Grant McCormack was cooking up and after Saturday she'd come to the same conclusion herself. She needed answers.

Licking her lips, she wasn't afraid to make eye contact because she wanted to judge his veracity when he spoke. Her respect for this man prevented her from being abrupt and so she chose to approach the subject with tact. "I've noticed that you've been distracted and erratic recently," she said.

His brows rose. "You've noticed a difference in me?"

She nodded and tried to stay loose, to appear as unthreatening as she could. "I know there's something on your mind, something going on," she said, offering a soothing outlet in the hope it would encourage him to talk.

When his lips thinned, her initial thought was failure because she thought she read displeasure. Leaning back, the chair reclined a little and his concern turned to a greater intrigue. "What have you noticed?"

If she wanted honesty, she had to give it. "You've been late to work. You were delayed in your return from New York. You've had clandestine meetings and are expecting mysterious clients to call the private line. Something is going on."

He locked his fingers together. "Are you concerned or is this you reprimanding me?"

Horrified that he would think her so haughty, she inhaled. "I would never reprimand you. That's not my place," she said. "But I am worried. As you said to me, you would help me out of any jam and I want you to know… I'm here to help you as well."

His gentle expression of concern had been replaced by a hard frown. "Your worry is noted, although I put in many hours here at Cormack Industries. My dedication to this company has never wavered. I treat my role here with great respect."

"I didn't… I didn't mean to suggest otherwise… But…"

The impulse to back away from the subject and apologize

engulfed her because it was clear that Grant had been offended by her suggestion he was giving less than a hundred percent. Her heart was hammering so loud that it reverberated to her eardrums and for a second she wondered if Grant could hear it.

But her gumption only returned when she visualized Raven walking out of her apartment after she had clammed up and claimed allegiance to Grant. She couldn't chicken out of being honest with the man she had defended. As long as she had faith in Grant's good intentions, she would remain his ally.

Raven wouldn't be coming back, but she still needed to know what was going on. That left her with only one option: to tempt Grant into proving that her faith was founded and her trust reciprocated. He had to tell her the truth.

"What is it, Zara?" Grant asked, making her realize she hadn't said anything for a while.

With a deep breath, she ventured to prove her trust. "I had a date on Saturday night," she said, crossing one leg over the other and brushing her hand down her thigh. "It didn't go particularly well and… I decided to come into the office to do a little work—"

"Your own dedication is"—the furrow in his brow grew deeper. He stopped talking for a moment and she assumed he'd put the pieces together—"you were here on Saturday night?"

"Yes," she said, with a gentle nod. "I overheard some of your meeting." Zara had thought it was better to lead with that than with the attack. But she reconsidered her approach when he flew up out of his chair.

"Zara! I… I expect far better from you. Eavesdropping? I didn't think that was your style."

Having never offended him before, she tried to backpedal, which made the pace of her words kick up. "I didn't," she said, rising to match his stance. The glow of his disappointment cut her deep. "I heard very little. When I realized you were here, I left."

"What exactly did you hear?" he demanded.

"Nothing," she said, shaking her head because his

disappointment merged with the anger that simmered just beneath his surface and she didn't want to face his wrath. "I just… I wanted you to know that you don't have to keep secrets for me. Whatever the time of day, you can call me and I'll come in if you need someone to record meetings and—"

"No," he said, holding up a firm hand that suggested his own panic. "That meeting is not to be recorded anywhere, do you understand? It happened in the way it did for a specific reason."

Grant was keeping secrets. If Raven hadn't brought that to her attention, Zara wasn't sure how long it would've taken her to come to that conclusion on her own. She and Grant had an honest working relationship and she couldn't figure out why that would change when there had been no big event to cause such a fracture in their rapport.

"You know that I'm with you, don't you?" she said, locking her gaze on his while lowering her chin a fraction. She touched the sharp tip of a pencil in the pot on his desk. "Whatever is going on, whatever you're doing… you're not alone."

Grant's anger and disappointment cleared and he scrutinized her for a few seconds. Whatever he was looking for in her, she wanted to portray her fidelity to the company and to this man who made good business decisions and had provided her with a lucrative career.

Raven was a tempting figure. Alluring in the sense that he was dangerous and fleeting, something that few women could hold onto. He'd come into a woman's life, smash it to pieces, and then fade into the night never to be seen again. Zara did not want to trash her own life only to be left with chaos when Raven had taken what he wanted from her. Grant and this company were the solid foundation of her life.

He must have gotten the message because his frown faded. "I'm setting up a deal," Grant said. "To sell a piece of tech that's been protected by those in the highest levels of Cormack Industries for decades."

"Decades?" she asked, and he again gestured for her to sit, which she did in time with him.

All previously frazzled emotion receded into their

familiar corporate calm. "Technology has evolved, and in recent years there have been great advances. However, not every piece of technology is some whizz kid's invention. Many things have been theorized for a long time. Some of our most elite R&D guys have been working patents filed in years gone by for products that were not viable with the contemporary technologies."

"And now this piece that you're trying to sell, it's viable." With a single nod, he smiled and linked his fingers in front of his chest. "I don't understand. If CI has refined this piece and gotten it ready for market, why not sell it through conventional means? Why have unrecorded meetings in the dead of night?"

"This piece is revolutionary," he said. A glint of excitement in his eye came closer when he leaned on the desk. "The bidding has to be private because whoever gains this prototype will require exclusive rights and they may further develop the product. Such information will of course be proprietary."

"You're handling the negotiations personally?" she asked.

Grant handling initial negotiations was unusual. Preliminaries were always done by vice-presidents or lower associates. If Grant wanted to be part of a significant deal, he didn't enter the boardroom with clients until the latter stages. And giving out the private phone number was unheard of.

"This deal was important to my father and to Frank," Grant said. "It's the least I could do."

Family. Grant never brought up family and he wasn't a man who liked to expose his vulnerabilities. But it was too much of a coincidence that Raven had mentioned the McCormack family and now Grant was bringing it up for the first time in their association. Tim's death, the meeting, her attack, it was all linked to this product.

At least she now understood one thing, if this was a deal important to his father, it made sense that Grant would want to handle it himself. "I understand," she said.

"I would appreciate it if you didn't mention what you saw or what you heard to anyone else," Grant said. "A sale is imminent and I wouldn't want to disrupt our chances of making a deal."

"Of course not," she said, shaking her head and straightening her spine to display her determination. "But if you need me… if you need assistance. You know that I'm here for anything you need."

"I understand," he said, widening his short smile. "You're a good girl, Zara."

"Thank you, sir," she said, and he barked out a laugh.

"We're long past the need for formalities," he said, steepling his index fingers under his chin. "How many times do I have to tell you that?"

"I take my role here seriously," she said, allowing herself to smile. "And I respect how hard you work and… after all you've been through…"

"Yes, okay," he said, getting up to come around his desk. Taking her arm, Grant helped her out of her chair and guided her toward the office door. "But 'Grant' will do just fine when we're alone."

"Okay," she said, clasping her fingers around his as he opened the door. "Thank you for trusting me."

"Thank you for coming to me," he said and his warm gaze reassured her enough to relax. "Now get back to work."

On leaving his office, she felt much better and couldn't understand why Raven was so disturbed by a simple business deal. Going back to her own desk, she was sure she'd made the right decision to discuss the situation with Grant who offered a benign explanation. The clients who wanted this piece of technology were determined and Grant was experienced enough to handle them.

Zara hadn't gotten as far as logging in to her computer when she blinked and got a flash of Tim's prone body on the ground. Her outstretched fingers curled into her palms and the frost that crackled over her shoulders lowered her gaze. The men in the parking garage came into her mind. If Raven hadn't been there to pull her out, to take on those men for her… she could be dead by now.

Grant made it sound so simple and for a second there she'd been appeased. A deal to sell a piece of equipment, there was nothing sinister about that. But there was something sinister about Tim's death and something sinister about secret late-night meetings when goons congregated in the basement.

Raven had told her on night one that Detective Kraft wouldn't be back in touch with her and he'd been right. Grabbing for her purse, she began to search for the detective's business card. Witnessing the death of a man should give her the right to follow-up on the investigation. Her fingers were working furiously when the phone on her desk began to ring.

Startled by the noise, it took her a few seconds to register the change in pitch. This wasn't her standard business line or the internal intercom; this was a call on the second line, the private line.

Licking her lips, she shifted her purse from her lap onto the desk and reached for the phone. Picking up the handset, she brought it to her ear with excruciating slowness because she wasn't sure she wanted to be any more entangled in this than she already was.

"Hello," she said. "Grant McCormack's executive assistant speaking."

"It's Sutcliffe," said an abrupt male voice. "Tell Grant we're on. Saturday at midnight, the Grand Hotel."

"The Grand… okay," she said. There was nothing threatening in that message and she actually smiled in relief as she stroked her fingertips on her upper arm and tried to relax herself.

"This demonstration better be successful or he's going to have a lot of pissed off terrorists on his hands."

Shock. The line died, but she didn't hear the buzz signaling it had disconnected. Frozen in her chair, the snarl in Sutcliffe's voice stayed with her and with each passing second, her insides got colder. 'Terrorists.' The word stuck in her head. What demonstration could be happening in a high-end hotel that terrorists would want to be successful?

This was no joke. She couldn't believe that Grant had been so casual while talking about this kind of product. CI didn't make weapons. They were inventors and investors in tech that could be adapted for medical and scientific use. They created hardware that helped people, not hardware that hurt people.

Shooting up from her desk, she abandoned her purse and headed for the door. She couldn't even remember if she had hung up the phone or not, getting to Grant was the most important thing. Knocking on his door, she went inside to see that he was on the telephone. When he saw her, he held up a finger while he finished off his call.

"Back already," he said after putting the phone back on its base. "What can I do for you?"

Her nerves were making it difficult for her to stand still, so she sort of swayed and forgot to blink. "Sutcliffe called," she said, gesturing with her hands, and his smile vanished. Waving her inside, he came across the room in a rush and closed the door behind her.

"What did he say?"

She tried to catch a glimpse of his facial expression, to see if he was experiencing guilt or fear. "That you were on for the Grand Hotel, Saturday at midnight."

Nodding, his eyes slunk away. "That was it?"

Still trying to read his emotion, she couldn't decipher panic. "What else should he have said?" she asked, hoping that he would be honest and explain Sutcliffe's declaration without her prompting.

"Nothing," he said, curling his fingers around her shoulders. He smiled again, but this time it was forced, and so it didn't serve to relax her. "There is a fundraising event in the hotel on Saturday night. Would you be so kind as to accompany me?"

"To the event?"

"Yes."

"At midnight?" she asked because that was much later than most corporate events.

"I wanted as few people as possible to be present," he said. "By that time of night there will only be a few people left in the public areas."

"The public areas?" she asked. "Should I be worried about—"

"You have nothing to worry about," he said, giving her shoulder a belittling pat. "I will have to meet with Sutcliffe and the other potential buyers. But I will need someone on my arm for appearances and to cover for me if anyone at the party asks questions about my whereabouts."

The idea of being present in a place where terrorists could be conducting demonstrations made her hands begin to shake. Knowing what she did, Zara began to fear she could be classified as an accessory to whatever crime may, or may not, be taking place.

When she didn't respond, he spoke again. "You said that you were available for anything that I needed. I don't need to be bogged down with polite civilities with a blind date and I don't have the time to conjure up a woman who won't require entertainment."

Zara had gone to corporate events with Grant before. Most of the time there were other CI colleagues there with them. But if this was a secret meeting in reference to a secret deal then he couldn't very well ask anyone else from CI to go with him, so she nodded.

"Great," Grant said. "I'll send a car for you around ten p.m.? We can enjoy the party for a while before the meeting."

"Yes," she said, and he opened the door for her again.

"Remember, not a word to anyone."

Shaking her head, she let herself be pushed over the threshold and heard the door close behind her. Grant was involved in something far more serious than she'd comprehended. Unable to believe he would volunteer to plot with such people, she speculated that he could be in over his head and need help of his own. Except he displayed no signs of being fearful, preoccupied maybe, but not nervous.

Zara began to get a feeling that Raven might be right about this impending doom and with Grant choosing not to be forthcoming, she set her mind to doing some investigating of her own.

***

THE FEELING OF FOREBODING never left her. For the rest of the day, Zara did as much research as she could in CI, trying to obtain details about older projects that had been rekindled. What she did find out didn't make her predicament any easier.

Having been under the misconception that she had the highest possible security clearance, she was surprised when she hit her first digital brick wall. Re-routing to a different system, she tried again, but got the same warning about her lack of security clearance. But she was learning how to convert frustration into determination—she wouldn't be beaten.

If she couldn't access the R&D systems that she needed to see, she had to take a different approach. Just like they did in the movies, she decided to follow the money. With each new file she opened and each new entry she read, Zara's sense of impending doom increased.

At the end of the day, other employees went home, leaving her to continue with the investigation that engrossed her. Even Grant came into her office to say goodnight, but Zara kept typing, kept printing, kept trying to put the pieces together, but still she couldn't find out what this damned product actually was.

Money was being moved, routed to strange areas and obscure labs giving her a rough idea of where the work was happening and who was doing it. The details on what they were actually doing were vague, so much so that she concluded they'd been concealed on purpose.

The lights outside her office went out and her attention sprang up from the glare of her computer screen to focus on the black abyss beyond this room. On Saturday night, she had gone to the parking garage after everyone else had left and she'd gotten herself in trouble. Raven had told her that she was on her own now, so she wasn't going to take any risks of walking into danger alone. The people who Grant was dealing with were serious individuals who wouldn't take kindly to her poking around in their business.

Throwing her things together, she shut down her computer, grabbed her purse and document folder, and then went for the door.

She got to the street and into a cab without encountering any unsavory characters and Zara knew she should be relieved. Instead, tears began to blur her vision. They weren't tears of fear or sadness, they were tears of frustration and regret.

Raven had been honest about his motivation for helping her and she had failed to see how he could help her—beyond the physical. The man could handle himself in a fight. But he was wily too and knew far more about her boss and his extracurricular friendships than she did.

At home, she skipped dinner and instead took an unused notebook from her stationery box and spread out on her desk to try to put the pieces together. There were holes in what Grant had told her. The more she studied, the more she realized that this had been going on for a while. He'd been lying to her for months.

This was not a new product and there was clear financial evidence to suggest that her boss had been working on this project for almost a year. Grant, who she had claimed to trust, the man she had believed to be harmless, had deceived her and all their colleagues. Unsatisfied and angry, Zara couldn't decide if she was naïve, blinded by admiration, or if Grant was just more conniving than she could ever have fathomed.

A creak in her living room made her lift her head. Prickling awareness kept her on ready alert, she was attuned to every whisper. Sliding her glasses from her face, Zara watched her office door and held her breath. If there was someone out there then she had no way to protect herself.

"Rave," she muttered, wondering if maybe her protector had come back to see her.

Dropping her pencil and her glasses, she pushed away from the desk and hurried to the door to peek out into the darkness of her living room. The space had never appeared ominous before, but the arched windows that stretched the length of one wall made her feel exposed.

Anyone in the building opposite could see into her apartment. Tim had been taken out by a sniper. There was no way for her to know if that same shooter had their crosshairs on her, as she stood there defenseless.

The columns in this open plan space had always been one of her favorite things about the apartment. Now they were in the way, a threat, providing cover for any assassins who could be loitering behind them waiting for their chance to take her down.

Convincing herself to be strong and that she could do this alone, Zara tried not to be paralyzed by fear. Except each of her breaths punched the air until she could hear her own panting. Her lungs burned as though they weren't getting enough oxygen.

Raven wasn't out there; he'd have shown himself by now if he was. The noise could have come from anywhere or anyone—a foe rather than a friend—and feelings of vulnerability held her immobile. These crazy people knew who she was and knew how close she was to Grant. Sutcliffe had assumed that she knew about this deal going down at the Grand hotel. Raven had told her that others were watching her.

Under the illusion she might see them appear, Zara didn't want to blink for fear an enemy would materialize like a teleporting demon. Except these people were humans, evil, despicable humans, but humans nonetheless.

Backing into her office, she slammed the door and planted both hands on it. There were no guns in the house and a kitchen knife would be a poor substitute if her attackers were packing hardware. Cursing Grant for putting her in this position, she couldn't believe that he wanted to keep her in the dark and to placate her, like her ignorance would be some kind of protection against those who might want to hurt or manipulate her.

Grant didn't trust her or maybe he just thought she was dumb enough not to see what was right in front of her. Except she hadn't seen it, not until Raven had given her the respect of warning her about the danger. Grant, she couldn't figure out. Raven had come to mean safety, his presence meant protection.

He was capable and at least some part of him cared about her, he wouldn't have tended to her injury and kissed her if that wasn't the case. She needed him now. Needed the security of his proximity because if she just let herself rely on him, to trust him, he'd be able to keep her safe.

Rushing back to her stationery box, she pulled it out and

tossed the lid aside to root around inside. She yanked out all the blue plastic filing folders then tipped the box upside down to empty it. Putting the blue folders and a roll of Scotch tape in the box, she opened a closet and added a box of matches to her cache along with her stored candles.

Ignoring her nagging hesitation about venturing out of the office, she marched into the living room and went to the central window to swipe aside the window seat pillows. Using the Scotch tape, she stuck the transparent blue folders to the window to create a blue stained-glass effect. Once that was done, she spread out the candles on the solid window seat surface and began to light them. When she was done with those, she went around her house collecting every candle that she owned.

Cramming the candles onto the seat, she lit them all and then stood back to admire her work. The floor was a mess with scattered cushions and used matches, but the light was brilliant. It illuminated the vast space she was standing in. But that wasn't the point. From outside that light would be a brilliant blue, just like the light Raven had shown her on the water.

Sucking her bottom lip into her mouth, Zara backed off to sit on the couch. He might ignore her. He might not even be watching anymore. But she needed answers. Not that her need for information had been the catalyst for this act. No, that had been her fear. If she was facing significant threats with lethal intentions then there was only one man who she knew could take on those threats and fight them with equal determination.

Wrapping her arms around herself, she brought her legs onto the couch to lie on her side. Her ankle began to throb again, signaling that her adrenaline was wearing off. Closing her eyes, she sent out a silent plea for Raven to see her signal. He had to come to her because if he didn't, she would never make it out of this alive.

SIX

SOMETHING WAS RUBBING her arm. Her sleep was so good that she didn't want to wake from it. Zara had been dreaming that Raven would come to her, that he would protect her. But that wasn't why she was so determined to remain in slumber. The dream took her back to their kiss. In her dream, instead of running away from her, he'd stayed and touched her, kissed her, taken her to her room, and proved his skills extended beyond combat.

"Raven," she breathed out as she let her eyes open to slits. "Raven?"

A hand on her arm made her reach out. When her fingers curled around the thickness of his upper arm, his identity became clear. The force of memory made her eyes and mouth open in a snap.

Pouncing up into a seated position, she dug her fingers deep into him and snatched his other bicep when she saw he was crouched beside her couch.

"Raven! Oh my God, you came. You actually came!" Throwing her arms around him, she squeezed him for a second before easing back. "Thank you, God, what made you come?"

He was glaring, but she sensed his expression was one of

surprise not concern. "The light in the window," he said. "I took it as a sign you wanted to talk."

Zara didn't like to confess her vulnerabilities to anyone, so she averted her eyes. "I got scared," she confessed in a whisper.

Irritation erased every confusion from his attitude. "You think that gives you the fucking right to summon me?"

Her fleeting smile probably suggested her appreciation. "You're still watching me." She sighed at the comfort that came with that knowledge. He hadn't abandoned her, even though she'd said he would get nothing from her. Impressed by the strength of his character, she was astonished that he valued her safety. No man from her past had put her before personal gain.

His stoic form barely moved but she registered the increasing heat in his gaze and that hunger cleared her earlier turmoil and replaced it with a completely new priority. Raven was here. She was safe. She could relax. No one would be able to hurt her now. Emotion shifted to explore the lust he examined her with and Zara was ready to do whatever it took to quench her own desire.

Raven was her deepest, darkest fantasy. A man so powerful and proficient, it wasn't just his prowess that made her heart beat faster and her core swell. Staring into him, she parted her lips and begged without words for an explanation as to why he was still stalking her.

"Not for the mission," he said.

Squeezing her grip, she tested the strength of his unyielding muscles with her delicate fingers. "If it's not for the job, then why are you watching me?"

His eyes narrowed further and in the oppression of this night, a frisson of fervor stoked her gut and made her breasts grow heavy. "You know damn well why," he snapped.

The force of his kiss thrust her head back, but that harsh passion made her feel desirable, like he was starving for her and unable to control himself. Making a man like Raven lose control gave her power. He was her guard and her savior. Somehow, he managed to lift her up, and made her feel significant—able to take on the world.

He scooped a hand under her skull to compel her mouth to his, giving him leave to direct her head and her mouth to where he wanted them. The size of his hand encompassed all her skull and with every move, his fingers tangled deeper in her locks. The sting of snagged strands and the mesh of matted hair were contrasted by the scorching desperation of his mouth and the assuredness of his tongue.

Balling his hand into a fist, he used his grip on her hair and the arm he clamped around her ribs to haul her onto her feet. Without breaking their kiss, he dipped down to snag her thigh with one hand and while hooking it high over his hip, he kept the momentum of their kiss going.

Caught up in the passion of their oral joining, she only knew they were in the bedroom when he sat on the bed, then lay down, urging her body forward to double it over his.

Kissing him was the most overwhelming experience of her life. The bulk of his tongue was in proportion to the girth of his body. Yet, as bold as he was, there was something consoling about his assertive mouth tasting hers.

The heady merging of their saliva was like swopping a reefer mid-draw or using the same coke straw. Without combining the drugs they each possessed, they couldn't reach the optimum high. For the first time, they experienced the right dosage for maximum impact and she felt like she'd been sucker punched by Venus.

Spanking her ass with a loud thwack, he yanked his hand out of her hair. "Grab a rubber," he said, nodding toward the nightstand without breaking eye contact.

God, he was arrogant. A couple of kisses and he thought they were going to have sex. But that steadfast confidence heightened her desire until she felt overwhelmed by his testosterone, which dragged her further under his spell. As she looked through the night into his fathomless eyes, she knew she was going to do it. This man was thrilling. He was dangerous and mysterious, and completely wrong for her in every way. But, damn, he made her feel good.

This was a man who a woman wouldn't get a chance with often. He was so capable and skilled in arts that before him, she had no idea were out there. Raven lived life on the edge, in the night, and she had a sense that he needed the light in her as much as she desired his darkness. Throwing reason and rationale out of their bed, she sat up to straddle him and leaned back to reach the nightstand. It was further away than she'd realized but his long fingers came around her hips and he steadied her weight, which let her push further.

If he let her go now, she would fall and probably break her neck, but being in his grip gave her stability. Opening the drawer, she reached beyond her vibrator for the box of condoms. Flicking open the top, she shook them out and grabbed the first one that came to hand.

When she whirled around and held it up in triumph, the first thing he did was whip her top up over her head and while she was still static and upright, he took the peak of one breast into his mouth. The sensation of his warm, wet tongue made her belly spasm and a whimper of ecstasy accompanied her weak arm falling across his shoulders.

His vast mouth could pamper a lot of her flesh. He breathed her into him while massaging her other breast with a rough hand and little finesse. Splaying his fingers, he spanned more of her and squeezed tighter.

Sucking her breast, he flickered his tongue over the apex then withdrew, making a pop sound when his mouth left her skin. Blowing on the damp mound he'd just tasted, barbs of aching awareness further stimulated her nipple and the direct link it had to the center of her.

He was doing all the work and she had no control here. But when she tried to regain her senses to be more active in their union, she failed. Raven enclosed her in his embrace and flipped her onto her back so that he could spoil her other breast with the same treatment as the first, and she was lost to a hedonistic oblivion of bliss.

Raven pulled back, and she basked in the anticipation of his next maneuver. Her expectation was excited further when she heard the rattle of his belt buckle. When it quieted, he made no effort to remove her skirt and she was about to question whether she should shed it when he kneeled up between her thighs and peeled off his tee shirt. Eager to view his impressive body, she scarcely noticed him snagging the condom from her limp fingers and thoughts of her own clothes evaporated.

Much to her disappointment, it was too dark in the room for her to pick out the specifics of his form beyond the odd ridge of a muscle. Her curious fingers extended enroute to his abs, but he got hold of them and pushed them to the headboard when he stretched out over her.

Swooping down to kiss her again, he sucked her bottom lip then sent his mouth on an expedition across her jaw to her neck. The tightness in her electrified abdomen made her body curl up around his. She couldn't open her eyes, couldn't breathe, because his mouth moved so slowly, yet it managed to enliven all of her at the same time.

His hand took all of her breast at once, and he sucked her opposite nipple. His caresses ceased to be at all gentle and he pulled back to clasp each of her knees. Pushing them down, she whimpered at the burn in her thighs, and was mortified to see him fixate on what he'd exposed beneath her skirt.

With extreme control, he lowered himself at this new angle. Just before he disappeared beneath her skirt, he glanced up at her and winked, and then his mouth was on her. She still wore her panties, but that meant nothing to him. He rubbed his tongue the length of her and fingered aside her underwear to suck the flesh he'd exposed.

With a flick of his tongue, she experienced the first frisson of orgasm. "Don't," she managed to say, fumbling her fingers into his hair.

But he didn't stop. He flicked her again and again, increasing his pace until she slammed the soles of her feet to the bed and bucked up into his mouth. Her dream had aroused her fantasy into reality, and try as she might, she couldn't stop herself from falling into a second climax when his tongue kept sliding over her, awakening each new crevice it found.

"Raven," she murmured.

Clenching her fingers in his hair, she closed her thighs around his head, but he got hold of her limbs, pried them apart enough to surge up, and looked her in the eye. "You know that's not my real name, right?" he asked, lowering his attention to her mouth as she nodded. "You still want to do this?"

Names seemed irrelevant when the prospect of annihilation hung on the horizon. Her thoughts were obscured by the hormones deluging her brain, but she managed to nod.

Kissing the corner of her mouth, he closed his forearms around her head. She was grateful of their support so she let the weight of her cheek rest against one before he sought out her mouth.

After fondling each breast, his hand slid down the center of her belly. He unzipped her skirt and gave it a shove. Complying with the unspoken request, she wriggled out of the garment and was about to reach for her panty elastic when he got there first. With one hand, he tore the delicate fabric away from her skin and flung it aside.

Shocked by this primal act, she pulled her head aside to break their kiss, but he wasn't perturbed by her surprise. "I destroy anything that gets in the way of what I want," he said and because he had one forearm still coiled around her head, he used his fingertips on her cheekbone to push her face and bring their mouths back together.

A man as bold as this was redoubtable and with that knowledge came heightened arousal. Arcing her spine, she pushed upward to flatten her torso on his. In return, he overpowered her with his magnificent weight, dropping it onto her and pressing her into the mattress. That was when she first felt the thick length of his dick forcing itself against the center of her body. Compelled against the soft, damp cushion she offered, it bedded its imposing length in her folds.

Tilting her pelvis to rub him deeper against her, she coated his silken rod with her natural lubricant. And because she was still sensitive from his oral gift, she whimpered and mewed each time she wriggled and accelerated her body's production of the slick juice that would ease his awaited invasion.

When he elevated his hips, she tried to object to the disentanglement. But he once again pressured the pads of his fingers onto her cheekbone and rolled her head to welcome his kiss. He loved to kiss. She could tell that by how long he spent trailing his tongue through each moist nook of her mouth. He pressed his tongue past her lips to let it massage its way forward only to retreat in a game of chase that made her tongue dart out to beckon him back inside.

His hips came down and she understood where he'd been when the latex encasing his member edged forward to seek her opening. He was leading with the pinnacle of his own pleasure and keen to meet his effort, she pushed up to welcome him. Her mouth opened in a desperate gasp when he slid himself all the way home with one sure jolting thrust.

In her previous experience of this initial moment of penetration with a man it had never occurred to her how delighted she was with her decision to be intimate with him. Right now, gratification was all she could feel. The intensity of her raw nerve-endings kept her wriggling, bucking, and gasping around the size of him conquering her.

Dragging his delectable member back, he plunged forward and seemed pleased with how she arched up to meet him. "You're a naughty girl, aren't you?" he said with a wry twist to his lips.

Her mouth opened wide when he thrust into her again. He kept on moving, making her gasp in every breath and meet every thrust. He remained above her, high enough that he could stare down and observe every subtlety of her expression as he moved inside her.

Extending her fingers on his pec, she curled her nails into him and he slowed to grab one of her hands and pull it up to his mouth. Smacking a kiss onto her palm, he pushed her hand back to his chest.

"You keep on doing that, baby," he said and began to charge back into her again, picking up the speed of his incursion. He dipped to suck her lower lip and when he rose, she was gratified to see the darkness in his eyes fixated on her again. "You leave your mark."

As if what he was doing wasn't enough, the snarl in his voice pushed her into a fierce climax that made her stab her nails into his shoulders and scream out. She had never screamed with such wild abandon during sex before. This was an outlet for the powerful force exploding in her gut, in her heart and in her head. All of her atoms wanted more of this, more of him, and when he kept pushing into her, she hauled her legs higher until they locked around his torso.

Crunching up, she caught his lip in her teeth and threw her hands to the back of his neck where she clawed at him, forcing him to kiss her with everything he had, with the same overwhelming need that was swamping her. He didn't miss a beat in his rhythm and when she flopped onto the bed, she used every ounce of reserve energy to meet his pounding.

Pushing away from her, he grabbed her hips and clamped them down on the bed to watch his final thrust that made his head go back. He didn't scream like she did, he let out a long string of curses that if she hadn't been so completely spent might have made her blush.

Withdrawing from her body, he didn't wait until the last of her orgasms finished their cascade. Meaning she was still blinking at the ceiling when the bed moved beside her and his form left hers. Her hands fell, one on her chest and the other on her forehead, and she closed her eyes.

"My God," she breathed out, struggling to form words. Her head flopped to the side to see him sitting on the far side of the bed. "I think I figured out who you are." He whipped around to face her direction, though she couldn't read his expression through the shadows. "You're a delusion, aren't you? I've actually gone completely insane and somehow you're my reward."

His body loosened then he rose to his feet and pulled his jeans up from where they hung over his ass. He fastened them and his belt again.

Being so caught up in the passion of their joining, it hadn't occurred to her to question what would happen next. "This where you run out on me?" she asked.

"Want me to spend the night?" he mumbled with a deriding snicker.

"Yes."

He turned and because he was right in front of the window, there was no prospect of interpreting the details of his features. "The question was rhetorical," he said, moving around the bed, past the corner chair he'd been in when she first met him. He came all the way around to her side of the bed and dipped to snag his tee shirt from the floor.

He was done with her. He'd gotten his ya-ya's in her bed and now he was going to disappear into the night. Raven was never going to be much of a cuddler, he was too guarded to let her in. But she didn't want to be abandoned without trying to reach him, especially not with everything she'd learned.

"You're not interested in why I wanted to speak to you?" she asked, pushing up onto her elbows, which got lost under the pillow her head had been resting on.

"Sure," he said. Unwinding his tee shirt and pulling it over his head, he stretched the material with his elbows to put his arms into the sleeves in an efficient, masculine manner, which made her sorry she'd turned their conversation to business. Not that she'd had any other choice because he was about to fade out of her life. "Hit me with it."

"Grant's keeping secrets from me," she said and his exhaled laugh didn't make her feel any better.

"Well, shit, sweetheart, that's what I've been telling you all along."

"I know," she said, scrambling up onto her knees to catch his ribs beneath his arms to keep him there with her. "I think he might be in over his head. That he might be in trouble."

"Isn't that a shame," he said in a way that made her think sympathy was the furthest thing from his mind.

She glowered. After building this man up to be some kind of hero, he was proving to be anything but. Disappointed, she wasn't ready to give up on him. "Don't you care about anyone?" she asked, falling back to sit on her feet. "Don't you care that something terrible could happen? Something that we could stop if we work together?"

"Okay," he muttered on an exhale as though he was only humoring her and didn't expect her to offer anything of substance. "What did you find out?"

Zara wanted to tell him everything, to spill the secrets of her boss and her investigation to Raven and have him help her piece together a solution. She wanted to trust him, but she had to be realistic. If Raven wasn't on the same page as her, or if this had all been some great ruse to gain her trust, she couldn't pour out her secrets to someone who had yet to reveal his end game.

Sex didn't make them a couple. It didn't mean that she had moved up Raven's priority list either. It just meant that they were both unattached and attracted to each other. Zara knew her heart had been touched by his determination to protect her. Having sex with him only enhanced her want to get to know this man better.

"How did you know other people were watching me?" she asked, opening her fingers on her thighs. "You said it the first night after Tim died. How did you know people were watching me? And how did you know that Detective Kraft wouldn't be in touch with me again?"

"Because Dennis and I go way back," Raven said and folded his arms across his chest. "What did you find out, Shifty?"

"Oh, I'm shifty? That's rich," she said.

"Once," he muttered and she lost his train of thought.

"Huh?"

"You screw a girl once and that gives her license to bitch. It never fails." Turning his attention to the floor, he stuck his feet in his boots. Although she couldn't see them, she figured he wasn't going to take the time to lace them. With a wide stance, he folded his arms again. "What do you want, Zara?"

Closing her arms around her abdomen, she didn't like being so physically exposed when she was about to reveal an emotional vulnerability. "I want your word that no harm will come to Grant, that you'll protect him like you protect me."

She couldn't reveal the whole truth to Raven until she was sure Grant would be treated as a friend. Yes, she was pissed that he hadn't been honest, but she had to believe that he was still the moral man she knew and that his actions were evidence of him being in hot water. If he was being coerced by blackmail or something similar, then she had to know Raven would help Grant, not attack him.

"I can't be in two places at once," he said, addressing this conversation as he probably would in any other scenario. Her nakedness didn't soften him and the sex certainly hadn't left him beholden. "And keeping you alive was a means to an end."

"Which is?"

"Information," he said. "I told you that already."

That may be true, but he'd declared himself as finished with her on Saturday night, and yet here he was. In light of tonight, she wondered if his goodbye was all part of the theatrics because he certainly hadn't stopped checking in on her. "But you walked away from me on Saturday. You said goodbye to me."

"Because you were sure that Saint Grant was gonna be your shining hero. Why do you think I came here tonight?"

"Because you were worried about me," she said, daring him to deny it. "Because you wanted to make sure I was okay. I don't know. Maybe you just can't help yourself. You've been watching me for God knows how long. Maybe months."

With one stride, he brought himself to the very edge of the bed then he bent to hook a finger under her chin. Forcing her face up, they were nose-to-nose when the darkness in his eyes met hers and this time a sinister glow had overtaken them.

The scorn of ridicule colored his words. "There's one thing you haven't figured out yet, baby."

"Oh, yeah, what's that?" she asked, determined not to shrink in the heat of his attempt to intimidate her.

"I was never watching you."

She didn't believe him and arched a brow to prove her doubt. "You just happen to always be in the right place at the right time?"

His volume lowered until his words were barely a breath that cascaded over her cheeks. "I was watching them."

"Watching…"

Dropping his finger, he backed off and folded his arms again. "I don't give a damn what you do with your time. I wasn't watching you. Why would I do that? I'm not interested in what you do. I'm interested in what you know. I've been watching the bastards who are watching you. I want to know what they're doing. I don't give a damn what they know. I know more than they do about the damned device."

Forgetting his disrespect and her confusion, she perked up. "The device," she said and rose onto her knees to curl her hands around his folded arms. "Tell me about the device."

"Oh," he said with too much glee to be sincere. "Now she wants information! Is that what the sex was for? Let me tell you, baby, I don't owe you a damn thing."

Mortified that he would consider her such a harlot, she stuttered before putting any words together. "The sex was not my attempt to…" she trailed off because she didn't know how to articulate what he was implying.

"Coerce," he said, ducking his head an inch. "That's what it's called. It's called coercion, and you're good at it, baby… very good at it."

"Don't talk to me like that," she said, not appreciating the lewd hue of his voice.

But when she slapped a hand onto his chest, she was reminded of their encounter. Instead of drawing her hand away after the slap, she kept it there and pushed into him again, curling the tips of her fingers to drag her nails over the fabric of his tee shirt.

"I could tell you were the naughty type from the minute I saw you," he said.

Lifting one arm from his chest, he extended a finger and used the single digit to push her hair back from her shoulder, exposing her breast, reminding her of her nakedness.

The thump of arousal began to build until her skin pulsed. "Is that why we had sex?" she asked, still obsessed with the act of driving her fingernails into him.

"We had sex because we wanted to have sex," he said. "Guys don't need to pin a deeper meaning on it."

"I'm not a guy," she said, letting her head fall to the side so she could look up at him.

"Which is another reason we had sex," he said and dipped forward to kiss her hairline. "Now, if there's nothing else…"

Ceasing their contact, he headed for the door. If he wasn't going to give her information, then she would just have to keep digging on her own. But letting him walk out now didn't offer a resolution to her true motive for lighting up the window.

Just as he opened the bedroom door to exit, panic made her call out. "What do I do if they come for me?"

He stopped and turned to look at her. Sagging back to sit on her feet, Zara remained in her kneeling position, hoping that he wouldn't leave her without some reassurance. She felt pathetic asking him for help, but she'd rather feel an instant of embarrassment with Raven than be defenseless if she was faced with goons like Kahlil's again.

His tongue pushed out his top lip and the impatience in his eyes left her hanging, wondering if he was going to offer any support. Then he muttered something and exhaled before disappearing into the living room.

Pouncing off the bed, Zara got as far as snagging her kimono from the back of the bedroom door when Raven reappeared in the room, carrying his jacket with him. On the cusp of asking why his outerwear was relevant, he tossed the jacket onto the bed and she noticed the pistol he was holding.

The black piece was small in his large hands. With practiced efficiency, he ejected the clip and checked the ammunition. Slamming the cartridge back into place, he grabbed the barrel and turned the butt of the weapon toward her.

"Here."

Her eyes went from his face to the gun then to the left and right. "What am I supposed to do with that?" she asked.

"Someone threatens you, you point and shoot. Have you ever shot a gun?"

Loosening her body, she shifted her shoulders in an attempt to portray nonchalance. "Maybe," she said, reluctant to reveal her ignorance.

With an eye roll, he came closer. "That's a no," he said. Grabbing her shoulder, he hauled her to him, and spun her around so that her back was to his chest.

Picking up her hand, he molded it around the grip then picked up the other hand to put it on the opposite side. "I'm not comfortable with this," she said, trying to relax her hands.

"What? You don't like it doggy style?" he asked, and she

expelled a syllable of a laugh.

They were standing upright, so where he got the idea of sexual positions from she didn't know. "That's not what I meant," she said. But he closed his hands around hers and raised the weapon.

"There's a round in the barrel, so we're not gonna squeeze the trigger. Bring it up until you can see down the sight. You see it?"

Light from the candles in the living room illuminated them, so yes, she could see what he meant. "I see it."

With his arms being longer than hers were, and his shoulders broader, she fit comfortably in the triangle his body formed around hers. Her shoulders pressed into the sturdy muscles of his upper arms as she focused ahead and closed one eye. "Pick an object and aim at it," he said. "Get comfortable with the weight."

"It's heavier than I would've thought."

"You've got eight rounds, okay?" he asked. "That means you've got eight shots to hit what you're aiming at. It's semi-automatic, so you can just keep on pulling the trigger."

"This is a nice gun," she said, bending her arms to try to get a better look at it.

"It's Swiss," he said, attempting to extend her arms again, but she resisted.

"Have you killed people with this gun?"

He ceased trying to get her to aim and curved his head around enough to look at her. "You worried about the police coming to your door looking for me?"

"You shouldn't be worried," she said, testing the weight of the gun. "All I can tell them is that I summon you with a secret light signal… you're like Batman."

"I'm not like Batman," he said, shaking his head and turning his face away when she smiled up at him. This time she let him hold her hands around the gun and bring it up so they could aim together. "He lives in Washington."

Laughing at his whispered quip, she nudged a shoulder into his chest, but that just made him curl further around her. It was nice to be in the circle of his arms and her previous fears dissipated. With this man and this weapon, she wouldn't be a victim again. Raven was still hard and although his quips suggested he was more relaxed, he was dry in his delivery. Still, she felt close to him, warm and sheltered. By giving her this gun and this lesson, he was enhancing her defenses, guaranteeing she'd be safe. That he went so far made her think she might be softening some of his tough outer shell.

"This doesn't seem hard," she said, closing one eye to aim at a spot beside her curtains.

"You want to squeeze the trigger, just increase your pressure."

"Okay."

"Remember to take into account your mark's movement. Don't aim at where he is; aim at where he will be. If you're outside, factor in wind speed and direction as well as other environmental factors."

"Other environmental—how do you know all of this?" she asked. Just like when they were in bed, he pressed his fingers to her cheekbone to direct her attention to where he wanted it to be, this time that was away from him and onto the gun sight.

"Keep the gun on you at all times and reserve yourself time in a shooting range as quickly as possible."

"Can I take my own gun?" she asked. "Won't I need permits and—"

He crouched enough to rest his chin on her shoulder, but he had to realize that he was losing the battle of getting her to focus. Having a weapon would make her feel safer, but Zara didn't want it raising questions in her life that she'd have no way to answer.

"I can get you the paperwork," he said.

"Will it be official paperwork?" she asked.

Twisting to try to get a glimpse of him, she got more than she bargained for when Raven glanced to the corner of his eye. In this position, their lips were almost touching and the temptation was too much to resist. Her questions and concerns faded. Being intimate with him had assuaged her troubles and the heated memory of what had occurred on her bed not so long ago still scented the room. Deserting the gun in his hands, she swiveled to clasp his face and kiss him again.

He didn't resist her tongue when she begged entrance to his mouth. Brushing her tongue along his, he closed his arms around her and she felt the imprint of the gun between her shoulder blades when he negotiated their movement to back her toward the bed. They fell onto it and as she sunk into the mattress, her head rose to give him access to her neck.

Catching a glimpse of the gun, which was still in his hand, pressed into the bed beside her head with his finger resting across the trigger guard, she couldn't stop staring at the firearm, which may one day save her life. His finger wasn't on the trigger, but she didn't know if the gun had a safety or if there was a chance it could go off at any second.

"You interested in me or my weapon?" he asked.

Snapping her focus around, she saw his face an inch above hers. "You're dangerous," she murmured, sliding her hands up his sides to his chest.

"Yeah, I am… I'm really bad news for a woman who can't handle trouble."

"I'm new to it," she said. "But I'm learning."

"Learn fast," he said and his heat became stern. "What are you gonna do if they come for you?"

"Aim and squeeze."

"Atta girl," he said and scooped a hand behind her head to bow it, giving him the ability to kiss her hairline. While his lips still rested there, he took one of her hands and guided it to the bed where he put the gun on her palm. "Close your eyes."

Much as she didn't want to tear her eyes away from his, she did as he requested. His weight left her and she strained to hear where he was or what he was doing. When there was no further activity, she opened her eyes. He was gone.

SEVEN

ON TUESDAY, Zara was determined to confront Grant and get the truth. Not that she wanted to do it in an inflammatory way. All she wanted was to talk to him, to try to get him to open up about what was really going on. Then he didn't show up.

Grant not showing up to work was an anomaly. He called to tell her he had some important personal business to take care of and when she tried to push for details, he shut her down and said he would be back on Wednesday.

Zara couldn't get much more information on the device or deal from the company network, so she searched a few of the terms she'd come across online. The Internet wasn't much use. There was no way to determine how reliable the information on the World Wide Web was. All she had to go on were a few names, and they were only first names at that.

By the afternoon, she was tapping her pen on her shoulder and beating her foot against the side of her desk. Sucking her lips into her mouth, she dug her teeth into them and then tossed the pen onto the desk. Answers could be in Grant's office, but she couldn't claim to trust the man and then snoop in his private space... could she? Glancing to her left, Zara saw her purse on the floor and thought about Raven's gun nestled in there. WWRD? What would Raven do?

Screw it. Thrusting her hands on the desk, she pushed up to her feet and fixed her door in her sights. She had been in Grant's office hundreds of times, many of them alone without any supervision. So when she used her fingerprint to open his door, the other assistant didn't even look up from her work. Stepping inside, Zara let the door close and then pressed herself against it. His blinds were shut, as were the ones in her office, meaning the only way she could be seen was from outside and given their lofty position, she wasn't concerned about onlookers.

This felt wrong. She shouldn't be in here for a dishonest purpose. Second-guessing herself, Zara was about to run out again, but Raven came back into her thoughts. He watched dangerous men who were watching her and he could only be doing it because he wanted to prevent them from doing anything wrong. Either that or he wanted the tech so he could wreak havoc of his own. But an evil man with nefarious motives wouldn't know Batman's personal address. A smile tilted her lips at his joke, the strength of his character and determination drove her forward.

Scurrying over to Grant's desk, she glanced around the surface, but it was clear. It always was. The three drawers to the side were where he kept his personal things. Having come this far, she wasn't going to back out now. So sitting in her boss' chair, she tried to open the top drawer. Yanking on it, she was thwarted. It was locked.

Picking a lock was beyond her expertise and if she tried to jimmy it, there would be evidence of what she'd done. It might have served her better to ask Raven for some secret spy equipment rather than a gun.

Ready to give up, she sat back in the chair and squeezed her lips to the side. Some people liked to have a spare key in case of emergency and a guy like Grant—who didn't carry much on his person when he came in and out—had to have a key stashed somewhere in the room.

Running her fingers under the edge of the desk, she splayed her palms and reached further. But there was nothing to be found. Falling from the chair onto her knees, she began to search the underside of the desk, but still didn't find anything.

Crawling over to the unit behind his desk, she checked edges and used the furniture to clamber up onto her feet. Checking under knick-knacks and inside books, she was frustrated again.

"If I was a key, where would I be?" she whispered to herself while scanning the room.

There wasn't much furniture and the door had no frame, so those places were out. Pinning the conference table in her sights, she grabbed the back of his chair to push it out of her way then stopped. The chair. Secreting a key somewhere around the conference table or anywhere else in the room would present the opportunity for a visitor to find it. But the one place a visitor would never need to touch was his chair.

Crouching, she felt along the back and beneath the arms. Just under the front right corner of the seat, she felt a lump. Ducking further, she discovered a rectangle of plastic that served as a pouch for a shiny, silver key. Pulling it out, she almost squealed, but saved her triumph for after she found what she was looking for.

Having already been in here a while, time was running short, she could be discovered at any minute, and if Grant called while she was in here the jig could be up. Climbing into the seat, she put the key in the lock and unlocked the drawers. Tugging it forward, it glided on its runners, granting her access. The top drawer was stationery. Gum. A pager. A Post-it pad and nothing else. Pulling the top sheet of the Post-it pad off, she kept it stuck to her thumb and closed the drawer to move onto the second drawer.

There she found a couple of contracts. A book of addresses, which were probably all on the computer. A calculator. An iPod. Some more stationery items. Scotch tape. Labels. Nothing. Onto drawer three. This was where he kept files, thus making it the toughest drawer to search. Her intimate knowledge of the company let her dismiss most of the documents with haste. Walking her fingers through them, she was about to give up hope when she got to the last file. This wasn't like the others. It was in a black folder with a red label.

Most CI files weren't in black folders and a red label usually meant the file was from the Research and Development Department. The number on the label intrigued her as well. "Zero, zero seven, nine, three." She had never seen such a small number. None of the R&D files she had come across in her time here came with a number beginning with zero.

Opening the file, the first page seemed to be a floor plan, though she didn't recognize it and the only writing on the page was in the bottom corner. "Project Game Time," she read.

There was no way she could read all the information in this fat file. Flipping to the last page, she discovered why the file number was so low. "A patent application," she murmured, scanning the document. "1974… forty years, but—"A knock on the door made her stuff the folder into its suspension file.

Shuffling the other files back to cover it, she closed the drawer and locked it. The knock came again, but she was having trouble returning the key to its slot under the seat. "One second," she said, sliding off the chair to stick the key in its hiding place.

After doing that, she dashed across to the door and paused to look at her empty hands. She had no reason to be in here and coming out empty handed might look odd.

"What is it?" Zara called out and spun around to seek out any reason for why she might be in here.

"Mr. McCormack is on the phone," the other assistant called through the door.

Zara squeezed her eyes closed. As odd as it was to exit without any purpose, it was odder that she was calling through the office door instead of just opening it, so she sprang around to reach the door. Pulling it open, she slipped around it, past the assistant and began to move to her own office.

"Thanks," she said. "Put him through."

Grant didn't ask her where she'd been or what she'd been doing. But that didn't prevent anxious sweat from seeping out of her pores, though that could've been a reaction of guilt rather than fear. Whatever it was, she didn't like working without a safety net. Her attention moved to her purse again. Zara had never thought she'd be the type of person to consider a weapon a safety net, but she did feel better that it was there, just in case.

***

EVERY TIME SHE HEARD the elevator, her eyes pinged up. It was Wednesday and Grant hadn't come in yet. So far, there had been no call from him to explain his absence. But she wasn't his superior—he didn't have a superior—so he could do whatever the hell he liked. The company kept on going without him. He'd done a good job of running it since his mentor Frank Mitchell died last year, so he didn't need to be here every minute, though he usually was.

After lunch, she was losing hope of seeing him. When the elevator pinged again, she glanced up with little expectation only to be confronted by the sight of Grant coming out of it with one of the female vice-presidents. Zara had never been so grateful for having a glass-fronted office. Grant's blinds were always closed when he wasn't in there. Now that he was back, the blinds would be opened and she would get her chance to talk to him.

That chance came much later on after he'd seen every vice-president who was on the premises that day. She was called in and out of the office for various administrative reasons. But it was as the outer office assistant was putting on her coat and venturing into the cold night, that Zara got her chance to talk to the CEO alone.

Grant was working with his office door open. She watched the outer assistant disappear behind the elevator doors, and then she turned around and tapped a knuckle on his door. He glanced up.

"Are you busy?" she asked.

"I'm always busy," he said, holding a hand toward his

guest chair. "You know that. You're the one who runs around picking up after me."

Her smile didn't reach her eyes, but she tiptoed in to approach his desk. "I was thinking about this product, the one that you're trying to sell in secret."

"Private," Grant said. "Isn't that a better word?"

"Private, yes, of course," she said and although she went to the guest chair, she didn't sit in it. "I can be of more use to you if I know more about it. I can pull together a marketing presentation and—"

"Conscientious, it was one of the first things I noticed about you," he said, stretching a superior smile across his face before taking a breath. "Your ability to take initiative and complete any task without complaint. You're a problem solver, Zara, and that's a valuable quality for an employee to have. It's rarer than you might think."

"Thank you," she said, unsure if flattery was his attempt to divert her attention from what she'd asked.

"Fortunately, that's not required in this case. I've been working with this product for almost a year. I know it inside and out. And my clients and I are past the hard sell. Now it's just a negotiation on price and utilization."

"I don't—"she frowned and shook her head.

Grant held up his hand to silence her. "Don't worry about it, Zara… I don't want you worrying about it."

Lowering his hands to the desk, he linked his fingers together and his brow came down. Without any further smile or civility in his expression, Grant was intent on getting the seriousness of his point across. "I just wanted to offer. To be helpful."

"Your first concern should always be for yourself," he said and she couldn't recall a time in which his tone had been this foreboding. "Remember to help yourself before you help others. These negotiations are precarious and with men who are extremely serious. We cannot risk offending any of them."

"I would never—"

"Don't venture into unguarded waters," he said. "This deal is not about money. It's about ideology and doing what my father and Frank failed to do."

"I was—"

"If I were you, I'd keep my nose clean," he said. "I will deal with these men because they are men who have a low tolerance for curious women."

From the glass in his eyes and the lack of energy from his form, she recognized those words for what they were: a threat. Grant had just threatened her. It didn't seem to be a friendly warning. He told her the waters were unguarded. Was that a hint that he did not intend to ensure her safety?

Backing away, she eventually turned and made a beeline for her own office. Grabbing her purse from the floor, she held it to her chest and stared at the wall separating her office from Grant's. Being closer to her weapon made her feel a bit better. But she was beginning to understand that Grant was not the virtuous man she had assumed him to be.

EIGHT

TRYING TO MAKE SENSE of the data laid out on her home-office desk was giving her a headache. So Zara removed her reading glasses and turned off the lamp, resigned to putting her investigation to bed for the night. While moving through the living room, she glanced at the candles on the windowsill and considered lighting them to beckon him. But Raven was no easier to decipher than what she'd left on her desk.

She took a shower and then lay down on her bed in the dark. The options before her weren't particularly attractive. She could quit her job and pretend that she had never heard of Grant McCormack, Raven, Sutcliffe, Kahlil, and the rest of them. But if there was a chance that these men were planning something nefarious, she would never forgive herself if people lost their lives while she turned a blind eye.

Going to the cops was another option, but she had no evidence to present to them. The only firsthand information she had was an off-handed comment made to her on the phone, and she didn't have concrete proof of that either. She didn't even know what this damn product was, meaning she couldn't tell authorities what to look for.

Spreading her arms the width of the bed, she steadied

her breathing. All she could do was try to obtain more information. Except she'd tried to approach Grant and every time he stonewalled her. Grant wasn't interested in her input; he was in league with the terrorists and happy about it.

Raven was an option. She could confess all to him and pray that he didn't take the information and bolt. She still didn't know quite how he fit into this scenario or whose side he was on. People always said that serial killers looked like everyone else. Maybe the same was true for terrorists. They didn't walk around wearing a button declaring their intent and they could probably be charming… not that Raven could be accused of that.

"What did I tell you?"

Recognizing the ease of his now familiar tone, Zara rolled her head to the side in time to see the floor lamp illuminate. Raven was seated in the corner chair as she'd anticipated he would be. Closing her eyes, she returned her head to its original position.

"Naughty," Raven said. "I said you were a naughty girl, didn't I?"

"What do you want?" she grumbled.

"Haven't decided yet," he murmured. His husky voice made her shiver, even with the heat of the shower still clinging to her skin, but the mental exertions of the day left her too drained to think about seduction.

"I'm not in a sexy mood. Can you come back tomorrow?"

"Busy tomorrow."

"How long have you been sitting there?" she asked, rolling her head and peeking at him out of one eye.

"Long time," he said. "You should probably turn on the lights when you're walking into your bedroom naked."

Rocking onto her side, she supported her head with a hand under her hair. "This may come as a surprise to you, Rave, but other men don't sneak into my bedroom to skulk in the dark."

"I prefer to think of it as loitering with intent," he said.

The lamp went off and the sound of movement

preceded his silhouette emerging in the frame of her window. Tipping her head back to look at him, Zara couldn't make out his features, but could tell that he was taking off his tee shirt.

"Uh, what do you think you're doing?" she asked, but he had already dropped onto the bed beside her.

One of his arms came around her ribs and he hauled her closer while his head fell to sample the line of her throat exposed beneath her supporting arm. "You opened the door," he said, tracing his lips back and forth on her jaw line. "Until you tell me it's closed again. You're fair game."

"I'm fair, what?" she asked, smacking his shoulder.

"You get as physical as you want," he said.

Rushing forward, he tackled her onto her back and pinned her down.

With his hands on her upper arms, and his shins over her legs, she couldn't move. "You're a physical guy," she said. "You understand the physical."

"Want me to teach you?" he asked, letting his jeans rasp the length of her exposed legs.

Lowering himself, he kissed her jaw again.

"You can talk me through it," she said and finished by muttering his words, "I'm fair game."

His statement didn't offend her. Having such a direct guy in her bed was something Zara needed. Questions existed in too many areas of her life. Conceding to simple sexual desire without extraneous stress in the equation was alluring.

"Is it words you want, baby?" he asked. "Is that what turns you on?" No man had asked her that question before. Usually actions took the place of words. "You want to hear what I'm gonna do to your fuckable body?"

That was another question no man had asked her and she was still pondering it, and the growing pulse in her muscles, when Raven's mouth moved over hers. Zara parted her lips and let him kiss her. She hadn't been objecting to the sex. Her objection had been to his presumption, and that complaint hadn't been particularly convincing even to her own ears.

"You lay it all out for me," he said. "I was thinking sex and you came in ready to perform. You're a good girl,

Zara."

"I thought I was naughty," she asked, and he caught her chin in his teeth.

The grip on her arms grew and she got a glimpse of just how strong this man was. His fingers cut so deep, she thought they might bruise her, but that ache stoked the fire smoldering low in her gut and she parted her legs to draw up her knees.

"Is that what you like, baby? You want me to talk? To get rough with you?"

Her heart pounced up to her throat when they made eye contact. In its place was a hollow haven of arousal that bubbled and simmered, popping and spilling lower, descending through her guts. Her head moved in a nod of its own volition and when his shrewd smile became lewd, she wondered what kind of brute she'd just unleashed.

"Push back," he murmured and she wasn't sure what he meant. "Show me what you've got… Fight."

Under normal circumstances, she would never try to fight anyone, especially someone with Raven's stature. But she tensed and tried to push up. Wriggling left to right, she got her feet to his hips and tried to push him away while pulling her arms back and forth, trying to work them out of his hold.

"Stop," he said. Although he hadn't had any difficulty in subduing her, she complied and went limp. "You see how that worked?"

"What? I—"

"When I said stop, you stopped." She nodded. "If we're gonna play games, if you want me to… take control. If no is gonna mean yes, I have to know when stop means stop."

"I don't understand."

"I'm happy to play with you," he said, lowering to kiss her and run the tip of his nose down her cheekbone. "I've been thinking about nothing else since I left you here naked with that gun the other night."

Exhaling her impatience, she tried to stem her frustration because somehow, she knew he would enjoy getting a rise out of her. He had kissed her, started to stimulate her, and then stopped to have a damn conversation. But she had to appreciate that he was being responsible because she hadn't realized that sleeping with him once would make her fair game, as he'd put it.

Now that she'd told him she wanted him to get rough, God only knew what door she had opened.

"What word will you use if you mean no?"

A safe word. As ridiculous as it made her sound, she had read about this. For couples who liked to get rough or push boundaries with each other, they came up with a word that could be used in place of a refusal. The possibilities began to flood her mind. The freedom this could give them in the bedroom provoked her hormones again until her toes tingled, forcing her to curl them into his hips.

"What are you going to do to me?" she asked, grinning past her pout. Trying to push up to kiss him, she was planted back on the bed. If this new chapter meant their kissing would cease, she would be disappointed. Kissing him was a wonder. The memory of it alone dampened her.

"Pick a word and then I can do whatever the hell I want until you use it."

Odd as it was, he was actually being respectful; he was taking care of her. In that moment, she stared up into his eyes and decided that there was no way he could be a terrorist. Terrorists wanted to terrorize and took pleasure in the suffering of others. She wasn't suffering. Granted, she wasn't his prey… except from the depth of his intensity now, she could be mistaken for it.

"Dagger," she said. "Because you're so cloak and dagger." He shook his head. "Why not?"

"Because I might bring one of those to bed."

That sent another shudder through her. Zara tried to free her arms so she could touch him, but he kept her pinned. "Taxicab," she said, growling in frustration. "Taxicab is our safe word. No chance of you bringing one of those into bed, is there?"

His eyes got heavier. "Excellent choice," he said and with that formality out of the way, he became fixated on her lips. "Taxicab it is."

Pressing down on her, he impelled his tongue into her

mouth. The motion of his kiss relaxed her and she opened and closed her fists. Still unable to touch him, she used her feet to do the touching for her. Coiling her legs around his thighs, she rubbed her feet down his hard calves, pushing into them with the balls of her feet, massaging the muscles until her toes hit his bare heels, then they ascended again.

He'd obviously removed his socks and boots while he was seated in the corner. Now all she needed to do was get rid of his jeans. When he loosened his grip on her, she slid her hands up his arms, expecting to get her chance to explore his body. Except he cut her chance short by picking her up in a bear hug. Coiling her legs around his hips, she locked her ankles at his lower back and stretched her arms out behind him, crossing them over, and linking her fingers.

Raven's wide kneeling stance gave them a good foundation and he didn't wobble once. Their eyes met and she leaned in to kiss him. While he was pampering her mouth, he shuffled forward and fell onto her. Zara caught the full weight of him for a split second before he shifted himself to one side, so that his body was still covering hers, but he wasn't above her anymore.

When he reached over her for the drawer, she assumed his intention was to retrieve a condom. Taking her chance, while he was on a mission, Zara combed a hand through his hair. She kissed his neck and shoulder while stroking his torso. Every inch of him was hard and she wanted to explore each of his muscles with her tongue. But knowing that her time might be limited, she chose instead to unbuckle his belt to try to get ahold of him.

The belt was as far as she got. He closed the drawer and returned his focus to her, squashing her roving hand in place with a slant of his pelvis. Stealing her mouth, she was basking in the fervor of his kiss when she heard the buzz. Still kissing him, she opened her eyes and tried to see what was making the noise.

She didn't see it, but she felt the tingle on her knee and she recognized the pinch of that cool metal. Gasping the air from his mouth, she grabbed his shoulders to force him away from their kiss. But he was already trailing the metallic object up the inside of her thigh.

"That's my…"

"Yes, it is," he said and licked her bottom lip. "You know what you have to say if you want me to stop." They had just made that agreement, and as mortified as she was at the thought of what he was going to do to her, she'd invited it. Asking him to push her boundaries had given him free rein to deliver her new experiences, even those that might fluster her.

"You're not gonna say no," he said, pressing kisses to her cheek, jaw, and neck. "You're naughty. You're a naughty girl who wants a bad boy to do naughty things to her. Aren't you?"

The pulse of her vibrator had paused high on her thigh. With his mouth open on hers, Raven moved the unyielding object higher to let it just touch her clit. The stab of pleasure made her cling to him, still their mouths remained open together, yet they didn't fuse.

"Relax," he said. "Let yourself feel it."

Sliding the cylindrical agitator south, he let it just enter her to tease her juices. Keeping it just on her threshold, Raven ducked down to kiss and tease each of her nipples to a point with his mouth.

When the invisible strings keeping her body together began to tighten, he shifted higher to lie the length of her with his weight braced on one elbow. The other hand moved the tormenting tool in circles, widening her entrance in preparation for him.

In no apparent hurry, he used a fingertip to circle the nipple closest to his supporting arm and kept on playing. Turning her body toward him, Zara tried to kiss him again. But he kissed her chin and rose over her only to then descend out of her vision, leaving a chill in the place his body had been. Parting her legs, he kissed her hip and ran his tongue across to unite it with the vibrator he'd moved onto her clit. Kissing each side of it, he moved the toy up and down over her and trusting it to do its work, he dropped his mouth and dipped his tongue into her.

Zara didn't know what to do with the rush of heat and arousal that was making it difficult for her to remain static.

To aid his work, he rested a forearm across her pelvis to pin her down. The buzz of stimulation made her yelp, and he reared up to kiss her. Experiencing her own taste on his tongue made her clutch his hair to force him closer. When she arched up into the toy, Raven pressed it into her sensitive spot, showing no mercy, and she yelped again.

Her unsteady breaths made her heart rate grow erratic. It thudded so hard that each pulse shook her throat. So squeezing her eyes closed, she sealed her mouth and swallowed hard.

But Raven's tongue glided through the seam of her lips, giving her no time to regain her equilibrium. "Pretty baby," he muttered. "Open those big browns for me." Letting her eyelids relax, she thought she was looking to him, but her world was one big blur, so she couldn't be sure what she was seeing. All that existed now was the panting gasp that scraped the back of her throat.

"I'm gonna watch you come," he said, running his mouth to her ear and sliding the vibrator through her heat to undulate it against her opening. "Nothing sexier than watching the way you breathe when you're hot for me. You want to come? Do you? Tell me."

"I want to come," she said, and he moved the toy in circles.

"I'm gonna watch you come like this…" Tracing the vibrator up and around her clit, he let it touch every intimate part of her. "Then I'm gonna fuck you until you come again. You've got a sweet pussy, baby. I'm gonna get to know it real well… Say it again."

"I want to come," she said, clenching her teeth in resistance to the building pressure that made her lightheaded.

Noting her defiance, he stroked her cheek with his stubble-roughened jaw. "Relax," he breathed and opened his mouth over hers. Distracting her with a kiss at the same time he massaged the toy over her again. Her forbearance failed and she was sent into a blind fog of endorphins that made every part of her spasm into a tense ball. "That was a good one."

The vibrator went off, but she didn't have time to

register that before he was kissing her and running his hands up and down her torso. While trying to blink, Zara couldn't breathe because her throat was so dry. But he kept on kissing her until her extremities began to tingle and she regained feeling.

Wrapping her hands around his shoulders, she spread her fingers and was impressed at the girth of his definition. Sliding them down his arms, she squeezed his elbows, then they shifted and she was flipped onto her face.

Grabbing her hair in a fist, he pulled it off her back, and kissed the nape of her neck. Then with the slightest of touches, he ran his tongue down her spine, sending a shiver through her that brought her to the brink of the precipice again.

"Rave—"

He smacked her ass, then kissed the globe and drove a forearm under her hips to pull them up. "This is gonna be fast and dirty," he said, insinuating a finger between her thighs to dip into the well he'd created in her with her previous orgasm. "You need to be fucked good and hard… it's gonna make everything feel all better."

She wasn't sure what it would make feel better, but she didn't care. She'd do anything he asked of her at this point. "Lift up that ass," he said and she pulled her legs under her. Both his hands came to the insides of her thighs and he forced her knees apart, giving her a wider center.

"Are you going to—?"

"I'm going in right here," he said, squeezing two fingers into her sensitized passage. "Hold on to the bars on the headboard. Don't let go."

Zara wasn't sure she had the strength to provide much of a lever point of resistance against what Raven could be capable of. But she lifted herself and did what he said. His fingers slid out of her and she glanced over her shoulder to see him lick them clean. His proceeding wink almost made her arms buckle, but her grip held true after she noticed that he had himself in hand.

Her excitement only faltered when she caught sight of his jeans, riding low around his thighs. Leaning over her, he pressed her cheekbone and forced her to look ahead. Scrutiny while screwing obviously wasn't one of his turn ons.

With one hand on her hip, Raven yanked her, angling her body to his liking, giving no thought to any preference she may have. But Zara was already panting and writhing in anticipation of what he was going to provide and had no desire to participate in the decision-making, not when Rave was so skilled.

The provoking pressure of him pushing inside drenched her with sensation. Displaying a lack of patience, Zara inhaled and closed her eyes. "Rave—"

He smacked her again, and she realized that he always cut her off when she used his alias. Sucking her lips into her mouth, Zara wriggled back against him, enjoying how his mass felt against her inner muscles.

"Now I'm gonna make you scream," he said, skimming his palm up her back, pushing down on his return to make her arch her ass up. "That's it, baby. Purr for me."

Drawing back, he left her body, so she held her breath and waited for him to return. The head of his dick stretched her threshold, and when she could bear it no more, she dragged in a breath and whined though she dug her teeth into her lower lip in an attempt to dam the whimper.

"That's all I wanted," he said.

One arm swooped under her and he caught her when he slammed into her. His pace was so furious that she had to cling onto the headboard even when he drove her forward enough to bump the top of her head into it.

With his steadying arm, he thrust deep and tilted her pelvis to a perfect position for optimum penetration. His bruising force pummeled her cervix and she clenched to slow his fury, but it didn't work. Except the speckles of her orgasm emanated outward and she tossed her head back to scream out. She had never experienced such breakneck bonding before. The pose, each of his actions, the urgency of his thrusts, all of it belonged in a cave somewhere thousands of years ago.

Losing her grip with her sweaty hands, she let go and he smacked her ass. "Hands!"

Despite the frenzy, he was aware of her every move and that attentiveness only increased her excitement. Keeping up his movement inside her, he lunged forward to grab both of her hands, which he picked up to plant on the headboard. Going back to his task, he held her hips and shoved into her once again before she heard his curse stream, this time hissed out from between his teeth.

Flopping onto her face, Zara made no attempt to speak or even move. Hyperaware of every cell, she closed her eyes and experienced every tremor and throb until their completion. She didn't know exactly where Raven was, but he stroked her arm, provoking her into turning her head toward the other side of the bed.

With her face still buried in the pillow, she was pleased to see that he was lying beside her. Although, he was on his side and wearing a frown that didn't suggest he was a man basking in the bliss of pleasure comparable to what she was experiencing.

"What's wrong?" she asked, lifting a hand to reach for his face, but he didn't let it get that far.

"I came here to earn your trust," he said, pushing her body away from his. "This was not how I intended to get it."

"You've never screwed a woman for information before?" Zara asked.

Rolling onto her side, she dug her elbow under the pillow he'd just vacated and rested her temple on her fist. For her, this was more than the mission he was on. He was pushing her boundaries and awakening desires in her that she never knew she had. Raven was special.

But she was getting the impression he didn't feel that way, from his anger and his inability to relax when he was having sex or trying to joke, she knew he felt damaged, that something in him held back because maybe he didn't believe he deserved having anything good in his life.

"I have," he said, sitting up on the far edge of her bed, facing the window. Not that he would see much. There was nothing but darkness beyond the curtain and even if it was daytime, all that was out there were the dumpsters.

"Why am I different? Why not screw me and ask me

your questions when I'm half-asleep? When I'm languishing in the endorphins of orgasm and my guard is down?" Hoping he might admit some vulnerability that would let her confess her own care for him, she asked leading questions.

He cracked his knuckles, then he tipped his head to crack his neck. "You're too messy to adopt as a typical asset. I've already revealed too much of myself to you."

Taking her fist from her head, she grabbed a vertical bar on the headboard and used it to push herself up in his direction. Kneeling behind him, seated on her own in-steps, Zara spread her hands on his back. "Whenever you make cryptic comments like that, you send my mind into overdrive. Why am I messy, Raven? What are you afraid of?"

He turned his head enough for her to see the silhouette of his profile, highlighted against the orange glow that emanated from the security light outside her window.

"Knowing the truth of who I am could get you into serious trouble. It could cost you your life."

"That's another cryptic comment, beau," she said. Splaying her fingers, Zara pressed her hands into him. Not that it was her intention, but her weight wasn't enough to make him move. That inherent strength was one of the qualities that fascinated her about this man. She kept on leaning into him until her lips touched his spine. "Why do you need my trust so bad?"

"You might be the only person alive who can help me avert disaster on a global scale."

That was less cryptic. Easing back, she dismissed the fizzing chemistry still at work within her. Languishing with her lover didn't seem right in the light of that kind of declaration. Since her phone conversation with Sutcliffe, she'd had her suspicions about what was going to happen, and this was the confirmation Zara needed about the gravity of the situation.

"How can I do that?" she murmured.

"I came here to earn your trust because I need information. But I also have to divert you from a certain course of action and if I don't… If I fail, then you'll fail, and that will cost lives."

"How am I going to do that?" she asked.

At no point in her diary did Zara have a date marked for a mass killing spree. All these things he said were going to happen—that she was going to be responsible for—she wasn't sure she could live up to that kind of expectation.

Leaving one foot on the floor, he twisted to bring his other knee onto the bed so he could face her. "I can't tell you that until I have your trust. Once I do. I'll tell you everything."

He was dealing with his own demons, but still prioritized saving lives. Searching his eyes, she read pain behind his detachment that made her wonder if he'd been hurt by women in the past. "Sometimes you have to give a little to get a little," she said, trying to coax him into telling her the truth about what was going on. Except his expression didn't flinch, he just kept examining hers, looking for a way in.

"How do I win your trust, Zar?"

"Well," she said, gasping in a smile and changing the mood because it was obvious that he was not going to open his heart to her tonight. Slapping her hands onto his thigh, she moved onto all fours then backed up enough to loop her arms around his neck and hang her weight on him. "You could start by spending the night instead of sneaking out while my eyes are closed. I've never seen you in the daylight before."

His features became hard and his patience was lost. "I want your trust. But I don't want you to fall for me. Emotions make things messy."

She wasn't sure she could stop that train now that it was on the tracks. His hook was the danger that shimmered from his posture and expression. But he cared about things, about innocent lives and her safety. Having never seen him with anyone else, she wondered if he was a loner, damaged and maybe a martyr to his own cause, whatever that was. But it was his complex character, as well as his seduction, that fascinated her and she wanted to know more, she wanted to know all of him.

"Is that why I'm a messy asset?" she asked, pausing before she kissed him. "Because you have feelings for me?"

"It's my experience that women run away with that feelings shit faster than men."

"If you want me to take a chance on you," she said,

tipping her head to the left to kiss him. "Then you're going to have to take a chance on me." Tipping her head the opposite way, Zara kissed him again. "Spend the night, Rave. Stay for breakfast and I'll tell you everything you want to know."

Grabbing her face, he pulled her mouth onto his. After a short, fiery kiss, he used his grip on her to shove her onto her back.

"I'm a man of my word," he said. Twisting, he drew one knee up onto the bed and supported her torso with his hands. "It's the most precious thing a man can give."

Optimism thrived. She wouldn't be afraid if he was here and she could offer him comfort. Having him here all night would give her the chance to prove that she could be a sanctuary for him and that their association didn't have to be all give and no take for him.

"Does that mean you plan to stay?" she asked. Nudging her fingernails into the nape of his neck, she scraped them back and forth.

Straightening his arms, Raven threw her back on the bed, then stood up and turned to come down on the mattress as well. Crawling over her, Rave stayed high on his hands and knees, caging her between his limbs, to stare down into her face.

"I'll have to stay to find out if you're a girl of your word. But after tonight, all bets are off."

"What does that mean?" she asked. Curling her hands around his shoulders, she stroked a path from his chest to his back, as far as her reach would allow.

"It means, tomorrow you give me your trust and I'll give you mine. But if you betray me, the consequences will be severe for you and everyone you care about."

She cared about him, but it was unlikely that he was referring to himself. Especially if she factored his scowl into the equation. "You would kill me for revealing you to anyone?"

"Me or anything I tell you, yes, I would."

Exhaling, she averted her focus while considering that she might have misjudged him. "A threat, well… today is the day for it," she muttered.

"What?" he asked, pressing her cheekbone to force her gaze back. "Who threatened you?"

"Nothing, never mind," she said. Grant probably hadn't meant his threat any more than Raven did. At the time, it shook the foundation of her belief in him, but she was coming to learn that she was ignorant about many things in her life.

"I shouldn't say this, but…" he blinked his eyes away and when they came back the darkness swirled in them. "I have… skills… that can facilitate the elimination of threats."

Just because he didn't use explicit terms didn't mean she was oblivious to his meaning. "Have you killed before?"

He didn't blink, but the line of his mouth curled at one end. "It's one of my two specialties," he said.

"I think I know what the other one is," she said, linking her fingers behind his neck. "Why do you keep your jeans on in bed?" Elevating her legs, she ran the inside of her feet up and down his thighs, which were encased in denim again.

"This isn't home turf," he said. "I've got to be ready for a threat to walk through that door any second."

Living on constant alert must be exhausting, but at least she didn't have to develop a complex or worry about flesh-eating diseases. Accepting this, she began to stroke again and he dropped onto his side. Pulling her to his chest, he kissed her hairline. Their limbs tangled and with her face against his collarbone, she exhaled and closed her eyes, ready to sleep with this man wrapped around her.

"Will you betray me?" he asked with his mouth in her hair.

Shaking her head, she sought his closest hand and squeezed his fingers. "No."

"My inner circle is small, very small, and if you're in my circle, you can't be in anyone else's. There is no way to play two sides in this war. You give me your loyalty and no one else. You have to be willing to die rather than give up the secrets of the Kindred."

"The Kindred?" she asked, tipping her chin. She couldn't see him, but her forehead rasped on his stubble.

"If we make it through the night, I'll give you one more chance to back out. After you're in, Zar, you're in."

She didn't know if she'd have to swear a blood oath, or if their association would be fleeting. Giving them both a chance to sleep on the prospect of this alliance was a wise decision. But if he were still here in the morning then she would be more assured that he wasn't an apparition of the night and he'd have another piece of her heart.

NINE

THAT MORNING Raven's ringing cellphone had woken them up. Before the first ring had completed its drone, he was up, seated on the edge of the bed answering the call. With a brisk, "Hang on a minute" into the handset, he'd put the device to his shoulder and turned his face in her direction, though he didn't twist his body far enough to actually look at her.

When he'd told her that he had to take the call in private, Zara forced herself out of bed with a yawn and wrapped herself in her kimono. She got as far as the kitchen before she realized she had been dismissed from her own bed. Since there was no point in arguing with him while he was on the phone, she went to work making breakfast, which it turned out she had plenty of time to do because it was half an hour later that she saw him again.

She was filling a glass of orange juice when he came out of the bedroom. "Good morning," Zara said, setting the full glass on the breakfast table next to the place she had set for him. Busying herself with presenting breakfast and setting the table took her mind away from the questions this development in their relationship raised.

Asking him to spend the night had felt like a good idea

at the time. But daylight was harsh and brought out every neuroses. They'd met under unusual circumstances and Zara wasn't even sure what a creature of the night ate for breakfast or how comfortable he was with being here. Had he stayed because he was interested in building a relationship with her or was it just for the mission?

She wasn't even sure what she wanted from him. It was obvious she would have to rely on him to guide her through whatever Grant was doing, yet he'd made no declaration that he would do so. Hanging on to the fact that he'd come to her even after saying he wouldn't, Zara figured this situation wasn't clear-cut for him either.

"Morning," he returned, but stayed close to her bedroom door, twenty feet from her current position next to the table in front of her open plan kitchen.

He didn't move much; she'd noticed that about him before. But his eyes scanned the space, left to right, up and down, but she had no idea what he was looking for.

Choosing to ignore his quirk, she tried to put him at ease with conversation. "Who was on the phone?" she asked.

"An associate," he said. Observing how he was fully clothed, and keeping his distance, she thought he might try to rush off. But before he did, she had to confirm one fact that had occurred to her while making breakfast.

Exhaling through her nose, Zara propped a hand on the back of the chair beside her and flicked her hair from her face. "Look, I know this is a dumb question to ask now, given, you know…"

"But?"

Loosening in deference to the inevitability of her question, she asked, "Are you married?"

Divulging no hint as to the answer, he stayed still. "Didn't you ask me that already?"

"No," she said, raising a finger and cocking a hip to swoop around the table toward him. "No, I asked if you had a girlfriend and technically a wife wouldn't be a girlfriend, would she?"

"Technically…" he said, tilting his head in a way that could concede her point.

She shrugged. "You seem like the kind of guy to whom technicalities would matter."

"I am," he said. "But I'm not married."

Getting her chance to look at him in the light, she paused to squint and brought her hands to her hips. Tall and broad she'd already known, but she hadn't realized how his dark brown hair had lighter tones through it that caught in the early morning sunshine flowing into her living room. The darkness remained in his eyes, but his complexion was warm, and the hard angles of his face fit with the image she had of him in her mind.

Rough around the edges, he had straight white teeth and keenness in his manner. Seeing him like this in the natural light, he became a completely different animal. Not a less dangerous one, but somehow more real, more human, like a man she could hold on to.

"That was a long call to be all business," she said. "Are you going to give me an excuse now and run out of here?"

"I kept my end of the bargain," he said. "I stayed until breakfast."

She didn't want him to run away, not when she felt like she was making progress. "You haven't eaten anything," she said, glancing back at the table. "I made blueberry pancakes. There's fruit and toast and juice." Zara silenced herself before she went into full-on rant mode.

"And coffee?" he asked, but he had to be able to smell it.

Smiling, she took that question as interest. Even if all he stayed for was the coffee, it was a start. "And coffee," she said with a nod. Tiptoeing over to him, she curled her fingers around his wrist and began to walk backwards, guiding him the direction of the table. Being with him here, like this, without the intensity of night, was strange. Still, he seemed as assured as ever, leaving her nervous about voicing her uncertainty. "You told me your word was the most precious thing you could give."

Implying he might be reneging on the deal was enough to provoke a frown. "Do I have your trust?" he asked, seizing the chance to talk business. Taking control of their movement, he grasped the back of her neck and turned her around to push her forward, though with his elbow bent, she was bumped along by the breadth of his rigid chest too. "You said if I stayed until breakfast that I would."

Business was his comfort zone and that was something she could identify with. "Sit and eat," she said, pleased, at least, for the chance that she might get some answers. "And tell me what the hell we're mixed up in."

Zara tried to move away, but his grip on her neck tightened to hold her against him. Burying his face in her hair, Raven dragged in a long loud breath that made her shudder and her thoughts of business diminished. "You smell like sex," he mumbled.

He spoke so matter of fact, but her waist quivered and lightened in response to his statement because it reminded her that they'd been naked together all night.

"I haven't been in the shower," she said, twisting around to face him so she could extricate herself from his grasp. Sweeping her hair from her face, Zara prodded a finger into his chest to delay making eye contact. "And neither have you." In the light, she hadn't been this up close to him, and it was unsettling that his stature was no less formidable during the day. She was imprisoned between him and the table. He let her go and leaned over to rest his hands on the back of the dining chair pressed to her spine, eating up the last slither of space between their bodies. "Which of course you wouldn't have because you don't get naked anywhere that isn't your home." Her mumbled words were a return to her previous awkwardness.

"Disappointed by that, aren't you?" he asked. Curling his fingers around her neck again, he tried to angle her face upward, but he had to use his other hand to tip up her chin and make it happen. "Come here."

On her tiptoes, she still had to crane her neck to meet his mouth when he kissed her, but her stiff muscles ceased to object when she got a taste of him. Although not a plundering kind of kiss like those he bestowed on her in bed, his tongue still felt the same. His strength reassured her enough that her feeling of being intimidated waned.

She felt herself falling, like she'd just slipped from a cliff and was hurtling toward the rocks and waves below. One landing would kill her, the other would set her free, and she had no idea, which would be her destiny. His kiss erased her anxiety and reminded her of all he'd done to protect her. He might be a thug most of the time, but he kissed her like she was his sun, the source of energy he needed to be as strong as he was. It could be that her feelings were a symptom of his impressive physique. Every time he touched her, he reminded her of his vigor. When he kissed her, he singled her out to be the center of his world. With him shielding her from harm, she felt like the most precious jewel in the world.

"God, you're tall," she said when he slid his finger away from her chin.

The corner of his mouth tipped up, and the affect that small change had on the intention of his gaze made her almost choke on her own breath.

Leaving her place in front of him, she moved around the circular table. He kept hold of her neck for as long as he could, but his fingers eventually drifted away. Retrieving the coffee pot from the kitchen, she filled two mugs that were on the table. Zara pushed one across the table to the position opposite hers, then seated herself and gulped her hot caffeine.

"Are you going to sit down?" she asked, lifting her eyes over her mug.

He was examining the table in such a way that provoked her to examine it too, except she saw nothing that would warrant such scrutiny. "I don't… I don't traditionally do breakfast around a…"

Glad that she wasn't the only one unnerved, and that she had the chance to put him at ease, Zara laughed and reached over to put a piece of toast on a plate. "Then I hope you enjoy this."

Straining his eyes toward the window, Raven blocked the daylight with an open hand and pulled out a chair. Sitting sideways in the chair, he put an elbow on the table and snagged the coffee mug to glug down the liquid, keeping his hand up and his attention on the window the whole time.

"I thought that spies liked to be able to see the door,"

she said, putting jelly on her toast, then pointing her knife at the front door which was in the corner behind him.

He didn't turn. "Someone comes through the door I've got plenty of time to turn around and shoot him in the heart. This here," he said, waving an arm at the wall of windows. "This is a fucking death trap. Have you considered window treatments?"

"How do you know what a window treatment is?" she asked, putting aside her knife to bite into her toast.

His gaze flicked to her. "Window treatments save lives, trust me. They're a pain in the fucking ass for a guy like me… and a life saver."

"I never would've expected you to say anything like that, beau," she said, picking up her coffee in the hand that wasn't occupied by her toast.

His sneer stuck to the windows. "The light shines clear in this window too," he said. "You're at a serious disadvantage in this place."

Having had similar thoughts about the sniper who took out Tim, she glanced at the windows then back to Raven before offering an explanation. "I love my windows and I love the light."

"You can love it when I'm not here," he said, pushing his mug onto the table and springing to his feet. "Do you have a hammer?"

"A hammer?" she asked, lowering her toast before she bit into it.

"Yeah, you know, bang, bang, nails, wall… I'll use the butt of my gun if I have to, but if I shoot a hole in your ceiling in the process… Do you have upstairs neighbors?"

Shoving away from the table, she put aside her toast and mug. Retrieving her toolbox from under the sink, she brought it into the living room and his expression lit when he took it from her and dropped it onto the floor. Falling onto his knees to scrape around in the haphazard arrangement of tools, Raven muttered something to himself. Eventually he rose with a hammer in one hand and a couple of loose nails in the other. He snagged the throw from the back of the couch and went to the window.

Zara sat back down and continued with her breakfast, catching an occasional glance over her shoulder at him as he nailed her throw to the wall in order to cover two of her windows.

"Better?" she asked when he was finished and was discarding the tools.

"The material isn't thick enough to provide complete cover," he said, backing away to admire his work. "Not with full sun working against us… But it will have to do."

Grabbing his coffee mug, he didn't sit opposite her, he came around and sat at the place beside her, but he pulled his chair closer to hers and sat side on again, still facing the windows.

"You hate windows," she said. This was the worst place in the world for him to be if he had a window or sunlight phobia.

"I just want to be closer to you, baby," he said, but he wasn't even looking at her, he was studying the uncovered windows further down the wall. He closed one eye and she touched his forehead, sweeping her hand in a crescent around his face to his chin.

Hoping to alleviate his concern, she made a suggestion. "Do you want to go back into the bedroom? There's only one window and it has a curtain. The sunlight won't bother you."

"If we go in there, we'll fuck, and we don't have time for that," he said. He removed her hand from his face and held it in both of his to kiss the back of her fingers. "Fuck it. Now is as good a time as any."

Further perplexed, she frowned. "For what?" she asked, her toast now forgotten.

"Death," he said and his eyes bounced to hers where he must have read her surprise. "I'm sorry. I'm not usually…"

She smiled, not worried about danger while Raven was around. "Awake in the daylight, I get it."

He dropped her hand and shunted his chair back so that they could no longer touch. "Who threatened you?"

His words were as clear and determined as his eyes and it was as if his previous agitation had never existed. Apparently, once he decided he was ready to die, everything else became irrelevant.

That he remembered what she'd said about being threatened surprised her, but again it hinted at the prospect of him caring for her. "Grant," she said, brushing crumbs from her hands. If this was it and they were going to be honest then they both had to answer some questions, so she wasn't going to play around.

"Why did he do that?"

"Because I asked him about the product."

"What do you know about it?" he asked.

"What do you know?" Zara wasn't going to be the only one answering questions and she wanted to make sure he knew that.

"You're sure you want to do this? You make this decision, you come inside, and there's no getting back out. You belong to me… Are you ready to be mine?"

If this was his way of asking her to choose him over Grant then he wasn't exactly being subtle about it, but she had to be impressed with how steadfast he was.

"Who was on the phone?"

"The chief. A man named Art," he said. "He was pretty surprised I spent the night here. I told him it would be worth it."

"Is that what this is? What the sex is for? Your way to buy the information you need?"

"I need an inside man," he said, bounding to the edge of his chair and resting his forearm on the table. "I need to know who Grant is selling the device to and then I need to take that person down before they can use it."

"They're terrorists?" she whispered, bringing her attention from his hand—which hung loose over the edge of the table—up to his eyes.

"That's right."

"Kahlil's boss, he's a prospective buyer and a man named Sutcliffe is too."

"Yes," he said, nodding slowly as if trying to ease her into revealing more. "Albert Sutcliffe."

"I spoke to him," she said, moistening her drying lips.

"What did he say?" Raven asked.

She could give him the details, but she was still basking in astonishment that a conversation like this was a part of her life at all. Except they had to make progress, leaving her no time to deal with the bombshell that terrorists were now part of her breakfast conversation.

Eager to know what she was up against, she made eye contact. "Tell me what it is," she asked, mimicking his composed demeanor.

Exhaling, he sat back, widening his stance with his feet flat on the floor and his hands linked on the top of his head. Conceding that this wasn't a time for a face-off, he loosened and dropped his hands.

"It started in the seventies," he said, touching a teaspoon next to the sugar bowl, which neither of them had used. "Research and Development at Cormack Industries filed a patent because that's what R&D Departments do. Someone had an idea and patented it. But technology wasn't up to speed with the minds of the engineers. It was put in a file and forgotten about. Periodically, it was brought back out and some work was done through the years. It wasn't until the nineties when miniaturization became more efficient that the possibilities grew. Finding appropriate software was difficult and wireless technology wasn't then what it is now."

"I still don't know what it is," she said.

Disregarding the spoon, he slid his forearm onto the table. "The original idea was benign enough. Doctors were spread thinly then as they are now and couldn't be in various places at once. It was theorized that a device could be built that could be preloaded with medications. Then, based upon measurements taken by qualified nurses and medics, doctors could administer the drugs from a remote location."

"What's wrong with that?" she asked.

"Nothing," he said. Shifting to the edge of his chair, he opened his hands to gesture. "In theory, there is nothing wrong with that and that's why they patented their ideas. It was in the eighties when remote access became a possibility that other uses were considered and then twenty years ago…"

"What?" All this might be old news for him, but she was amazed at the breadth of what she didn't know.

"The connection was made to incorporate forms of medicine that could be aerosolized, preventing the need for needles, and that was when Grant McCormack Senior put a stop to it. He shut down the project, fired anyone who disagreed with him and demanded that the files be shredded."

She squinted, not understanding why he would make that decision. "Why would he…"

Still giving nothing away about his own sentiments, Raven explained the facts. "Because a machine that can expel specific quantities of a gas at whatever intervals its master dictates is a terrifying thing. Maybe not by itself, but we're on the cutting edge of technology here. Advisors were talking about AI and how the idea could develop until doctors weren't needed at all. They speculated that patients could be kept in isolation cells while a doctor worked from an office, treating patients who would be hundreds or thousands of miles away." He paused, giving her time to absorb the possibilities. "McCormack Senior didn't like that vision of the future. Talk became about integrating defibrillators and writing code that could help the machine decide to keep patients alive based upon pre-determined criteria."

Amazed, she wanted to hear more. "Oh my God," she exhaled.

"Protecting a system like that from hacking and other abuses would be a full-time job. So engineers offered suggestions of a kill switch hardwired to shut down the device… but that's incorporating an inherent weakness, right? 'Cause what's to stop the hackers getting to the kill switch and taking out all the patients in the institution with the click of a mouse?"

Okay, so she could understand how someone wouldn't want to be a part of that. "So why wasn't it over after that? If McCormack Senior was so against—"

His brows rose a fraction. "Because twenty years ago, before his orders could be carried out, something happened to Grant McCormack Senior."

"What—" Her mouth opened as her eyes crept around to him. "The accident."

"If you want to call it that," he said, sitting back again.

"Accident, murder, whatever, McCormack wasn't breathing anymore. The company went through an appropriate mourning period and Frank Mitchell took over in lieu of Grant Junior coming of age."

Processing the epic possibilities that could become realities if this device fell into the wrong hands, Zara tried to be pragmatic instead of emotional. Taking a breath, she brought them to the present. "So why is this an issue now?" she asked. "If everything was destroyed…"

"It wasn't," he said. "About five years ago, after the discovery of ultra-thin aluminum batteries, Grant Junior was digging around in the CI archives trying to figure out where the innovation could be applied to defunct ideas. That's when he found this old dusty project and brought it to Frank.

"Grant thought it was the right time to develop it. Miniaturization was possible. We had the software for remote access and wireless is about as good as it could get. It wouldn't work over thousands of miles, but it would do for a single hospital. Frank vetoed it and flew into a rage about this being why his best friend Grant Senior had died. Frank demanded that it never be mentioned again."

"A year," she murmured, making some mental connections. She pushed out her chair enough to turn toward him. The timeline coincided with the death of Grant's guardian. Had he waited until Frank had died and then gone against his mentor's express wishes? "Grant told me he'd been working on this product for almost a year. He said he was doing what his father and Frank failed to do." All the pieces fit and she couldn't doubt that Raven was telling the truth. "But why terrorists?"

His shoulder rose in a slack shrug. "I don't know. The right minds would have to be on the development of the technology to bring it into the twenty-first century. The last we know it was worked on was before Grant Senior died. Maybe Grant can't get the tech up to standard without drawing attention to what he's doing. But as for Grant's motives for doing this… I haven't figured that out yet."

"The original patent was filed March third, 1974," she said.

"How do you know that?"

"I saw the paperwork."

"He let you see it?" he asked, either impressed or incredulous.

"I…" Squirming in her seat, she righted the spoon he'd been toying with. "I might have snuck into Grant's office when he was out and uh… maybe, uh… broken into his desk. Though it's not breaking into something if you find the secret key and unlock it, is it?"

Any hope she had that he would reassure her vanished when she lifted her attention and discerned the hint of amusement in his expression. "You're a good girl, Zara."

Her mouth fell open and the air rushed out of her lungs as though she'd just been punched in the chest. Rising up, she wanted to put space between them. In the act of backing away, the chair she'd been sitting on clattered to the floor on its side, but Zara didn't think to right it. Still retreating until her shoulders hit the wall beside the throw he'd pinned to the wall, she couldn't breathe.

Raven was on his feet in a crouch, reaching for her as he approached. But, as one of her hands ascended to close over her gaping mouth, the other flew out in front of her and he stopped. It was obvious from his expression that he didn't know what to do about this unexpected development. From the strength of her abrupt action, he had to think she'd just flipped her crazy switch.

Except she hadn't. Zara wished it were that easy. She'd just figured out who he was and the jolt of that revelation made her forget how to breathe and about every danger in their lives. When her fingers did eventually descend from her mouth, she still couldn't close it. The shock was just too much.

"Fuck," she murmured.

"What? What is it, baby? Talk to me."

Her hands were shaking. She'd never experienced such instant cold, but then she'd never had a surprise as profound as this one. "You… you're Brodie," she whispered and he staggered back wearing his own stunned expression. "That's how you know so much about this device and the company. And why you know about Grant Senior and Frank. That's how you know where Grant was on the night of his parents' death... You were there. You're... you're Grant's little brother."

After a brief pause, his arm swung out and up to press the back of his fingers to his mouth. Rubbing them back and forth, Raven took his time to absorb what she'd discovered. Then, rising to full height, his shoulders went back.

"I guess I got the right girl," he said. "You're a helluva detective. How did you figure that out?"

Explaining it to him helped her to make sense of her clarity. "You said those words to me last night and I don't know... there was something familiar in your voice. I didn't think much about it. But now, looking at you when you said it... Grant said the same thing to me, he called me a good girl, and you used the same inflection. It just... You're his brother, aren't you?"

Good humor was gone and his harsh expression matched the steel reinforcing his stance. "That's right... What are you gonna do about it?"

This new piece of information only caused more questions and confusion. "Why can't you...? Why can't you just go to him and ask what's going on?"

Averting his eyes, he took his time, no doubt trying to figure out how to explain himself. "I haven't spoken to my brother in"—his bottom lip came out at the same time one of his shoulders popped up and down in a shrug meant to dismiss what he was thinking—"ten years, maybe fifteen... Yeah, fifteen," he said as though he had just figured that out. "I was eighteen."

Feeling more connected to him now that she knew the truth, Zara tried to locate her composure. "He never talks about his family," she said.

Holding himself at a distance from his emotions, he kept his gaze fixed on her. "That's one thing we have in common then."

"But after your parents died..."

Reconnecting with the emotions he usually tried to hide, anger bled into his words. "After my parents died, he refused to go back to the house and I refused to have anything to do with the company that killed my father. Frank took Grant and I went with Art, my mother's brother… and that was it."

Mystified, she couldn't believe it was so simple. "That was it?" she asked, keeping her distance. "You're brothers."

The man who had been looking after her, the man she had kissed and had sex with… he was her boss' brother, she still couldn't believe this was true.

"By blood only," he said. "Grant got the company and I got the estate. We have nothing to do with each other's lives."

Brodie McCormack hadn't been heard of for years and Grant had never ever mentioned a brother. Replaying her experiences with Brodie, she realized he'd revealed more of himself to her than she'd given him credit for. Taking her to White Falls to show her his childhood home, the land he had to still own, that was about more than discrediting Grant. He was trusting her with his location. Grant wouldn't have been the only one to see his parents die on that water beneath them. Brodie knew Grant had witnessed the atrocity because he'd seen it too.

Now she knew who he was, knew his family, and his upbringing, which helped her to understand the glimmers of polish beneath the tarnish he used as a mask. "You're a myth. You vanished when you were a teenager. People think you're dead. You took me to White Falls and showed me that light… The McCormack land is a myth, just like the youngest McCormack son. The light on the water, on the peninsula, is that where you live?"

"When I'm in the country, yeah," he said, audibly displeased at the turn of this conversation. He wasn't happy that she'd figured out his identity. "We've got some pretty nasty security though, so I wouldn't think about coming trick or treating."

"Don't joke, Rave—" Except now she knew his full name and it wasn't Raven. As many questions sprung up as she had answers. Now that she knew his lineage, it made sense why he cared so much about this specific case. But she didn't understand how he'd become so hard, where he'd learned to fight and shoot. How had one brother become so coarse while the other was so refined?

"Are you gonna tell him?"

Zara hadn't realized she'd been absorbed in examining her floor until he spoke. Lifting her chin to focus on him, she couldn't answer his question, because she didn't know why his anonymity was so important. But his mind had gone to Grant and to his own secret, proving how concealing his identity was his predominant concern.

She had to understand what they were facing. To give them both a chance to recalibrate in light of this new revelation, she chose to share information that was rightfully his given his connection to CI. "What do you know about Project Game Time?" she asked.

"Nothing," he said. "We didn't know the name of the mission. I have a guy, a friend, who can get into any computer system known to man, but we didn't know what we were looking for."

Clearing her throat, she explained. "There was a document at the front of the file, titled Project Game Time and there was a floor plan with some measurements but no names."

"Unless we know what the floor plan relates to—"

"I have a feeling it's the Grand Hotel," she said, edging closer when she saw him move toward her. "I don't know for sure. But Sutcliffe said on the phone that the demonstration was going to happen at midnight on Saturday at the Grand Hotel."

"Fuck, you're good, baby," he said.

She didn't flinch when he brought his arms around her and she took the squeeze of his embrace as a measure of his admiration for her covert work. "There's more. A lot more. But I... I have to get to work."

"What kind of more?" he asked, loosening his clinch, his gaze dimmed on its descent to her mouth.

"I followed the money and Grant's right, this has been going on for a year... and I don't think you'll like what he's been doing in that time."

"Okay," he said, nodding as if to reassure her, he used a finger to hook her hair from her face. "You don't have to worry about a thing anymore, baby. You belong to me now.

You're always gonna be safe."

She shook her head and although he looked ready to appease her further, Zara spoke first. "That's a beautiful sentiment, but I have a feeling I'm going to be the guinea pig."

His brows lowered in a glower. "The… what?"

She inhaled and her worries made her words crackle. "Grant asked me to go with him to the fundraiser at the Grand on Saturday night. He's picking me up at ten p.m.," she said. Given all she'd learned, her apprehension about the event had increased. She wasn't so sure she could trust Grant to make sure she was okay while surrounded by evil.

The set of his jaw tightened and he ground his molars as he released her from his arms and turned away with such force that Zara had to grab the chair beside her to catch her balance. Remaining static and quiet when he walked away from her, she awaited his response.

Eventually, he stopped pacing and a split second later his hand rose to rub the back of his head. Then his hand flew out to punch the column beside him and the plaster burst in a shower of powder and paint, making her jump.

He whirled around and the fury on his face made her shrink. "I don't know what to be madder about," he shouted. "That you agreed to go on a date when you knew it was gonna be dangerous, or that you agreed to go on a date with your boss while you were fucking me!"

Surprised by his anger, she quickly recovered and knew she could respond in kind because she felt confident that he would never use his strength to hurt her. "First of all," she said, countering his argument and his tone. "You're not pissed that I'm going out with my boss, you're pissed that I'm going out with your brother. Second, he asked me out before you and I ever had sex. And third, what the hell gives you the right to dictate who I date when you're probably out screwing every night? I'm sorry, did I miss the part where we promised each other a happily ever after?"

With one bound, he got in front of her. "You're under my control now."

"Am I?" she asked, glaring at his scowl.

She wasn't scared of him, not his size or his strength or

his mood, because he'd stayed with her, watched over her. She understood more of the man beneath the façade. With all Brodie McCormack had been through—losing his parents, abandoning his birthright and his brother—it was amazing that he was standing here in front of her.

He and Grant had come from the same womb, but they were polar opposites. Grant needed a panderer to pick up after him whereas Brodie needed a challenge. From her experience with the younger McCormack, she'd come to understand that in order to gain his respect, she had to match his ferocity. Because he was a no-nonsense type of guy with laser-precision focus.

"Yeah," he sneered.

With a parched throat and a hammering heart, she maintained eye contact. "What makes you think that?"

"This," he said.

Grabbing the back of her neck, he pulled her up to the ends of her toes and planted his mouth over hers. With balled hands, Zara beat at his chest, but there was no force behind her punches and she didn't try to back away when she could have.

His tongue delved deeper and she sucked it hard, closing her mouth enough to scrape her teeth over him and return his wrath. Pulling their bodies apart, he swept everything off the table to make space for what he planned to do to her.

Zara untied her kimono to signal her compliance and ready herself for his passion. But this man didn't stop to ask for her blessing, he stole her waist, threw her down onto the surface, and came down on top of her to show her exactly what he could do at a breakfast table.

TEN

TARDINESS WASN'T A GREAT start to her workday. But she couldn't say that her day had started out badly overall, not after enjoying ecstasy in a tryst with her lover. So wearing the widest smile she'd ever had, Zara made her peace with running behind at CI and appreciated the solitude of her office. It gave her much-needed time to process the new information rattling around in her head. Not least of which was the identity of her lover.

Raven was an abstract guy who was all danger and mystery. Learning that he was in fact Brodie McCormack, brother of her boss and son of a business tycoon, she felt much more secure with him and with what they were doing. Raven was elusive and it would be impossible for a real relationship to endure between her and a phantom. Caring for Brodie McCormack was real. He was three-dimensional flesh and blood. His severe manner suggested he'd gone through a gauntlet of torture since losing his parents and she couldn't stop her thoughts from flitting back to him.

Her breakfast table hadn't endured their morning escapades. He'd promised to pay for the plaster damage on the column and the broken furniture, but to Zara, those things were irrelevant. Clarity left her in awe. He had trusted her with so much, not just about the device and its history, but with his own identity as well. Granted, it hadn't been a voluntary admission, but he hadn't tried to deny it or dismiss its relevance.

Having the knowledge of who he was, when so few people did, gave her a secret that had the capability to unravel Raven's world. During her research into Grant McCormack and CI, half a decade ago, before she was employed here. Zara had learned of the existence of a younger McCormack brother.

After the death of their parents, the younger brother disappeared off the grid, leading many in the media articles she read to believe that he had been killed in the accident, or had suffered some terrible fate not long after it. Although as far as she knew, there was no official death certificate on public record.

Curiosity bloomed within her. At several points during her day, Zara drifted off into a daydream and wondered about the mysterious life of the man she'd accepted into her life. It was no longer her singular mission to uncover the details of Grant's corrupt business dealings.

Zara wanted to learn the truth about Brodie McCormack as well, of where he'd been and what had happened to him, since there was no record of him after the age of thirteen. The media had reported that there were no school records or college transcripts, no criminal convictions or official certification. At the time of reading those articles, she'd been intrigued, but not enough to question or investigate them.

Finding out about Brodie's past wouldn't be done under the radar. For one thing, if he discovered her poking into his business uninvited, he would retract his trust and may hurt her, as he'd warned he would if she betrayed him. Getting to know Brodie would have to be done the old-fashioned way, using her feminine wiles, and it helped that he seemed to be partial to exploiting them.

This morning he had disappeared while she was in the shower. As disappointed as she was to find that he was gone, she wasn't concerned. It was actually encouraging that he had gone without drumming into her the need for secrecy about his identity. That was how she knew that she did indeed have his trust. Her declaration had been vindicated: by giving her his trust, he'd earned hers in return.

At some point, he would appear back in her life. When he did return, Zara would share the rest of what she had learned. Once everything was out in the open, she hoped that he would begin to clue her in about how they were going to take these people down.

Throughout the day, her thoughts bounced back to her night and her morning with Raven—except now, she would have to think of him as Brodie and that might take some getting used to. Being preoccupied with thoughts of a man was supposed to be a part of immature youth, something she thought she had gotten over. This wasn't a time to be scatterbrained by sex and potential intimacy, with terrorists on their tail and possible destruction of life. She would have to keep her head in the game.

Speculating about how this might play out, Zara was typing up a report Grant needed when her computer froze and that was something that didn't happen given CI's technological capability. Removing her hands from the keyboard, she was about to reach for her phone to call the IT department when a white window popped up on her screen and letters began to appear as though someone was typing on her computer in real time.

"We need the file number."

The cursor jumped to the next line and flashed there as though she was expected to respond to this command. Glancing around, she wondered if this was a test, or a con of some kind. Nothing like this had ever happened to her before. She doubted CI had the ability to freeze out a user and override her computer like this. Given her position in the company, there would be no need for an internal user to be communicating with her like this when an email would suffice for a legitimate query.

"Who is this?" she typed into the window.

"Irrelevant," came the reply. "All I need is the number."

"I don't know what you're talking about," she typed back. Although she didn't know any hackers personally, she did know that people could be conned into giving out information they didn't want to give over a computer.

"He was right about you." The words came up a letter at a time and she re-read them when the sentence was complete.

"He, who?" she wrote because she wasn't going to admit to her connection to Raven or Brodie when this person could be luring her into a trap.

"Your lover."

Still unconvinced about this intruder's motive, she stayed vague. "Which one?" she asked, folding her arms on the desk, hoping that Brodie was standing behind whoever this digital interloper was.

The concept that she could have more than one lover would piss him off, if his reaction about her going to the Grand with Grant was anything to go by. But she wanted him riled, his passion fired hers, and the memory of his possessiveness aroused her so much that she wriggled in her chair and pressed her thighs together.

"The one you made pancakes for this morning," came the response and she could almost hear Brodie's voice snapping at her, though she still wasn't sure who she was communicating with. "The one who punched a hole in your apartment."

Okay, so that was sort of confirmation that she was talking to Brodie or someone associated with him, except those things could be known by anyone watching through her windows. Suddenly, she understood what Brodie meant about her windows being a weakness.

Not ready to show her cards, Zara was still aware that she could be communicating with an enemy masquerading as her lover. "If he wants information, he can ask for it himself," she responded and sat back in her chair to await the response to her sass.

She didn't have to wait long. "We are Kindred," came the reply. "You belong to us."

Disturbed by the cultish reply, she thought about the

friend Brodie had referred to, the one who could access any computer. This had to be that guy because CI's digital security was top rate. It would take a pro to sneak under the corporate defenses.

"How do I know you are who you say you are?" she typed because she didn't want to walk into any kind of trap. Brodie would tell her to be cautious and she understood the need for that vigilance.

"Taxicab."

Zara blinked twice at the word. So their private safe word was apparently some kind of code of identification now and that made her squirm for less lustful reasons. If Brodie had given out that piece of information, what else had he told his unit?

"File number?" the words came up on the screen beneath their safe word, and although she was embarrassed, she was assured that this person was in Brodie's inner circle.

"00793" she typed. Almost as soon as the last digit flashed onto the screen, the window vanished and her previous project came back up unaffected by the interruption.

Agreeing to trust Brodie had come with extras she hadn't bargained for. When she saw him next, she had to get answers about this group. She had to know what being involved with them was going to entail.

***

IT WAS DARK when she left work. Grant had been in meetings for most of the day, so she'd seen very little of him. Since she knew a McCormack family secret, she was quite happy to avoid her boss because she wasn't sure how her poker face would hold up. Although she'd managed not to rouse his suspicions yet, so that gave her optimism.

With her arms full of files, Zara unlocked her apartment door and pushed it aside. Artificial light filled the space, which should have been dark. It was joined by the sumptuous scents of food, except there shouldn't be a soul here.

Fear didn't spear her as it might have before, because

with the lights on, the space wasn't ominous. Brodie had never turned on lights and made himself at home, but ensconced in the promise of his protection, she was assured he'd appear to take down any threats if the need arose.

"Hello?" she called out and an unknown man appeared from behind the closest column with a paintbrush in his hand.

"Are you gonna stand there all night and let the bought air out?" he asked and disappeared behind the column again.

Her confused brow wrinkled. The stranger's presence was unexpected. She had no idea why he would be here. "Uh, who the hell are you?" she asked, coming inside and kicking the door shut with her heel.

"Handy man," he called without showing himself.

Relaxing her expression and her shoulders, she recognized bullshit when she heard it. "Handy man," she repeated, not believing it for a second.

Approaching his position, she took note of the new dining table in place of the old one. The stranger came into her field of vision and she examined the patched column he was painting. When Brodie promised to do something, he didn't mess around. Although she hadn't known it was his plan to invite strangers into her home to do the work.

Dumping her files on the table, she swung her purse from her arm and discarded it while glancing toward the kitchen where she saw pots simmering on the stove.

"What is going on?" she asked, taking her jacket off, putting it and her keys beside the files.

"Dinner," he said, wiping his brush with a cloth and putting it in a box of tools he had on the floor beside him.

He could be as nonchalant and unthreatening as he wanted to be, his response didn't begin to explain why he was here.

Her patience for these anomalies in her life was wearing thin. "Who are you?" she asked again.

Unimpressed and expectant, she turned her back to the kitchen, and propped a hand on the back of one of her dining chairs and awaited an answer with the air of a critical parent. The man was tall and lithe, he had dark gray hair with flashes of white through it, but he was attractive and alert. Still, that didn't mean she knew who he was or why he was here.

Wiping his hands on a rag hanging out the pocket of his overalls, he dropped it to offer his hand. "Art," he said. "And you're our secret weapon."

"Our?" she asked, shaking his hand because it was the polite thing to do.

Some of the wind had been taken from her sails. Brodie had referred to Art as the chief. This man would know everything about what was going on.

Just then, at the far end of her apartment, Brodie came out of her office flicking through her desk planner. "You're late," he said, without taking his eyes away from her planner.

Agog that he would be so presumptuous as to go into her office at all, she couldn't ignore the infringement of her privacy. Without an ounce of shame, he was flicking through the pages of her personal planner. It didn't matter that there was nothing incriminating in there, she was just amazed at his gall.

"What do you think you're doing?" she asked, watching him read as he approached.

Still reading her notes and appointments, he didn't conceal his actions. "Getting to know you better," he said.

That was the way to do it. Everything was in there from doctor's appointments to the dates of her cycle. Zara took notes about birth control and medications as well as when bills were due and grocery lists. As soon as he was close enough, she snatched the planner from his hands and snapped it closed.

"Try asking me a question," she said.

Earlier, she had considered how she would get to know Brodie through time and experience. Apparently, he wasn't as patient or respectful.

"Fixed your column," he said with a sideways nod in the direction of the repair.

"I see that."

"Art cooked," Brodie said, glancing at the kitchen

behind her. "I don't cook."

Riled by Brodie snooping in her office and by this new person in her apartment, her anger grew. She didn't want to be railroaded and had thought she and Brodie were forging a relationship of trust, now she wasn't so sure.

"What the hell have I gotten myself involved in?" she demanded, folding her arms around the book she'd stolen from Brodie. "Information! You said you wanted information, not to take over my life!" Color caught the corner of her eye and her mouth fell open at the sight of the curtains now hanging on either side of each of the windows that she'd been too distracted to notice before. "Window treatments?"

"They save lives," Art said.

Brodie was behind him, doing a terrible job at concealing his amusement. Zara no longer needed to wonder who had mentored him in his life lessons.

Touching her thumb to the tips of her first two fingers, she lifted her arm, but words failed her. These men had been in her apartment for God knew how long, cooking, building furniture, and hanging curtains… She was actually nervous to go into her bedroom and office for fear of what else she'd find.

"Take your work off the table," Art said, extending an arm to rest a placating hand on her shoulder. "We'll eat and you can tell us what we need to know."

Art crouched to clear up his tools, then carried the box toward the front door, all the while she pinned the stink eye on Brodie. "This wasn't what I signed up for," she hissed at him.

With one stride, he got close enough to snag the back of her neck and yank her closer so he could plant his lips on her hairline. "Art taught me everything I know," he murmured to her. "And he'll be the one looking out for you when I'm not around."

As if this was enough of an explanation, he turned her around and smacked her ass to urge her toward the table. Gathering up her things, Zara used the time to absorb this turn of events. She put everything away and went into her bedroom to change her clothes. Thankfully, nothing in there appeared to be any different.

When she came back out, the curtains were all closed and the men were seated at the table with food piled on their plates. They were eating and talking in hushed voices that she couldn't hear until she got up close, except when she did, they stopped talking to look at her.

"Where do you want to start?" Art asked as she lowered herself into the place set for her. "You know what the device is?"

She nodded and looked at her plate. There was rice and chicken cooked in a sauce that smelled delicious. It had been a long time since someone had cooked for her. As tempted as she was to try the food, she didn't have much of an appetite.

"Eat," Brodie said with his mouth full, pointing his fork at her plate. "It's good."

"I'm sure it is," she said. The men were hunched over their plates, scooping the food up in huge forkfuls that filled their mouths. This wasn't a civilized meal to linger over; these men were using their fingers in place of knives and gulping from full water glasses. Pushing her plate away, Zara folded her hands on the table. Both men stopped eating and glanced at each other before focusing on her.

"It's a huge insult not to eat food someone has prepared for you," Art said. "It doesn't matter if it's sheep stomach or monkey brains, you eat it. Some tribes will see their children go hungry just to feed new friends."

Dampening her urge to scream at them both for their boldness, she called on the professionalism she used at CI and made herself breathe until she could loosen her shoulders enough to be calm when she spoke.

"Forgive me if I'm not particularly hungry," she said. "And you're one to talk about insults. You've come into my home uninvited and overhauled the place."

"Repaired damage done by us and improved your safety," Art said, swallowing down his food. "Nothing was done to hurt you."

"I told you that you belong to me now," Brodie said. "Once you're in our inner circle there are no half measures.

You're in all the way."

"So trusting you means trusting your uncle and your crazy friend who commandeered my computer earlier?" she asked, losing grip of her temper. "Aren't you pissed they left all the hard work to you? What did you do? Survey the women who previously slept with all of you to figure out which of you was best between the sheets? That's a tough job you have, beau. How many assets do you have to screw your way through before they promote you to Chief Muff Diver?"

"Zar—"

"Let's deal with our business," she said, feeling a distinctive chill when she looked at Brodie. "You said that the right minds would have to be on developing the device and I can tell you who they are. Three weeks after Frank Mitchell's death, there was a restructure of the Research and Development Department at Cormack Industries. Three of our best engineers were laid off and removed from the company payroll. Except they weren't."

"What happened to them?" Art asked, discarding his fork onto his plate.

"It took me a while," she said. "But I traced them through a secondary funding scheme, set up as a fresh investment project to appear like a new subsidiary."

"Appear like?"

"There was a huge injection of cash into a single account although each of the amounts was so small it would be deemed irrelevant. Cormack Industries does a lot of work with new energy initiatives. We have premises in the Arctic Circle, uninhabited islands offshore that research wave power and various plants throughout the country working with wind power. Pinning down which specific location these men had been relocated to was very difficult."

"But you found them?"

"It's called the Winter Chill Project, but it's Game Time," she said, fixing her attention on Art. "They're based in a remote part of Quebec, on the east shore, which allows equipment to leave the docks here and travel up to them without having to worry about customs and such. CI has their own transportation and one of the engineers is a keen sailor.

They bring in what they need in small batches, so that they can be transported on vessels small enough to come into the private slip they have near their facility."

"How did you put these pieces together?" Art asked.

"At first it was a series of coincidences," she said. "Today I found out that they had requisitioned a large quantity of chemicals cultivated by a lab we have in Florida."

"And that's…?"

"Enough to make me suspicious," she said, maintaining a professional distance. "All of the vials are number coded. I haven't yet deciphered what was in each of them. But I do know what the Florida lab does."

"What?" Brodie asked her and she slid her eyes toward him.

"They work on vaccinations and the eradication of viral diseases."

"Fuck," Brodie exhaled though there was little expression on his face.

"My thoughts exactly."

Art lifted a hand to get her attention. "Can you be specific about where they are?"

"I know their GPS location," she said. "They're so remote and well-hidden that you won't find them on any map."

Art nodded and inhaled as he switched his focus to Brodie. "What do you want to do, Rave?"

Brodie reclined in his seat to link his fingers at the back of his head. "Taking out the lab is an option," Brodie said. "But I'd bet if they're planning a demonstration on Saturday that whatever they need has already been brought into town."

"Agreed," Art said. "We have to find out where it is."

"We know how it came into the country," Brodie said to him. "Swift found nothing on the system. All traces of the project have been erased. He's pulled up all the historic data, but that's useless. There's nothing new."

"Grant's a smart motherfucker," Art said. "He wouldn't risk digitizing anything. Frank might have caught a whiff otherwise."

"He didn't start working on this until after Frank died," Zara said.

Art glanced her way, wearing a frown. "He might not have moved on his ideas, but I'd bet he was developing this plan since he first laid eyes on Game Time."

"Where would they be storing it in the city?" Brodie asked, leaning forward to rest his arms on the table. He twisted to address Art, and the older man shifted in his seat to face his nephew, making it obvious that they were done educating her.

"It will have to be a dual strike," Art said. "We'll have to take out the storage facility here and the Quebec base at the same time or he'll just regroup."

Brodie shook his head. "We can take out the base whenever we want, Chief. Grant has what he needs for the demonstration already. We have to think about what comes next. It's Thursday now, I say we try to find the device he has here, whether we find it or not, I'll take out the Quebec lab on Saturday. "

Her anxiety level had been increasing since she agreed to go with Grant to the Grand. Without knowing exactly what he planned, she couldn't know what to expect. Accidents could happen and when playing with potentially live ammo, people's lives could be at risk, including hers. And if Brodie was in Canada, he wouldn't be around to keep her ass safe.

"So we're not even going to try to stop the demonstration at the Grand?" Zara asked, but neither man answered her question. It was as if she had ceased to exist. "We don't even know what they're planning, what this demonstration will be. It could be their intention to hurt people and I'm going to be there. I think I have the right to know if—"

"Calm down," Brodie said, barely offering her a glance. "We're not going to let anything happen to you."

"You can't guarantee that if you're not going to be in the country," she said. She didn't like the way the men maintained focus on each other and dismissed her like an irritating gnat. They might be seasoned professionals, but she was the one walking into the fire. "What about everyone else at the Grand party?"

Brodie's eyes rose in their sockets as if he was counting to ten or telling himself to ignore her because she only had to be tolerated for a short period. "Grant won't hurt folks," Brodie said. "He wouldn't draw that kind of attention to himself. But we do need to figure out where he's keeping the device here in town. It will be useful to monitor its movements."

Art nodded at his nephew. "Swift's in town and ready to go."

"Yeah, but Falc is in Mexico with Wren," Brodie said. "This is us."

"Swift has men."

"Who are not trained for this," Brodie said with a deliberate look. "You know his position... I can take out the trio of scientists in the Canadian location. Dismantling their base will be easy after they've been eliminated, especially if it's remote. I can do it in daylight if I have to."

"Swift and I will work on locating the inventory Grant has down here. We'll destroy the compound when we find it and take down the targets."

"Leave the targets to me," Brodie said. "Sabotage the device if you get the chance to do it without engaging or revealing yourself. Maybe if Grant fucks up the demonstration, his customers will lose interest. But just in case I'm wrong about his intentions, we'll need to research how to destroy the virus and unless we know which one it is…"

"We'll patch Wren into the communications."

"Got it," Brodie said. Both men nodded at each other and rose from the table at the same time.

"Whoa, wait a second," she said, leaping up and holding out her hands. "What was all that?"

"Preliminary planning of the op," Brodie said. "We'll nail down the specifics once we have a full briefing."

"An hour?" Art asked and Brodie nodded. "Excuse me."

Art left the table and took a phone from his belt, dialing it as he headed toward her office. Brodie went over to the couch to retrieve his jacket from the backrest.

With whiplash at the sudden planning and abrupt action, Zara was trying to catch up. "You're going to Canada?" she asked.

"Yeah, write down the coordinates we need."

Too many possibilities. Too much potential for danger. She couldn't let Brodie go on a mission that seemed like suicide. "You're going up to Canada to take on three men? What if the virus is there? Are you going to attempt to destroy a toxic chemical that could kill you if you screw up?"

Brodie nodded but wasn't looking at her. "And the device too, if it's in production," he said, putting his arms in his sleeves. "The schematics will still exist, but without his men and his resources, Grant will be slowed down. We'll disable him once the imminent threat is dealt with."

Shocked at his detached implication, she blinked twice and tried to decide who she should be more worried about, Grant or Brodie. It didn't take her long to decide who was the more lethal of the brothers. "Disable him? Disable Grant? What does that mean?"

He was still aloof while his thoughts were clearly elsewhere, maybe on thinking up ways he could 'disable' his sibling. "We're not gonna kill him… unless we have to."

Shaking her head, she cupped her chin and took a step toward him, wondering if he was insane. Despite his obvious proficiency, she couldn't deny her feelings for him anymore because Brodie was still the one she was most worried about. "You can't kill Grant and you can't go up to take on this mission alone."

Oblivious to her apprehension, he was preoccupied. "Why not?" he asked, fixing the cuff of his jacket. "Is there more information that—"

"It's dangerous," she said and moved another step in his direction in hopes of gaining his attention. "If you go up there, you could get yourself killed."

"Walk in the park," he said, without considering her warning.

Determined, she wouldn't be ignored, Zara put herself in front of him. "No," she said, grabbing the edges of his jacket when he began to sidestep her. "I can't let you do this."

Now when he did look her in the eye, all she saw was focus, but it wasn't on her. "We have to slow him down to give ourselves a chance to mobilize. If we don't, Grant sells the device and people get hurt, is that what you want?"

She was deflated and bewildered. "No… no, but there… there has to be another way."

"We're open to suggestions," Brodie said. But she was still trying to think of something when Art came out of her office.

"Time to split," Art said. "Swift will buzz Falcon."

Brodie removed her hands from his jacket and moved in time with Art in the direction of her front door. Except if they left now, she wouldn't see them again.

In a last-ditch effort to stop them from walking into harm's way, she reached for the one thing that might make them think twice. "I'll tell Grant," she exclaimed. Both men stopped to turn and glare at her. "I will. I can't let you do this. It's insane."

"What did you think we were gonna do with the info?" Brodie asked. "Write it in a journal?"

"There's law enforcement and—"

"Bureaucracy slows progress and doesn't yield results," Art said. "If you're going to jeopardize the mission then—"

"No," Brodie said, opening a hand toward his uncle who was just behind him. "Baby—"

"Oh no," she said, shaking her head and backing up toward the couch. "You're not going to sweet talk me into changing my mind. I gave you that information because I thought we were going to expose the danger. I didn't think you were going to go all gung-ho and endanger yourself."

"I told you not to fall for me," he said, losing the softness he had used in his attempt to placate her.

"You think this is about us?" she scoffed. Their relationship was secondary to their lives. "This is about stupidity. What will happen when you all get yourselves killed? Am I supposed to finish the job on my own?"

"We do this all the time, girlie," Art said. "You don't

understand how highly trained all of us are. This is a piece of cake. It's actually one of our less dangerous missions because it doesn't require direct contact with any of our targets."

"He said he was going to take out three of them," she said, jabbing a finger in Brodie's direction.

Art's mouth opened before he laughed a long hysterical stream that made him press his hands to his ribs. "You think he has to go near anyone to kill them? He's a marksman. Do you know what that means? He can hollow out a dime from two hundred yards," he said, approaching her. "The three of them will be dead before the first guy hits the floor. Then all he has to do is saunter over there and blast the place to high heaven." Slapping a hand to Brodie's shoulder, he gave him a yank. "Come on, Rave."

"You're a murderer," she murmured.

"An assassin," Art said.

Brodie's eyes stayed on hers and their darkness intensified. She had made so many excuses for him and believed him to be safe because he protected her. Zara had been alone with a man who was a killer for hire. A man she had been naked with and slept with had the ability to kill with impunity. While her connection to him seemed to strengthen every time they were together, she speculated on how a killer got rid of a woman when he was finished with her.

"You're not…"

"What did you think I did with my time?" Brodie asked.

She had to admit that his fighting skills and involvement in this situation suggested he didn't live a wholesome life and he had stated that he excelled at killing. "Okay," she conceded. "If you think you can do this without getting yourselves hurt then have at it. But Grant isn't to be hurt… and don't come to me for anything else. We're through."

"You don't get to walk away," Brodie snarled and moved out of Art's reach to come toward her. "You were warned that there was no exit once you were in."

Standing up to him, she remained steadfast. "What are you going to do?" she asked. "Shoot me? You have everything you need. I've told you everything. Destroy everything and then Grant will have nothing to sell and the world will be safe again."

"Kid," Art said in a sedate tone and Brodie's head snapped in his uncle's direction. "Release."

Brodie flashed his growling gaze to her again and then whipped around to follow his uncle, who grabbed his tools and opened the door to depart. Once they were gone and she could no longer hear them in the stairwell, she began to clean up.

Her stomach grumbled so Zara sat down to fork a couple of pieces of chicken into her mouth. The food was good, incredible in fact, but her appetite wasn't up to finishing anything. She boxed up the remaining food and washed the dishes, trying to lose herself in mundane tasks.

In need of a distraction, she went into her office and the first thing she did was look for her file on Game Time. It was gone. Flopping into her chair, Zara closed her eyes and let her head fall back. She'd been played. Even though she'd wanted to believe Brodie was righteous, she had been conned, probably as hundreds of women had been before her.

ELEVEN

PURDY'S WAS CROWDED the following evening when she went in for her usual Friday drink after work. Zara liked that the buzz of conversation filling the establishment muffled some of her thoughts. One glass of wine didn't manage to numb her, so she had a second. Her life was a mess. She'd betrayed her boss and fallen for his brother, who it turned out would rather jump head first into a hazardous, possibly life-threatening situation, than admit to her his true feelings on any subject.

After being handed her third drink, she began to gulp, and only stopped drinking when someone sat on the stool beside hers. Having managed to snag a table in the corner, she hadn't expected company. Being social was the last thing on her mind, and probably beyond her capability with the volume of alcohol pulsating through her bloodstream.

"It's busy," the man said.

His dashing smile and lingering gaze made her sigh and plonk her glass down on the table. "If you're looking to get laid, I'm really not in the mood," she said, glad of the gumption that the wine gave her.

His head jerked an inch as though he hadn't been expecting such a direct statement. "How about a little conversation," he said, laying his arms around his bourbon glass.

She was past the point of objecting to his presumption and she planned to go home as soon as she finished her wine. So if the guy wanted to sit and babble for the next ten minutes, she wasn't going to fight with him. Most men did what the hell they wanted to; one berating conversation wouldn't affect the arrogance of his gender.

"You are a looker," he said and she picked up her wine to avoid focusing on his leer. "I'm glad I came to see for myself."

That sounded sinister enough that she lowered her glass from her mouth to examine his cold expression. His eyes were iceberg blue. His nose was crooked, indicating it had probably been broken in the past. A scar on his neck attracted her scrutiny. It looked to be deep enough that it was a wonder he survived the initial wound.

"Excuse me?" she asked.

"Routine is a godsend," he said. "And you are a creature of habit, Zara. Guys like me appreciate that." Scanning the room, he nodded and smiled at her again. "This is a nice place."

Not interested in the details of the setting, she kept her eyes locked onto him. If he knew who she was, then he wanted something. Intoxication began to decrease and she moved her leg to confirm her purse—containing Brodie's Sig—was on her lap. "Who are you and what do you want?" she asked.

"You want to watch the company you keep," he said. Edging even closer, his smile began to fade. "You wouldn't want to be standing too close to Raven when I put a bullet between his eyes, would you? Brain matter doesn't come out of silk, honestly, that shit stains."

"Who are you?" she asked and the haze of intoxication lifted. "Are you a buyer?"

With a brief laugh, the corner of his mouth twisted. "A buyer? No," he said. "I don't give a damn about the device he's chasing or who it kills. I care about Raven and watching him die. I'm here to ask you to pass on a message." Getting closer, his arm brushed hers. "You tell him that payback's a bitch and I have my eyes on his prize… Canada is lovely this time of year."

"What does that—" He shifted back to his original position, downed his drink, and then got up and left as quickly as he'd appeared. Fixing her eyes on her wine glass, Zara second-guessed whether any of that had really just happened or if she'd imagined the whole thing.

Deciding that the potential threat was too serious to dismiss, she abandoned the rest of her wine and sped out of the bar in search of a cab.

***

BRODIE HAD WARNED her about security at is house, but Zara assumed that the place wasn't impenetrable. She got the cab to drop her off half a mile from her destination, for three reasons. One, folklore around here said that no one lived on this piece of land. As a woman on her own, she would look odd strutting up to a derelict property. The cab driver would likely remember her as a nut and might tell someone about the peculiar fare.

The second reason was she didn't know exactly where the front entrance was. Having never been here before and with Grant never mentioning it, the layout had been something she had failed to commit to memory.

The third reason, which some might say was juvenile, was she didn't want those inside to see her coming. They were supposed to be on her side, but she feared making a target of herself.

The cab driver dropped her off at an address near a club she used to frequent. It was the only nearby address she could deliver to him with confidence because she didn't know the area well and the point was to make this trip as forgettable as possible. Brodie couldn't object to her showing up if she proved she'd taken precautions to safeguard his obscurity.

On arrival, she paid her money, got out of the car, and loitered on the sidewalk like she might be meeting someone. It was only when the cab was out of sight that she began her journey.

Her shoes pinched, and if she'd known that this trek was on her agenda, Zara would have put on different footwear that morning. But these shoes went well with the black suit dress and jacket she wore to the office. The discomfort in her feet did make her consider aborting this job a couple of times. But the mental picture of the man in the bar kept her moving forward.

Brodie wouldn't be watching her anymore, not now that he had the information he wanted. If it hadn't been for the development in Purdy's, Zara would have had no reason to see him again. Despite her anger at being used, she couldn't dismiss the new player who was threatening Brodie's life.

Just because she was pissed, didn't mean that she wanted him dead, so she couldn't pretend she hadn't heard the warning. No doubt Brodie would argue that he could take care of himself and she knew that to be true—if he knew the threat was coming at him.

The walk took much longer than she'd anticipated. The gates to the property were further away than she'd assumed they would be. There were no lights to illuminate her route anymore; she'd passed the last streetlight on the block the cab had left her on. The closer she got to her destination, the more daunting the environment became.

A brick wall stood ten feet high and had iron railings above that with razor wire coiled around it, revealing that Brodie's parents had been the paranoid sort. That they had been so uneasy about strangers made Zara uneasy too. The boundary of the McCormack property stretched the full width of this peninsula and although she couldn't see the house, she knew it was there somewhere.

Nothing about this picture was inviting. Trees and bushes crowded around the wall, indicating the land had been left to ruin. Yet the wall was in top shape, betraying that someone had maintained the perimeter. She ran her fingers along the rough gray stone as she looked for an opening.

Her hope for a nice wrought iron gate she could slip through unnoticed began to dwindle. When she did find the way in, she was shocked to see a huge metal beast of a gate painted as black as the night around it.

There was no handle to open it. Figuring there must be some way to operate it, she searched for a good ten minutes before standing back and admitting defeat. Brodie had told her not to just show up and now she knew why, because it was nothing more than a big fat waste of time.

Taking another step back, Zara considered how she could get the message to him. But she couldn't hack into anyone's computer, and if he wasn't watching her then the light in her apartment window would be useless.

As she was about to turn and go home, there was a thud and then an electrical whirring sound. Less than five seconds later, the gate began to slide to the left. It was opening. Brodie had been telling the truth about security because she hadn't made an intrusive approach that could have drawn someone's attention. Yet they'd known she was here.

Another thud signaled the end of the gate's movement. It had only opened a couple of feet, but that was enough space for her to get through. Edging closer, Zara swallowed away her apprehension and proceeded forward. This could be a trap. A security system might be programmed to let people in only to decapitate them with a huge swinging axe or something. But having come this far, she ventured forth.

The ambient light faded further when she inched through the gate. Taking a step forward, she was overwhelmed by how overgrown the grounds were. They were reminiscent of a fairy tale forest where the unsuspecting heroine was gobbled up by the hungry wolf.

Another thud sounded and the gate began to roll back. She watched it close and with that, her chance of escape was lost. Light suddenly blared on and she whipped around to see the headlights of a jeep illuminating her and the flora all around her. Holding up a hand to shield her eyes, she saw someone move across the beam of light and come closer.

"He said you were tenacious." The voice belonged to Art and her hand lowered a little. "You've got a set on you girl, showing up here after threatening us."

"How did you know I was here?" she called. "Or are you going to tell me it's a coincidence that you were just driving by?"

"Recognizing a coincidence is the first step to solving a mystery," he said as though he'd said the words a thousand times before. "What are you doing here?"

He sounded more impressed than peeved, so she stepped in his direction. "I have a message for Brodie."

"He's not home. You're lucky about that. He never would've let you in. Only five people have been in his house in the last twenty years."

Zara assumed she was about to be flung off the property. It was probable he'd let her in just to tell her not to draw attention to the place by snooping around. "Well, I—"

"How would you like to be the sixth?" he asked and was close enough now to hold out a hand.

Dropping her shielding hand into his, she knew this wasn't going to be as simple as delivering a message.

***

ART SAID NOTHING in the jeep on the way to the house, which was much further from the gates than she'd thought it would be. After driving for around two miles, the house emerged from the darkness when she had given up looking for it.

Three floors high, it was constructed with a dark gray stone that made the gothic towers appear even more ominous. Art drove to the side of the building and down a ramp through an open garage door into an underground parking area. When he turned off the engine and got out of the vehicle, she did the same, though she wasn't quite sure what was going to come next or why he'd allowed her inside when Brodie wasn't even here.

"I just—"

"Upstairs," Art said, already moving away from her.

Zara hurried to catch him up to him. He pressed his thumb to a dull blue pad next to a door, and she recognized the CI fingerprint recognition tech. He took her up a spiral staircase and through a set of doors. One wall of this space was open in a series of pointed arches. Stepping out from beneath the standard-height ceiling, Zara had to re-inhale the oxygen taken from her lungs at the sight of the cavernous entryway, floored with the most incredible wood that she had to stop and admire it.

"It's Macassar ebony," he said. "The house is gothic revival." Moving through a pointed arch behind her, he took her hand to bring her into the main space. The double wide stone staircase drew her eye up to the vaulted ceiling three stories above.

"It's incredible," she said, almost unable to believe it. The pointed arch windows high above them were made up of smaller rectangles. Some were clear glass, some were textured, and others were colored.

"It has a twin," he said.

"A what?" she asked, absorbing the features of this incredible space with wide eyes filled with wonder. There were a series of black doors forty feet from the foot of the stairs, which she assumed were the front doors.

"Two identical homes were built simultaneously by Grant Senior in the seventies. This one on the east coast and the other on an island off the coast of Washington state."

Still open-mouthed, she drank in the atmosphere of this echoing marvel. "Why?"

"Because my sister had her husband wrapped around her little finger," he said and this got her attention. Art's sister was Brodie's mother and Grant Senior's wife. "My family was originally from the West Coast and my sister didn't like to be away from our mother back then. Grant Senior built the other house for our mother."

Taking on one project like this would've been a challenge. Two could be considered insanity. "That must have cost a fortune."

"Yes, it did," he said with a half-smile and a nod. "He was showing off and my mother, Brodie's grandmother, was a very difficult woman to please. Come through to the kitchen."

Art guided her through a series of doors and passages.

Eventually they came out in a large kitchen set at the side of the house. It had a twenty-five-foot ceiling and the same style of windows as the entry way did. These were high above as well, stretching across the wall above the stove at the height of the second story.

The room was huge and in addition to the wraparound units and the double-width stove, there was a dual height island, and a den area with a couch, and a couple of armchairs around a coffee table, which sat beneath a wall-mounted TV.

"I just made coffee; would you like some?" he asked. "Or there's wine in the cellar if you'd—"

She held up a hand and waved it in time with her shaking head. "I've already had two and a half glasses."

"If this is a drunken booty call, you really should've called first," Art said, skirting the kitchen island to reach the coffee pot. "Brodie isn't home."

"You said that already. Forgive me for asking," she said, putting her purse on the lower portion of the center island and curling her fingers around it.

He glanced over his shoulder as he poured black coffee into two mugs. "What?"

"Why did you let me in? I got the impression last night that you didn't think much of me."

"I was the black sheep of my family," he said, carrying the mugs down the opposite side of the island and indicating with an eye roll that she should follow him. When they got to the couches, he sat and put the mugs down on the low coffee table. "Brodie and me spend most of our time in here, in our bedrooms, or using the facilities downstairs. The houses were built structurally the same but the boys have remodeled in their own ways over the years."

She wasn't sure who "the boys" were, but she wanted to know where Art's story was going before asking about anything else. "You were saying," she said, attempting to get the conversation back to where it had been. "About being the black sheep?"

Opening his mouth, he took a large lungful of air before continuing. "I was the second of four children. There was eight years between me and my eldest sister, Melinda, that's Brodie and Grant's mom."

"Why did you take Brodie after she died? Do you have a wife and kids of your own?"

"Neither," he said, reaching for his mug. "I lived here with Melinda when I was in the country. Brodie idolized me. I spent my life traveling, learning from indigenous people, backpacking, trekking, and mountaineering. He loved to hear my stories. After our mother died, Brodie's grandmother, Melinda didn't see much of our younger sisters. One of whom was a single mom and the other had serious issues with her problem child. After Melinda died, we found out it had been written into her will that I should become guardian of the boys."

Intrigued, she speculated. "But you didn't want to be tied down?"

"I wouldn't say that, but... Grant Junior took to business; he idolized his father and trotted into work with him as often as he could. He was fifteen when his parents died, it had been his birthright, and his lifelong ambition to take over at CI... no one thought it would be so soon. Brodie wanted nothing to do with the company. That was when Frank and I sat down with the boys and they made their decisions. It was never our intention to keep them apart, but... Brodie started traveling with me, Grant went to college, and our paths rarely crossed... especially since Grant refused to come here to the manor."

"This is fascinating, but..."

He smiled. "What has it got to do with my reaction to you last night?" he asked.

Nodding while freeing her feet from her shoes, Zara retrieved her mug from the coffee table and cradled it with both hands as she brought it close to her body. Then twisting herself to face Art, she drew her legs up onto the couch and tucked them beneath herself. "I thought you didn't like me."

"When I was young, I was a bit of a crusader. I thought myself a bit of a... hero, I guess. We built homes for those who had lost them in natural disasters and fought injustice as we found it. I had more than a few contacts myself and I made money by tracking people down or getting information. Over the years, one thing led to another and we found ourselves going after bigger and bigger fish. Brodie took to fighting and shooting like a tiger takes to his stripes. Eventually I was obsolete. Support staff for this tower of a man who really was a hero. Brodie has killed dozens of men, hundreds of them, and I guess he's lost a bit of his humanity because of that. But everyone he's killed, he's killed for a reason."

The ferocity of Art's pride made him lose the easy, approachable demeanor he'd had on receiving her. She couldn't think of any parent who would defend their child with more vehemence than Art took on when talking about Brodie.

"I think he still has a lot of humanity in him," she said, sipping her drink through the delightful steam rising from it.

He relaxed and drank from his own mug. "I think so too. I'm incredibly proud of him. He didn't go to school or college. He didn't get married, have kids, and live a traditional life… He turned into me… only a better version of me, the version of me I wanted to be but couldn't."

"You're protective of him," she said, understanding his frosty reception yesterday. "Were you worried I was some sort of Mata Hari?"

Considering her words, he took his eyes away from her, choosing instead to enjoy his coffee for a while before putting it on the table and answering her. "The other day, when he wasn't in his bed in the morning and I called him… When I heard he was at your place… that he'd spent the night…"

"You were a worried parent," she said, wearing a smile. Brodie was all man, all grown up, and capable of caring for himself. It was funny to imagine someone waiting up for him.

"No," Art said, shaking his head. "No, I… he spends all night out a lot of the time because he works at night, he scouts at night. He spends two thirds of the year overseas, and it's not like I don't know that he can take care of himself. He stays out all night for the job. He's never stayed out all night for a woman."

"Never?" she asked, struggling to believe such a thing.

Leaning forward with open hands, he let his palms join and fall together as he angled himself toward her. "Don't get me wrong, he's had plenty of women. That's an area he never needed any coaching in," Art said and she saw the paternal satisfaction swell in his chest. "Sometimes when we're abroad somewhere he'll spend the night with a girl, especially if we have nowhere else to sleep that night or we need cover. But here, at home"—his lip turned out as he shook his head—"never happened."

Fishing for information and maybe a compliment, she tried to be casual when she probed further. "There's never been anyone special in his life?" she asked, especially interested as to what "plenty of women" might mean.

Before he spoke, Art seemed to debate with himself whether he should be honest. "There was a girl once, Mischa. He met her in Italy and did some work with her father. But… Mischa was cosmopolitan, social… She didn't mind having him locked in a cage for her private use, but she wouldn't be seen with him in public."

"Brodie wouldn't have minded that," Zara said, learning that jealousy tasted more bitter than coffee. "He doesn't like to be seen in public."

Art was shaking his head and wearing a sneer of revulsion. "She was cold and ruthless. Brodie was blinded by her beauty, but I could tell, she was rotten all the way to her core. She did some work with us and she took a… psychopathic enjoyment from it. We called her Cuckoo, she hated it, but Tuck and I agreed it made sense. She was half a step away from asking Raven to kill just to get her off. That was when I knew enough was enough."

So Art had been instrumental in ending the relationship. Brodie would listen to his uncle's advice, but she was surprised to hear he hadn't fought for his woman if there was a chance of love between them. Maybe the association had been more sexual than emotional.

Taking another drink of the delicious coffee, Zara shrugged off her distaste at the turn of the conversation. Pushing her mug onto the table, she sidled a little closer. "I wish I could say he got carried away with me, but it wasn't any emotional connection that made him stay," she said. "I told him to. I told him if he spent the night and had breakfast with me that I would tell him anything he wanted to know."

Art's lips slanted up. "You might think that's the reason. But I know my nephew. Painting him into a corner like that… you gave him an excuse to do what he wanted to do anyway."

"Maybe." She shrugged.

"Cuckoo made me wary of what a woman could do to him. But you… you're not like her. You're exactly what he needs."

Art's optimism made her draw back a little. "Like I said, I wouldn't read too much into it. He wanted information from me and he got it. It just so happened that he got some sex into the bargain."

"When we first started researching you," Art said and she squirmed at the notion these men had been investigating her. "It was because Albert Sutcliffe's men were watching you. We wanted to know what had them intrigued. So Brodie went to check you out and when he came back… it had been years since I'd seen him smile like he did that night. He never smiled like that with Mischa… You had him at that very minute. I don't know how or why, but you did."

"He told me he thought I looked naughty the first time he saw me," she stated.

Art held up his hands. "Hey, what happens between a man and his woman—"

"I know that he's told all of you the dirty details," she said, pointing at her coffee mug. "How else would you know I drink my coffee black? And your friend on the computer knew intimate things about—"

"My friend on the computer was kicked out of the room when you started questioning who he was… which was very smart by the way," Art said, turning his whole body in her direction. "You should never admit details when you don't know for sure who you're talking to. Brodie kicked us out after your question about lovers. We didn't get back in until he was done."

Art could just be telling her what she wanted to hear. "If that's true, why didn't he just announce himself?"

"It pays to hide your identity from others and you have to be humble enough to realize there's always a chance that someone is watching you."

They were concerned about insulating themselves but weren't so concerned about her safety. "So you were happy for them to know that I was giving out company secrets, just not who I was giving them to?"

"Look here," he said, elevating an arm onto the back of the couch. "Brodie has gone above and beyond to keep you safe. He's risked exposure for you and he has never done that for another soul… I taught him better than that."

Lifting her own arm to the back of the couch, Zara laid her hand over his. "I'm sure he's very grateful for everything you've done for him."

Fixing her in his sights, Art's eyes grew heavy. "You cut him deep," he said, sliding his hand back a bit, though his fingers stayed under hers. "Last night with that murderer bullshit."

Never had Zara thought she would be involved in anything like Game Time. Terrorists and ambiguous "demonstrations" weren't meant to be a part of her life. Last night, she'd acted on impulse, speaking before she had a chance to process. "I didn't know what he did," she said, shrinking in light of the truth.

Her actions, her words, they did hurt Brodie. All along, he'd been honest, and had never made himself out to be a saint. The shock of being drawn into his world made her lash out because being taken advantage of was her greatest fear.

Coming from a small town, Zara had wanted people in the big city to believe she was street smart. More than once she'd had it proven to her that she wasn't as savvy as she wanted to believe. Since arriving here, she had come a long way, so far that those in her hometown probably wouldn't recognize her.

Art's scowl was a return to his disapproving parent manner. "He saved your life, that's what he did, and you should be grateful for that."

"I am," she said, thrusting her shoulders back to beseech his gaze. "Please don't think I'm not, I... I guess I was reacting rather than thinking because I was hurt... It's not like he and I made any promises to each other. But it just... I tell him I trust him, then his buddy communicates through my computer and I come home to you erasing every shred of evidence that he ever existed in my life."

Art relaxed some. "You were hurt. You thought you were being dumped."

She wasn't going to deny the truth. "I thought he used sex to get what he wanted and I was disappointed in myself for letting it happen. He told me he was watching the people who were watching me. Who was that?"

"Tim Sutcliffe was supposed to sweep you off your feet so that you'd talk him up to Grant. His uncle, Albert Sutcliffe, was meeting with Grant in New York that Monday and it was at that meeting that Grant led him to believe you knew everything about the deal."

Her eyes narrowed. "Why would he say that?"

"Grant probably wanted to cover his ass and saying he has an accomplice helps to insulate him and makes others believe he is not ashamed of what he's doing. Divulging that his actions were a secret would open him up to blackmail and the threat of assassination."

"Oh my God," she exhaled, curling her fingers around her throat. So she was his safety net and the one who was supposed to ask questions if he suddenly vanished. The sad truth was, if Grant had disappeared, she probably would have gone on a crusade to find him without any idea of the danger she'd be walking into. "Are they still watching?"

He shrugged. "Brodie's been keeping an eye on their positions and so far, it looks like you're in the clear. I guess they didn't expect to lose young Tim. It's probably not worth the risk of someone else's life to have you watched. Who knows what would happen if anyone else tried to move in on you, especially now that you've got Brodie's attention."

"Do they know that?"

"That you're with him? No." Art shook his head. "No one can see into your bedroom and Brodie's discreet. He knows how to cover his tracks."

Of that, she was sure and she made a note to be more careful herself. Tim had found her in Purdy's, as had the man with the scar. Threats didn't always look scary. In fact, every time she'd been approached by one, they'd been outwardly pleasant, except for Brodie. Though he wasn't exactly a threat to her... maybe.

"I don't suppose it matters now that our... whatever it was... is all in the past."

Art's eyes moved up to fix on something, which caused her to glance over her shoulder. But she saw nothing unusual. "We're about to find out if my nephew's through with you," Art said, pushing up off the couch.

"How?" she asked. Searching the wall to try to find out what had caught his eye, yet she still saw nothing.

"You're going to learn that this house has more secrets than you can possibly imagine."

Art poured a third cup of coffee, then ducked to produce a bottle of scotch from a drawer. Retrieving two heavy based crystal tumblers, he put them on the center island and unscrewed the liquor bottle to pour out two measures.

TWELVE

SLIDING DOWN, Zara tried to hide her presence. Art's actions indicated that Brodie was about to arrive and she doubted he would receive her with glee. Peeking over the back of the couch, she watched Art start to screw on the scotch lid and sure enough, a few seconds later, the kitchen door bounced open, and Brodie came in.

"You owe me two hundred bucks, Chief," Brodie said to his uncle and tossed something metallic into the air, then caught it in his palm. Displaying the item between his thumb and forefinger, Zara was amazed to see him holding the biggest bullet she'd ever laid eyes on. "You sent me out with one round and I came back with one round. Figure that one out."

"How did you kill him?" Art asked, tightening the bottle lid.

For some reason, that was the moment Brodie's attention snapped around. By her reckoning, Art hadn't betrayed her presence. But Brodie had become aware of her all the same, and the minute he did, he lost all traces of triviality from his mellow expression.

"What the fuck is she doing here?" Brodie asked. Flicking the round into his hand, he used it to point at her while scowling at Art who was coming around the island with the two crystal tumblers.

"Not to mess with tradition," Art said, holding a glass toward Brodie who took it. The men clinked glasses and downed their drinks in one. Apparently, it was a tradition to get liquored up after Brodie took someone down.

"Now answer me," Brodie said, wiping the back of his hand across his mouth.

Art took both empty glasses over to discard them in the sink. "She showed up at the gate, what did you want me to do?"

"Ignore her," Brodie said, as if she wasn't here. "Just like we do with every other trespasser. She would never have gotten past the fucking gate and even if she did—"

"What?" Art asked, grabbing the third coffee mug, he took it over to Brodie. "Security would've taken her down. Is that what you wanted? 'Cause apparently you've got a spare round if you want to erase her yourself."

"Very funny," Brodie said, taking the proffered coffee.

Art came over and sat on the couch with her again. "Brodie had an out-of-town job today," Art said.

"Oh," she said, twisting away from Art to see Brodie was still just inside the kitchen door, where he had been since he came in. "Do you work out of town much? Art says you spend two thirds of the year overseas. That must be tough."

"Did he now?" Brodie said, flashing a glare at his uncle before he discarded his mug on the lower part of the kitchen island to move closer to the couch.

"Wait a minute," she said, losing her timidity when clarity struck her. "An out-of-town job? Did you go to Quebec? Did you—"

"No," Brodie said and glanced at Art. "We're doing the job tomorrow, after Tuck gets here. We'll be leaving at first light."

She wasn't convinced, but his certain gaze didn't lose any of its anger. "Brodie, if—"

"I said I didn't," he snapped. "You calling me a liar?"

Her accusations were only pissing him off, and she'd guess he wouldn't get so defensive if he was lying to her.

"No," she said, shaking her head.

He'd asked for trust and he'd never lied to her before. If he would openly admit his identity when confronted with it, she had no reason to believe he would deny destroying Winter Chill. Admitting his identity to her was a bigger risk than confessing complicity in the Quebec job. Also, if it was done, she couldn't sabotage them. So by her reckoning, he had no reason to lie.

Brodie wasn't appeased by her denial. "What else did Art tell you?"

Switching her gaze between the men, she reclined against the arm of the couch to look up at Brodie over the back of it, hoping he wouldn't start a fight with his uncle just because he'd been hospitable. "I didn't come here to cause any trouble."

It turned out that Art wasn't the cause of his annoyance. "Why did you come here?" Brodie sneered. "Because I remember telling you not to."

Reminded of the man in Purdy's and his warning, she forgot all other grievances. "I had to see you," she said, clambering onto her knees to rest her torso on the couch, but when she stretched her arms to reach for him, he didn't come near enough to reciprocate. So she gave up on trying to pre-emptively console him and let her limbs flop onto the back of the couch. "I came to warn you."

His eyes flared and his head bobbed forward as though he'd been struck by surprise. "Warn me?"

"Yes."

Widening his stance, Brodie folded his arms and she assumed the bullet was enclosed in his fist. "This ought to be good, because if you think that you or your CEO boyfriend can take me down then—"

Why he kept bringing up her association with Grant, she didn't know. He'd known about her employer before he approached her, it was why he approached her. But she didn't like to be accused of a crime she hadn't committed and she had never considered Grant a boyfriend, she had never even thought of him in a romantic way.

"Listen, bucko," she said, infused with irritation. Shoving

her hands to the couch, she pounced off it backwards and rounded it to bring them face to face. Without her shoes on or the height of the couch, she wasn't nearly as scary as she wanted to be. Still, she carried on because she deserved the right to defend herself. "We've covered this. Grant is not my boyfriend. We've attended a million corporate functions together and he has never once grabbed me and kissed me or pinned me to my own bed and told me to fight him off—"

"I didn't tell you to fight me off."

Scowling, she was met by his nonchalance. "We were both there, you know what you did."

"What we did, baby," he said, reducing the space between them. "And you wouldn't have stood a chance at stopping me from taking what I wanted from you no matter how hard you fought."

Their sniping provoked more than their tempers. Hormones began to simmer until she could see her arousal reflected back in his leer.

"I know how to get you to stop," she said, letting her lip curl at one corner as her brow arched.

Pouncing forward, he grabbed her face under her jaw and crowded her against the back of the couch betraying his own arousal in his enlivened gaze. "You've got a smart mouth, Bandini," he murmured with a snarl in his voice that made her center pound in unison with her heartbeat and the thump in her throat.

She couldn't change the man, she had to respect who he was, and who he was fascinated her. "I don't remember closing the door on you, McCormack," she said and with her panting permission, he swooped down and planted his mouth on hers.

Grateful when he lifted her up to sit on the back of the couch to bring them closer, Zara hooked her legs over his hips and clung onto him. Brodie came forward, urging her into a backwards slant that kept her off-balance and in need of his anchoring body. With one arm around the bottom of her rib cage, he kept his hold of her face to dictate their devouring kiss.

His tongue sank into her mouth and that defiant force

battled hers. They were both as stubborn and as arrogant as the other. He could try to intimidate her, but she couldn't deny her carnal reaction to him. This man was her button. With a look or a word, he could race her in a way every other man failed to.

If she believed for a second that he had used her body against her to extort information, then that doubt was erased when he thrust her face away and glared down at her with a vicious devotion bleeding from his drowsy eyes.

The heat of his gaze provoked her into trying for another kiss, but he held her back and the victory in his smile made her stab her nails into the sides of his neck. Dragging them down to the neck of his tee shirt, she snagged it downward and then with an open mouth, she lunged up and closed her kiss over his throat.

The rumble of his satisfied growl vibrated her lips, but she lapped her tongue up and sucked her mouth away only to spread kisses across the front and side of his neck.

"Bet you're glad I let her in now," Art said.

His smiling voice came from behind her, so she guessed he was still seated on the couch. Giving in to her desire for Brodie freed her in a way that erased all burdens from her life. Sitting on the back of this couch, wrapped around the man she was tasting, felt so right. This was what safety felt like. What security and stability felt like.

This may have started as an enigmatic attraction, but it had grown into something more. With every fact she learned about him, her appetite was whetted to learn another and another. One more word. One more kiss. She wasn't sure it would ever be enough. Until she had stood here facing his spitting fury, she hadn't known the depth of her own obsession, now it was undeniable.

"Are you staying over?" Brodie asked, sinking his lips into her hair and she stopped her kissing to tip her head back.

She hadn't come here with the intention of being intimate with Brodie again. But the intensity around his darkness grew and Zara comprehended the truth behind his question. If she stayed now, she was staying for good. He'd told her that once she was in there was no getting out. It seemed that time had come.

More sure of her desire and infatuation with this man than she'd been of anything before in her life, she didn't hesitate to reply. "Yes," she whispered and as her lips settled together, she let her smile breed his.

"Starting a new tradition?" Art asked.

Using Brodie's body to keep herself secure on her perch, Zara twisted enough to catch sight of Art's knowing expression. Brodie's arm slid away from her back, forcing her to cling tighter to him. But he pulled one of her arms away from its embrace and skimmed his hand downward until it touched her palm. His thick digits splayed and insinuated themselves between hers. She hadn't expected to feel lumps and callouses adorning his skin, but he worked with his hands so she shouldn't have been surprised.

"You're gonna get lost in this house a dozen times before you learn the route from here to the bedroom," Brodie said and he snagged the back of her neck to pry her body away from his so he could look her in the eye. "Don't ever get scared in this house." She nodded but was daunted by the prospect of this labyrinth of a building. "We have every eventuality covered. Every exterior door and window are alarmed or booby trapped."

"Booby trapped?" she repeated and thought about her fear at the gate. It turned out there was a chance she could have been decapitated by a flying axe after all.

His expression remained static. "You have nothing to fear if you trust me."

Playing with him, she asked, "The booby traps will know if my confidence in you wavers?"

"No," he said, glowering at her as he squeezed her neck to chastise her for her tease. "The traps are in peripheral parts of the building we rarely use. You won't have clearance to enter sensitive areas, which might be rigged. But I'm telling you not to go snooping."

She had never been so grateful for a lack of security clearance in her life. "Okay."

"Come on," he said. Releasing her hand, he crouched to wrap an arm around her ribcage. But before he could lift her up, she pushed his chest and loosened her legs.

Going to his bedroom would lead to intimacy and when Brodie was touching her, rational thought became impossible. She had to tell them about the guy in Purdy's before leaving this space or she probably never would. "Wait," she said, shaking her head. "I have to tell you something."

He huffed. "You can't talk while I walk?"

"You can't go to Canada."

"Oh, shit," he said and let her go to walk away.

Holding on to the couch, Zara hooked her heels up on the edge of the wide back. "You can't."

"I thought you came here for..." Flipping around, he opened his arms in a shrug. "Why don't you want me to go, baby, huh? You think I can't take out three nerds?"

"One of those guys is a black belt," she said. "But it's not your abilities I'm concerned about."

"Then what is it," Art asked, giving her a chance to tell her story.

"I was at Purdy's tonight," she said and knew that needed no more explanation because they knew her schedule as well as the guy who had accosted her did. "And I was approached by a guy who told me to give you a message."

When Brodie's body heat radiated to her, she turned back in his direction. "What message?" Brodie asked.

His curiosity was an improvement over his previous irritation. "The last thing he said was that Canada's nice this time of year," she said. "That has to mean... he has to know about your mission."

Almost on top of her, his sudden anger began to tinge his features as though he was preempting the answer to his next question and assuming the worst. "Did you talk to anyone?" Brodie asked through narrow lips. "Did you tell anyone about—"

"About what?" she asked, practicing her own glare. "No, I didn't tell anyone about what happened last night in my apartment. Why would I? I would have to admit how you got that information, wouldn't I?"

Art chimed in with a statement cryptic enough to make Brodie proud. Now Zara understood who had taught her lover to be so vague. "It's got to be—"

"No," Brodie said, pinning a scowl on his uncle. But by cutting him off, Brodie actually gave credence to Art's unspoken suspicion of the perpetrator's identity by responding to the prospect without it having to be uttered. "He wouldn't have approached Zara."

"Sure he would," Art said, leaning over the back of the couch beside where she sat. "What else did he say, girlie?"

Trying to remember the conversation, she turned her lips into her mouth to buy herself some time. "He said… payback's a bitch and he has his eyes on your prize," she said and when Brodie backed off this time, she saw the deliberate look he dropped to his uncle.

"There's nothing we can do," Brodie said.

"There's one thing," Art said.

Zara was lost because again they were carrying on their conversation as though they were alone.

"Have you got time to track him?" Brodie asked.

Art exhaled in defeat. "No. He's a fucker."

"What else is new," Brodie muttered.

"I don't understand," Zara said, seeking an answer on their faces. "Who is he? He said he didn't care about the device or who it killed."

"He's a guy set on revenge," Art said. Brodie was walking away from her again, so she turned and slid a leg over the couch so that she was sitting astride the backrest.

"How do you know who he is?" she frowned and tilted closer.

"Slick looking motherfucker with a scar right here," Art said, lifting his chin to indicate the line of the scar on his neck and she nodded. "His name is Griffin Caine. He's something of a groupie. He followed Brodie's work for years. But he was just too erratic to be brought inside."

"He threatened Brodie's life," she said. "But he… called him Raven."

"Brodie's been Raven for years," Art said. "Sometimes even he forgets who he really is."

"Being back here, so close to home and dealing with CI… it must be bringing back memories," she said, glancing at Brodie, but he was retrieving the bottle of scotch and not listening to them.

Bringing her legs up, she crossed them and balanced in her seated position atop the couch.

"It hasn't been easy for him," Art said, watching his nephew pour out a large measure. "When we first heard what Grant was doing... We were in Egypt and... it's funny how your demons can find you no matter where you are, isn't it?"

"I can talk to Grant," she said, lowering her volume and hunching a little closer to Art. "I'm not convinced he's a lost cause. If we can figure out why he's doing this—"

"He's doing it to punish our father," Brodie said. She had thought he wasn't paying attention but it turned out she was wrong. He tossed the liquor down his throat and poured out another measure. "He's doing it for spite. Our father died for this damned piece of metal and plastic and Grant wants to show him that it was for nothing. That our father's sacrifice meant nothing."

Absorbing this declaration, she considered how well the brothers knew each other. "How do you know that?" she asked. "You said last night that—"

"Because he's right," Brodie said, rotating the glass full of scotch back and forth in his hand. "Grant is right."

Art jumped up from the couch to head in his nephew's direction. "Did you hit your head tonight? Breathe some crazy-making fumes? You don't support this. People will die! Innocent people!"

Snapping around, his fury burned from his eyes. "Yeah," Brodie retorted. "But if Caine knows about it..." he glanced past Art to focus on her. "He thinks she's fair game."

"You invited this," Art said with impatience, yanking the bottle of scotch away and sending the bullet Brodie had discarded on the counter, clattering onto the floor.

"You're saying this is my fault?" Brodie said, slamming his glass on the counter.

"You knew it was a possibility. You knew that as soon as you found a woman to care about—"

Depressurizing his anger, Brodie exhaled his resolve. "This is what he's been waiting for," Brodie said, retrieving his glass and turning his mouth down into it. He didn't deny Art's declaration that he cared for her. "This is why he's been dogging me for years. Killing me wasn't enough."

"No, it wasn't," Art said, speaking in solidarity. "But you're not going to fall apart now. Caine is the least of our problems. We've avoided him this long. We'll just keep avoiding him. You know that half his fun comes from the chase. He's not going to put a bullet in Zara until you're there to watch it."

Her observational role suddenly became interactive. "In me?" she asked, scrambling off the back of the couch to dart toward the men. "Why does he want to kill me?"

"It's a long story," Art said. "Needless to say, their feud is rooted in a situation involving a woman."

"Feud?" Zara asked, resting a hand on the countertop to support herself in case this story got any worse, although she couldn't imagine how it could.

"Caine was in love with her and she didn't want him," Art said. "The story is irrelevant to the fact that he hounds Brodie at times like these because he enjoys watching people suffer. It would be the highlight of his life if Brodie made a mistake."

Narrowing her eyes, she sought an explanation. "Why would—"

"Because he has anger management issues and narcissistic tendencies," Brodie said while examining the contents of his glass.

That sounded like someone else she knew. "It's a wonder you two were friends," she muttered.

He didn't entertain her sarcasm. "We were not friends," Brodie grumbled and drank more of his alcohol.

"We focus on this mission and deal with Caine later."

"This mission is fucked from the start," Brodie said. "We still can't figure out where the fuck Grant is stashing the device in the city. The fucker is smart. He knows better than to digitize anything. Frank taught him the virtue of doing things old-school."

Brodie elevated the glass toward his lips. Zara put a hand on Art's chest to urge him aside. Then she slipped into the narrow space between Brodie and the counter to seize his glass before it could reach his mouth.

"Well, it's not in the bottom of that bottle," she said, handing the glass off to Art who hurried it away before Brodie could snatch it back. "That's one place down."

"What are you doing?" Brodie asked her and his body swayed forward, pinning her to the solid granite at the small of her back. "Worried if I drink too much that the equipment won't work when we get upstairs?"

"I'm looking forward to finding out," she said, scratching her nails up the fabric of his tee shirt and around his neck where she linked her fingers and used his strength as leverage to pull herself higher. Pouting, she fixated on his mouth and exhaled a murmur of want.

Seeing him stressed made her want to calm him. She wanted him to relax, to erase his worries and remind him of her warm body because she wanted to be a sanctuary for him. Brodie was an outlaw, the kind of man who wouldn't shy from any fight and she was in awe of his abilities.

To be a part of his life, to be a place of safety and comfort for him, would be a privilege. From what she'd gleaned from him and from Art, Brodie hadn't exactly had an easy life, but she wanted a chance to offer him security and relief.

His hum of pleasure encouraged her. "Come on," she whispered. Hoping he'd trust her enough to let her in, she tried her best to be unthreatening in her seduction. The last thing she wanted to do was set him more on edge. "Relax for me, beau."

The force of his arm clamping around her stole the air from her lungs and he hauled her up to join their mouths just as she wanted him to. The bitter liquor still flavored his tongue but she reveled in that taste and the broad masculinity of the man who lifted her from her feet and onto the kitchen counter. Quickly putting himself in charge, he parted her knees and dragged his teeth on the inside of her lower lip as he broke their kiss.

Art appeared in her peripheral vision, but even as Brodie turned to look at him with business written all over his face, she couldn't stop staring up at this man who was beginning to take her over.

"We still have time," Art said. "Tuck and I will take care of business. We'll find out where it is."

"Who is Tuck?" she asked, exhaling her hormonal mist to pay attention to the conversation again. "Where is he?"

"Tuck uses the alias Swift," Art said. "He is our computer whizz, the guy who got into your computer at CI."

"Oh," she nodded, stroking Brodie. "Is he here?"

"No, he went back to his own lady tonight," Art said. "He hasn't been with her for a while and he promised her a visit."

Perking up, she glanced at each of the men. "He has a lady?" she asked, reassured that if he had a girlfriend, he had to have some redeeming qualities.

"Kadie," Art said.

"What's she like?"

"We've never met her," Brodie said, sliding a hand up her back to grasp her neck again. "Tuck likes to keep a nice thick, clear line between Kadie and anything that could get her hurt… which is basically everything in his life that isn't her."

Squinting, she moistened her lips. "And she's happy with that?" Zara asked.

It took a strong woman to watch her man go off into battle regularly without any idea of where he was, what he was doing, or who he was with.

"Who knows?" Art said with a shrug. "Swift is a private guy, so I wouldn't ask him too many questions when you meet him."

This was a night full of surprises; at least this one wasn't unpleasant. "When am I going to meet him?" she asked Art but looked at Brodie.

"He'll get back into town tomorrow," Brodie said.

Art's concern was increasing. "Everything depends on us finding this piece of kit."

Her role in this situation had been to get information, so she felt compelled to do what she could to get more.

"I'll find it," Zara said and lay across the counter to snag her purse on the opposite edge.

Brodie took her hand to help her right herself and she

began to dig in her purse.

"How are you going to do that?" Art asked her.

Pulling out her cellphone, she held it up. "I'm going to call Grant and ask him where it is."

She started to speed dial, but Brodie plucked the phone out of her hand before she could connect the line. "Two pieces of advice," he said, giving the phone to Art, who took it away toward the couch. "First… and this is more of a house rule… don't ever call anyone outside the Kindred Circle from this house, you hear me? No one."

Not used to such orders, she saw one immediate problem. "How do I know who is in the Kindred Circle?" she asked, leaning back on her hands.

"Here's a clue," Brodie said, gesturing between himself and Art, who was returning to them. "You're looking at the only two members you know."

That didn't help because she couldn't contact these men even if she did want to. "I don't have either of your phone numbers."

He didn't exactly light up, but he swept her hair over her shoulder with the back of his hand and scrutinized her neck. "Excellent, so there will be no confusion," Brodie said.

Ready to push boundaries, she teased to see how far he would let her get. "What if I want a pizza?"

Brodie wasn't for playing. In fact, he did deadpan better than anyone she'd ever met. "Then you go down to the basement, get in a car, and drive to the pizza place."

If she did spend any more time here, she would have to get used to there being a no takeout rule, which wasn't great because she was a terrible cook.

"What's the second thing?" she asked.

Planting his hands on the counter on either side of her hips, he loomed over her. "Don't go running to Grant every time you need to fix a problem."

That seemed to be more subjective than the previous rule. But it was an old habit. Grant and she had worked together for five years and when she was uncertain of something or needed help, Grant was the man she called because all her issues were CI related—her life had been dedicated to that company for half a decade.

"Okay," she nodded. "You're right, I… I need to start thinking of him as the enemy, don't I?"

"He's sure not as great as you fucking think," Brodie grumbled.

It wouldn't be easy for her to switch her thinking because Grant had been her boss for so long. They had spent late nights together, sat in long meetings together, brainstormed, problem solved. Now that part of her life was over and she had to realize that Grant wasn't the unthreatening, easy-going CEO she believed him to be.

Except she was only here because she was connected to him, because she had access. If she couldn't use that access, then Brodie would have no further use for her.

"Grant knows where the device is and we want to know," she said. "I don't want to get hurt, but I have to be able to help you."

"Damn," Brodie mumbled then righted himself to look at Art. "Maybe we should just lock her in one of the guest rooms. It's a shame we don't have Zave's custom built suite."

Horrified to hear that they knew a person who had a custom suite obviously designed to imprison people, she wasn't going to let her aversion to the suggestion of being locked up go unregistered.

"You're not locking me in anywhere," she said, sitting up straight. "Why does your friend Zave have a custom built suite?"

"To lock up women," Brodie said as if this was the most normal thing in the world.

Drawing her eyes from him, Zara chose not to ask any more questions when she wasn't sure she could handle further revelations. "My suggestion makes sense," she said. "I'm not going to tell Grant that we want to know. I can be… discreet. I know about this product and I know that Sutcliffe wants to meet him at midnight tomorrow, right? So I'll just ask leading questions. I'm here, with you, in a safe place, no one can hurt me here."

Brodie didn't seem to be moved by the confidence she had in her powers of manipulation. "The last time you asked

Grant about the device, he threatened you."

Grant's threat had shocked her at the time too. Despite the revelations about her boss' character, she still couldn't envision him actually putting his hands on her in anger. "He would never hurt me. I have worked with him for five years and he's always been kind to me," she said, sliding her hands onto Brodie's sides. "He has a soft spot for me."

Still not swayed, his brows stirred a fraction lower. "It's not his soft spot that concerns me. It's any hard ones he might be packing."

He probably meant guns, but that wasn't what Art heard. "Hard ones or hard ons?" Art asked, wearing a half smile. He folded his arms as his hip hit the counter. She'd wager that the manor's few guests had been male, the "boys club" atmosphere was thick and Art's jeering was probably just typical teasing. "You've seen the way Grant looks at her."

Brodie's lack of patience for his uncle's teasing was very telling. Clenching his jaw, he wouldn't even look at Art when he answered him. "Yes, I have and I told you not to talk about that again."

"You're both crazy, he's my boss," she said, coiling her legs around Brodie's.

"I know you're a small-town girl, Zara, but you're not that naive," Art said. "You were hired at an executive level without previous experience in the company. You flew through the ranks quicker than anyone else has. Grant has given you almost unrestricted access to the systems. It's called grooming."

Forcing herself not to gape, Zara searched their features for a sign they were teasing her because she couldn't believe Art's claim to be true. "He's not grooming me," she said, but Brodie didn't jump to her defense. "He doesn't want to sleep with me."

Though his expression didn't betray much, Brodie seemed to peer deeper into her.

Art almost appeared to feel sorry for her, except he hid it behind a veil of amusement. "I think his admiration for your morals might have turned his attraction to you into something deeper."

"Which is why we're never gonna talk about that again," Brodie said to his uncle with a tone of finality, like a parent putting a full stop at the end of an argument with an insolent child.

Grant was nice to her, sweet sometimes, but he had never been forward. He had never harassed her or made her feel uncomfortable in any way. Staring at Brodie's chest, she tried to remember any time she'd got an inclination that Grant might feel something more than professional toward her. But she couldn't, then again, she hadn't thought him the type to consort with terrorists either. It turned out that she didn't know Grant as well as she thought.

Languishing in her ponderings, Zara almost forgot that she was in company. "I wonder what he'll do when he finds out I've had sex with his brother," she murmured without making a conscious decision to speak.

"He won't be cracking out the champagne, put it that way," Art said, not attempting to hide his laughter. "Take the girl to your room, kid." Art hit his nephew's arm before he sauntered toward the door. "I'll buzz you when Tuck gets in."

Art left the room just as another thought struck Zara, one that made her perk up and make eye contact with her lover. "That wasn't what this was, was it?" she asked, nudging Brodie's chest. "Some kind of one-upmanship? Like a sibling rivalry?"

Now he lost his patience with her though he seemed to check himself before opening his mouth. "You keep trying to find deeper meaning in us having sex," he said. Grabbing her neck, he tipped her head back and brought his nose down to meet hers. "Here it is: you're hot as fucking hell and I'm gonna keep riding you until you tell me to stop. Because fucking you is the only thing I've ever done in my life that doesn't feel amoral."

Coming from him that was high praise, her heart bounced against her ribs in jubilation. She could tell that wasn't something he confessed lightly. "What if I don't tell you to stop?" she asked, tipping her chin to catch his mouth in a quick kiss.

"Then I guess you'll be moving in, baby," he said and

stole his own kiss, which as always didn't end in a hurry.

THIRTEEN

BRODIE LINKED THEIR FINGERS and pulled her off the kitchen counter. Zara reached for her purse when he began to drag her toward the exit, but she didn't manage to snag it because he was moving at quite a pace.

Leading her through passages, he opened a door and ran up two flights of stairs without letting her go. When they got to the top, he opened another grand door and tugged her into a long hallway. Switching their course, he guided her through another door and then swung a left into a narrow corridor with only one door at the end.

Glancing back at their wake, she kept advancing headlong in the direction Brodie towed her in. "I hope there's not a fire," she said, knowing she'd be lucky to find a way out let alone the kitchen.

He stopped at the end of the corridor and pressed the print of his thumb into the center of a regal doorknob, which had the same fingerprint recognition pad on it that she'd seen in other parts of the building.

"If there's a fire, we go out the window," he said, before opening the door and drawing her forward to let her enter first.

The huge wooden framed bed was situated in front of a

recessed double window. There were a couple of doors to the left and a seating area to the right, where there was an entertainment center done in the same finish as the bed.

She was about to turn and compliment him on his dark, masculine decor when the daunting snick of a heavy lock sliding into place made her comfort disperse into dread. When she whirled around, Brodie was within breathing distance, so close to her that the wall of his chest blocked her view.

"I said you were naughty," he said. Scooping a hand under her hair, he twined his fingers in her locks and pulled her head back at an angle so harsh that it made her neck ache. "I was right… You disobeyed me."

"Yeah, and look how great that worked out for you," she said, matching his snarl.

"You made a big mistake coming here." With a wide stance, he kept her legs between his and walked her backwards in the direction of the bed. He offered her no help when she lost her footing, so Zara had to grab on to him to keep herself semi-upright. "Everything in this house belongs to me, and now that includes you," he sneered. "No one will look for you here. Haven't you heard? The world thinks I'm dead and this place abandoned. This is the end of the world for you, baby."

Something as solid and rotund as a log hit the dip of her spine and she exhaled her trepidation when she groped behind her and found she was pressed into the frame at the foot of his bed. There was no way to get away from this man, no way out of the room. She was his prisoner. Instead of being terrified, a quake of excitement tremored through her.

Brodie let go of her hair and began to unbutton her shirt. She clung to the timber at her back and held her breath, not uttering a word when he dragged her shirt out of her skirt and tore open the last two buttons to bare her torso.

She boosted herself up using the bed as a support and encouraged him on by opening her mouth on his jaw to rasp her teeth on his stubble. She wasn't afraid of him. She wanted to provoke him. To unleash the truth of his darkness that he tried so hard to hide. But before her tongue could meet his skin, he grabbed her face and urged her away.

He scowled, aiming his hostility toward her mouth.

"You're my plaything now. My house means my rules."

Shoving her jacket and her shirt down her arms, he twisted her elbows to yank the apparel off and cast it aside. Unsatisfied with what he'd revealed, he ripped the fabric strip connecting her bra cups to expose her breasts.

He bent his knees to collect up her half-naked body and closed his mouth on one breast while perching her on the frame of his bed. Hooking her feet on the plank that supported the mattress, she opened her legs around him to arch herself into his imploring mouth. He sucked and licked one breast and took the other in his palm to fondle it. Then, sucking his mouth free of her bosom for long enough to lick his fingertips, he swirled and circled her nipples between them, alternating his fingers and his mouth, until the cramp in her belly made her hiss.

Massaging her nipples with the pads of his thumbs, he kissed the corner of her mouth. "Oh, she's pretty," he said with perverse pleasure. "Knows just what that hot body can get her."

Her constricted lungs barely allowed words to seep from the threshold of her mouth. "There's only one thing I want," she ground the words out through her gritted teeth.

Zara combed her fingers into his hair as he moved south to kiss her chest again. When he snagged her nipple in his teeth, she coiled her digits tight against his scalp.

Pulling the taut peak in his mouth with him as he retreated, he only released it when it would come no further. "You think you'll find it here?" he asked.

Sliding her hands through his tresses, to his jaw and up to his face, she compelled his head up, away from its task, so that she could look him in the eye. "I already have," she said and wrapped her legs around him.

As her ankles locked, he reached around to grab them and wrench them apart. Using his hold on her limbs, he yanked her forward, forcing her to stand. One of his strong hands drove itself beneath her waistband and sent her skirt fluttering to the floor, before he stepped back to get a better view. Left in only her panties and stockings, she was fired up by being on show for him, and from the reaction in his jeans, she'd say he liked what he saw.

"She's naughty," he muttered as though to himself. "Do you like dressing dirty?" With one arm, he lunged forward to capture her. He yanked her body onto his so tight that she struggled to breathe. But she loved the way he held her, how his strength could overpower her. Despite what he was capable of, he could never use that strength or his lethal skills against her. Having immunity from him was a thrill in itself. "You dress to drive men wild?"

"I dress for me," she said, trying to push away from his embrace simply because she knew she couldn't.

Using his mass, he crushed her against the end of the bed. She was lost in the intensity of his eyes but yelped when he snatched her panties and ripped them away from her fizzing skin before he let his other arm enclose around her.

When he bowed nearer, she tipped her head back to avoid his kiss, because riling him enlivened her. But he opened his mouth and sucked the neck she'd exposed for him.

The bite of power in that kiss made her yelp. "Oh, God, Brodie," she said, throwing a hand up into his hair.

He pulled back wearing a sneering smile that wreaked of pleasure. "That's better."

Grabbing her hips, he picked her up and threw her over the footboard onto the bed where she landed in a bounce. He was already hauling his tee shirt up over his head and she scrambled away, going as far back as to settle herself on his pillows.

Seating himself on the edge of the bed, he bent to unlace his boots and in that brief interlude, a thought struck her. If so few people had been in his house, then Brodie may never have had sex here. The women he slept with overseas probably knew him as Raven and she wondered if he had ever slept with a woman who knew his real name.

When his boots were off, he stood up to unbuckle his belt and watched her as he pulled open the buttons on his jeans. Her eyes flicked up, she registered his scrutiny, and that was when she realized she was chewing on her bottom lip in anticipation of seeing this man naked for the first time.

"What you drooling at, pretty baby, huh?" he asked,

pleased with himself for discovering her impatience.

Without denying her fervor, she changed her position. "This is home turf," she said, crawling on all fours across the bed to reach for his jeans, but he caught her hand before she made contact and pulled it up.

"My rules," he said, lowering himself to kiss her once. Zara lost herself in the sweet zeal of his rapturous tongue trying to mate with hers. "Open those legs for me, baby, real wide."

She did as much as she could in this position high on her knees with her wrist locked in his grip, elevated above her head. While his mouth kissed and nibbled on hers, the heel of his free hand landed on her pubis and he curled his fingers around to rub them up and down the slit in her body, coating her in her own juices.

"Mm," he hummed. "I think no panties should be a new house rule." He pushed one finger into her and began to screw her with the single digit. "I'm gonna take what I want from you, baby... I want that tight fucking pussy dripping before it tastes my cock. You're gonna get damn used to being naked and ready for me. This place is where you'll worship my dick, 'cause you've got a whole lot to learn about the consequences of disobeying me."

Panting, a whine left her throat and she moved her hips in time with his hand. His finger slid all the way out and before she could object, two slid in slow. She gritted her teeth and tried to sink deeper onto him but he pulled her arm taut to drape it around his neck.

"Hold on to me," he murmured, caressing the forearm he'd locked around his neck. He kissed her jaw then her neck and lifted his lips to her ear. "Rub your clit for me, baby." Still hanging around his neck on one arm, she did as she was told with the other, clinging onto him tighter with every new burst of sensation.

As she pressed her fingers to herself and began to stroke, her fingertips made contact with his two digits, which were still fucking her. They made quite a team. Soon, she was tightening her arm and pulling herself closer, higher, using his body as an anchor for hers, which was so near the brink of oblivion that stars began to blur her vision.

"Stop," she panted and pulled at his wrist, trying to get his digits out of her. "Oh, God, Brodie, if you don't stop I'm gonna—" but she didn't have enough oxygen to breathe or speak. Throwing the other arm around his neck, her body bucked into his hand and she called out his name.

The sound had barely left her lips before he crouched and hauled her arms up over his head to free himself of her hold, then she was pushed onto her back and he hooked his solid arms under her thighs. Zara didn't realize he was on his knees at the side of the bed until his tongue plunged into her.

"Brodie!" she yelped, though she wasn't sure if she was objecting to what he was doing or encouraging him to continue.

Her engorged tissues were still trembling, but he licked through her, delving his tongue in deep and pursing her clit between his lips to flicker it with his tongue. Every time they'd been together, he'd showered her with attention. He got some kind of pleasure out of each orgasm he granted her.

The men in her past wanted only what she could give and didn't care to give anything back. But she was beginning to worry that Brodie would think her selfish or ungrateful since she had never returned the favors he blessed her with.

"Wait," she said, but her extremities were shaking.

Her fingers and toes had lost all feeling and every nerve in her body was on a quivering alert, preparing for the next deluge of pleasure he was working her toward with his mouth. Grabbing his hair, she tried to pull him back, but her breathing was growing more uneven with every second.

Pushing a hand onto the bed and using the other to pull his head, she managed to sit up. But when she looked down and saw him there between her thighs, with her legs over his shoulders, the sight was almost enough to finish her off.

"God, that's hot," she whispered.

One of his arms curled around her pelvis and he massaged her tummy with the other. "Lie down," he said. "And we'll see if I can get you to boil over."

"No," she said, stroking his hair and his face. "Come up here, come with me."

Fixating on her stomach, he revealed his strategy. "I plan to come right here," he said, trailing a moist fingertip from her belly button to her cleavage. The shimmer of pleasure it caused made her squeeze her internal muscles, that in turn made her thighs tighten, and his pride grew. "You like that? You want my hot spunk all over your horny body? You want it bad, baby, don't you?" He began to rise higher on his knees. "You want my scent soaking into you?" he kissed her. "Want me to brand every inch of you as mine?"

As he came higher still, she was forced to lay back. He stayed within an inch of her mouth as he rose over to lie on top of her. When he kissed her again, she got the chance to wrap her arms around his head. She couldn't stop touching his hair, his back, his shoulders, his face. Every part of him that her fingers met made her arousal intensify until she was grinding her pelvis up into his.

The metal spike on his loose belt buckle kept spearing the soft flesh on her abdomen as she undulated, but the sting didn't slow her down. Brodie kept on kissing her, rubbing his hands down her sides, over her breasts and eventually under her ass to reposition her on the bed so her head was on the pillows she'd been sitting on before.

Relaxing her legs, she used her hands and feet to shove at his open jeans and when they were out of the way, she curled all her fingers around the impressive girth of his dick and angled her hips to push herself up. Guiding him to her opening, she rolled the apex of his arousal up and down the seam of her body, kissing the head of his dick with her intimate lips, then let it slide up to caress her hypersensitive clit. Drawing back, she took a breath and thrust herself up to take the first inch of him into her.

He tried to retreat, but she kept pushing, determined to take all of him. He grabbed her hips and pinned them down then abandoned her mouth to glare down at her. "You horny little minx," he said and although he was frowning, she smiled.

"I want it," she said, wriggling in his grasp.

"You're a dirty girl"—he reared up to flip her onto her chest—"you think you can ride my cock bareback?" he asked and spanked her. Groaning, her knees dug into the bed, raising her ass higher. "You don't say when, I say when."

Grabbing her thighs, he pushed them up under her until her bent knees touched the underside of her vulnerable breasts. Three of his fingers plunged into her and he worked them back and forth so fast that she had to bite the pillow beneath her face to stop herself from calling out again. After delivering another climax, he smacked her ass and snatched one knee to whip her over onto her back again.

"I'm gonna train you real good," he said, kneeling between her legs and falling over her to brace his weight on his hands on either side of her. "You're gonna need a strong hand."

He rose onto his knees and examined her body, sprawled in front of him as he towered over her. Her legs were parted on either side of him, and he pressed his thumb into her clit making her yelp again and wriggle against the resistance he offered.

"Tell me you belong to me," he said, kneading his thumb into her, never breaking that contact as he spoke. "Tell me!"

Lost in the mist of approaching orgasm, her body was languishing in the chemical overload this night had brought. "I belong to you," she cried out, barely able to see him past the weight of her eyelids.

"This snug, sweet cunt only reacts for my dick now, only mine, right?"

She curled her fingers into the blanket they lay on and whimpered out a confirmation. Struggling to keep her eyes open, she writhed down on his thumb. "My pussy is yours," she managed to say then yelped. "Brodie, please, beau, fuck me."

"Soon," he muttered and pulled his thumb back to push it through her folds into her drenched opening. "Tell me it all belongs to me, your hands, your mouth… your tits, your ass. All of you."

"All of me," she called between ragged breaths. "All of me! I'm yours, Brodie!"

Pulling out his thumb, he put it in his mouth to suck it clean then dropped his weight forward, so he was looming over her again. "Zara," he asked, looking her in the eye. "Do you mean it?"

"Yes," she said, opening her arms and closing them around the back of his neck. "Yes, Brodie, baby, I mean it."

Pulling him down to kiss her, she forgot about the sex and the pound of excitement prickling through her and kissed him until she tasted his soul. She didn't feel his arm move, but when the thick crown of his cock pushed into her, the pressure of him stretching her made her forget to keep kissing him.

But he didn't forget. He kissed her mouth, moved his amorous attention to her neck, then rose to look at her face as he pounded into her. The heat of him was different, the slick motion of his member moved faster and faster in her until she was no longer capable of thought. When she said his name, the shadows in his eyes burned to a thick ebony.

Clawing her nails down his back on the impact of her orgasm, she was still calling for him when he pulled out of her to shower her abdomen in the seed he'd promised to bathe her with. Unleashing a string of profanities, he squeezed himself out over her and she arched to accept his gift.

The air was hot and smelled of sex and sweat, but all she could feel was the warm glow of contentment. He bowed over her and lost his mouth in her damp hair beside her ear. "Next time it goes in your mouth," he said and her smile actually grew.

Expecting that he'd let her sleep now was premature. He scooped her up and carried her into the huge bathroom adjoining the bedroom. It had its own central Jacuzzi bath and double sinks. But he carried her past those, slid aside the textured glass of the shower door, and put her on her feet.

Brodie turned on the water before going to grab towels from a concealed closet in the corner.

"Your house is amazing," she said, leaning against the cool tile and stretching out an arm to test the temperature of the water.

There were two showerheads, one at either end of the cubicle, and jets on the walls, as well as a built-in tiled seat. But he'd just turned on one showerhead, so she guessed they were going to get cozy. She bent to roll off her stockings and threw them out past the open stall door.

"Thanks," he said, hanging the towels over the top of the screen and pulling his jeans off to toss them aside on top of her stockings.

Getting to see him naked in all his glory made her teeth clamber for her lower lip again. He was magnificent, sculpted, and muscular. His body was athletic indicating he did more with it than just lift weights, and his dick was so long and fat that she was enticed to leap forward and grab hold of the appendage as though she had never had the pleasure of experiencing it.

He entered the shower, and slid the door closed, then opened his palm toward her, so she gave him her hand. "Did you mean what you said in there?"

"Which part?" he asked, putting a bar of soap into her hand. Pulling them both under the water, he pressed the soap she was holding to his torso and began to move it in circles.

She got the message that she was supposed to do the washing so she took over. "About us being only for each other?" she asked.

Soaping his body gave her the chance to learn his form. She examined his scars and spent extra time washing his tattoos so she could learn their shapes and designs. All of them were black ink. He had one on the ball of his shoulder, one between his shoulder blades, and another on his chest. She crouched to get a better look at the one he had on his thigh.

"Maybe," he said. "I guess."

That wasn't exactly the resounding confirmation she was looking for, but at least it was a confirmation. The water washed the soap away from his body and she was about to rise from the floor when his hand landed on the top of her head.

Bringing her eyes up, Zara looked for an explanation. It came when he closed a fist around his now erect dick and guided it to her mouth. Nudging his head against her lips, she opened and let him push himself into her mouth.

Closing her lips around her teeth, Zara sucked on him as he controlled the pace. "Damn," he hissed, moving faster. "I just found my new hobby."

Sliding his hand down to the back of her head, he pushed her onto him and he worked himself deeper. His curse came half a beat before he exploded in her mouth and the thick milk spread on her tongue. He withdrew but balled his hand on her wet hair to pull her head back.

"Show me it's gone," he said and she opened her mouth wide to prove that she'd already swallowed him down. "Wash up and then come to bed." He patted her head and rinsed himself then left her alone on her knees under the shower spray.

So he wasn't in the mood to put words to what was going on between them. He'd shut down her questioning fast enough to make that clear. Zara rose and let the heat of the water steam her sinuses as she washed her hair.

FOURTEEN

WHEN SHE CAME OUT of the bathroom wrapped in one of Brodie's towels, Zara could just make out the outline of Brodie's form in the middle of the bed in the darkened room with the aid of the bathroom light behind her. The covers were draped over his pelvis and he had a forearm lying across his eyes. She was pained to turn off the bathroom light because that would mean giving up her view of his ripped form.

Being here at his home granted her the privilege of seeing him relaxed and exposed. Scars marred some of his body and they added to her questions about his past. She'd seen him fight, Art had told her of his ability with weapons, but all those skills hadn't saved him from every blow.

"Lose the towel," he grumbled and his heavy voice startled her.

It didn't matter that he hadn't taken his arm away from his eyes, somehow, he'd known she was there.

Casting the cloth from her body, she crept toward the bed and tried to figure out where he wanted her. His legs were parted and one arm lay far from his body. The bed was large, but so was he, and he managed to take up most of it, leaving no obvious space for her.

"Are you gonna stand there all night?" he asked.

No, she wasn't, so she sat on the edge and ran her hands through her jet hair before moving close enough to rest her head on him. He flinched at the contact and his arm darted off his face before he lifted his head to scowl at her.

"My hair is wet," she said, assuming the chill in her locks had startled him. Brodie closed his eyes and covered them again, so she settled to lie against him. His breath began to slow and he lowered his arm from his eyes to rest it around her. "Do you have a preferred side of the bed?"

"The middle is my preferred side, get used to it."

Smiling, she turned her face into his hard chest. Bringing her knees up, Zara slipped her feet beneath the covers and ran her dainty toes up and down his bare shins. To most, it would be odd how fascinated she was with a guy's legs, but his nakedness proved how comfortable he was. He stayed half-clothed when he was in places he didn't consider secure, having him naked now was an honor.

"Are you still mad that Art let me in?" she asked.

"We don't let strangers in," Brodie said.

"I'm not a stranger," she said, splaying her hand on his diaphragm to stroke the width of him. "I like Art, he's very proud of you."

"He wasn't exactly nurturing, but he gave me what I needed," Brodie said, tightening his arm to lock her against him. "He's a good guy."

A good guy, Brodie meant it, but there was a lack of sincerity when he said it. He could be talking about any guy off the street. She wondered if he played down his connection to Art because he was used to not letting others see his affection for the man, or if Art had just raised him to believe that feelings were vulnerabilities that could be exploited.

"I was nervous coming here," she said. "I didn't mean to intrude on your personal space, but when that guy sat down with me in Purdy's... I couldn't ignore the threat he made. I took the risk and did what I had to... would you have done it any different?"

"It's not the same thing," he said and his arm slid back up to cover his eyes.

Sitting up, she held her weight on one straight arm beside his body. "Why is it not the same thing?" she asked and rested a hand on the arm he used to cover his face, urging him to bring it down to look at her.

Close to slumber, he didn't look impressed that she was asking him to explain himself. "Because if a guy threatened you, I'd slit his throat, and you would never know it happened."

Closing her open mouth, she swallowed and could only stare down at him. Brodie might not wax lyrical about having feelings for her, but his possessiveness empowered her and betrayed that he wasn't as detached as he tried to portray. While she'd never considered herself the type to advocate violence, she had never faced such life and death situations before, now she understood its necessity.

Moving her hand to his abs, she stroked it up over his chest to his throat and then down to the comforting rhythm of his heart. "I'm glad I figured out who you are," she said. "When you first showed up in my room, I was… scared and confused, but…"

"What are you now?" he asked, laying his arm on the bed, curving it around her ass beneath the arm she still supported her weight on.

A smile began to grow. "Still scared and confused," she said, exhaling a laugh before she made eye contact. "But not about you. You've become the one thing in my life that I can rely on."

Tracing the edge of his thumb in an arc over the top of her ass, he managed to stoke her desire and appeal to her heart at the same time. "I'm not a reliable guy. When I get pissed off people tend to get dead and I can't tell you what will set me off or when. Sometimes I just wake up in a bad mood."

"And you go looking for a fight?" she asked, concerned for his safety, which was ridiculous because Brodie didn't need anyone to worry about him. "What pisses you off?"

"It pisses me off you're with Grant every day," he said. "It pisses me off that I can't keep my eyes on you twenty-four, seven. I promised to keep you safe and I plan to keep doing that. So you can scratch scared from your list, baby. I've got you covered."

It wasn't a declaration of commitment, but it gave her an opening. "And how long will that be for?" she asked.

One lazy blink followed another. "You're asking if this is going anywhere?" he asked, cutting through the bullshit. "Don't do that. Planning the future is a dumb waste of time."

Dealing with death and disaster all his adult life had made him cynical. "Sometimes you have to plan, so that you know what to avoid," she said. "When I was growing up, my dad wanted me to run the house, my friends were getting knocked up and married. I was never supposed to make it out of that town and if I hadn't been so damned set on getting out of there, I never would have."

Letting his eyes close, she could tell that he was tired. "You're strong, baby," he mumbled and pulled her down onto his body. "You go after what you want."

She had to make decisions on what she wanted and go after it, because she'd learned young that no one would hand over her dream life to her. Except she'd given up hope of ever being part of anything profound that could change the world, until Brodie strolled into her life and showed her that the chance was still out there.

"And you destroy what gets in the way of what you want," she said, reminding him of what he'd said to her.

Tired, with his guard down, and the intimacy of the moment at its height, he sighed. "When my parents died, I locked myself in this house for months. Art was my only contact with the outside world, he kept me alive."

Pained by what he'd endured, her empathy seeped to her words. "You were still a child, you'd just lost your mother and father," she said, understanding why his reaction had been so strong.

After losing her mother, she'd been lost too. But her father hadn't seen anyone's grief except his own, so Zara hadn't been allowed to shut herself off.

"Art didn't put pressure on me to do anything or be anyone. For the first time, I got to be myself. When he was tired of being stuck here, he walked into my bedroom and told me to pack."

Surprised, she guessed that's when his international adventures began. "Pack? Where did you go?"

"We went to India. I got my first tattoo there and being part of something so different to everything I'd known was invigorating. I forgot everything I'd left behind. Living a life without the expectation of my parents changed me. I promised I would never tie myself down again, that I would always be free."

Making such a decision at thirteen was extreme, but he hadn't reneged on it. Art's nomadic lifestyle had become Brodie's and was probably why Brodie had never thought to finish his education or get a traditional job. He had responsibilities now, sure. But he was still as free as the bird he took his alias from.

"You're lucky to have had experiences like that," she said. "I always wanted to travel, but I've never made it out of the States."

"You're bogged down by responsibility," he said, moving his hands to squeeze and stroke her ass. "For some reason you're addicted to working for my brother."

"I'm not addicted," she said, climbing up to lie on top of him, parting her legs over his hips. "I'm easily replaced and I don't want to lose my job."

"You think you'd lose your job 'cause you took a vacation?" he asked and his head tipped back as his eyes became curious. "When was the last time you spoke to your dad?"

Talking about her family always made her uncomfortable. "A while ago," she said, opening her hands on his chest. "He doesn't need me anymore. I let him down by leaving town."

"That why you're scared Grant will replace you?"

She pounced onto the defensive. "I'm not scared," she said, trying her best not to get angry with him for pushing her buttons. "Why don't you tell me what happened between you and your brother?"

"That's ancient history," he said, rolling onto his side

to push her body off his. "Get some sleep."

Grateful that he'd opened up to her at all, she nestled close into him and he swept an arm around her to hold her near. Zara quite liked that his central position forced him to hold on to her. When she ran her feet up his shins again, he lifted a leg over hers to pin her feet against the mattress.

"You keep doing that, you won't get any sleep," he mumbled before he yawned.

It had been a long night, he'd been working, and was tired. He was also just like every other man and would probably do whatever it took to avoid having "the conversation." Still, there was no rush. She'd made headway by just being accepted into his home. For now, incremental progress would have to be enough.

***

SLEEPING WITH BRODIE was easy and waking up with his fingers playing inside her as his mouth sampled her neck was nicer. That happened twice through the night and she had ideas of waking him up in her own special way when morning came.

Except when it did and she woke up, she was alone. Brodie wasn't in the bedroom, the bathroom or what she discovered was a walk-in closet. Taking a few minutes to examine his clothes, she learned he didn't venture far from tee shirts, jeans, and hoodies though he had a few leather jackets as well.

One of the units in the closet was locked and required fingerprint authorization. She wondered if he had a Rolex collection or something similar that he wanted to protect. Most of the closet was empty, but if he was used to globetrotting, he probably got used to traveling light.

Being this close to his private possessions made her feel closer to the reality of who Brodie was. Glimpsing his underwear, his toothbrush, his shampoo, it was all so normal and yet he didn't let anyone else this deep into his inner sanctum, so being able to touch these personal products made her feel special, valued, and grateful for his trust.

She showered and did her best with what she found in the bathroom to make herself presentable for the day. There was no way for her to dry her hair, but it was the weekend. She didn't have to worry about work, so she could let her hair go a little crazy. It seemed the rest of her had. But she liked the new adventurous side of herself that Brodie brought out and she looked forward to pushing those boundaries even further.

Her stockings were gone. Her panties and bra were torn, so all she could put on was her skirt, shirt, and jacket. Examining her rumpled appearance in the bathroom mirror, she removed her jacket because it looked ridiculous to be so buttoned up when her clothes were crumpled and her hair was drying in its natural wave. But when she took it off, she was mortified to see the outline of her nipples through the sheer material of her shirt, so she put the jacket on again.

Having delayed the inevitable for long enough, she ventured into the hallway, and tried to remember which way to go. The bedroom door closed behind her and the click of the lock made her jump. The blue fingerprint pad secreted in the knob flashed, indicating that she was locked out, so she couldn't go back inside even if she wanted to.

The first turn was easy because there were no other doors in this narrow section. She went to the end and turned right. But when she got into the next section, she wasn't sure of what to do next. She tried a couple of doors and found a couple of different rooms, but no stairwell.

Trying further down the corridor yielded no results. When she began to panic about how long she'd spend getting lost before someone came across her, a door behind her opened and Art hung into the space wearing a smile.

"This way, girlie," he said, holding the door open for her.

Grateful for his help, she went through the door and started down the stairs. "How did you know I was lost?" she asked over her shoulder. "I thought I was going to be wandering the house for hours."

"Brodie turned on the motion sensors when he came downstairs," Art said.

This statement made her pause, but Art passed her and continued to descend. Shocked that anyone had such high-tech security in their home, Zara speculated about the number of enemies these men had. "You have motion sensors?"

"Infrared too," Art said, looking over his shoulder at her. "But he wouldn't let us turn that on."

"Us?" she asked.

Art had picked up speed on his descent, so she hurried after him, determined not to get lost again. Instead of going down just two flights, they went down four and she was about to question their destination when he pressed his thumb to the door in front of them and opened it to reveal a long black corridor, which ran in both directions.

"You can't go wrong down here," Art said, holding the door open for her.

Strips of electric blue light in the upper coving lit a series of black doors, which flanked this black space.

Once she absorbed the striking lack of features, she looked to Art. "What's down here?"

"All of Brodie's favorite rooms in the house. Though I guess if you stay over often enough that might change."

He let the stairwell door close and put an arm around her shoulders to guide her down the corridor. "We have gyms and work out spaces. Shooting range, combat training, everything he needs. And of course," Art said and stopped in front of a door that looked just like all the others to her. "Main security."

He touched the panel by the door with his thumb and the door whooshed open. Inside was a large conference table with half a dozen chairs around it and a control desk that had at least forty different monitors in a bank in front of it.

"Wow," she exhaled, amazed by all the blinking lights and the pictures on the screens showing various areas of the house as well as external images, from the grounds, and further afield. Periodically, the picture on each screen changed and she wondered just how many areas of the world they were capable of monitoring.

"Coffee?" he asked.

Art was already retrieving the coffee jug from the machine set up on a table near the door. She only half-nodded because she was still watching the pictures flashing on the screens. Approaching the control desk, she saw lots of buttons and lights as well as three built-in keyboards and she wondered what it all did. Looking back up at the color screens, she watched traffic building up on the main road perpendicular to CI, the picture changed and she saw the CI main entrance.

"You're watching my work?" she asked, taking the coffee mug from Art when he came to her side.

"We watch everywhere," he said. "We're a small group, so technology helps us out a lot."

"How do you afford all of this?"

"Inheritance and murderer for hire pays damn good."

Another screen changed and the flicker caught her eye. When she recognized the picture, she stepped toward it and the shock of what she saw made her almost drop her coffee. "That's my apartment."

"Yep," Art said. "The one in your bedroom goes straight to Brodie's phone." She whipped around ready to protest, but he laughed and held up a hand. "I'm kidding."

"I thought he wasn't watching anymore," she murmured, turning back to the picture of her apartment. It was taken from outside the front of the building. The camera had to be set on the building opposite hers. But with her vast amount of windows, she could see right into the full panorama of her own living room.

Art leaned in to whisper in her ear. "I think it's unlikely that boy will ever take his eyes off you."

The sound of the door made her whirl around in time to see Brodie coming in with another man. Both of them were shirtless, glistening with sweat, and panting. From the way their hands were taped, she guessed that they'd been fighting, but she saw no bruises or blood, so she hoped it was all in the name of training.

"If you could make that shot, I'd be out of business," Brodie said over his shoulder to the man behind him who was unwinding the tape from his hands.

"I could make it," the man said and that was when

they noticed her.

"Hey," Brodie said and jabbed a thumb behind him. "That's Tuck."

"It's a pleasure," Tuck said.

She apparently needed no introduction because no one offered Tuck her name. While Tuck finished unwrapping his hands, she examined him. His form was ripped, implying that he had to train as much as Brodie did. That they had to keep themselves in such good shape was a testament to their occupation. Tuck's hair was lighter than Brodie's, and it had flecks of much lighter blond through it.

She felt like she should say something. "How is Kadie?" she asked. Brodie and Art looked at her, and she remembered what they'd said about asking him questions.

Tuck didn't seem to be perturbed by the question. "Infinitely understanding," Tuck said, rolling the wraps up and closing his hands around them. "That's how I can be sure she's not screwing around on me. She never knows when I'll show up or when I'll slip out again."

Art barked a laugh. "I dread to think what you'd do if you got there and found another dude in your place."

Tuck slapped a hand on Brodie's back as he passed him. "That's what I've got my buddy here for." Tuck went to the control desk and turned the swivel chair around so he could drop into it.

"You say the word and I'll take the fucker out," Brodie said, going over to prop himself on the control desk next to where Tuck was sitting.

"What have you got for me, pet?" Tuck muttered, stroking his hands up either side of the keyboard before he cracked his knuckles and began to type.

Zara's eyes widened when she saw how fast his fingers moved. The lines of letters, numbers, and symbols that scrolled on the basic screen built into the unit just in front of his keys meant nothing to her. Watching him work was making her seasick, so she went back to looking at the pictures on the bank of monitors.

"Where are all of these places?" she asked, waving a hand in the general direction of every feed.

"All over," Brodie said, twisting to look at the screens she was watching. "Tuck can tap into any existing camera, and over the years, we've planted plenty of our own."

A picture flashed up on a screen to the left. She recognized the pointed arch windows, the floor, and the stone staircase as the ones she'd seen upstairs. But the carpet on the stairs was different to the one she had seen in this house. Going around the control desk, she got closer to the screen to examine it in more detail. An older woman came into view and she waved a pointed finger at her.

Glancing back at Art, she sought confirmation. "Is this the other house?"

"Yep," Art said with a head bob.

"You told her about that?" Brodie muttered with displeasure.

Art shrugged. "Everyone knows the house exists. I mean the plans are out there for anyone who looks," Art said. "It's not a secret."

"Who is she?" Zara asked, peering closer at the woman ascending the stairs.

"Tuck," Brodie muttered and Tuck pushed along to a different keyboard. He typed something then gave Brodie the nod.

"Hey, Bess," Brodie called and the older woman on the stairs jumped and spun around. "Say hi to the camera."

"Oh, Brodie," she scolded, raising a hand to her chest. "You are going to give me a heart attack!"

"Wouldn't do that, not while the doctor isn't home," Brodie said, leaning back and turning his smile down. "Just checking in. Any trouble?"

"What trouble would I have on an island inhabited by myself alone?" she called out into the air, so Zara assumed she couldn't see in here.

"Told Thad I'd check in," Brodie said. "Call if you need anything."

"Zave will be back with the Liberated tomorrow. You don't have to worry about me… that boy and his gadgets," she muttered and carried on up the stairs and out of camera range.

With half a smile, Tuck reached over and tapped the keyboard beside her then went back to his. "I've got two possible targets," Tuck said. "But I wouldn't bet my nanite processor on either of them."

Brodie nodded and when Tuck turned his chair toward Brodie, Art crossed to stand between the two men. She didn't know what a nanite was, but the others seemed to understand what he meant.

Brodie spoke first. "Give me the addresses and—"

"You have other business to take care of today," Tuck said and got up. "I'm going to shower, then Art and I will check them out." He headed for the door with Art following him. "Keep your powder dry, buddy!"

Tuck and Art disappeared and when the door closed behind them, she rounded the control desk. Brodie didn't move or acknowledge her for a good thirty seconds.

He pounced to his feet. "Ready to roll?" he asked.

"Ready to…" But he was already on route to the door, so she went with him.

"I'll get changed and take you home. Grab your stuff and I'll meet you in the garage." He paused and seemed to reconsider this. "I'll shower in the gym. You can wait for me in there." That was a preferable option, as she would probably get lost again if she went off on her own.

The next set of doors he took her through led to a fully equipped gym. He sat her on a bench and disappeared through a swing door, which she guessed was where the showers were because six minutes later, he came out washed and ready to leave.

She'd tried not to think about how detached he was acting toward her because she'd assumed he was maintaining his masculine façade in front of his uncle and colleague. But as he took her through the house to retrieve her shoes and purse, his familiarity didn't increase and his possible reasons for being so impersonal were beginning to concern her.

When they had her things he took her to the garage, where she noticed a vast number of vehicles, at least six bikes and four cars, though there was space for more. He retrieved two helmets from a metal cabinet, one of which he handed her before he went to maneuver a motorcycle out of its space.

"I can't get on that," she said.

"Why not?" he asked, glancing down at the bike then back at her. "You've been on it before."

His confidence never wavered. She wasn't sure how understanding he would be about her reluctance. Climbing on a bike when she was such a mess and only half-dressed didn't sound like a good idea to her.

"Yeah, but…"

He stashed her purse in a secret panel then got on and started the engine. "What's the problem?" he asked but gunned the motor. When he winked, she had to concede a smile. "You can handle this much testosterone between your thighs… I've seen it."

"It's not the testosterone I'm worried about," she said, coming closer and raising her voice when he revved the bike again. "I'm not even wearing underwear." Opening her jacket, she showed him the proof and he took his time checking her out.

He turned off the bike and leaned back, though he didn't get off it. "I can't take a car out of the main gate in daylight," he said with a half shake of his head, which might have been apologetic, yet wasn't quite. "I can't do it, baby." All this secrecy was new to her, but she understood why he couldn't take that risk. "Cab fare?"

Well if it was that or nothing, she would have to live with it. "Okay," she mumbled and moved nearer. "You be careful tonight… Can I have my purse back?"

Opening her hands toward him, she waited for him to comply.

He scowled. "I'm not gonna let you just walk out of here," he said, alighting the bike while pulling his wallet from his pocket.

She pushed it away. "And I am not going to let you pay me for my services," she said. "I have money for a cab."

"Fuck," he mumbled, and shoved his helmet onto the bars of the bike. Going over to the cabinet again, he selected a set of keys from the several on offer and came back toward her, pointing the key at her as he spoke. "If, by some miracle, we get away with this. Do not tell Art."

"Away with what?" she asked and the lights of a shiny, gray Audi flashed when he pressed a button on the fob. "Wait."

The first time she'd been on his bike, she hadn't had the time to think about the merits of risking the ride. Throwing caution to the wind again, she pulled on her helmet, and hiked up her skirt to climb onto the bike. It almost tipped, but he lunged forward and caught it.

"Nothing sexier than a woman on a bike," he said, dropping the car keys into his pocket. "You're badass, baby."

He shirked his jacket and wrapped it around her. It was huge, but it would serve to keep her warm. After he hopped on and put on his own helmet, he pulled her arms around him and she resolved to keep herself close.

When he revved the bike and blasted forward, she whooped and clung even tighter than she had before. He probably wouldn't be able to breathe, but he didn't complain. The grounds were as much of a mess as she'd imagine last night.

There was no clear path out, he swooped the bike one-way and the other. Zara would bet that he was testing her, but as she got more used to the motion, she relaxed. Brodie was proficient. He wouldn't put her in a position where she could get hurt.

On reaching the boundary, they didn't go out the main gate. They went through a narrow opening between the wall and the natural cliff face that rose at this point of the landscape. Further down this alley was a gate that was only a few feet wide and it was already closing before they were all the way through it.

She wasn't sure how they activated the gate, but with their tech, they probably had a built in button somewhere. The wall carried on along the cliff for a few feet, then Brodie zoomed across the top of the slope that led to the beach and then they were on public roads. No one else was around and because there wasn't much around here, there never would be. They had their secret entrance and now she understood what he meant about not bringing a car out of the main gate.

They pulled up behind her apartment, between the dumpsters where he'd parked before. Brodie turned off the bike and dismounted. Her legs were wobbling after he lifted her off the bike, probably because of the vibration and the adrenaline. Pulling off her helmet, he curled a hand around the back of her neck to steady her and retrieved her purse before he guided her upstairs.

She unlocked her apartment and went inside, but he didn't come in behind her, causing her to stop and look around for what the problem was, only she couldn't see one.

"This is all gonna be over soon," he said, loitering on her threshold. "Once Grant finds out about Quebec, I'd guess he'll cancel your date."

"It's not a date," she said, putting her purse and helmet on the dining table. "Are you going to come in?"

He spread his hands to opposite sides of the doorframe. "Work to do, baby."

"If you weren't planning on coming in, why did you bring me home?"

"It's what's done, right?" he said. "Didn't other guys bring you home after...?"

Trying not to let him see her eye roll, she dumped her house keys next to her purse and went back to him. "Do you see any of those guys around here?" she asked and his narrowed eyes darted to the side as he tried to figure out what she meant. "If I wanted to be with a guy who acted in a traditional way, do you think I would've let you kiss me in the first place?"

Leaning further into her apartment, he took a breath and she pinched his tee shirt between her thumb and forefinger. "I don't want you to be anything that you're not, Brodie. I know there will be times when you'll have to be in other places doing other things. I'm not going to throw a tantrum if I have to get a cab once in a while."

Squinting at her, he didn't sound pleased. "That sounds like the future talking."

Moving closer still, she liked that he was hanging into her apartment in the way he was, because it gave her the opportunity to talk within a few millimeters of his lips. Letting their breath merge, she kept her voice to a whisper, though her smile probably wasn't coy.

"Isn't that what we're doing?" she asked, dipping her body closer, letting her head tilt one way while his went the other. It was as though they were kissing without erasing that last tiny space between their lips.

"You're something special, Zara Bandini," he said, mirroring her murmuring tone.

Feigning coyness that she knew he would identify as a tease, she flirted with him. "I'm your something special, Brodie." Raising her brows, she asked for confirmation. "Aren't I?"

The genuine sorrow on his face made her breath stick in her throat. "I wish you could be, baby, I really do." He tried to lean in to kiss her, but she backed off and erased their intimate flirtation.

"What are you saying?" she asked, fearing his implication.

His pity faded to let his mask of indifference rise, making it clear he didn't want to be having this conversation. "Last night, I think I got… caught up in, you know… you were in my house, that's never happened before and… it was nice, to live the dream for a night."

"Live the dream?" she asked almost unable to believe what he was saying.

"Come on," he said, releasing a hand from the doorframe to reach for her wrist, but she curved it out of his reach. "I can blow through here when I'm in town if you need a ride. And if there's ever a boyfriend giving you shit… I'll take care of him for you."

Her brows rose. "If I…" Folding her arms, she told herself to calm down before she spoke, but it wasn't easy. "I should slap you in the face, you know that?"

He opened his arms. "For a guy like me that's practically a marriage proposal," he said, but she wasn't taking humor as his honest response.

"Tuck manages to maintain a normal relationship," she said.

His head bobbed in concession. "If normal is seeing

her three times a year, then yeah, I guess he does. Recently, he's different about it… He knows he has to end it soon. He's strung that girl along for like… I don't know, five years or something."

"Why does he have to end it?"

He stepped just over the threshold and bent his knees to come to her height. "Because guys like us don't have normal."

"Did you ever stop to ask whether or not I wanted normal?" she asked him. "Huh?"

This made him falter and he straightened up. "Well, what do you want?"

"I want you," she said without wavering. This time yesterday, she might not have been quite so definitive in her answer. But spending the night with him had concreted her feelings and they ran far deeper than the physical.

"Baby, I'm not for sale." He was trying to build his walls, trying to be the untouchable outlaw, but he couldn't quite disguise his regret.

"Damn right you're not," she said. Grabbing his tee shirt, she twisted it in her fist, and he let her pull him forward so she could close the door of her apartment. Her confidence in the face of his letdown intrigued him enough that he let her say more. "You, Brodie McCormack"—she pushed up onto her tiptoes to bring her face as close to his as she could—"belong to me now."

The curl of his lips was trying to contain a laugh, but she could tell he was sort of impressed by her assertiveness too. Few people would get away with taking control of any situation he was a player in. He could snap her neck in a heartbeat and she would have no way to fight him off if he chose to turn on her. To him, she was an amusing amnesty from the intensity of his life, that she thought she could coerce him into anything against his will was laughable, and she knew that.

But she was sure of her desire to explore him and their relationship further. Zara had to prove her dedication by fighting for her place at his side. Not content that she'd made the ferocity of her certainty clear, Zara let her hand trail down to his belt buckle. Seizing it in her fist, she spun around and made for her bedroom, dragging him along behind her. That he came along with her at all was proof that he wasn't done with her yet.

FIFTEEN

"I DIDN'T HAVE TIME for that," Brodie said a while later.

They were on her bed, both lying on their chests, but he was about halfway down the mattress so his face was in line with her ass. His fingertip trailed up and down the arch of the globe and then across to the other one before he gave her a hard smack.

"I couldn't let you walk away. If I did, I'd probably never see you again," she said, enjoying the tingle his hit had caused. Turning her face in the pillow, she looked down at him, and whispered the truth. "I'm not ready to lose you."

Taking his focus from her ass, he contorted to look up at her while maintaining his lying position. "You don't understand what my world is and you can't compare me to Tuck. He doesn't have mortal enemies… I do."

"You're worried about Caine?" she asked. Lifting her head onto her hand, she balled the pillow inside the crook of her elbow. "You wanted to dump me because you think some guy might try to hurt me?"

"I don't do well with being out of control," he said, returning his focus to her ass.

She cast her eyes to the ceiling and almost laughed. "I never would've guessed." Parting her legs to run her toe up his leg, she was disappointed by the denim barrier between their fleshes. "What would we have to do to make this place secure enough that you could relax?"

"I can relax here," he said, giving one of her ass cheeks a squeeze.

"Relax enough to get naked, I mean."

"Ah," he said with a smile in his voice. "That won't happen, baby."

His hot breath cascaded over her flesh making her hypersensitive. But he slid up the bed and pushed her onto her back to kiss her. "You have to leave?" she asked and he nodded on his way to kiss her again. "You'll be careful?" He nodded again and seemed unable to take his eyes from her mouth. "Brodie…" Maybe it was the quiver in her voice, but his gaze flicked up to hers. "Will you come over? Tonight? When you're done?"

"I don't know when I'll be back," he said, drawing a circle around her nipple with his fingertip.

Trying not to seem desperate, she did want to convey how determined she was that he should visit her. "It doesn't matter," she said. "I know that you can get in here, you've done it plenty of times before… There's a spare key in the kitchen drawer. Whatever time it is—"

"You're not worried about Grant?"

Preoccupied by her stroking fingertips that enjoyed the plains of his chest, she inhaled. "You're right that he'll probably cancel when everything goes wrong for him tonight."

"Okay," he said. "If I get back in time and there are no hitches… I'll come over."

Stretching her arms around him, she crossed them and jabbed her nails into his shoulders. "And wake me up?"

"How would you like me to do that?" he asked and she was amazed at the power his vague smile had on her.

"Surprise me," she whispered and he exhaled a laugh into her mouth before kissing her once more.

The phone beside her bed began to ring and as much as she wanted to ignore it, Zara knew that Brodie had to leave anyway. With a final kiss, he sat up, picked up the receiver, and handed it over to her.

"Hello?" she asked, watching Brodie stretch his back when he rose from her bed.

The sinew of his muscles begged to be touched and she pulled up her knees when moisture began to gather between her thighs. One of her hands fell to her center. Brodie turned around and he registered her positioning after a double take.

His intrigued expression was punctuated by a head tilt and he moved to the end of the bed to pick up his tee shirt from the floor, while keeping his eyes pinned to her hand.

Yanking his tee shirt over his head, he put the backs of his hands together and gestured for her to open her legs further. She arched into her laugh and it was then she heard something on the other end of the phone.

"Hello? Zara?" When she recognized the harassed tone, she sat up, and crossed her legs, zooming all focus onto the phone line and away from Brodie's stimulating form.

"Grant?" she asked and Brodie stopped buckling his belt. "Are you okay?"

"There's been an accident," Grant said. "At the Quebec plant where my men were working to perfect the product."

"What kind of accident?" she asked and gestured for Brodie to come over. When he sat on the bed, she hung over his shoulder and tipped the phone so they could both hear.

"There was an explosion. Our men are dead."

"Oh my God, that's awful," she said, making sideways eye contact with Brodie. "How did it happen? What does this mean?"

The agitation in his voice made her feel sorry for the man she was supposed to be wary of. "That there could be a delay in delivery and that might upset our buyer... I was going to go into the Sutcliffe meeting alone. But I... I might need your support. Would you be able to meet me at the hotel, upstairs, before the event? I need to tell you some things."

So she wasn't going to be an innocent bystander, he wanted her face to face with the terrorists. Despite what Brodie and Art had told her about these men following her, somehow knowing they would get a close look at her face made her uneasy, but she couldn't think of an excuse that would get her out of going to the event. "Sure," she said. Brodie pulled away enough to turn and shake his head. She looked away, but his fingertips touched her cheekbone and he forced her to look at him.

"At the Grand, same time, ten o'clock."

"Sure," she said. "I'll meet you there."

"Thank you," Grant said. "I don't know what I would do without you."

"Of course."

Grant hung up and she pressed the red button on her phone then leaned over to hang it up. "Are you fucking insane?" Brodie demanded before her hand had even left the handset.

She turned back to him. "I panicked," she exclaimed. "He's my boss, I've always followed his orders. He'd have been more suspicious if I refused. It's a public place, what can happen?"

His anger was visceral, one of his hands went to the back of his head. "It's a public building, not a public place. There are conference rooms and bedrooms. Plenty of places inside where he can get you alone with terrorists. Terrorists, Zara, do you understand that?"

Considering his distress, she brought her legs around so she could sit on the edge of the bed to examine his stance. "On the bright side, you don't have to kill anyone tonight."

"Don't bet your pretty ass on that yet, baby," he said. Coming forward, he sat on the bed beside her. "Can you call the Grand for me and find out what Grant has booked? Find out if it's a bedroom or a conference room? What time is it now?"

"Almost four," she said, peeking at the bedside clock.

"Okay." He ran his hand up and down through his hair at the back of his head. "Six hours. That's enough time to scout the location… I don't like that we don't have the routine down, but Tuck can spot me. I'll grab Maverick and—"

"Maverick?" she asked, noting that wasn't a bird alias like the rest of them.

Concentrating on developing his plan, he muttered his response. "My rifle."

He'd named his gun. Her eyes drifted south as she speculated on what else he might have named. "I don't understand. What's your plan?"

"You're gonna find out where that room is and if it's not at the front of the building, you need to change the reservation, okay? You're his assistant. You can come up with a reason why you'd need to do that, right?"

"Sure," she said, taking his wrist to pull his hand down from his hair. "But I don't..." Clarity hardened her own expression. "You're going to... you're going to shoot them."

"I'm gonna do whatever it takes to keep you safe," he said, touching both her cheekbones and sweeping his hands downward to cup her head. "You trust me, don't you?"

Her furious nod didn't hesitate. "Of course I do," she said.

"All you have to do is stay out of my line of sight. That's all you have to worry about," he said. "I can do all the rest if you just ensure I've got a clear shot. Make sure you've got a drink before they arrive, and if something happens while they're in there that makes you uncomfortable—drop the glass."

"Then what happens?" she asked.

"I'll clear the room."

Twisting closer, she brought her other hand to his wrist. "You would kill everyone in the room without further explanation because I drop a glass?"

He was a weapon at her disposal. Empowered and awe struck, her anxiety lessened. With the Kindred watching her back, she had nothing to fear.

"Dropping the glass gives you the excuse to hit the deck," he said. "Trust has to work both ways. You'll be on the inside and it will be the responsibility of the rest of us to keep you safe. We don't stop to ask why when we get a signal from a partner."

"What about Grant?" she asked. "How can you make sure he—"

"The only person whose safety I will guarantee is yours," he said. "Any other collateral damage is acceptable."

"Brodie," she exhaled and searched his eyes for a few

seconds.

Nothing in her experience with other men was comparable to how sexy this man's determined gaze was and it was fixated on her. Sliding her hands onto his shoulders, Zara climbed over to straddle his lap and seized his mouth with hers again. Now that he wasn't going to Canada to take down the lab, he had some free time and she intended to take full advantage of this opening in his calendar.

***

"I DON'T LIKE THIS," Brodie said through the earpiece Tuck had given her to wear before she left her apartment. It was so tiny that she worried it would be stuck in her ear canal for good. But he had assured her that it wouldn't. With her hair down to conceal it from anyone who got too close, she was confident it would remain discreet.

"No shit, Sherlock," Art's voice came through too.

Zara kept walking along the sidewalk toward the Grand Hotel. It was dark and those who were in town at this time were dressed up for dates and functions. Given her mission, the gold, scoop neck, silk dress she wore was activity appropriate, but it didn't match her mood. Seeing so much sparkle was unsettling when she knew there were criminals loitering around who might be tempted by the jewels.

She herself was wearing a sparkling necklace, provided by Tuck, with a tiny camera secreted somewhere behind the diamonds, but a mugger wouldn't know that it was a spy gadget. If they decided they wanted the piece, they could take it from her and would probably beat her to a pulp in the process.

She tried her best not to move her lips and kept her volume low. "I hope I don't get mugged," she said, touching the necklace.

"It would be the worst night of his life if a mugger touched you," Tuck said. All three voices could come down the one line into her ear. "Rave's got you in his sight."

Horrified by the prospect of an accident, she reminded herself not to gasp. "You better not be pointing your gun at me," she said, smiling at a couple who passed her and may have heard her talking to herself.

"My gun is always pointing at you, baby," his voice rumbled through her ear to the back of her neck and she suppressed a shiver.

Clearing her throat and her smile, she held the chain strap of her purse and went through the Grand's revolving door and into the lobby. The marble floors gave way to a sumptuous carpet that led to the elevators. She called one and wondered if she'd lose her connection with the guys when she went inside the shaft.

The elevator came, so she stepped in and selected the fourth floor where Grant was set up in a business suite. The doors closed and she was thankful for the minute she had to herself before facing possible death.

"You should've called up," Brodie said and she got her answer about whether or not she would lose them. "Going straight up surprises him. That might make him nervous... he might have come down to the lobby and public is better."

"You're just worried she'll walk in on him jerking off," Art said.

"We've got him in sight and he's alone," Brodie said, sounding more like he was ignoring Art than answering him. The elevator doors opened and she inhaled before she exited to bolster herself for what was to come. "Remember what I said, baby. I'm right there with you."

Reaching the door, she knocked and then turned the handle to go straight in. If this were a business meeting, as she was supposed to assume it was, then there would be no reason to wait for a response.

Grant was already there and was pacing in front of the window. He didn't look up when she came in, so she closed the door and went to a decanter in the corner. Taking her purse off her arm, Zara laid it down and poured two measures.

It wasn't until she took the drinks over and stepped into Grant's path that he stopped and actually saw her. "Zara," he said and took the glass she held up toward him.

"You look like you need a drink," she said, wearing a warm smile meant to comfort. He took the glass and gulped the liquid without attempting to disguise the trepidation of his mood with a traditional toast. She sipped from her own glass and watched him drink.

"Watch it with the hard liquor," Art said through her earpiece. "That's enough."

Sustaining a conversation and presence in this room would be difficult while being a part of another conversation going on across the street at the same time. "I think we both could use the courage," she said, more in response to Art than to Grant.

Grant kept drinking until his glass was empty, then he went to the large leather couch that faced the window and collapsed onto it, resting the glass on the back of the couch.

"Come and sit here," Grant said, bringing his glass down onto the seat.

Doing as she was told, she took his empty glass and put it on a side table with her own. "I have a clear shot," Brodie said and she tipped her chin away for fear Grant would hear their voices. "That's your only warning. If he puts his hands on you"—she slid down the couch away from Grant. "Better."

Grant didn't support her retreat though because he shifted toward her. "Thanks for meeting me."

"Sure," she said, unsure of what to do when he dropped a hand onto hers on the seat of the couch. The contact was slight; she just hoped Brodie didn't notice it.

"I asked you to meet me because… I want you to help me."

"Of course," she said. "Anything I can do."

"You're a good girl, Zara," he said, bringing his hand to her jaw.

With a laugh meant to be light, she pulled his hand down from her face. "How many have you had to drink, sir?"

His eyes searched hers. "We're more than boss and employee, aren't we, Zar?" he asked, inching closer still.

"I don't… I don't know what you mean."

"I can trust you, can't I?"

A few weeks ago, she might have been offended that he would question her allegiance. Now the lines weren't so clear because she was in league with his brother who was trying to put a stop to his illicit business deal.

"You can trust me," she murmured, turning her head enough that the men in the opposite building wouldn't be able to see her mouth. Not that it mattered; they could hear everything.

"Good," Grant said at the same time Art said the same word in her ear. His eyes moved from his slacks to the couch, to the floor, to the wall. So while his body position didn't change much, his turmoil was obvious. "I've been struggling with something for months now. Making decisions alone which could affect many lives."

Ready to listen to what he had to say, she tried to remain calm. "What kind of decisions?" she asked and couldn't believe this was the moment he was going to confess all to her.

His gaze stuck on his knee, he inhaled, then moistened his lips. "Many years ago CI began developing a device," he said and she had to squeeze her lips together. "It was meant to be for medical use that was its initial purpose…"

Trying to forget the danger, she imagined this was all new information. "We develop a lot of medical devices," she said, urging him on.

With a distant almost longing in his voice, he beseeched the spirits or perhaps they were the demons that haunted him into this course of action. "My father didn't agree with its potential," he said, opening his fingers over hers and tracing the seams of her closed fingers with the tips of his.

This was a genuine moment of vulnerability and she felt guilty that he was revealing himself to her without being aware of their audience. But that was her human compassion ruling good sense because with the potential for danger tonight, she was so grateful to have Brodie watching over her and she touched the edge of her necklace before returning her thoughts to Grant.

"You never talk about your dad," she said, opening her fingers to trap his, so that he couldn't keep stroking her because such an action felt intimate and she did not intend to get that close to this man. She was happy with the one she'd chosen.

Some of his regret receded and he strengthened his jaw. "I don't talk about any of my family," he said. "They're still out there. My father had no siblings, but my mother did… They're out there, but…"

When his attention drifted up to the window, she was struck by the irony. Grant was staring out and two of his family members were staring right back, only he didn't know it. "But?" she asked, trying to ease him into carrying on.

With a loud inhale, he straightened his shoulders. "It doesn't matter," he said, shaking off his previous melancholy. "When we find ourselves alone in the world, we have the freedom to make grander decisions and that's what I'm doing with Albert Sutcliffe."

"Is he the confirmed buyer for this device?" she asked.

"There are two other interested parties, but Sutcliffe has been the most persistent. I think his ideology is the most worthy."

That was a terrifying statement. It was bad enough when she thought that this was all about money. If Grant was not only in business with these men, but also in league with their ideas and politics, CI could become a very different kind of institution. "His ideology?" she asked.

He twisted and met her eye with a determination she recognized from someone else she knew. "I need a confidante. Someone to help me. To understand."

"To understand what?" she asked.

"How important this is," he said. "These men, the men I've been dealing with… they're serious and determined. I can't lie to you, Zara. Meeting them could endanger you."

"Endanger me, how?" she asked, reminding herself that she wasn't supposed to know these men were terrorists.

His tight smile wasn't reassuring. "I'll do everything I can to protect you. We won't let it come to anything serious."

"Thank you," she said, hoping that this was the right reaction to such a statement. "But if this deal is in any way dangerous, you shouldn't go through with it. Why is this deal so dangerous?"

"Because once we sell this device, it's possible that it will be used for a sinister purpose."

Taking her time to think about how she might react to this revelation if it was new. She explored his features for a few seconds. "What, like a weapon?" she asked, drawing her hands away and moving further down the couch, but he followed her again.

"No, it's not... you'll see later exactly what it's capable of. Sutcliffe wants a demonstration and that's why it was so important that you and I talk before the meeting. I wouldn't want you to think I kept anything from you."

"A demonstration? I don't want to be present if people are going to be hurt." She moved to rise, but he caught her wrist when she was halfway up and tugged her back down.

He didn't let her go, just pulled himself closer. "No one will be hurt," he said. "You have my word on that. No one will be hurt tonight. What these men want to do is make the world a better place and we can be a part of that, Zara. You and me."

"I don't want to be a part of anything that is going to cause suffering."

"Dial it back," Art murmured in her ear.

Zara tried to temper her reaction because it was important for the mission that they knew where this device was and what it was capable of.

"I have worked so hard to make it perfect, Zara," he said. The saddest part was that he clearly believed what he was saying.

"I'm sure the men in Quebec who died thought the same thing... What happened to them? You said there was an explosion?"

Coming across as the consummate professional, his detachment from the loss of life was unnerving. This wasn't like talking to Brodie who was used to death and destruction. As far as she knew, Grant was a novice, yet he put on a good show.

"I don't know yet. I'm going to travel up there tomorrow to investigate. Everything there was destroyed. Luckily, I had already moved some supplies down here and the compressed drug was kept separately." When his gaze drifted away, he was frowning, lost in his resolute thoughts. "The fact that someone knew to attack us there is concerning. Very few people knew that the plant was there."

Managing to preserve her ease, Zara tried for more information. "I don't remember seeing a research station there in the company reports."

"It was kept secret for this very reason. To produce and use this product requires vision that few people have. Some would set out to destroy it. It's possible we have a saboteur who may have a misguided idea of why he was destroying our research. Or…"

It was her turn to be determined. Without taking her attention away, Zara hoped their connection would force him to be honest. "Or what?"

"One of our bidders was sending a message." He was honest in his suspicions at least, but he had no answers to offer her on why the plant had been destroyed.

Coiling her hands in her lap, she nibbled her lower lip. "I don't like the sound of that."

His gaze stuck to the lip she was worrying in her teeth. "Will you come with me?"

Surprised by the question, her other thoughts vanished. "Where?" she asked.

"The plant. Tomorrow."

"Oh," she said, tightening her grip on herself.

"Say no," Brodie said through her earpiece.

"Say yes," Art followed up and she sucked her lower lip into her mouth as she tried to think of a response.

With a smile, she tried to ignore the implication of the request. "I can make reservations as soon as I get to a computer," she said, hoping he might tell her to do it this minute. "I can coordinate your trip from here. There is no need for me to travel—"

"I meant with me," he said and his hand rose toward her face, but she intercepted it.

"That's very sweet, Grant," she said, looking left and right while trying not to be too obvious about leaning away. "But uh… we should keep things professional."

The heat in his eyes was anything but professional, so she

deliberately slanted her shoulders in hope of concealing this exchange from the men watching through her necklace. "You're one of the most incredible women I've ever known," he said. "You remind me a lot of my mother."

"Oh," she said, not sure if that was a compliment or not, given he was talking about romance. "That's uh... creepy."

Grant laughed and he seized her hand again. "I meant it as a compliment. She was a wild woman, tenacious and confident. She was fearless, very intelligent and she had a great spirit."

"Thank you," Zara said, making a mental note to ask Brodie later if she reminded him of his mother. "I am flattered, really, but"—she pulled her hand away from him—"I'm sort of seeing someone."

"You are?" he asked, his surprise made him draw back.

"Yeah, she is," Brodie said through her earpiece in a growl that made her tremble.

"I am." Covering Grant's hand, she gave it a platonic pat.

"Is it serious?" he asked and she noted how her earpiece became silent.

"That seems to depend on his mood." Muffled laughter echoed in her ear, but she kept her smile steady on Grant.

"You deserve the best. I hope he knows how lucky he is to have such a gracious woman."

Grant linked their fingers and stood to pull her to her feet. "We should go to the party downstairs, show face, and write some checks. We'll come back up here when it's time."

"Wait," she said, not moving when he tried to guide her along at his side. "I still don't understand about this demonstration. When is it happening?"

"Tonight," he said. "Midnight."

"So the device is here on the premises?" she asked. "Where is it?"

He widened his smile and drew a finger along her jaw. "You'll find out when it's time."

Trying to catch a look over her shoulder, she couldn't object when he took her out of the suite and down to the party. But she could use some direction from her cohorts right about now because there was danger here and Grant was leading her straight into the fire.

SIXTEEN

GRANT HAD TAKEN HER to the party in the Grand ballroom and furnished her with a flute of champagne. Art told her to put the alcohol down, but with frayed nerves, she was hesitant to comply. At least she was until he reminded her the camera in her necklace would go into the ladies' room with her if she needed to pee. After that, she stopped drinking and just used the glass as a prop.

Maintaining a distance from festivities, Zara chose to remain on the fringes of the room and not to interact. "I want to dance," she said, keeping her back to the wall and her glass over her lips as she watched the glitterati mingle. "I wonder if my new boyfriend dances."

She didn't really want to dance, but she'd been here for nearly two hours and she imagined the men in the building opposite were getting as restless as she felt. So she decided to needle Brodie while he could do nothing to prevent her.

"Let him take you to Rio during Carnival and you'll find out," Art said through the earpiece.

Imagining the lives of the people she was watching and those of the men supporting her tonight, she was struck by the differences. "You know, this whole experience has made me realize…" she murmured. "Adventure is all around us."

"Stop talking," Brodie said in a monotone that betrayed his displeasure.

Her initial thought that he was just being grumpy and impatient was replaced when she realized her support team couldn't see her here in the ballroom at the rear of the building. But they could see the frontage, where they could be witnessing anything, and withholding the information from her.

"Should I be worried?" she asked and then explained herself. "We're worried about a chemical agent and we know this device is on the premises."

"Can you see Grant?" Art asked her.

The last time she'd seen him, he was on the dance floor with a blonde. Zara stepped out of the shadow to examine the partygoers and spotted Grant in a small group of serious men.

"Yes," she said, aware of her frown but unable to remove it. "He's networking."

"As long as you keep him in sight, you'll be safe. He's not going to unleash any noxious gases while he's in range," Art said in a cool but reassuring voice.

Zara relaxed because that made sense. "You're a smart guy, Art," she said, returning to her dark cocoon and her teasing. "It's a wonder you let yourself be dragged down by that lug head you live with."

Art laughed but Brodie spoke up, "Pretty baby, you let that smart mouth run away as much as you like, it can spend all night apologizing. Spend less time talking and more thinking about that."

Hiding her smile, Zara sought out Grant again to check his position. Except he was coming through the crowd toward her, so she erased the smile Brodie had put on her face. "Four men just entered the conference room," Art said, returning to the cause at hand.

Taking her weight off the wall, Zara composed herself in time for Grant arriving at her position. His grave expression made her skin prickle into gooseflesh, but she tried not to display any hesitation because her boss had to believe that she was strong enough to face this without folding.

"It's time to go," Grant said, offering her his arm.

Upholding her air of naivety about the situation, she smiled and took his arm, allowing him to lead her out of the ballroom.

"Two more targets in the zone," Art said through the earpiece.

Two voices. Two locations. It was difficult to follow both without revealing the truth of what she was doing to Grant. Over time, it would probably be easier to slide in and out of the present moment as the Kindred blathered in your ear. But Zara was concentrating on Grant, letting him guide her toward a dangerous situation she wasn't trained to handle and her trepidation was making her ears ring.

When they got to the elevator, Grant stepped away enough to press the call button. "I appreciate your support," Grant said. "Your loyalty is valuable to me. I don't want you to think I underestimate it."

Grant took her arm again when the elevator came and they moved into it together. "What's going to happen up here?" she asked. "I can be more valuable to you if I know what to expect."

"Good," Art said in her ear. "Find out what he anticipates."

Grant didn't respond right away, in fact it felt like an age before he said anything, to the point that Zara began to wonder if he was just going to ignore her question.

"I don't know exactly what will happen," Grant said, curling his fingers over hers at his elbow. "Whatever does happen, play along and I'll explain later."

That wasn't the reassuring answer she'd hoped for. But it would have to do because they got to their floor and Grant ushered her along the corridor toward the conference room they'd been in before. Her heart began to race. As much as she tried to keep her breathing steady, her fingers began to shake. She couldn't ask for comfort from her protectors. With Grant so close, she had to be mute.

"I'm there with you, baby. All the way," Brodie murmured in her ear.

Much to her surprise, her fingertips were on the line of diamonds around her neck. They must have risen to the jewels to seek solace from Brodie. Knowing that her lover had sensed her need encouraged her to carry on and she took a deep breath before Grant opened the conference room door.

She had expected people to be here, but not so many, or maybe not so many ominous ones. The sight of six intimidating men made this once generous space feel much more confined.

"Albert Sutcliffe," a broad man in a brown suit came to her and held out a hand.

She glanced at Grant for some kind of direction, but got none, so she gave Sutcliffe her hand. "Zara Bandini," she said in introduction.

He kissed her knuckles and made eye contact while the others in the room paid her no attention. "I apologize for the trauma you incurred on the night you met my nephew Tim," Sutcliffe said to her.

Grant had moved away from her side, but only by a couple of feet. Still, he said nothing to the revelation Albert Sutcliffe had just made, implying he hadn't been paying attention to the exchange. Grant probably had enough on his mind. It hadn't occurred to her that the connection might be referenced, and so she didn't know how to react. She was saved the trouble of fumbling through the encounter when Grant parted from her to shake the hand of the man in a brilliant white shirt and a stylish hat.

"Kahlil," Grant said, shaking his hand.

"My superior is not happy," Kahlil said, drawing his eyes away from Sutcliffe. "We want to conclude dealings."

Sutcliffe didn't appear as cold as Kahlil and so far, they were the only two to come forward. It was obvious they had no love for each other and Kahlil didn't even try to appear accommodating.

Sutcliffe didn't give Kahlil a second look. He maintained his attention on her and Grant. "Once we are satisfied with the results, dealings will conclude in my favor," Sutcliffe said. A man came in behind him to punctuate Sutcliffe's arrogance with a menacing glare. Apparently,

Sutcliffe hired men to do the cold, evil thing for him.

"You are all too eager." The voice came from the couch facing the window that she couldn't see because Kahlil, Sutcliffe, and his man were blocking her view.

"Nykiel Sikorski," Art said. "He's a crazy motherfucker."

The men who were restricting her view parted at the same time someone rose from the couch. The very tall man was sleek and wore a silver-gray suit that made him look expensive. While she wouldn't call him particularly cold, there was an ice in his demeanor. One that suggested he experienced little emotion.

"Let us see what we have before we start wars with each other over it," Sikorski said.

He went to the conference table and pulled out a chair to seat himself. The other men followed his lead and did the same. Two men dressed in a similar manner to Sikorski stayed standing in front of the window and she was conscious of how they might block Brodie's line of sight.

"Take a seat, Ms. Bandini," Sutcliffe said, gesturing at the seat beside his.

Instead of sitting there, she smiled and selected the seat closest to the door, furthest from the men, which just happened to be at the foot of the table. If Brodie had to take action, she didn't want to block his shot or become an accident.

Grant remained standing and made eye contact with her before retrieving a laptop from a side unit. He moved to the head of the table and opened the computer. Then, after pressing a few buttons, he laid it down for all to see.

Although it was a large screen laptop, it took a few seconds for her to realize what she was looking at. It was a movie or… video feed. Taking in the faces and the features in the room, clarity hit her.

"That's the ballroom downstairs," she said, setting her eyes on Grant.

"Yes," Sutcliffe said, as though what she'd said was explanatory not an exclamation.

"I've got it," Tuck said. "We're watching the feed

with you." Now she understood how useful Tuck's skills could be. He had obviously hacked into Grant's computer, giving the men supporting her a view of what she was seeing.

"I'm staying on you, baby," Brodie said, more interested in protecting her than seeing what was going on.

Relying on Grant's earlier statement that no one would get hurt, Zara watched the screen. People were milling around, sipping their champagne while glad-handing. Nothing remarkable was happening. Unsure of what she was supposed to be seeing, Zara kept watching. The people were happy to be at the event and no one seemed to be sick.

Everyone was silent, in this room and the one across the street. They all seemed so intent and she waited for the penny to drop. "That's one way to do it," Tuck muttered.

"Check this, Rave," Art said in the earpiece, but he wasn't talking to her.

"I'm not taking my eye off the room," Brodie said. "Talk me through it."

"Do you see it, girlie?" Art said, though she couldn't respond.

No one in her room was speaking yet, so she peered closer at the mute screen, attempting to decipher the significance of what they were witnessing, but she couldn't figure it out. The woman with the sleek blonde French roll in the center of the screen tossed her head back in a wild abandon not typically seen at these events, that was her first clue. When a man propped a hand on the shoulder of a colleague to support his weight, Zara saw that he was laughing. Every face she looked at was contorted in hilarity.

"Nitrous oxide," Grant said, leaning over to hit a key on the keyboard. The screen froze, then he closed the laptop lid. "This device has proven it can disseminate any gas. We at CI have some compressed concentrated canisters that can be sold with the device. The technology has been refined by our best technicians and can be controlled from anywhere in the world."

No word about what had happened to those technicians though, and she glimpsed each face for a sign that might imply one of these men were culpable. Nothing jumped out at her. Nothing except how surreal Grant's pitch was. It was reminiscent of any usual presentation at CI. Except this wasn't a normal day at the office. Grant was selling death today, though one would be forgiven for not realizing it.

Grant carried on. "Plant a few of these devices in major cities, in hospitals, stadiums, in airports, you trigger them for short amounts of time intermittently, and it would take months for authorities to trace the source. In that time, if you used something communicable then it's spreading, even while the device is dormant."

Zara's mouth fell open and she wanted to call out in protest. Until now, she'd been able to bargain away Grant's guilt, believing that he didn't wish anyone harm or that he didn't understand the gravity of what these criminals would do with the technology. There was no mistaking his intention anymore.

Sensing her need to object, Brodie preempted her outburst. "Easy, baby," Brodie murmured in her ear, making her shiver, and reminding her of the precariousness of where she was.

The others in the room were unfazed; none appeared to be horrified as she was. "We will have to consult with colleagues," Sikorski said, speaking for the group without their permission.

Grant nodded as though he'd expected this and it was traditional for there to be a pitch before negotiations commenced. "I understand," Grant said, bending to spread his hands on the table. "Final bids will be expected within two weeks."

"And delivery?" Sutcliffe asked and the three prospective buyers all awaited an answer.

Explaining delivery was Grant's worry. "We have plans to make," Kahlil said. "We will not delay for—"

"Something unforeseen occurred," Grant said. His look in her direction suggested that he wanted support or back up. As far as she was concerned, he was looking in the wrong place. "Our main production facility was compromised and my men were killed."

Now it was their turn to appear horrified. A delay

would be unacceptable, but they were fine with killing hundreds or thousands of people. Zara had never considered the priorities of terrorists before. Apparently, they worked to deadlines on a calendar just like the rest of the population. "Interesting," Sikorski said, drawing out the word. "You have some enemies of your own. Disgruntled customers?"

Grant shook his head. "I assure you that we produce only the highest quality merchandise."

Sikorski was unsatisfied. "If an unhappy customer did not cause the damage, was it an industrial accident?"

"We are investigating," Grant said. "CI is a multinational with a superb health and safety record. I lost good men at that facility and I assure you that I will find out what happened to them… exactly what happened."

Being at the foot of the table, she couldn't see the expressions on each of the bidder's faces, which were turned to Grant at the opposite end of the table. Grant looked at every man individually with a stern frown that almost accused them of knowing more than they were revealing.

Sikorski was the first to rise, with Kahlil and Sutcliffe not too far behind. Once on their feet their goons joined them. They waited half a beat and then departed in one drove with Grant bidding the three main men farewell with a handshake.

Watching him treat this like any other business meeting and these men like clients who should be respected, flummoxed her to the point of putting her in a daze. These men were terrorists with nefarious intentions. Grant was not only supporting those intentions, but he was facilitating and accelerating them.

Disregarding the support crew she had in her ear, when the door to the conference room closed, she and Grant were alone, but the atmosphere crowded the place until she almost choked with claustrophobia.

"Well, that didn't go as badly as I expected," Grant said and touched his palm to his temple for a brief moment. "I thought they'd push for a delivery date. But until I find out what happened… I don't know what we can salvage or how long it will take us to produce more devices. With limited resources... Anyway... sorry, that's not your concern. What do you think?"

When he turned, she got her first good look at him. The wide set of his hopeful brows and the looseness in his jaw baffled her. Taking a moment to process, Zara curled her lip over her teeth to bite out her frustration.

"What do I think? What do I think?" Her outrage gained momentum. "I can't support this," Zara said, thrusting away from the table to storm over to him.

His brows fell until the harsh slices altered his expression into anger, indicating he hadn't expected her to have this reaction. Grant didn't shrink or apologize. "Zara, you have to understand—"

"I can't," she said, stopping a couple of feet from him. "You're talking about murder on a huge scale. Why would you believe that this is a good idea? How could you have instigated—"

"The technology could be used for so many purposes," he said, gesturing with his hands. "People have died for this. People have to see what it's capable of. It's the only way anyone will take it seriously."

She couldn't believe these excuses anymore. "You're trying to downplay what just happened, but I was here, Grant. You're going to be party to murder and for what? Money? Is that what this is about?"

"No!" he objected and stormed past her toward the top of the table. "We have always been a pioneering firm and forward planning is key to keeping us on top. The world is changing, Zara. We're becoming segregated by ideology. In the future, countries won't exist as we recognize them today. We at CI have to align ourselves with a purpose."

Unable to believe her ears, she dipped her chin forward. "Align ourselves with a purpose," she murmured, in disbelief. "You mean you want to get into bed with these people? This is about more than money and investment in the future... you want to get into the war game."

Still adamant, he gestured with a stern hand. "I want us to be decisive. I want people to know what CI stands for. I don't want polished soundbites and politically correct ad campaigns. I want to take action and after this, no one will doubt that the CI giant can make changes in the world on a grand scale."

Shaking her head, some of her gusto dispersed into disappointment. There was a time she would have walked through fire for this man. She had built him up, respected him, believed in him. "I can't believe you're saying this," she whispered.

He softened his posture and his expression but his words were as vehement. "I have to prove that this will work. All my father cared about was his damn company and his misguided morals."

"Misguided?" she said, finding some starch to bolster her. This was not a time to be shocked and meek, this was a time to stand up and push back against a harmful force. It had just never occurred to her that she could be working under a man who was so unethical. "Your father wanted to protect people. He wanted to build machines that would help people, not hurt them."

"And I will not be limited by his lack of vision. The world is changing, Zara, and if you can't see that then you're as narrow-minded as he was. People like Sutcliffe and Kahlil or Sikorski are the future customers of our company. Have you seen the state of our economy, of the global economy? Governments can't afford our products and they're cutting the budgets of those who can. We have to look at reality and stop pretending that we live in this utopian world that doesn't exist!"

"Is this their ideology? Or yours?" she asked, approaching the table again. "You sound like… this kind of rhetoric… Grant, the security services hunt down people like you."

"No," he said, shaking his head and slamming a hand to the laptop. "I want to work for the benefit of the world and no one can deny that there are people who need to be stopped before they come for us. How will you feel if you walk away from this and next month a hundred people die in a horrific attack?"

Widening her eyes, she lifted her hands. "That's

exactly what I'm worried about!" He didn't appear to understand her perspective. With her hands opened toward herself at shoulder height, she beseeched him as she walked closer. "People will die, Grant, civilians will die. If you put something like that out into the world, you can't take it back. If you give it to these people, they will use it and you can't direct how they do that."

"You don't understand," he muttered like he was disappointed by her lack of foresight. "I want to hurt those who call us infidels and disrespect any religion except their own. We have to fight back. Our government's hands are tied. We're fighting an inferno with a bucket and spade. We need the ocean, Zara. I want to be the ocean."

"The ocean," she sighed.

Western nations had been attacked without notice and their civilians killed in unwarranted attacks. Few would argue that those transgressions weren't atrocious. The world was facing a new age where individuals could operate under their own volition in acts of war without the support of their governments. But those misdeeds didn't justify others taking the law into their own hands.

"You don't understand," he murmured again and his shoulders sagged until his hands landed on the table.

Releasing the tension in her shoulders, her arms fell to her sides. "No, I don't. You have to stop this, Grant and until you do…"

Rising from his position bent over the table, his scowl intensified. "What?" he asked. "Until I do, what?"

Shaking her head, she was surprised at how emotional she felt about what she was going to say. "Until you do, I'm not coming back… if you want someone to fuel this insanity then you better keep looking. It's not going to be me."

"Now, Zara, just wait a minute."

"No," she said, backing toward the door when he started to come toward her. "I'm sorry, sir, but I can't be a part of this."

Turning around, she hurried to the door and got out of there as fast as she could without looking back. Her reaction hadn't been a part of any plan and she hadn't expected to end this day by quitting her job. Putting one foot in front of the other, she concentrated on the deep carpet that wasn't conducive to an upset person who was walking in high heels. She got to the elevator and pressed the call button about five times.

Those in her ear were silent. At least she couldn't hear them through the noise ringing in her ears. She felt like she was listening to a car alarm while submerged in water and she just couldn't focus. The elevator came and she went inside, but she had to blink at the buttons for a few seconds before registering which one to press.

When the doors closed, she let herself relax on an exhale, and opened her arms to support herself on the rail at the back of the elevator. Closing her eyes, Zara couldn't remember the plan. There had been talk of what to do if everything went wrong, but none of what to do if everything went right.

Though she couldn't fathom how what had happened could be construed as right by any measure. What she really needed to do was to go into the restroom, wash her face, and give herself a good shake. But she didn't want her audience to know how rattled she was, so she kept going.

On getting out of the hotel, she stormed down the block while fishing in her ear to remove the tiny piece of tech linking her to the team. Tipping her head to make sure it didn't get lost, she peeled the thin transparent film from her ear and pressed it into her palm. Quelling her urge to toss it aside, she kept it because she didn't know how much it was worth or if it could be traced.

Replaying what had gone on tonight, she got mad when she came out of her daze and began planning her next move. Grant wasn't willing to listen to her and she would be no use to the Kindred now that she'd quit her job. But that didn't mean she was going to bow her head and forget what she'd learned.

Half a dozen blocks away from the hotel, she began to think about hailing a cab. Her daze was wearing off and sense was coming back, if she walked the couple of miles to her apartment, her shoes would end up hurting her feet, and she didn't need pain on top of everything else.

Just before she stepped off the sidewalk to cross an alley, the roar of a motorcycle sounded. But paying little heed to it, she kept on moving, that was until the vehicle came into her peripheral vision. It roared forward and stopped right in front of her. Taking her gaze from the front tire blocking her route, she saw that Brodie was the rider, and this encounter was no accident.

"Baby, you're a natural," he said with a lopsided smile that made her want to slap him.

Finding that her anger had not entirely receded, she growled. "Get your bike out of my way."

Either he ignored her mood or he didn't care, because he carried on without addressing it. "The guys are heading back. We have a debrief. It's time to go home."

"I am going home, back to my apartment," she said and tried to back off.

But while still straddling the bike, he lunged toward her to hook his solid arm around her waist. He hauled her close and held her against his thigh so she was near enough for a kiss.

His breath heated her cheek. "That place isn't safe for you tonight. Only one place you'll be safe tonight, baby, and that's on your back under me."

Grinding her teeth, Zara didn't want her fury to explode in this public arena. "Let go of me," she murmured.

"You're pissed," he said and his smugness wasn't concerned. "Atta girl… use it."

Bending forward, he pressed his face into her hair and tried to kiss her neck. But she tilted her head toward him to refuse his mouth access. Slapping her palms onto his leather jacket, Zara shoved at him enough that his arms and expression loosened, but he didn't actually let her go.

"Who the fuck do you think you are?" she demanded, using the anger as he'd suggested. "I can't believe I ever listened to anything you had to say. You were there tonight. Did you hear the same thing I did? Those men are dangerous and they plan to level the world. How dare you expect me to go anywhere with you! You want to know where I'm going?

To the cops! As soon as I heard what this was about, I should've gone to the authorities to let them deal with it. But I didn't, I got swept up by you and by this idea of vigilantism and adventure, like I could make some kind of goddamn difference. People have already died and maybe—"

"What?" he snapped, echoing her mood. "The cops could've saved them? Those guys were crooks, all of 'em. You go to the cops now and what are you gonna tell them? You have no evidence, not one shred, and you won't have anyone to back up your story. You'll sound like a nut!"

Undeterred, she pushed her shoulders back. "Better a nut with a clean conscience than a crook with a guilty one."

With his own anger, Brodie argued with her. "You go to the cops now and that's it, you're out. Grant won't take you back. You'll lose our protection. And you'll become enemy number one to every man you met tonight. How long do you think you'll last out there by yourself?"

"Better dead than useless," she said, smacking the earpiece onto his leg then reaching around to unfasten the diamonds. He flicked the earpiece away but stuffed the diamonds into his pocket after she handed them over.

"The earpiece begins to breakdown once it's deactivated," he said. "It uses your body heat as a power source."

She didn't care about how anything worked anymore. Zara just wanted to go back to her mundane life. "You can take down the cameras you have watching my apartment too."

Narrowing his eyes, the snarl returned to his voice. "We're a little busy trying to save civilization," he said. "Call your cable guy for tech support."

Shaking her head, she refused to feel guilty. "You have no right to be angry at me. I've done everything you've asked me to do," she said.

"I didn't ask you to abandon the team," he said, his voice growing huskier.

Distraught and disoriented, she didn't know what to think anymore. "Your team… they're your team, not mine. When you're through and I'm useless to you, you'll move on… they're your team," she said and let her gaze fall to the thick breadth of his thigh wrapped in dark blue denim.

In a maneuver that surprised her, he grabbed hold of her chin and forced her head up until their noses almost touched.

"You don't think you're a member of the goddamn team? Five people have had boots on the floor in my house over the last twenty years. You want to know how many women I've fucked in that bed? One. You. I'm sorry if we didn't roll out the red carpet, baby. We're a low profile bunch. Most fuckers in this world think I'm dead, fewer people than that know Tuck's real name and Art would never have brought you in if he didn't intend on keeping you. You want to end your association with me, pretty baby, that's just fine. But don't you dare insult those men who have trusted you with their identities and therefore their lives… You came to us. You sought us out."

His rage was offense. This was his way of processing hurt. But she couldn't let him change history as it suited him. "You researched me, you have a camera opposite my apartment," she said without retreating from her staunch position. But he was right. Art, Tuck, and Brodie had trusted her with their secrets. Zara just hadn't realized how profound that was and hadn't understood that it inferred her acceptance on the team.

"What we do is look out for each other and you are a part of that now, Zar. That camera protects you. It was designed by my cousin, Zave, who lives in the twin house," he said, tracing his fingers up to her cheekbone. "We call him Falcon. He's a hardware genius. He designed, developed, and built every device we use. Priority one for the Kindred: we watch each other's backs. Falc can build anything we ask for and Swift can write any software to run it. Between them, they have built the Kindred an impressive arsenal of weapons and gear to reinforce priority one. Like your necklace and the earpiece, those kept you safe. If you weren't a part of the team, you wouldn't have had any of it."

Her anger had lost some of its steam, but she still had questions. "Why didn't you shoot tonight? I thought the plan—"

"If you'd told me to shoot, I would have," he said. Both of his hands touched her cheekbones, he let them drift down in an arc, allowing his thumbs to trace the apples of her cheeks.

Touched, aroused, angry, confused, it was all so exhausting. Losing herself in him was easy, especially when his focus on her was absolute and she felt powerful to have such a man enraptured in her.

"Without question?" she whispered.

"Without question," he said and his eyes descended to her mouth.

"Because I'm part of the team?"

"And because you've got me by the balls, baby," he said.

Reading a softness in his features that she'd never seen before, she was reminded of his voice in her ear promising that he was with her, and of his refusal to take his eye from the gun scope while she was surrounded by those dangerous men.

Drowning in his scrutiny, she wasn't sure he was aware of the conversation anymore. Whispering her hope, she exposed her own vulnerability to him. "Could it be that another part of your anatomy is in play?"

"My mouth?" he asked, perplexed by her statement.

He didn't see how she was in knots for him, didn't understand how much she needed him to admit his devotion to her because until she knew he wanted her beyond this mission, she would be in a continual state of tension, of fear that he might turn his back on her when all of this was over. "Your heart," she said, abandoning her anger and relaxing her weight to his thigh where the rumble of the bike carried through him to her.

"It doesn't matter, does it? If you're leaving the team, we'll never see each other again."

Because he would shut her out or because he didn't think she would live long if she followed through on her threat to go to the authorities, she didn't want to ask which he meant.

Leaving the team was probably a good idea for her, if for no other reason than it might spare her a heartbreak, but she was fast losing her ability to defy him. "The cops have the resources—"

"Trust me," he said, narrowing his eyes and his lips at the same time, imploring her to believe him. "Come inside, all the way. Commit to us."

Zara knew that talking in terms of the team made it easier for him to ignore the truth of what was happening between them. Without the heat of her anger, she longed for the comfort and security of the Kindred, and of him.

"What do I have to do?" she asked.

He reached to the back to free the helmet meant for her then held it toward her. "Get on the bike and come back to base."

Holding eye contact for another few seconds, she relented and took her helmet to pull it on before using her grip on his shoulder to climb onto the bike.

He turned up the collar of his jacket and hunkered low while Zara wrapped her arms around his torso. He pulled her arms tighter and revved the engine a couple of times before taking off. She still had so many questions about what had happened tonight and what their plan would be going forward. Hoping that she would have the chance to figure everything out at this debrief, she resolved herself to not making any decisions until after it.

Just because she was not as worldly or street smart as these guys didn't mean she should be dismissed. She had people skills that none of the men had displayed. Constant conflict and working in intense situations had hardened them all and any social skills they may have once had were diminished. Art was kind, Tuck seemed indifferent to her. But Brodie could barely hold a conversation without it being overtaken by some emotion or other, and he had the discretion of an M1A1 tank on a freeway.

Taking up with a bad boy intent on taking down terrorists and quitting her job had not been on her New Year's resolutions list. Her life was unrecognizable to how it had been just a few weeks ago. Her eyes had been opened and now that they were, she couldn't close them again. Grant did not intend to listen to her or to be swayed by her. She just hoped that the Kindred were different.

SEVENTEEN

"GET ON IN HERE. What took you two so long?" Art asked when she entered the manor kitchen under Brodie's arm.

The lower part of the kitchen island was laid with four place settings. Art and Tuck were already gobbling down the food in their shallow bowls and a bottle of wine stood between the two vacant place settings. Art got up and went to the stove to pile two pasta plates full of spaghetti and meatballs. Bringing them to the empty spots, Art put them down and returned to his own meal.

"This is the big debrief?" she asked when Brodie sat on a stool and reached for the red wine. "Spaghetti and meatballs?"

"Would you rather have something else?" Art asked her, slurping up a noodle.

The food wasn't what surprised her. The lackadaisical manner of the men who had just gone through the same night she had was what perplexed her. "No, I... I was just expecting something else."

"A darkened room with a swinging light bulb?" Tuck asked. "That comes after. Right now, we eat." Tuck pointed to her seat with his fork then twirled it in his plate to gather up more spaghetti.

"Sit down and eat, girlie," Art said.

Going to the couch, she supported her weight on it and bent to take her high-heels off. "This dress is silk and cost a month's salary," she said, wiggling her toes, which were screaming with delight at being granted their freedom. "There's no way I'm getting spaghetti sauce on it."

Brodie left his food and went to a tall, broad closet in the corner, saying nothing about his intention. "But you got on the back of his bike?" Art asked and Tuck smirked with him.

Brodie closed the closet then tossed something black in her direction. She caught it and opened it up while he went back to his food.

"Problem solved," Art said when she revealed the fabric to be one of Brodie's tee shirts.

Pulling it on to protect her dress, Zara was grateful for the food because she had some nervous energy to replenish. "How does this work?" she asked, gulping the wine that Brodie had poured for her.

"You start by not getting drunk," Brodie said, taking the glass away from her and putting it back on the tiled surface. "Get some food in you or you'll pass out. Alcohol's the only thing you've had tonight."

The sight of the trio's satisfaction made her appreciate what the sustenance offered after a stressful night. "What's the worst that can happen to her in here?" Tuck asked. "You take advantage of her? You're gonna do that anyway."

Brodie didn't deny it. Art smiled at his nephew, which made her look at him too. She was surprised to see him looking right back at her. "What?" she asked, glancing at her plate as she twisted her fork in the pasta.

Brodie was still examining her and the scrutiny was making her squirm. "I'm just trying to imagine what it would be like to have you not giving me grief while I fuck you."

Tuck laughed and Art appreciated the joke but seemed to be waiting for her reaction. With a slack jaw, she glared at her lover. Brodie was the one who talked during sex and he definitely gave her more grief, but she understood banter and was happy to play the role he painted her into.

"When you stop needing a step-by-step tutorial, maybe I'll stop giving you grief," she said, turning her frown upside down much to the amusement of Art and Tuck.

Brodie wasn't dissuaded from his mighty position. "High maintenance is what you are. You're full of demands," he said, dropping an elbow to the counter and his fork into his plate.

"In bed is the only place in the world where I'm sure you're paying attention," she said, elevating her chin and narrowing her eyes. "I know how to get what I want and when to ask for it."

Brodie's long arm trespassed in her personal space. He hooked a hand beneath her stool and dragged it across until it bumped his. "You know where to find what you want," he muttered.

His face sank and she leveled her posture to align her mouth with his. "Right here," she whispered, resting her weight on him while her nails dragged over his leg to the inside of his thigh.

"Atta girl," he exhaled and eliminated the remaining space between their mouths.

He did love to kiss and she could lose herself in the sensation of his fierce tongue as it toyed with hers. His hand slid across the back of her stool and she loved how the arc of his arm created a barrier between her body and reality, and she was in no hurry to get back.

The bitter wine on her tongue and the tangy sauce on his intensified the experience of taste and scent in the potency of their kiss. Even though she hadn't tried the food yet, she would have to compliment the chef. Nothing had ever tasted so good.

"I guess we should get down to business," Art said and she forced herself to stop kissing Brodie when she registered Art's authoritative tone. Brodie wasn't as affected, his arm snaked up, and he pressured her cheekbone to ease her back into their kiss.

With her hands on his chest, she succeeded in putting

less than an inch between them. While he might be used to being so open in front of Art and Tuck, she was conscious of how quickly their ardor could escalate and wasn't sure she'd be able to conceal her want. "You'll have me all night," she mumbled on him.

"I plan to have you a helluva lot longer than that," he said. With his eyes open, he kissed her bottom lip, then deferred to their audience and shunted her back to her food. Except by now, she was so out of breath that she couldn't focus on the plate. "Eat."

On his command, she took her fork from the bowl and did as he told her to on autopilot. Stabbing a meatball, she took it into her mouth and when the medley of flavors filled her senses, she released a long moan that stopped the men in their tracks.

Swallowing the meatball, she swirled her pasta around her fork, eager to take more now that she knew how good it was. "This is incredible," she purred, opening her mouth wide to slide her fork inside slowly. Closing her mouth around the cuisine, her eyelids sank down to meet and she moaned at the pleasure of the taste extravaganza.

"Wow," Tuck said with a laugh in his voice that made her eyes open.

The hacker was wearing a smile, which was countered by the assassin's glower. "What?" she asked Brodie.

"I'm the only guy allowed to see that face," Brodie grumped.

Art was grinning, making it appear that Brodie was the only diner with a problem. So choosing to ignore him, she smiled at the chef. "It's really good," she said to Art and he bowed his head in appreciation.

"Yeah, we figured you liked it," Art said.

"You'll need to write down the recipe," she said, though she knew she would never be able to master his skill in the kitchen if this was any measure of his capability. "Is there anything you can't do? You seem to be amazing at everything."

"Are you flirting with him?"

Whirling back to her previous view, Brodie's

expression hadn't changed much, though it was edging closer into outrage. "I'm not flirting," she said, slack-jawed and wide-eyed as she glanced at the other two men seated with them.

"The guy is practically my father," Brodie stated. "You were on a date with my brother tonight. First my brother, then my mentor and—"

"It wasn't a date," she said, shoving an elbow on the edge of the counter to lean closer to him. "And I was simply complimenting Art for preparing this delicious meal. It tastes better than the only thing you've ever put in my mouth—"

"Okay," Art said, rising to his feet with his hands open, in a gesture probably meant to calm them all. "Let's get the business stuff out of the way, after that you two can bicker like a married couple as much as you want."

"It's great television," Tuck said, clearing his plate.

Before he said anything else, Art went to the stove and retrieved the pot of food to put it in the center of their dining space. Touching her shoulder to get her attention, Art gave her a squeeze. "There's plenty more, girlie, fill yourself full."

"Now you're doing it!" Brodie said, his fork clattering into his plate. Tuck laughed and she sucked up her spaghetti then used a fingertip to wipe the sauce from her chin before she spoke.

"You're the best lover in the room," she said, supporting her weight on the crossbar of her stool to push toward him. Smudging the sauce from her finger to his lips, she smiled after he sucked her digit in a seeming show of acceptance. When he released her, she sat back down and began to gather more pasta onto her fork. "At least I think you are. You're the only one I have experience with." Filling her mouth with food, Zara smiled at Brodie, causing Tuck to laugh again.

"Letting him have a woman was better in theory than in practice," Art said, dishing more food into his and Tuck's plates.

"That's always the way, Chief," Tuck said, hunching down over his plate. "You think your kid is ready for the responsibility, but it's always you who ends up picking up after it and feeding it."

"I tidy up after myself, thank you," Zara said, then realized she'd just agreed with the analogy that compared her to a pet.

Art put the spoon back in the pot and sat down. "What's the next step?" he asked, putting a stop to the fooling around. "Grant picks a buyer, right?"

"Right," Tuck agreed.

Their previous banter was forgotten and she kept eating as she listened. "He's swaying toward Sutcliffe," Brodie said.

"And we all know what a mistake that would be," Art said and the other two men nodded in agreement.

Brodie wasn't eating anymore. Tuck was gobbling up his second plate. And she felt a bit stupid for asking a maybe obvious question. "Is there a good choice?"

"Kahlil probably," Tuck said.

"Kahlil," she said, thinking about the men who had attacked her in the CI parking garage. "Do you know who he's working for?"

"The Saudis," Brodie said. "There are certain… elements in their own back yard who they would like to get rid of."

"What about Sikorski?" she asked.

All of them shook their heads without a moment of hesitation. "He's a scary sonofabitch," Art said. "He runs one of the most lucrative Bratva gangs in the northeast. Word is his jacket isn't hanging on the most secure hook with the boys back home, if you get me. He's volatile 'cause he'd sacrifice good sense in favor of making a statement. The last thing anyone wants is a terrorist who has something to prove."

With his fingers linked over his plate, Brodie had lost his appetite. "The problem with the Russians is they have so many enemies," Brodie said. "We could never guarantee who they would use the device against."

Still seeking answers, she searched their expressions. "So why is he in the running? If Grant knew—"

"He's charismatic," Tuck said, pushing his half-full plate away. "He owns a huge mansion and has parties which are invitation only, gentleman-only invitees."

"Why would there be no women—"

"Oh, there are women," Art said. "But not the type who are invited."

"Oh," she said and suddenly she wasn't particularly hungry anymore either.

"Few people have Sikorski's respect. He's a tough man to impress," Brodie said. "He's extravagant and can have you eating out of the palm of his hand. But he'd just as soon stab you in the back if it served his interest on that particular day."

"Or have one of his flunkies stab you," Art said, topping off his wine glass and Zara's too.

Tuck leaned back in his stool and linked his hands at the back of his head. "Yeah, he wouldn't want to get blood on his fancy suit."

Their knowledge would be useful, but something in their tone made her curious. "You're all talking as if you know him…" she said but got no explanation. "Have you met him?"

"Our paths have crossed, but he's not a man you want to eyeball," Tuck said.

Looking at Brodie and Art, she received no translation. "I don't know what that means," she said.

As the other two men were considering their plates, Tuck answered. "He's heard of us."

"Heard of you, Swift," Art interjected. "You're a legend."

"A myth," Brodie said, scraping the last of his food together in the center of his plate.

Righting himself on his stool, Tuck picked up his wine glass. "Least I'm not dead, like some people at the table," Tuck said, balancing the glass on its base and raising his brows at Brodie.

They'd made jokes about Brodie being an apparition and she'd considered his existence herself. But something occurred to her in that moment which caused her to frown. "Does Grant know you're here?" she asked. "Does he know you're alive?"

Now that his plate was empty, Brodie shoved it away.

"Doubt he cares," he said, snatching up his glass to gulp down the remainder of the liquid.

For a man born to privilege, he ate like an animal... except when it came to her. He wasn't sloppy when his head was between her thighs. That was probably the only place in the bedroom where his etiquette was impeccable.

"What do you think?" Brodie asked and she snapped out of her daze to make eye contact. "Were you listening?" Being honest, she shook her head. "What were you thinking about?"

"Uh," she said, taking her glass into her hand to buy some time. "Just who Grant will choose."

"That's what we want to know," Art said. "You know him better than anyone at the table."

Considering all the business deals she'd witnessed at CI, she sipped her wine and tried to reach a conclusion. "Grant likes people who are straightforward," she said. "He doesn't like quiet, reticent people. He believes those kinds of people have something to hide. He also doesn't like to be embarrassed and likes to believe that he can predict the progress of a person or their company based upon his deal with them."

"Then Sutcliffe it is," Tuck said. "Sikorski is the most likely to embarrass him since no one can project what he would do. He could say one thing and do something else."

Art nodded. "The Saudis are secretive and dealing with Kahlil he probably sees as beneath him."

"What do we know about Albert Sutcliffe?" she asked, sitting back to enjoy her wine.

"Born in the UK, he moved over here with his parents when he was eight," Art said. "He inherited his father's company and his estate but lost most of it through bad investments and unfavorable divorce settlements. He dabbled in politics twenty, thirty years ago, but liked women and voicing his honest opinion too much. He was seen as a radical with delusions of grandeur and lost most of his credibility after that."

Interesting as his history was, Zara heard nothing that could be considered a motive for terrorism. "So what would he want with a—"

"He believes that geopolitical problems should be solved with tit for tat and he's built up something of a cult following," Art said. "When he gets the chance, he voices his dislike for the West's response to problems in the lesser privileged parts of the world."

"And so we should just eradicate those who disagree with us?" she asked, unable to grasp how someone could think this was a legitimate solution. None of the men disagreed with her and their expressions validated her thinking. "Okay, so we don't want him to have the device either."

"There is no good choice," Art said.

"Then why didn't we take them out?" she asked, directing this question to her lover.

"We didn't take them out," Brodie said, emphasizing the first word. "Because we don't need three powerful organizations coming after us. We're gonna wait until Grant makes his deal and lets down the unsuccessful bidders, then we wait and watch. When the handover is going down, then we take out the involved parties and destroy the device."

That made sense because carnage at the hotel could have brought hundreds of people after them. Kahlil was a puppet and his employers wouldn't like their man to be executed. The Russian Brotherhood wasn't known for being understanding. And who knew how many followers Sutcliffe had.

But as sensible as that solution sounded, it left her with one question. "What about Grant?"

She knew her question wouldn't win her any popularity contests, but she had to know what they planned to do with her former boss on the day of the handover when the Kindred planned to eradicate Game Time and its purchaser.

"Do you care?" Brodie asked. The tone in his voice wasn't grumpy anymore. Instead, it was deep and curious.

Though it could've been her imagination, she was sure that all of the men leaned closer to her. "I do," she said. "But not because I want to sleep with him or because I believe in what he's doing. He's been good to me. He's your brother.

You should care too."

Brodie stood up to grab the wine bottle from beside Tuck. Dropping onto his stool again, he filled up his glass. "He stopped being my brother fifteen years ago."

"What did he do to you?" she asked, wondering what had happened to sour the fraternal relationship when he was eighteen.

Brodie took his attention away from the group, signaling his intention to ignore her question. "We're not going to harm Grant," Art said, probably knowing better than to push Brodie in company.

Eating some more of her food, Zara finished her wine and thought about the night. Grant was Art's nephew too. She didn't know anything of their relationship, but she could understand that he wouldn't want his nephew harmed. After Grant's comments about family in the conference room, she doubted he'd had recent contact with any of them.

Tonight had been a learning experience. Now that the adrenaline was wearing off and the new day was coming nearer, she had to think about sleep. Sliding off her stool, she began to gather up the plates, but when she got around to Tuck, he took them away from her.

"You did the heavy lifting tonight," Tuck said. "That gets you off dishes duty."

A hand took hold of her neck and she was drawn backwards against Brodie's solid form. Tilting her head to look up to him, he lowered his mouth to kiss her.

"Bed?" she asked.

"Bed," he said, pulling her back and under his arm to lead her toward the door.

"Night," she managed to call before the kitchen door swung shut.

EIGHTEEN

BRODIE KEPT HOLD of her neck and used his elbow on her shoulder to guide her through the house to the stairway.

"I love this house," Zara said when they began to ascend the stairs. Although she wasn't an expert yet, she was definitely beginning to recognize the route.

He wasn't really listening. "You, what?" he mumbled.

They got to the top of the stairs and she spun around to press herself against the door before they could go through it. "I'm sorry."

Reaching around her, Brodie got the door open an inch, but she used her weight to block him. "Sorry for what?" he said, exhaling his impatience.

Saying her piece meant something to her, she just wished he would understand the depth of what she'd gone through. "Tonight. I freaked out. I was ready to walk away and if I had—"

"We don't leave a man behind," he said, with his thumb on her chin, he held her face. "It's cute that you think you had a choice."

Spiders of awareness crept across her skin, making even the tiniest of hairs stand upright. With her eyes fixed on this man, her man, she opened herself to the possibilities of the night and the achievement she'd made.

This night was a watershed, her acceptance into the team, and she'd done it. She had been useful to the mission, followed orders, kept her cool. All of those stimulants bombarded together in an upsurge of sensation that exploded in her gut and shimmered to each of her extremities.

The sight of him may arouse her. The way he looked at her certainly did. As did the entitlement of his touch, the scent of his skin, and the sound of his husky voice. It all worked for her. Now that she had it, had him, he had become a part of her soul and she didn't want to live without him.

Brodie was a man to be revered. Modest as he may be about his skills, he had kept her alive tonight and valued her above everything else. That kind of control was intoxicating. Being a priority for a man like Brodie gave her authority and while it was a power she wouldn't dream of abusing, it was liberating to have the kind of security that only a man like Brodie could offer.

She had influence over him, but whether that clout extended to anything beyond their sexual connection, she couldn't yet be sure. Resigning herself to existing in the now, Zara lifted her chin and emphasized her bosom with her posture.

He didn't want to get serious tonight, forcing him into any admissions or denials would lessen the legitimacy of whatever he said. So to prove her dedication, she chose to needle him with the ultimate ambition of satisfying them both.

"Art said you were attracted to me when you first came to check me out," she teased, drawing her fingernail up his arm and across his chest to pinch the fabric on his sternum.

"You'd rather I thought you were a dog? I notice women I want to fuck."

With the goal of rousing him to a state of frenzy similar to that which was taking her over, she pushed on with her tease and let her eyes wander down his body, playing it coy. "The way he said it was like it was unusual, like I was different. I think maybe Art was worried."

"Like you were trouble?" he asked and pushed her.

With a thump, her back hit the wall and the air leaving her lungs made her gasp. In the same breath, he came down to her level for a brief tongue kiss. "He's a smart guy. He gave me some amount of grief when I spent the night at your place."

Pleased that she was getting his attention, she toyed with his tee shirt some more. "He told you to leave me that morning, didn't he? Is that why you were on the phone for so long?"

Keeping his mouth close to hers, Brodie ducked to keep them parallel. With his face so near, she couldn't leave the trap of his ensnaring eyes. "At first, of course he did, 'cause you're a liability," he said, opening his hands to rub them down her sides and up over her breasts in a coarse perusal of what he was about to gain full authority over. "Women are messy."

"Sex is messy," she said. Digging her nails into him, she sucked her lip into her mouth in an attempt to lessen the volume of her shorter breaths. "What you're talking about are relationships and that's not what we have, is it?"

It wasn't clear to her if he understood the importance of this conversation. He seemed preoccupied by her body and the vision of her mouth. But maybe the distraction would aid her in getting to the truth. "You are…"

"I'm what?" she asked when he didn't finish.

"Hell if I know," he said and she couldn't blame him for losing his train of thought because her rational mind was in disarray, jumbled by the tsunami of emotions she'd endured on that night. "You were off limits from the first day, keeping a clear head is the best way to ensure an op goes down without a hitch."

"I'm part of the team," she said, touching the corner of his jaw with a fingertip and curving her body into his emboldening touch.

"Part of the team for this mission, you said. I told you that my inner circle was small… no one's ever been…"

"Excommunicated," she said, struggling to even out her breathing. "So what will you do with me when this mission is over?"

The more relevant point was what he planned to do with her in the present. They were still in a shared hallway, but her body was prepared for a much more private event. "When this mission is over…" he said, kissing her and trailing his lips along the length of her jaw. "It's dangerous to make plans beyond tomorrow, baby. Stick with me and you'll learn that."

In a brief moment of clarity, her features contorted with the unsettling reality he was presenting. "Does that mean that one day… you don't plan to come back?"

Opening his hand over her intimate core, he massaged her through her dress and she gratefully forgot about her concern and surrendered to the insistence of his libido. He wanted her ready and she was already there, but that didn't stop him from urging her closer to the edge. Dragging his hand up her body, he held her chin to lock their focuses on each other.

"Everyone's headed for that one day," he said. "All of us have to accept that one day there won't be any coming back."

"You've lived your life with these clean lines," she said, watching her fingers play on his chest, tracing the lines of the muscles beneath the material of his tee shirt. "Bad guys and good guys, right and wrong."

"If you think it's clean then you haven't been paying attention. Alliances are flimsy and allegiances spin on a dime. Why do you think I keep my circle small? I can count on one hand the number of fuckers I trust."

In need of his validation, she tried to kiss him, but he slanted back out of her reach. "Am I on that list?"

"You're in my house, aren't you?"

"What does that mean? Taking a woman into your bed doesn't mean you trust her."

"No, it doesn't," he said. One of his hands snaked down to her hip. He compelled her along the door to force her against the frame while the other hand clamped around the back of her neck to pull her mouth to his. His fingers dug in and his strength made her submit, but she'd learned that getting rough was safe with him and her favorite way to play.

"Do you trust me?" she asked, but his patience for

talking was wearing out. He swooped down to kiss her neck and her lips curled in their own surrender.

"I told you, you're a natural," he said and when she resolved herself to him being evasive, she exhaled and drove her nails into his shoulders to jump into his arms. Endorphins commanded their priorities, in times like these a person would struggle to get, or give, a reasonable answer. Zara wasn't even sure what she wanted him to say, but she knew what he made her feel.

"It's invigorating," she said, squeezing her thighs around him while the width of her smile made her cheeks ache. Trying to decipher her mood and meaning, Brodie's gaze darkened. "It's like… the danger, the things that could have happened tonight…" Maybe it was inspiration from the wine, but she opened her fingers in his hair and dipped forward to suck his earlobe into her mouth. "I'm ready to be safe now, beau."

"On your back and under me," he said, opening the door and carrying her toward the bedroom. "The safest place on earth."

"On home turf," she said, rummaging between their compressed bodies to loosen his jeans.

"Desperate to get me naked, baby?" he asked, dropping her onto her feet and crowding her against the bedroom door as he pressed his thumbprint onto the handle.

Her skin fizzed with anticipation, the weight of him pressing her into the door made her wriggle in search of extra stimulation. "You've got to catch up, baby. It's time for the panty check."

Being part of a gang intent on protecting what was right aroused her. Now that she had recovered from the initial shock, she could replay the evening and comprehend how lucky she was to be alive. The thrumming pulse of renewed life worked her heart and her blood through her veins at an invigorating pace. Relishing this thirst, she dragged her teeth on his jaw. That contact provoked his appetite enough that he grabbed her neck in a vice grip and opened the door.

"Get in there," he said, propelling her forward into the bedroom. She was still trying to regain her balance when the door slammed and he came over to snatch her again. "I've tried to be gentle with you, Zar. I really have."

Using his clamp on her neck, he bent her over the end of the bed and wrenched up her dress. Tearing away the fabric he found concealing her, he rubbed the length of his fingers through the seam of her until she relaxed enough that the digits could wheedle their way inside.

Curling and straightening the two fingers he had working her lust, he kept stirring them until she was panting. "You're wet already," he snapped, withdrawing his hand from her, he brought it to her lips. "What does that taste like?"

Still bent over under the force of his hand on the back of her neck, she parted her lips and he rammed his fingers through her teeth. "Suck," he demanded and she did. "You know what that is? That's a dirty, horny girl. You could've gotten yourself killed tonight and that got you off!"

Twisting her head away to empty her mouth, she gasped. "I was never in danger."

"You think those fuckers wouldn't have taken you out?"

"They might have tried," she panted. "But they never would've succeeded."

"Tough girl, are you?" he sneered, tracing his fingertips around her mouth. "You couldn't take guys like that on."

"You could," she spat out, groping to the side until her palm hit his torso. "You would never have let them hurt me."

"So sure of yourself?"

"So sure of you," she said, massaging the hard muscle under her hand. "It's such a turn on to have you out there, watching me. You held my life tonight. The only one who could've hurt me, was you."

Swiping her hand away, he curled down around her. She arched her ass into the ridge of his erection, but he ignored that act to growl in her ear. "The night isn't over yet."

With his grip tightening, she was crushed further down causing her to fight for breath. The quest for oxygen distracted her so much that she missed the unbuckling of his belt. The next thing she knew, he was fucking her.

"You want to get rough with bad boys? Then they're gonna get rough with you. You're not tough," he said, pulling out and slamming into her. "You're so fucking wet. You been thinking about my cock all night? Huh? Is this what you wanted? To be bent over and fucked like the naughty girl you are? You want me to teach you a lesson about what you're best at?"

Withdrawing, he pulled her upright only to then force her onto her knees. Her mouth was already open before he had a hold of himself. But he shoved himself into her mouth and maintained his previous pace. "That pretty pout is good for this right here. I'm gonna fuck your face until you learn that the only time you open it is for this. My cock. You hear me?"

She nodded and he pulled out to haul her up again as she was gasping. The ferocity of his glare made her grab for his arm to steady herself but he whipped her around to bend her over and went back to screwing her. This time he kept her hips and yanked them back every time he surged forward.

"Fucking this pussy deep is the only way to teach you," he panted out. "You think of this when you go waving my fucking assets around to other guys. The only man you open your legs for is me. Let that tight cunt worship my cock and she better be dripping before you disappoint my dick."

"Oh, God," she called. The deep-seated ache in her loins exploded in a tight pinch that made her scream out in a frenzy of pleasure and pain.

This man, this incredible man, owned her exactly as she wanted to be owned. He knew how to play with her, how to take what he wanted. And the pleasure his body got from hers was what got her off.

"That's all you want," he said, taking himself all the way back so the throbbing head of his cock was stretching the threshold of her body. "This is what you wanted, isn't it, Zar? You wanted my cock to take what it wanted. You wanted me to fill that cunt. I get whatever I want from you, don't I? You'll let me use you for this, as a fuck toy, because you're desperate to please me… is that right?"

"Oh, God, yes, Brodie," she said, trying to wriggle back to take more of him. But he held steady and grabbed the back of her neck to keep her face down and immobile.

"You're for me," he said, squeezing.

While still pinning her, his other hand stroked its way from her ass to her hip and kept on going until he was toying with her vulva. He rubbed, pinched, and flicked her clit in a series of erratic maneuvers that actually made a sob of bliss come from between her parted lips. Her eyes closed and she tried to concentrate on resisting the abyss of orgasm. He'd already taken her over that precipice while he had achieved no climax himself.

"I'm not wearing a rubber," he said, bowing his body over hers. "Is your pussy hungry, baby?"

"Mm-hmm," she managed to whimper while working her hips against his digits and trying to consume more of his cock in her center.

He tutted. "Naughty girl, you know how wrong it is to let a guy screw you without a rubber? You are a horny girl. You'll let me do whatever I want." The heat of his breath left her hair and he stood again. Taking his hand from her center, he seized her hips and yanked her back to sink himself into her again.

Using that tight grip that bit deeper with every pull, he forced her back as he came forward and each smack of their colliding bodies grew louder and louder. On another climax, she screamed again and came up enough to reach back for his wrist. He shook her off to deliver a final series of punishing pounds and then he cursed out a sentence filled with her name.

It was while they stood together like this that she realized he had actually come inside her. Smiling, she flopped forward over the end rail of the bed and let herself grow boneless.

"You're something else, Bandini," he said and pulled himself out of her body.

From his tone, she couldn't tell if he was being serious, joking, or scolding her. Making herself stand and turn, she chose to go with the second, although he was already turning away, so she couldn't find any translation of his tone in his features.

"I'm your something else," she said, trying to play it cool but realizing that some part of her not-so-subconscious was trying again to gain his view on the validity of their relationship.

Spinning around, he swiped her jaw and pulled her so close that her nose brushed his. "You don't get it, do you?" he snarled. "I don't do holidays and birthdays. I don't do, 'Good morning, sweetheart' and 'hi, honey, how was your day at the office?' I don't do nice and sweet and... I've been trying to be something I'm not with you and it fucking tears me apart to know that if you got a glimpse of the real darkness in me, you'd run screaming for your life."

"Don't you get it?" she said, pulling his hand down from her face and linking their fingers as she moved in close. "It's because of the darkness that I want you. I want that danger and that excitement. All my life I've craved the adventure you take for granted."

Shaking his head, he was unconvinced. "You want it because it's new and you think it's a game."

She wouldn't be patronized. "In that conference room tonight, with those men, those dangerous men, I knew the stakes. I knew there was a chance that they could hurt me. But I wasn't afraid... I could feel you with me, in me, and you gave me the strength to stand tall without fear."

His anger grew dominant in the face of what he perceived to be her naivety. But she got it, understood his fear, and it wasn't enough to scare her away. "One day I might not be there and if you wade into this life now, because of me—"

"We're all headed for that one day," she said, quoting him.

Grazing her cheekbone with his fingertips, he bowed to get closer. "I won't let you give up your life for this, for us."

On a rush of anger, she slapped his hand away from her skin. "If you don't want me, then say it. Don't hide behind feigned virtue."

Retreating, he spun away while rubbing the back of his head. Zara waited for him to cut her down. When he about-faced, he let his hand fall. "Of course I fucking want it! But I'm a selfish prick who takes what he wants. You need to look out for you and I am not what's best for you!"

"Maybe being with you is my selfish too," she said.

After the adrenaline of the night and the hype of their lovemaking, this was no time to be making decisions about forever because she was terrified he would veto any chance of a future.

Taking his tee shirt up over her head, she stripped out of it and her dress, before crawling onto the bed and under the covers. Brodie didn't join her. He leaned on the bedframe she'd been bent over during their fuck-bout.

"We've got the morning-after pill downstairs in the—"

Ceasing her smoothing of the covers, she frowned at him. "Why would you have—"

Showing her a palm to quiet her, he shook his head. "It's part of Zave's kit."

"And that should mean something to me?"

"He and Thad, they… it doesn't matter. But Thad's a doctor, so he keeps us stocked with all the meds we need."

Maybe when she was further embedded in the group she would understand what Zave and Thad were into. So far, all she knew was that Zave had a custom-built suite for locking up women and that he worked with Thad who kept the morning-after pill stocked with the first aid kit.

"I'm on the pill," she said, sitting up to lean against the grand headboard.

With his hands spread wide, he supported his weight on the footboard of the bed. "You stopped taking the pill three months ago."

"And your investigation skills become even more intrusive," she said, but was actually impressed by how far reaching their detective work went and how accurate it was. "I had a couple of wheels left and I've already called my doctor for a refill."

"Why did you do that?" he asked.

She would've thought that was self-explanatory but she wasn't averse to letting her actions speak for her. Pulling back the comforter, she kicked it down out of the way and stretched her nude body across the bed. "Because I wanted to be ready for whatever you might throw at me," she said, wearing a smile.

Zara hadn't known what would happen between them, but she knew that boundaries were something they would stretch with each other. Having him inside her blurred her lines of sense and being able to cut loose with him was the most exhilarating experience of her life.

NINETEEN

SUNDAY WASN'T A DAY off at McCormack Manor. Zara woke up alone and after getting lost, stumbling into a couple of guest bedrooms and a poolroom, she managed to find her way to the kitchen. There she found a stream of coffee. Art kept filling her with the caffeine while teaching her how to make his spaghetti sauce that he was preparing in bulk to freeze.

Art took her down a set of stone stairs at the back of the kitchen behind a false wall, which led to a walk-in freezer, a wine cellar, and a dry store. Art loved to educate her about the house and Brodie's history and it was obvious that he doted on his nephew.

Once Tuck was finished working out with Brodie, he swept her into the basement to give her a brief tutorial of the security system and took her fingerprints to give her clearance for the house, cars, and systems. Art ventured in to give them coffee and food before taking her on a tour of the building. There were parts of the house they didn't venture into and he made no comment on those, so she didn't ask.

Tuck and Art were entertaining her in the control room when Brodie stuck his head in the door and demanded that she go with him. She expected sex and was surprised when he took her to a shooting range located on the premises and proceeded to teach her how to shoot. Much as she tried to flirt, he was all business… at least until she asked him to prove his own skills, at which point she dropped to her knees. If blowing a guy while he was unloading an automatic weapon didn't show trust, she didn't know what would.

Waking up on Monday, she panicked when she fumbled on the bedside and read Brodie's watch. Zara was already in the shower before she remembered that she didn't have a job anymore.

Reality fatigued her, but she couldn't go back to bed. Dressing in her outfit from Saturday night, she found Art in the kitchen, and wasn't surprised to find him already pouring coffee for her when she walked in.

"Thank you," she said, taking the mug to slurp down the bitter roast that warmed her insides.

"All dressed up, are you leaving us?" Art asked.

"I have to find a job," she said, bending to snag her shoes from the floor behind the couch where they'd been since Saturday night. Taking them and her coffee around to the coffee table, she sat down, gulped more coffee, then put it down to bend and put her feet into her shoes.

Art came over, drying his hands, and sat in the armchair at the head of the coffee table. "Tuck and me were talking," Art said. Curving both hands around her mug, she raised her brows in question as she drank. "You're a good girl, smart, capable, and social, which is something the rest of us lack."

"You do okay," she said, finishing off the coffee then rising to head for the pot. "And you make great coffee."

Filling her cup, she drank some more. "You're young and beautiful, I'm not much of an inside man at my age."

Art wasn't disguising his flattery and she was suspicious about what he was trying to sweet talk her into. "I'm sure you've seduced your share of assets," she said, coming over to sit on the couch again, feigning ignorance to his fawning because she wasn't sure she wanted to know what he wanted.

But it turned out that Art got to the point fast. "We

want you on the inside, permanently," Art said and she put the cup on the table because she couldn't refuse to acknowledge his request, she had to face it.

Art might want her on the inside, maybe Tuck did too. But that Brodie wasn't the one asking her made her suspicious. "What does Brodie say to that?" she asked, wondering if Brodie knew Art was talking to her about this. "You're talking about future missions." Which was something Brodie had been reticent to commit to.

He softened. "You're good for him," Art said and moved over to sit with her on the couch to take her hand. This was about more than the job; Art was asking her to be with Brodie. "Do you like staying here?"

Withdrawing her hand, she squirmed. "Don't pressure him," she whispered.

"I'm not press—"

Her night in Brodie's bed, talking to him and being with him, affirmed her desire. She wanted to pursue their connection, to further explore her growing feelings. But Brodie was accustomed to being an island, so it would take time to ease him into a relationship, she would have to be patient, which meant Art would have to be patient too.

"If you push him, I'll lose him," she admitted, glancing over her shoulder toward the door in fear that they'd be caught having this clandestine conversation.

Art wasn't as nervous. "I know how to handle my nephew," he said. "And I don't want to pressure you, 'cause I don't want him to lose you… I don't want you to underestimate how important you are, do you hear me?"

Acknowledging, and appreciating, his honesty, she nodded. "I hear you," she muttered with a blush of discomfort.

He caught her hand again. "He needs you and he does care—"

"Art," she said then the door opened and Brodie came in with Tuck. The two of them stopped talking to examine her and Art as their sudden silence was conspicuous.

"All good?" Tuck asked, but she didn't look at him as he examined everyone.

"Okay," she said, grabbing another swig of coffee. "I have to go." Leaping up from the couch, she bypassed the furniture and snagged the back of Brodie's neck to drag him down for a kiss.

He caught her waist and hauled her close. "Where you going?"

"I'm going home," she said, balling her fists on his chest. "I have to get changed, haven't you noticed that I've been wearing your clothes all weekend?"

"No," he said, leaving her to go to Tuck, who was retrieving water from the fridge.

Spinning to rest her hands on the back of the couch, Zara addressed Art, but spoke so everyone could hear. "The guy who is supposed to have super keen awareness doesn't notice when I'm wearing clothes that are ten sizes too big for me."

Art smiled, but Brodie replied when he and Tuck were on their way back to the couch. "That's because whenever I look at you, I see you naked. Your clothes don't matter a fuck to me."

Brodie rested his body weight on her, so she was forced against the back of the couch. Tuck lowered himself into the armchair.

"Women are weird about that shit, man," Tuck said. "You should probably let her pick up a few things."

With the permission of the other men granted, Brodie grabbed the back of her neck and pulled her in the direction of the exit. "Then I guess we're going out. I've got shit to do anyway."

Guiding her down to the garage, he pulled out the helmets for the bike then went to a second cabinet to retrieve a firearm. She had no idea what shit he had to do that involved a gun, but she was quickly learning not to ask the obvious questions because they often led to obvious answers like that he intended to harm someone.

He got on the bike and pulled her on behind him then handed over a helmet. "What should I say if the cops ever come to question me about what it is that you do?" she asked.

"We have cyanide capsules for that eventuality," he

said. "Remind me to get you one when we get back."

Holding the helmet in front of her, ready to pull it on, she gazed down into the abyss inside it. "Oh my God," she said.

"I'm kidding," he said and rose to kick the bike into action. "If I go to jail one day, I go to jail… It'll boost my street cred."

She pulled on her helmet only seconds before he fired out of the garage. Being mixed up with men who lived on the wrong side of the law could never end well, but that didn't put her off. The longer she hung around with them, the greater her chance of being pulled in and getting herself into trouble. They might exist in a gray area, but these were the good guys, and she was proud to be a part of this team.

***

BRODIE LEFT HER at her apartment without any promises of returning. Zara wasn't worried. Their paths never diverged for long and sure enough after less than an hour of being back at home there was a knock on her front door.

With a smile, she shook her head and left the dinner table where she'd been sitting with her computer and crossed to open the door.

"You chose not to pick—" But her words stopped when she saw Grant McCormack on her doorstep instead of Brodie. "Grant, hi."

"Hello, Zara. Can I come in?" Grant asked, standing as tall as ever, yet wearing a more humble expression than she'd ever seen him wear.

Hurrying back a step, she widened the gap to allow him inside. "Sure," she said, hoping that someone at the manor was watching the camera and would prevent Brodie from coming back, or that Brodie would take a while to do whatever he was doing, so he wouldn't walk in on this encounter.

"What can I do for you?" she asked, directing him into the kitchen. "I wasn't expecting to see you, well… ever."

"I came to offer you your job back. I hoped this

morning when I came in that I would see you… that maybe…"

"That I had changed my mind?" she asked, pouring each of them a coffee then leading him to the dining table, where she closed her laptop and sat down. "You're right. I was angry on Saturday night… but you have to see this situation from my perspective."

"I do," he said, taking the seat beside hers and lunging forward to scoop her hand into his. "But I also know you didn't do anything rash after we parted ways."

"Like going to the police?" she asked and almost wanted to tell him that he had his younger brother to thank for that. "I thought about it…"

"Why didn't you go?" he asked, flattening his hand on top of hers on the table. "Was it because you thought that maybe… that you started to understand my position?"

Not even close, but she couldn't tell him that. If she had been brought into this by Grant having never met Brodie, then she would be freaking out. She would have gone to the cops and probably been laughed out of the room because as Brodie said, she had no proof and no witnesses.

Grant would never admit the truth. She had no way to track down Sutcliffe and the others. If Tuck was having trouble collecting evidence with his superior skills, the cops would have no chance of finding anything.

By this point in proceedings, she would have been collecting bottled water and canned food and probably buying herself a plot of land in Montana to dig herself a bunker. But meeting Brodie had changed her outlook on so much and she could see now that being close to Grant was their ticket.

Gaining inside information had been her purpose since the beginning of this. The opportunity that Grant was presenting her with served the means of the Kindred and that was where her loyalty was now. Lying to Grant was still difficult, being honest and respectful toward him was an engrained behavior, one that she'd have to shirk if she wanted to foil the deal.

Trying to think like a Kindred member rather than a CI employee, she projected empathy as best she could. "I understand what you're trying to do," she said, sweeping her hand around to bring it closer to her chest trying to be subtle about putting a barrier between them. "But I don't trust the men you're associating with. They're dangerous... I could tell that just by standing in front of them. Are you sure you want to deal with these men?"

"I have little choice," Grant said. "This is not something that I... I'm no criminal mastermind."

Taking the opportunity to separate herself from him, she slid her hand out from under his and sat back, bringing her coffee mug to her chest at the same time. "Well, at least you admit that what you're doing is illegal. I'm glad to hear that you understand that."

His disposition unfurled with optimistic honesty. "I want to be a part of something bigger, a part of history."

Ensuring not to be too hasty about insinuating herself back into his confidence, she questioned him. "And you think you can right all the wrongs of the world with a device made to kill people?"

"The right people," he said, shuffling his chair closer to hers. "You have to understand that with this device we can pinpoint its use."

He was bullshitting her. Stating the truth, she tilted her head. "You were talking about hospitals and airports."

"That's grandstanding," he said, waving a blithe hand and leaning in with his eyes intent on hers. "This could be placed in a room where we know certain people are going to be. With the press of a button, those people could be infected and they'd carry that disease back to their nests... It's like killing termites or ants. Have you seen how exterminators work?"

"But you're talking about people," she said. "And you can't guarantee that there won't be civilian casualties."

"In war, there is always collateral damage."

"This isn't war, you're talking about execution."

Something in his dismissive air reminded her of Brodie. They could both talk about the potential for suffering with a complete disconnection to their humanity. Brodie she could understand, he'd taken dozens of lives. As far as she knew, Grant was a stuffed shirt who had never seen any form of combat firsthand. "And haven't governments been assassinating hostiles for decades? For centuries? We can be a part of that."

Now she had a chance to harvest information that could prove useful to the Kindred. "What do you know about these men you're dealing with? How did you get connected with them?"

"Kahlil is a senior member of a petrochemical company that CI has done business with for years," Grant said. "It was during a conversation with him at a conference years ago that I learned of the existence of this device. Apparently, his superior had been in negotiations with my father regarding it. During those negotiations, my father ordered the destruction of all documentation and shut down the project. I brought it up with Frank and he had a reaction which intrigued me."

His story pretty much matched Brodie's, so she was confident they were both telling the truth. But it was interesting that while the older brother had seen opportunity, the younger one had seen only danger. Brodie respected his father's reticence while Grant resented it. "If your father wanted no one to have this device, then how can you disrespect his memory—"

"I have reason to believe he died for this device."

Brodie had made similar overtures about his parents' boating accident not actually being an accident. "Your parents died in your father's boat."

"It didn't explode on its own," Grant said. "Certain people believed my father was the barrier to selling the device. If he was out of the picture, they thought they would get their hands on it."

It turned out that those people were right, it had just taken longer than they might have hoped. "Shouldn't that be enough to put you off selling it?"

Shaking his head, Grant's lip curled and disgust consumed his expression. "I think it's ridiculous that he left us, that he jeopardized all our lives for a product. He and my mother paid the ultimate price. Yet I'm the one left picking up the pieces. I had to live my life without their guidance and with the notion that my father prioritized misguided ideals over his own family..." His anger was visceral, he'd been carrying it for so long and yet it lurked just under the surface of his preened exterior.

"Grant—"

"I want to prove that his sacrifice was for nothing, that all it took was a different point of view," he said with an insistence that clouded his decorum. "I can sell this item and make the world a better place. He lacked vision, but I can conceive of a future where CI leads the way in eradicating threats to our fundamental freedoms."

"And then you'll prove that you're a better man than him, is that it?"

"You think this is about pride?" he asked, leaping up out of his chair. "Maybe it is, maybe it's about pride in myself and my ability. Pride that my father should have displayed. He could have made the negotiations work and if he had, he would be here."

"So you're punishing him," she said, putting her mug down and resting her elbows on the table. "You're never going to get even with him, Grant, he's dead. You want to punish him because you're angry, because you're hurting, and I guess all those emotions were stirred up again when you lost Frank last year."

"My motives are irrelevant," he said, putting a stop to her analysis and resuming his starched company stance. "I want you to come back to CI, to return to your previous role. We will never have to discuss this again."

Pretending to consider this, she left her coffee and rose to move toward him. "With the knowledge that I have, I'm already complicit in whatever happens." There was no avoiding her role in this charade. Grant wanted to sell Game Time and the Kindred still didn't know where it was. They had to know when the exchange was happening so they could put a stop to it.

"You have no need to fear criminal prosecution," Grant said. "I've ensured that we will be insulated."

She didn't doubt his skill when it came to writing up

contracts. No doubt they had been written in language that implied CI was selling the device for sanctioned medical use, but she knew its intended purpose and she knew that Grant knew it too.

Spending the weekend with Brodie at the manor had given her time to process what had happened on Saturday night. She was still scared for her own safety but was under Brodie's protection. Without her inside at CI, near Grant, there was a chance the Kindred could be ignorant to the successful bidder's identity and miss the exchange. They had only gotten as far as they had because she had been able to do research and report back.

The Kindred still needed someone watching Grant who had access to the information they needed to save lives. When she thought about it in terms of the potential loss of life, she saw that she had no choice and had to take the opportunity that Grant was presenting to her.

"I'll come back," she said, implying that she was unsure of her decision. "But I want to be a part of these negotiations. I want to see this through to the end. You need someone to be your conscience. If I'm not happy, I'm going to make sure you know it. I don't want you to do anything you'll regret."

"Zara," he murmured, closing the final stretch of space to place a hand on her cheek. "It would be my honor to have you at my side. But you need to know, this is going to happen and I won't let anyone get in my way."

Smiling, she didn't shrink in the face of his veiled threat. "You're not going to let anyone hurt me and you certainly couldn't hurt me yourself. Why don't you let me look through the paperwork you have, maybe seeing the files on this device and your progress, will help me to understand."

His chin rose a fraction, but he was distracted by his fingers, which began to stroke her face. "I'll let you see everything that I have... because I trust you, Zara. And you're right, I couldn't hurt you... just as I believe you wouldn't hurt me. You won't go to the authorities because if you were going to, you would've done it already."

That was true in a physical sense. But she was

betraying him and he'd be hurt when that was revealed. "Did you go to Quebec yesterday?" He nodded. "What did you find?"

"Not much of anything," he said, still caressing her face.

"There are forensic teams you could hire to look into what happened if—"

"I've thought about it. The circle of people who know about this deal is small. The circle of people who know and are capable of murder and destruction is smaller. I don't need forensic technicians to tell me who did this."

"You know who it was?" she asked and his simple smile made her shiver. "Who?"

"My brother."

Shock hit her so hard that she had to spin away from him to hide her reaction. Returning to the table, she sat down and hooked her fingers into the handle of her mug to bring it close to her body so she could use it as a shield again, only this time it was an emotional one. "Your brother," she whispered.

Grant came back to the table too and brought his chair to hers before he sat down. "You weren't expecting me to say that."

"No," she said with a slight shake of her head. "I can honestly say that I wasn't expecting you to say that." Captivated by the liquid in her mug, she tried to think of how to handle this development. Brodie had promised he wasn't culpable for the destruction in Quebec.

His forearm aligned with hers and he linked their fingers, palm to palm. "I don't talk about him that much… I don't talk about him at all," Grant said while they both fixated on their joined hands. The heat of guilt made her want to silence him and confess all. But her selfish curiosity wanted to know if Grant would reveal more of the relationship that Brodie kept so secret. "I haven't seen him for years. Once in a while I hear a whisper and I figure he's still out there, doing what he does."

"Which is what?" she asked, maintaining their physical link, trying not to hasten her anxious breathing.

"My father was ruled by my mother. Anything she

wanted, she got. He was deeply in love with her. After they passed, we found out that it was my mother's wish for us to live with our Uncle Arthur, her brother. I had never gotten along with the man. He was wild and intense," he said, toying with her fingers. "But my younger brother was seduced by the adventures our uncle sold. Frank fought for me and I was left under his guardianship. My brother and uncle left the country and it was a number of years before they came back. By then, Brodie was as wild as my uncle, wilder even. He carried so much anger and I thought I understood it. I thought it was about losing our parents."

"But it wasn't?"

Grant breathed into the nothingness between their flush bodies and she was sure the chance for an answer had passed… then he spoke. "I think he blamed me for not going with them. I was in college by then. I was getting my MBA and was running CI almost full time as well. I was polished and educated, Brodie was… unrecognizable to me. I tried to talk to him, but we had nothing in common. We argued and… Well, Brodie had forgotten how to articulate, he was like an animal. Arthur ruined him."

Torn between her want to comfort and her want to question, Zara remained still. "Your paths diverged."

"Yes, exactly," he said, sliding his fingers deeper between hers.

Unable to decide if Grant's accusation was true or not, she had to figure out how he'd concluded that Brodie was the perpetrator. "Why would you think he would return now? Or attack you this way?"

"Because he's become something of a vigilante. Frank and Art kept in vague touch through the years, though they kept that a secret and Frank only made the occasional cryptic reference about it. But from my understanding, Brodie learned to hunt, to fight and to kill. He's worked in many countries and thwarted many plots. I don't know the precise details, but I got the general sense that Frank was proud of Brodie's life. Although I would presume it was a vicarious pleasure because Frank was as straight-laced as they come."

She wondered if Art told Brodie about what Frank

felt or if Brodie too was kept in the dark about the particulars of those conversations. "Wait a minute," she said, having another thought. "Is that why you're so determined to do this? So determined to make some grand mark on the world, because you believe Brodie is doing that?"

His thought about his answer before he gave it. "His life is an adventure and I would be lying if I told you I didn't wonder what my life would've been like if I had gone with Art." Parting their linked digits, he got up to stroll toward her window. "I look at my life and realize I've done everything as I was supposed to, everything that was expected of me. Growing up, the other kids called me 'Saint,' because I never misbehaved. I've always toed the line."

"That's a good thing... isn't it?" Before Brodie, Zara had been a company gal too, but he had opened her eyes and changed her perspective on the way she lived her life.

"I think I thought that if I was the best then I could somehow match up to my father and make him proud. But he's gone and I know now that I don't want to be like him. I don't want to live my life buttoned up and righteous. He prioritized his ethics over the family he was supposed to love."

Twisting in her chair to observe him looking out of her window, she rested her cheek on her hand. Grant craved adventure, just like she did for so long. It made her realize just how easy it was for a person to conceal the truth of their desires

"So you want to be like Brodie?" she asked. "You think his life is so great?"

"I think he does what he wants and doesn't live his life constrained by rules. He does the daring things that others won't. Art turned him into a killer. But he's a hero as well."

"Whose hero?" she asked. Pushing up out of her chair, she gave into the urge to go to his side and offer comfort. But with the idea that her lover could have deceived her rattling around in her mind, she needed some comfort of her own. Hurt and angry, she wanted to give Brodie the benefit of the doubt. She wouldn't be appeased until she heard the truth. By the strength of Grant's certainty, somehow she doubted Brodie would be making the denial she wanted to hear. "You're building him up as this idol and yet you've admitted you haven't seen him for years. He could be a villain. He could be a criminal out to serve his own agenda. Don't do this because you're trying to match all your brother's deeds with one swing. You don't know the man he is."

Slipping a hand onto his arm, she received no response to her proximity. "I know he's the type of man with the means to find our secret plant. I know he works with a band of highly skilled men. And I know he would rather stop me than see me succeed. Just as I know he would rather use covert means than to face me man to man," he said, clasping his hands at his back and staring out of her window, probably straight into the camera that fed into Brodie's control room.

"You're sure it's him?" she asked.

Brodie had been out of town on a job when she'd gone over there on Friday night. He'd asserted it wasn't in Quebec. When he and Art were making plans for the operation here, he'd said the job would be done on Saturday and they'd led her to believe he had a mission on Saturday before Grant called and revealed what had happened in Canada. If Brodie had done it, then he'd known the truth before Grant's call to her, he'd known it all through the first night they spent together.

"You're right about one thing, Zara. He is a ruthless man without conscience. I know that from our last meeting fifteen years ago. He lies and he deceives. There is nothing and no one who can sway him from his objectives. He would seduce and discard a person once they have served their purpose. He's incapable of love. Incapable of delivering truth. Art trained him to follow orders and to treat people as temporary assets to be used as long as they serve his needs. Brodie will be whatever he needs to be in order to complete his task and then he vanishes into the night without so much as glancing back."

Chilled by the idea that Grant could be describing her position, she began to try to figure out why Brodie was not more determined to find and interrogate the person or persons responsible for the attack in Quebec. The stories she had been told of their tight knit group and never letting anyone inside could be just that: stories. Tuck and Art were soldiers in arms and the three could convince a person of anything. Like that she was the only woman to have set foot in the house for twenty years.

Pondering this, she noted that Grant had turned to look at her. "If we're going, we should probably get back to the office," she said, having faced as many truths as she could handle for the moment. "You have meetings this afternoon."

"Yes, of course, you're right," he said, shaking off his tumultuous mood.

"But we could have dinner," she said, in need of time to process this before she probed further. "Once I've had a chance to look over the paperwork, I would appreciate an opportunity for us to talk about it."

"Excellent idea," he said, curling a hand around the ball of her shoulder. "Will you let me drive you to the office? I can bring you back after we've eaten."

Her smile was her assent. After a quick change of clothes, Grant took her to work. She would have questions for her boss after reading his notes, but the questions she had for her boyfriend were stacking up too, only she had no idea when she might have a chance to ask them.

TWENTY

WORKING AT CI gave her a grounding that she needed. Grant let her peruse the Game Time paperwork, but as soon as she opened the file, she wished she hadn't. She was only wading deeper into a mess she couldn't clean up. Distracting herself with the documents, Zara chose not to focus on the unknowns, but to focus instead on learning as much as she could.

Dinner with Grant filled in plenty of blanks about uses and applications. But she still speculated about the motives of each prospective buyer while her mind kept wandering back to the possibility of Brodie's involvement in Quebec. Grant seemed adamant that Brodie was the only one who would be motivated to do such a thing.

Internally admitting that she'd been swept into the fantasy of Brodie, she chastised herself for being drawn into the allure of his mystery and letting it blind her. Brodie was dangerous, but his capability wasn't what upset her. It was the lie. Zara had bought into his assurances that she was a part of the team, now she had to face the possibility they'd been dishonest with her.

Grant took her home after their meal. Although he made a not-so-discreet play to invite himself up for coffee, she declined and excused herself, blaming the hectic day. When she got inside, she dumped her purse on the kitchen table, took the combs out of her hair, and began to strip on her way to her bedroom.

What she really wanted was a shower and a good shake, but she was too tired to follow through. So she went into the bedroom, crawled onto the bed, and closed her eyes with hope that the new day would bring clarity.

"Still walking into the room buck naked without turning on the light, baby."

He called her "baby" except his words weren't familiar. She might be face down on her own bed and have no impetus to cover herself up, but he sounded like the stranger who had surprised her on the night Tim was shot.

With a ball of dread tangled in her gut, she had to ask him straight, without teasing or games confusing the matter. "Did you do it?" she asked, rolling onto her back and taking the blanket with her to protect her modesty, which seemed sort of ridiculous given all they'd done with each other.

"One night with Saint Grant and he's got you back under his spell. He's good."

Sitting up in the middle of the bed, she crossed her legs and held the sheet to her chest. "And how good are you?" she asked, anger enflamed her. "It didn't take you long to turn me… and you still haven't answered the question. Did you do it? Did you kill the men at the Quebec plant?"

"Yeah," he drawled without urgency or apology. "I did."

Falling back onto the bed, she stared at the ceiling, letting her hands lose themselves in her hair. "I knew it," she murmured. "As soon as he said it… It just made sense."

"Saint Grant, there to save you from the big, bad wolf."

Bolting upright, she tucked in the sheet so that she could gesture with her hands. "You can't turn this around on him. This was all you. When was it? The night of the out-of-town job, right? The night you promised me you weren't up there."

"I didn't promise nothing. You'd already threatened to tell Grant. We had to get it done before you could rat us out to your boss. Tuck and I left soon as Art and me left here."

"I didn't go to Grant! I didn't—"

He flew up out of the chair. "We didn't know that then, did we? If there's one thing you should learn from me, it's to never make empty threats!"

"But false promises are okay?" she asked, rearing up high on her knees to mirror his position at the end of her bed. "You said I was one of the team!"

"We don't take chances when—"

"What was the one bullet thing about? If you killed them then how did you come back with one bullet? How did you kill three men without firing your only shot?"

Looming closer, he held up both hands. "With my bare hands," he growled and she didn't like the shadows in his blank eyes.

"Why would you do that?" she asked, wondering if he got some sort of perverse pleasure from an up close kill that he wouldn't get with a rifle from far away.

"I never leave evidence unless I have to," he said. "Those guys weren't expecting us. We were in and out, but the device was already gone. We walked in on them destroying evidence."

"All this time," she whispered, understanding that his discrete manner and tone signified the end of the trust she'd thought they were building. "You went in there and killed those men—"

"Back to the murderer bullshit, are we, sweetheart?" he asked, strolling into the light of the window to project his silhouette over her on the bed as she sank back to sit on her heels.

"I'm not pissed that you killed them," she said, without the ability to garner anger in the face of such heavy sorrow. "I'm upset that you lied. All this time and you didn't trust me. Even after all I told you, after Saturday night and letting me play a part... asking me to risk my life, to put my life in your hands, and all the time it was a lie."

Her heart pumped so hard that her throat began to close. She wanted to cry for her stupidity and at his for wrecking what could have been a good thing for both of them. "I told you on the first night that getting you into bed was the easiest way to get information from you," he said. "I was honest."

"No, you weren't," she said, shaking her head, her focus sunk to the mattress. "If you cared about me at all and were any kind of man... You would be honest now that you've been caught. You had a chance to tell me the truth and you chose to lie to me."

"It was only a matter of time before this went to shit," he said, sliding his hands into his jeans pockets. "So now you know... that's it."

"I guess so," she said, exhausted, but wondering why neither of them sounded particularly angry.

He was so deadpan, she couldn't work out how he really felt about the conclusion of their association or if he'd invested his heart in their union at all. "Maybe next time you won't be so quick to trust a guy with your secrets or to open your legs for him."

"Oh thanks, you're such a pal," she said, more snide than angry.

He went toward the door and she expected him to leave, but he paused just before he went out. "Were you gonna tell me?" he asked.

"Tell you what?"

Pivoting, he stalked to the side of the bed. "You give me shit for lying and then you do it yourself."

"I'm not lying," she said. Locating her rage, she levered back onto her knees and walked on them to the side of the bed where he stood. "I have always been honest with you!"

"Honest about what you were doing today?" he sneered, wearing only disgust. Moving in until his knees touched the mattress, his trained aloofness slipped. It was his anger that made him violate her personal space, using his height to tower over her.

"I know enough about your practice to know that you knew I was with Grant at CI," she said, refusing to be intimidated by him. "Don't even pretend to be jealous about dinner. You couldn't care less about me, so who I eat with is nothing to you!"

His voice dropped an octave, and the rumble made her swallow and reconsider her emboldened position, though not enough to make her back down. "I don't give a fuck that you ate with him, I give a fuck what you spent your afternoon doing. He gave you free access to everything we've been trying to get our hands on for months."

The files. He was pissed about Game Time, not about her lack of devotion to him. "Yeah, because Grant trusts me! I understand how that kind of fidelity is alien to you."

Rage made him raise his voice and her guts trembled in reaction to his threatening conduct. "You bounce from one guy to the next! What did I tell you about allegiances in this game? How could you think I'd trust you? I trust my men, men who have proved themselves capable! Not some chick in a skirt who doesn't have the cojones to hold her nerve. What could you possibly offer to the Kindred except a pair of tits for the guys to shake during down time!"

Lashing out at her, showing his anger, verified that his control had gone. For the first time, she got a sense that his need to hurt her demonstrated how his heart had gotten involved, except it was clear to her that he resented her for making him vulnerable.

"This is not a game! And you can't ask for my allegiance to remain true to you when I find out you've been lying to me all along. That day was the first that we started working together and it was a lie! All along, everything was a lie!" The fact that he'd fallen for her, if he had, was incidental, and an accident, and Brodie didn't like to be out of control.

Tracing a curled finger down her cheek, he bowed closer to her mouth but she recoiled. "Breaks your fucking heart, doesn't it, baby?"

"Get your filthy hands off me," she grumbled and reared up to shove him. "Get out of my apartment! I mean it, get lost and don't you dare come back here, Brodie. Stay the fuck away from me!"

He scoffed in a mix of amusement and disgust. "I've taken all I need from you," he said, sauntering backwards and opening his hands at his sides. "Why the fuck would I come back?"

Turning his back on her was so easy for him. Zara couldn't so easily switch herself off. She wanted to scream, wanted to throw something at his thick head to see if she could make a dent. But she wouldn't give him the satisfaction.

Listening to him leave, as she had that first night they met, she breathed into the silence and then flipped herself over to bury her face in her pillow. Oblivion was a long way away. As much as she tried to deafen and blind herself in the sanctuary of her pillow, Zara knew it was a fool's errand.

She needed freedom from her thoughts, freedom from her stupidity, and freedom from her analytical mind that wanted to poke holes in every genuine moment she thought she'd shared with Brodie.

Visions of him were imprinted on the inside of her eyelids. There was no escaping him. But it wasn't shame or anger that dominated her mood. The sickness in her gut and the weight in her chest was heartache. There was no other term for it.

TWENTY-ONE

A WEEK WENT BY and life returned to normal. Attending meetings with Grant in CI and taking her work home with her was so normal that it was bizarre. When staring at herself in the mirror, Zara questioned whether or not Brodie, the terrorists, and the device had ever actually been a part of her life or if she'd imagined the whole thing.

The two-week deadline would be up on the next Saturday. So if she expected to affect the decision she would have to find a way to bring up Game Time with Grant soon.

After working much later than she should have in her home office, Zara took a shower. While drying her hair, she anticipated getting some sleep and waking up with a better perspective. She left her bedroom to turn off the lights and check the door only to discover that someone had already killed the lights in the living room.

Brodie usually commandeered her in her bedroom. The figure she noticed sitting on her couch now was more respectful of her private space, but still hadn't gone to the trouble of knocking and requesting entry as a normal person would. But Art did teach Brodie everything he knew, so she shouldn't be surprised that the uncle took such liberties too.

"Well," she said, pausing to take a deep breath. "I

expected one of you sooner than this."

"Rave?"

She folded her arms. "No, I figured it would be you or Swift. I know how stubborn Rave is and he made his feelings about coming back pretty clear."

"The boy is an idiot," Art said, shifting forward and resting his elbows on his knees to clasp his hands.

"An idiot who you trained," she said, maintaining her distance. "What do you want?"

In many ways, Art's betrayal was more hurtful than Brodie's. He portrayed himself as a sage individual who knew the ways of the world. Yet he had chosen to talk to her about his nephew and Zara's relationship as though he was trying to form a bond with her and she'd bought it.

At least when Brodie spoke of their relationship, he was vague and non-committal, seemingly, as confused as she was about what they had and where it was going.

"I told him to tell you the truth from the start."

"At the start you wanted him to dump me," she said, not relenting her high ground. "Or was that a lie too? Was it all an elaborate ruse to make me believe I meant more to you all than I actually did?"

Even saying the words made her feel foolish because she had believed it, every word of it. Before meeting Brodie, she would never have classified herself as a desperate woman. Looking back she would assert herself as being happy without a man, she didn't need a relationship for validation.

But she had been desperate for adventure and being a part of the Kindred for however short a time, made her feel that she was a part of something bigger. Grant's inferiority complex was starting to make sense to her.

"At the beginning I didn't know what you were. I knew he was caught up in you, infatuated. But after that first night, when we had dinner in here together, I knew it was something more. Because even in spite of your shitty mood, you glowed when Rave came near you."

"Then you left here and decided to start bullshitting me. Sorry if I don't buy your story." Art got up and she glanced toward the window then sidestepped to move herself into the shadow of one of her columns. "Is he out there?" she asked.

Art stopped and glanced at the window. "What?"

"Is Rave out there? Setup beside one of your illegal cameras ready to tie up loose ends? Where is it you're supposed to have me stand so he can get a clean shot?"

"He wouldn't," Art said, losing his contrition and replacing it with anger. "He's in love with you. I don't think he's ever been in love. He could no more hurt you than you could take a shot at him."

She narrowed her eyes. "I wouldn't test your theory at this point. Are they watching? Are they in your ear? What is it you want me to say? I'm not interested in helping any of you anymore. You've lied to me for so long—"

"The only lie was that we weren't responsible for Quebec. Everything else was genuine."

Except she had no reason to trust him. "Why would you lie when—"

"Because when you first heard us discussing the plans, you panicked and had a fit then claimed you were going to tell Grant. Rave, Swift, and me, we've been doing this a long time and we're of one mind when it comes to what needs to be done. We made a decision and we acted. Rave said he didn't want to burden you, but I... Calling him a murderer like you did—"

"Yeah, I know, it cut him deep. You said that already."

She could be facetious and try in vain to hold onto her anger but the truth was that she had more anger toward herself than toward anyone else. She wanted to believe Art's declaration of Brodie's love, despite all the evidence contradicting that assertion, and that gullibility just took her back to self-loathing.

"It did," Art said.

"Tell me why you're here tonight. Going over the past serves no purpose. It's just a waste of your time and mine... and the time of your buddies listening in."

"No one's listening in," he said, opening his hands wide enough to spread his jacket to show that he had no weapons. No weapons didn't mean he was alone. He was part of a flock who hunted and hid together. Each knew the other and she'd been taught that their priority mission was to watch each other's backs, so it was doubtful that he was out alone.

"I don't believe you," she said, dropping a shoulder to the column and rolling her eyes upward. "Just say your piece."

He gnashed his teeth before snapping. "Rave told us not to come near you again. Told us you were unviable and off-limits. It's unlike him to be so protective of—"

"Rave," she muttered and peered at him as she shifted her weight to her feet again. "Why do you keep using his alias? You don't trust me? You think I'm recording—"

"When we're away from base, we always use aliases," Art said, closing the space left between them while lowering his volume. "Anyone could be listening."

Making eye contact helped her find clarity. "You've bugged this place too, you or him. You heard my conversation with Grant?"

"More is the point that Rave heard it," Art whispered and she brought a hand up to cover her dry mouth. "You said some hurtful things, girlie."

"I was making a point," she exhaled. "If your goal tonight is to make me feel sorry for him then you're underestimating how your audience feels." Fortifying her confidence, she wouldn't let her compassion overwhelm her sense.

But he wasn't deterred by her statement. "I know exactly how you feel, girlie, and you're as sunk as he is. You won't get me to believe anything else. You're not angry with him, you're hurt, and that's why you're acting this way. Your pride was bruised when you thought maybe he used you. Your heart too."

Vicious in her retort, she wanted to scream. "He did use me," she said, setting her jaw and averting her attention.

With a curled finger on her cheekbone, he brought her eyes back to his. "He loves you, button. Trust me on that."

When she blinked two tears skittered down her face and on an inhale, she lifted her head out of his reach and stepped back. The touch was too reminiscent of Brodie's, and she didn't need that now, not when Art's words were so close to home.

"You should go," she said. "I need you to leave now or I'll have to call the authorities."

"You wouldn't call them on either of my boys," Art said, not doing the gentlemanly thing and departing at her request.

"Please," she said, pleading with him to let this be.

"Our mutual friend went to great lengths to conceal his association with you. While we had regular access to your apartment, we scanned the environment to preclude any chance of being surveyed. But make no mistake, not all threats were neutralized. I came here to let you know there may be others who know you're playing both sides."

"Playing…" Believing it was his intention to rile her, Zara chose not to rise to the bait. "You can be assured that my loyalty is not split. I have been with Grant McCormack for half a decade and he has never endangered me."

"Never?" he asked, proceeding his word with a gentle nod. "Like putting you in a room with terrorists?"

"He wasn't the one with the gun pointed at my head," she said, letting her vehemence speak for itself. "I won't be drawn in by your kind anymore. I don't need advice. I don't need assistance. I need to be left alone."

She glared into his soft expression and tried to imagine how he had trained Brodie to kill. This man had two faces: one was kind and unthreatening but the other had the capability to cut down a man without a blink. The trick to surviving the Kindred's gauntlet was not to be drawn in by that first face.

Zara would only survive this ordeal by not blinking first. Taught by these men not to show weakness, she remained steadfast until Art retreated and eventually left her apartment.

Only when she was alone did she let herself sag. Though she hadn't admitted it to him, she was disturbed by the idea of being listened to in her own home. It had been bad enough to think people were watching her, to think of them hearing her as well was just too much. It was one violation too many.

Going into her bedroom, she got dressed and packed a bag. An interested party may follow or trace her location, but she would still be out of the web that was closing around her and for one night, that would have to be enough for her.

***

A NIGHT IN A HOTEL didn't settle her. Zara woke up at frequent intervals and had to remind herself that she wasn't at the manor.

Brodie had broken into her psyche and she'd come to expect him at her side or in her periphery at least. Getting over the treachery of his actual motivation for coming into her bed meant also accepting that she was now in a precarious situation without a safety net.

At work, this reality played itself over again in her mind until she resolved herself to do something about it. So marching into Grant's office without declaring herself, she was seated in the guest chair before he diverted his concentration away from his computer.

"I don't think you should do this."

Placing a hand on the lid of his laptop, he pushed it down, then locked his fingers together on top of the machine. "I have just sent an encrypted message to all parties. Sutcliffe was the successful bidder. His bid was actually the lowest, so you can be assured that this was not about the money."

Mortified that she hadn't had any influence over the progression, the inevitability of what would happen next took her fear to a new level. "I thought you were going to consult with me," she said, having not expected him to have acted in such haste without due notice.

"I didn't want you to have the burden of this decision."

"The burden of being an accessory to mass murder? Is that what you meant? Because it's what we both are." Rising from her seat, she leaned over the desk. "Brodie wouldn't want this. He wouldn't want you to… to collaborate with these people. Please… he… you said that he killed the men in your lab… did you think about why he did that? Maybe it was a warning."

His eyes widened. "You think he was threatening me?" Grant asked, sounding more annoyed than intimidated and she could practically see his competitive hackles rising.

"No, I meant warning you that this isn't a good idea." As

much as she didn't want to give Brodie any points for personality, she did want to get through to Grant. "He could've come for you if he wanted to hurt you, to defeat or outmaneuver you. He could have attacked you, but he didn't. He tried to take away your opportunity to make this deal, to do harm. In effect, he intended to take away your ability to harm yourself." Stepping back from the desk, she sank back into her chair. "Maybe that's what he was trying to do."

Saving people from themselves seemed to be a specialty of Brodie McCormack's. The burden of living with complicity was heavy enough to slow a person. Art had told her that Brodie believed he'd lost his humanity, at least some of it, and Brodie had told her that he hid his darkness from her. With his deception followed by his rejection, he had saved her from him. Just like he'd tried to save Grant from making this deal.

"What do you know of his intentions?" Grant asked, dismissing her. "You don't know how coarse and uneducated he is. Brodie fights dirty and he has never intended to help me in his life. All he cares about is himself and winning."

Except if that were true, he'd have taken Grant out of the picture and coaxed her back into his bed for sport. But she had no way to convey that to Grant without betraying her own association with the brother Grant loathed.

"Delivery is to be made within the week," Grant said. "I'll need you to make plans to ensure the secrecy of the handover."

And after that statement, he opened his laptop and went back to work. She wasn't going to start an argument, because she could tell she wasn't getting through to him, but she had bought herself a clue as to who might.

TWENTY-TWO

GOING HOME and waiting until after dark, Zara lit all the candles in her blue window and waited for him to come to her. She was ready for his taunting and happy to accept the humiliation of extending this invitation, which he would no doubt try to amplify when he showed up. Mocking her request for his presence with any insistence would be more telling than he realized.

If he did show up after declaring to no longer need her, he'd be revealing the truth of his addiction and confirming Art's assertion. If he didn't show up, it would prove that he really did have no further use for her and that he wanted nothing more to do with her.

After cleaning up and putting away her laundry, Zara came into the living room to find that the candles had been extinguished. Glancing left and right, she sought out friend or foe.

"This better be good," his deep voice drawled.

Whirling around, she found him leaning against the far wall near her bookcases. It was dark, just as he liked it, and he had shown up himself rather than electing to send an agent on his behalf. He was here. She wondered if her signal had given him the excuse he needed to return to her.

"I know how to end this," she said, keeping things business as that seemed to be the demeanor he was projecting.

"And you want a gold star for figuring that out?"

"I need your help." His laugh was short and bassy but distinctive in its lack of sincerity. "I don't care if you disappear from my life after this. I've figured it out and you are the only one with the power to prevent this… talk to your brother."

"That's your masterplan," he asked, pushing off the wall. "You think me walking into Saint Grant's apartment is gonna change his mind about this?"

"You've underestimated your influence over him. We all did. I think losing Frank set this chain of events in motion. He was the last family that Grant had. Being alone made him reflect on his life and it changed everything for him. He had nothing left to lose and nothing to stand up for either."

"What the fuck has that got to do with me?" Brodie asked, coming nearer.

Maintaining her posture, she vowed not to lose her nerve. "He envies your life, covets it maybe. He believes he made a mistake going with Frank as opposed to going with Art. He wants the adventure that you take for granted."

He stopped moving and slowly his head began to shake as a whisper of a disbelieving laugh left his lips. "Man," he murmured. "You two are made for each other."

Setting her jaw, she tried to remember that she was asking for help and so shouldn't argue with him. "You don't—"

"Grant's life exists in a light I've never had," he snarled and his own resentment bled into his words. "Constantly living life under threat is not an adventure. Scrutiny leads to paranoia. I can't walk in the open. I exist in the shadows and anyone who tries to venture into my darkness has to abandon the world. Living life alone is not as easy as people like you think."

He'd stopped walking toward her, so she took the final steps to erase the remaining distance. Anger began to fade. Her heart belonged to this man and although he sounded resentful, like he hated the world and welcomed his isolation, she could hear pain in his words. Calling him here was meant to be for the greater good, she wanted to tell him how he might be able to reach Grant and prevent any atrocity from taking place.

But she wasn't as good at detaching herself and she couldn't view Brodie as a business associate. She had lain naked with this man and shared secrets. She'd entrusted her life to him. Maybe Art was right when he said Brodie hadn't wanted to burden her with the truth of Quebec. Either that or Brodie was trying to maintain barriers because he was afraid of what loving her might do to him.

His and Art's relationship was deep but masculine, Brodie wasn't used to the softness of a woman. Zara had feared what would become of their relationship after the mission, but it wasn't even over and she was losing him already. Someone had to open themselves, to take the risk, and she knew now that person would have to be her.

"I know you've lived your life in pain. That the things you've had to do to help others have changed the essence of your humanity. You've faced struggles that—"

She tried to take her hands to his face, but he ducked back and sidestepped to avoid her, probably because physical contact may make him forget he was supposed to snub her. He walked away, but she spoke again, keeping her back to him to give him the moment of privacy he probably needed in the face of what he'd just admitted.

"Grant needs to hear it and he needs to hear it from you," she said. "He needs to understand what your life has been and what this decision will mean for his humanity."

"His humanity is his problem," he mumbled.

Turning around, she could only see his back because he stood in front of her couch, facing the kitchen. "This isn't about salvaging your relationship with your brother," she said, calculating her words and their pace. "You have the ability to change Grant's mind-set and to end this before anyone gets seriously hurt."

"People have already died."

He was being deliberately obtuse, but she wouldn't fall into the trap of combatting his attitude because it would only end in them fighting. She had to get through to him, had to make him see that she wasn't like the others, that she understood him and understood Grant.

The only way she could affect change and divert the possible disaster Game Time would cause, was by making these two men stand toe-to-toe.

Crossing to him, she kept her tone soft. "I meant anyone innocent… You're strong, stronger than the rest of us. I know you can get through to him… you got through to me."

Splaying her hands on his shoulder blades, she tried to soothe him. But the contact made his head whip a quarter turn so he could spit his words over his shoulder. "I used you."

"I don't believe that anymore," she murmured, skimming her hands up, over his shoulders, she curled her fingers around the collar of his jacket and eased the leather back to coax him out of it.

Twisting enough to drop the garment onto the coffee table behind them, she rested her lips on his tee shirt covered back and dragged her nails up to his neck because she knew how that action stimulated them both. Art's words and her own experience with this man helped her to see through the bullshit. He was as scared as she was and if she let him push her away then she would lose him for good.

Handing over trust meant handing over a piece of yourself and being vulnerable. Letting yourself love someone meant standing naked on a battlefield, waiting for your love to protect and liberate you. If that person chose not to love you back, chose not to fight at your side, the only possible outcome was annihilation.

Zara wasn't ready to admit defeat. "You told me to leave my mark on you," she murmured into him, hoping she could provoke him into getting physical with her because it was the first step to breaking down his barriers. Except he didn't respond, she kissed and caressed, but he stayed there rigid in front of her. "Please," Her voice cracked under the burden of what she was trying to accomplish. "Don't hide from me anymore, beau."

Maybe it was his attempt to get away from her, but he inched away from her and turned to sit on the couch. But his new position presented her an opportunity. She might make a fool of herself by being so unguarded, but she took the risk of ridicule and raised her skirt to straddle his lap.

Stroking her hands up his chest, over the mass of his shoulders and past his neck onto his face, she tried to get lower to make him look at her but he turned his head left when she went right and vice versa.

"Look at me, beau, please. I'm right here. I need you," she whispered, caressing his jaw because she needed to breakthrough.

She didn't want him to hold her at a distance anymore. She needed to feel that they were in this together because without him, she wasn't strong enough to fight alone. Brodie was used to fighting alone, and she wanted to prove to him that he didn't have to be isolated anymore. She had told him that she wanted his darkness, that she didn't want him to change. She had to trust him because if she didn't, he would never trust her.

He gritted his teeth. "I lied to you," he said as if that and his feigned anger was enough to break their bond. He wouldn't let himself look beyond her chest and that was enough to prove her suspicion about his lack of conviction.

Splaying her vertical fingers on his cheeks as her smile formed, she wasn't angry with him anymore. "I know," she breathed out. "You're a complete bastard most of the time. But I can't lose you."

His gaze leaped to hers and the new angle gave her the chance to plunder his mouth. Trying to break through his barriers, she whimpered her joy on his entwining tongue when his hands spread on her back.

Still open mouthed in desperate need of validation, she matched the strength of his heavy tongue as it slid over hers. With her weight balanced on his hands and forearms, he lifted and twisted to put her on her back and squash her into the cushion of the couch with his weight.

After a long period of indulgence, their mouths parted and when she expected him to start stripping her or taking liberties with other parts of her body, he didn't. Reading his scowl, she took her hands from his torso to his face and tried to figure out why he hesitated.

"We can't do this out here," she said, deciphering why they'd stalled. "Because of the cameras. We could draw the curtains or move through to the bedroom—"

"Swallow," he grumbled and her contentment ceded to confusion.

"Excuse me?"

"You never asked where Raven came from," he said. "A 'Raven' is a KGB term for an agent whose job it is to sexually compromise a female in order to complete their mission."

In want of another kiss, she tried to respond in an appropriate way. "That's apt I guess," she said, curious about why he'd brought that up now.

"A 'Swallow' is what they call a female agent tasked in the same way."

"You're giving me my own code name?" she asked and kept on stroking him.

When she tried to take another kiss, he resisted. "You're playing me," he said. "I'm sort of impressed by how you've taken to the job. It takes some people years to adapt to deception like this. I was right. You are a natural."

Offended by his implication, the heat of arousal that had permeated her began to grow frosty. "You think I'm using sex to—"

"You need me, don't you?" he snarled. "Isn't that what you said? I'm an easy mark, you've done me before, so it's not like you're in for any surprises."

"This is a surprise," she said, thrusting her hands onto his chest to try to move him, except he didn't retreat. "I was trying to get through to you. I'm so sick of the bullshit. Not everything has a sordid, secret meaning. I get that you're used to people trying to manipulate you. But all I wanted to do was show you that I forgive you for lying to me and to give you a chance to trust me."

Cruel satisfaction crept onto his expression. Figuring her out—as he thought he had—made him feel superior. His entitled hand opened on her waist and snaked up over her breast.

"I'm not gonna talk to him. You won't get what you want," Brodie said. "I have been doing this way longer than you have. I know how to play dirty."

Dampening her hurt and feelings of dejection caused by his belief that she could be so callous, Zara returned to her previous confidence. He didn't have the same clarity about their relationship that she did. She knew how she felt about this man and wasn't ashamed of it. He was still playing his games. They were back to square one. She had to win his respect again and the only way to do that was to match his confidence.

Proving her conviction, she countered his statement. "If that were true, you wouldn't have told me that. If you thought I was going to use sex to coerce you into working for me then you'd have fucked me and then revealed your intention, or lack of it. What do you think will happen if you have sex with me? Are you scared you'll feel obligated to—"

"I'm obligated to no one except myself and I can do what the hell I like with your body," he snapped. "You'd have no way to stop me."

"Why would I?" she asked with full confidence that if she used their safe word he would stop. "I still want to be with you, I haven't closed the door."

Wriggling beneath him, she began to unbutton her shirt. Without patience, or perhaps in a show of dominance, he grabbed the material away from her and ripped the sides apart. Exposing her bra wasn't the point of the act. Proving her lack of fear and her intention to follow through, even if he didn't speak to Grant as she requested, was the point.

His hands got rougher as they groped her chest, but she wasn't going to wither, in fact, she arched herself into his fondling and let herself moan.

"I'm not gonna change my mind," he said, yanking the sleeve of her shirt and the strap of her bra down from her shoulder to bare one of her breasts. "I'll use your body then walk out of here and you won't see me again."

He ducked to suck her nipple hard. "You've said that before," she murmured, worming her fingers under his tee shirt when he rose up again.

His breathing was becoming as erratic as hers, and she was having trouble keeping still. "I don't care how many candles you light in the window," he said, bowing to nip her lower lip. "I won't be back. I won't help you. I won't do what you want me to. I work for myself. I don't care what you need."

But with the mass of him weighing her down, Zara was in increasing need of just one thing. To convey that, she parted her legs and tilted her hips up to grind herself against the stiff want growing behind his fly.

"Then why are you here? If you don't care about what I need, why did you come?"

Elevating his weight, he picked her up and turned her over to force her onto her belly. Hanging over the arm of her couch, her arms flailed in a reflex which sent the end table and lamp clattering to the floor leaving her with no way to hold herself up. Brodie was already ramming her skirt up out of his way and disposing of her underwear with one practiced tug.

With one leg kneeling on the couch, he pinned one of her legs to the backrest, while the other was on the floor pinned down with his foot on top of hers. Open to him, two of his long fingers plundered her first.

He fucked her hard and fast with those digits until she was lubed up enough for his cock to take what it wanted. She hissed when his hand slid away and he smacked her ass before she heard the unbuckling of his belt.

"This is as much love as you'll ever get from me," he growled and then the rounded summit of his dick slid between her folds.

Holding her breath while he forged his way into her, she pushed back and began to undulate her hips, trying to squirm and pull him deep into her.

Each long, abrupt thrust garnered the speed needed to get her to the finish line. Even when he withdrew, her body pulled him back in, sucking his shaft so far into her that the crest of his member met her cervix, making her cry out.

"You're addicted, beau," she panted as he fucked faster and faster. "You can't help yourself. You want me too much."

If all he wanted to do was use her for his own gain then there was no need for this. If they were being watched or listened to then this encounter was more likely to compromise them in harm not favor. Brodie knew that, he was smarter than she was when it came to this stuff, yet he'd done it anyway.

Driving into her, he pushed his dick deep, stretching and sating her insides while her hormones begged for more. "I'm here to teach you a fucking lesson," he hissed. "You let yourself be used by guys like me and your pussy is gonna see a lot of action. Guys will fuck anything that moves. It means nothing to me. You mean nothing. You've got a snug cunt, ripe for fucking, and you deserve everything you get if you keep asking to be punished. You think I'd say no to a fuck like this?"

Sweat made her clothes cling to her tingling skin. The vast room had been cold, but the heat of this encounter was already fogging the windows. "Like what?" she gasped, swaying her hips side to side and with him still within her, her walls massaged his shaft. "A fuck that feels so good?"

He spanked her hard. "Fucking an innocent little flower who's so idealistic that she really still believes I'm one of the good guys. You need to wisen up, baby. You stay this naive much longer, you'll never make it out of this alive."

He came out then plunged into her again. Taking her to the cusp of climax, he pushed in and pinned her hips down to collect her arms. Pulling them back, he made her shoulders concave and locked her wrists in one hand against his shoulder before taking the back of her neck to jerk her head up.

"You know we've got every second of this on tape. If you think about stepping out of line or compromising the Kindred, we'll make sure your precious Saint Grant gets his very own copy of it."

Maybe screwing her out here had been his plan all along if he wanted leverage to keep her quiet about her association with him. But blackmail only worked if a person wanted to keep something secret because they were ashamed.

Spitting her hair from her mouth, she smiled, though she knew he couldn't see her amusement. "I'm not threatened by the idea of our association becoming public," she said, wheezing out her words, and his grip loosened a fraction. "We concealed it while it was advantageous. You needed Grant to trust me and he does. He trusts me so much that I figured out his motivation. He's trying to live up to your example. You're the only one who can make him see sense. If the cost of my clarity is him finding out about us, then come to the office tomorrow and we'll screw right there on his desk."

For a second, he said nothing. "You've got a smart mouth, Bandini," he ground the words out of his hoarse throat.

Confident that she had impressed him, she tried not to crow. "All the better to blow you with," she said.

For half a minute, neither of them moved or spoke and Zara craved a glimpse of his expression, though she knew it was unlikely to betray much about his true thoughts. His mood became more explicit when he cursed into the night and spanked her before returning to his uniting of their bodies.

Still consumed by the intensity of their joining, each of his plunges into her wrought such friction that he conveyed his rage, though its cause could be any of a number of things that she couldn't fathom now. Orgasm ripped through her with such ferocity that her head came back in time with her riotous scream and she wished for the ability to touch him.

She had no time to go limp; he hauled her back and called out a stream of vulgar curses, which no longer made her flinch. When his balls were empty and her void filled with his load, he released her to hang over the arm of her couch. She listened to him fastening his jeans before she planted her palms on the arm and pushed herself up to sit.

Standing toward the other end of the couch, he said nothing while she gathered the edges of her shirt together.

"I won't visit him," Brodie said. "Your scheme didn't work."

"Yes, it did," she said, though she wouldn't have categorized her need to see him as a scheme. "I had to know if I could trust you, to know if you still cared." Taking her focus to the unlit candles, she exhaled. "If you didn't come, I knew that it was over. I didn't summon you here for sex, but that solidified the truth."

"The truth?"

She shrugged at her ponderings. "Maybe our lives are too

different. Maybe you lied to me to push me away or maybe you did it because you never trusted me." Lifting her hips to wiggle down her skirt, she let her shirt stay loose over her chest. "But you do care about me, Rave. Deny it all you want, but I know you do."

"I never got what Grant saw in you," he said, narrowing his eyes. "Over the last few years he's seemed more together, more grounded and once we started investigating you, Art suggested that maybe you were the reason because you were so responsibility motivated."

Curious, but oddly relaxed, she stayed loose. "Now what do you think?"

"I think if anyone's ideology has influenced him, it's not yours. Do you really think that this can end without innocent lives being taken? Those guys in that lab, the ones that Tuck and me executed. They died following Grant's orders. They were guilty of doing their jobs, they didn't ask questions, didn't know anything about Grant's plans. Why do you think he had different labs doing different things? The guys in Quebec had no idea what the Florida lab was doing. Grant is being covert because he knows that what he's doing is wrong."

Zara wasn't as naïve as Brodie was accusing her of being. She'd known the truth. She just hadn't wanted to face up to it. Grant was wrong and conspiring to commit murder on a mass scale. Brodie actually went out into the world and killed who needed to be killed without hesitation, regardless of who they were, their knowledge base or motivation.

"What's your point?"

Coming to her, he bent over her to grab her chin and wrench her head up. "You need to wise up. I am a cold-blooded killer. Sharpshooting might be my specialty, but I'm just as capable of cutting a man down up close. These hands," he said, holding up the one that didn't have a grip on her. "These hands that you have had all over your body, playing in your snatch, your hair, your mouth. The hands you have let smack your ass and squeeze your tits. Using the hands that you wish were dedicated to your pleasure, I've strangled men. I've cut them and snapped their necks. I've beaten men to death, while listening to them beg for their lives. Every man who gets the chance begs for fucking mercy. Do you want to know how many get it?"

Frustrated that he wouldn't admit what they had, she was losing her patience. "I know what you are," she said, whipping an arm up to bat his aside so she could surge to her feet. Her action forced him to straighten his spine, but that was all he did. He didn't move away, so her body was flush to his. "I don't want you to apologize. I don't need you to explain or to change. I'm not naïve, but you're blind."

Lunging down, he didn't retreat from her anger. He got up close, proving his physical superiority. "I'll use you every chance I get," he said, dragging his sneering eyes to her mouth. "I'm not a good guy who can save you. I'm a bad guy who doesn't want to be saved."

Except he did have some morals, some love. If he didn't, he'd have taken out Grant long ago and this whole problem could have gone away. Then there was his uncle. Brodie loved Art, they had been integral in each other's lives since Brodie's birth and Art had control, proving that Brodie wasn't quite the monster he portrayed himself as.

Searching for hope, she pleaded with him. "Why can't you accept that I don't want you to change?"

"So you'd be happy if I kept lying to you, every mission? Because I will. I don't lie because I have to, I lie because I'm good at it. I like keeping secrets because trust is a weakness and it takes a long time to earn it."

"You lied about Quebec to save me from carrying that burden and because you knew I had to face Grant without giving away the secret. And you probably doubted my poker face." Because she hadn't known how good or bad it was then either.

"Stop making excuses for me," he said, growing tense.

"I'm not, I…"

Bearing down, he squinted and lowered his voice to a murmur. "If I'm such a good guy, why did I never tell you that I was the one who killed Sutcliffe's nephew?"

"Tim," she exhaled and couldn't maintain her certainty any longer. "You shot him while he was kissing me."

"That's right, baby," he said and his sneer grew smug.

"You think I had to take him out then? I could've done it before he went into Purdy's or after he fell out of your bed."

"You were protecting me?" she asked, hazarding a guess as to why he chose that moment.

He scoffed. "It was sport. There was no need to kill him right then. But, bam, you should've seen the look on your face." Confronted by his amusement, her knees buckled and she dropped to the edge of the sofa and leaned forward to cover her mouth. "Scaring off Sutcliffe was the goal and we didn't want his kid recruiting you and giving him an edge. Didn't scare the man out of bidding. That was a bust. As for giving him an edge… I guess we'll have to wait and see who picks up the prize."

Brodie swept up his jacket and began to walk away. Zara cast off her shock and stood with a proud chin to project her fortitude. "Actually, a bidder has already won. All parties have been notified of Mr. McCormack's decision. Arrangements for the delivery of the device are being made as we speak."

He spun around and pinned his glare on her and now that his amusement was gone, it was her turn to be smug. "Who?" he croaked and the darkness around him seemed to progress beyond the metaphorical.

"That information is proprietary," she said and tried to keep her breathing even when he erased the gap between them. Slanting his weight forward, he drew a fingertip over one cheekbone and met her defiant eyes.

"Now you're getting it, baby," he whispered, reeking of a depraved sense of achievement. "Sex is free, trust costs lives."

Understanding his detachment, she tried her best to match it and met his eye with her head held high and her hands on her hips, devoid of all emotion. "You don't have to worry about me giving you either again," she said.

Two fatal events had occurred since she'd met him and she now knew they'd both been perpetrated by him without her knowledge or inclusion. He'd had ample opportunity to clue her in and he'd chosen not to. Bereft, Zara wondered what else he had hidden from her.

If he wasn't going to be forthcoming without her

pressuring him, then she wasn't either. Protecting herself had to be her priority. He'd made his own priorities obvious and she was nowhere near his list.

"I guess you should consider yourself excommunicated," he said, but grabbed her chin to push his mouth onto hers.

Shoving away from the intimate contact, she wiped a hand over her lips before folding her arms. "Ditto."

A sinister smile caught the corner of his mouth. He swept around, marched to her door, and departed. Loosening her body, she exhaled and looked skyward. The camera outside the window at her back would still be monitoring her so she didn't want to betray how shaken up she was.

Having given the audience enough of a show tonight, Zara took herself into the shower to rid their joining from her body. She had been so sure that his showing up would prove how much he cared for her. Instead, his presence had reinforced just how little she knew about him.

Feeling more alone than she had before, Zara went to bed without answers or reassurance and she had no plan for how she would face the next day.

TWENTY-THREE

IGNORING THE INEVITABLE wouldn't make it go away, despite how attractive that prospect was. So Zara made the time to go into Grant's office with her notebook just before lunch. She had to open a dialogue about Game Time, because even if she couldn't stop the handover, she had to be prepared for what she was going to face.

"I need to know where the device components are so I can have them brought to the meeting," she said when she stopped in front of his desk with her pen poised, ready to write.

With a smile, he disregarded what he'd been working on to give her his full attention. "Perfect timing," he said, bending in his chair to open a drawer from which he pulled two envelopes. The first he held up for her to take. "Reserve a rental van to be picked up at the date and time in here, use the alias and payment information that's in there."

The more information that she had, the more likely it was that she would be able to prevent disaster. By giving her such limited data, it became clear that without being explicit, Grant didn't want her to have too many of those details. Having kept the secret of his plan for so long, it was probably second nature by now for him to be cagey, but Zara was disappointed to lose the chance she'd thought she had.

Trying not to show her disappointment, her pen fell to her side, but she kept the smile on her face. "How long will we need it for?"

"No more than twenty-four hours," he said. Without closing the drawer he'd retrieved the envelopes from, he righted his chair at his desk before revealing a detail she had been trying to avoid. "Sunday is when it's happening."

"Sunday," she said, sliding the envelope into the back pouch of her notebook. It wouldn't have mattered if he said it was happening that night or next month, Zara wasn't sure she was ready for the pressure of subverting the plot single-handedly.

Grant nodded. "Yes, all the information you'll need is in that envelope. I'll deal with informing Sutcliffe."

Somewhere along the way, Zara had learned how to cast off shock with haste. Dealing with new information, processing it, and moving on were vital components to not missing important facts and to staying alive. "What is the other envelope?" she asked, eyeing the beige paper he was smoothing onto the desk surface.

He pushed it across the width of the desk with a single finger, and then smiled up at her as he locked his digits together. "That's your loyalty bonus."

"My what?" she asked, raising her eyes from the rectangle to his.

"Your loyalty bonus." His features seemed to dance in delight. "Go on, open it."

Putting her notebook and pen on the desk, she picked up the envelope that she dreaded opening. But his joy left her no option. He failed to contain his anticipation and that left her with a dragging anxiety, which she had to subdue.

So while focusing on the tucked in flap, she reassured herself that the envelope contained nothing sinister. Slipping the heavy triangular section of paper out of the vee holding it in place, she put a thumb inside to slide out the thin sheet inside.

She knew straight away that it was a check, the shape of the paper and its smooth printed surface were giveaway characteristics. Hesitating before she turned it over, Zara reminded herself to temper her reaction to whatever it read.

"A hundred thousand dollars?" she asked, not doing a great job of tempering anything.

"I know it's not much in light of what this deal will pay us," he said, returning to the open drawer to retrieve something else. "Catch."

On instinct, her hand leaped up to catch what he'd tossed as per his request. Uncurling her fingers, she saw the flash of a Mercedes sign and closed them again in a snap. Her horrified eyes shot to his, but he was grinning in triumph.

"It's in your new spot downstairs. Do you want to take it out for a spin? We could go somewhere for lunch."

Glancing from the hefty check to the car key, she exhaled and sank into the chair just behind her. "This is hush money," she murmured and the weight of sorrow brought tears to her eyes.

"No!" he declared. "Think of it as payment for services rendered. I would never have gotten through this final stretch of the deal without you."

That didn't make her feel any better. She felt like such a failure. Her best wasn't good enough. She couldn't dissuade him. She'd tried. And although she wasn't sure if terrorists signed contracts, Grant had already accepted an offer and wouldn't go back on his word now. Maybe if he had the strength of someone like Brodie on his side, he would have the confidence to stand up to a tyrant like Sutcliffe. Not too long ago, she'd have considered herself able to call on the Kindred for support. Not anymore.

The truth had finally sunk in. She was alone, not part of any team or a greater cause. Alone. Raising her focus, she found herself bolstered by the confidence and enthusiasm in Grant's eyes. She wasn't alone and never had been. Grant was a constant in her life. He'd been with her at the beginning, middle, and end of this escapade and his loyalty to her had never wavered.

Returning his smile, she folded the check and picked up her notebook to slide it in the back pouch. "Where do you want to eat?" she asked.

It was like her life had reset itself, being back here at CI going through the motions, her life was returning to its pre-Brodie routine. All that would change if this deal went through.

Leaping from his seat, Grant strode to the hat stand by the door where his jacket was hung up. "I know this great little place where it's private. I'll guide you. It's not on GPS. It's not open to the general public"—he swung his jacket around his head to drive his arms into the sleeves—"we're going to do amazing things together, Zar, amazing things."

Considering that this could be the beginning of her new career in enabling terrorists didn't make her feel any better about being part of this process. Dubious, she joined her boss beside the door and fought to maintain a grin. She should be grateful that he was spoiling her, but each dollar was soaked in blood.

Not long ago she'd thought herself capable of making a difference, but now she questioned every decision she'd made. Grant's methods were different from Brodie's but his intention was the same, to work to achieve safety for the vast population of this planet. Setting her mind on understanding Grant's position and his ultimate goal, she wasn't ready to give up.

Grant paused before opening the door to glance back at her. "I hope your boyfriend won't be upset about the amount of time we spend together. After the success of this deal, I can only imagine that our time in each other's company will increase. How is your relationship progressing?"

Relationship, that word was a joke. It implied fidelity and honesty. She'd had neither with Brodie. "It's not," she said. "We broke up."

"Oh," he said, loosening his fingers from the door handle and bringing himself around to face her.

"Yeah," she said, hoping he wouldn't ask for details.

"I'm sorry to hear that," he said, in such a way that he sounded anything but. "What went wrong?"

Wasn't that the question of the century? No doubt it was one she'd never get the full answer to. "Different values, I guess," she said. "He lied to me about a couple of important things."

"It's never wise to begin a relationship in a lie," he said, gathering her hands into his as he became more serious. "Did he hurt you?"

"Physically, no," she said, her gaze slid sideways. "But I thought we had something with the… potential to go all the way… I'd have done anything he asked me to."

Loving a guy like Brodie meant handing your life to him. She imagined that if he chose to love a woman he would make it his mission to safeguard the gift of her love and that no feat would be unachievable if his lover was in need.

But she wasn't that woman. Zara tried to give him a second chance, she tried to make amends. But Brodie didn't want that chance, wasn't interested in salvaging what they had. As it turned out, what they had was an illusion and no one could grasp and hold an apparition. The sickness in her heart still made breathing feel like a chore when she thought of him.

Grant's thumbs stroked over her skin. "If you want him taken care of…"

Letting her eyes creep up to his, she tried to figure out what her boss was implying. If Brodie had said that to her, she'd have known exactly what he meant. Grant's meaning was a bit more ambiguous. She could send Grant to Brodie to "take care of" him and hope that the brothers would reach an accord, which might prevent the transaction with Sutcliffe from taking place.

But she knew each of the men well enough to doubt that eventuality. Even if they spoke rather than tearing strips of flesh from each other, neither would surrender their position. Especially not in favor of something as tentative as good sense.

"Thank you, but I think it's best left as it is."

"Okay," he said, warming his expression with optimism. "Lunch will cheer you up, let's go."

Opening the door, Grant offered his arm. She took it and allowed him to escort her to her new vehicle. The rewards of the dark side were flashier, though Brodie claimed to be the one who resided in darkness.

Zara's thoughts returned to her former lover with such

frequency that she began to chastise herself for thinking of him. She was holding on to a dream of what she wanted him to be: hers. If she kept doing that, she would never let him go or find happiness.

Never thinking about him again was a tall order, but it was the only option available to her. She would never see Brodie again. She had no reason to. Her life, her future, depended on forgetting about her association with Raven.

Thinking of him by his alias rather than his birth name separated the enigma from the man. Brodie was the man she loved and Raven was the man who would never let him reciprocate her devotion.

TWENTY-FOUR

SUNDAY. All Grant had told her was that he would pick her up after three. It ended up being almost five by the time she got the call. When he did arrive, he was in the van she had hired for him. She got in, received a muted hello and then the journey was silent until she couldn't take it anymore.

He hadn't told her where they were going, but they were heading south in the direction of McCormack Manor, not that she assumed that was their destination. The sun would be setting in an hour or two and she didn't relish the idea of being alone in the dark under threat of attack.

"Is Sutcliffe coming alone?" she asked, speaking loud enough that her words could be heard over the pounding of her heartbeat.

"He's bringing two men," he said and added some reassurance before she could voice dismay. "They will only be there to load the device securely in the back of their vehicle for transport."

She and Grant were alone, without back-up, and she was disturbed by the idea of how they would hold up against two trained thugs. Grant was a novice in these sorts of dangerous, clandestine affairs, and she feared that he hadn't considered everything that could go wrong.

Despite the termination of their intimate relationship, she wanted to know that Raven was perched on a roof nearby with his crosshairs pinned to anyone who might do her harm. But there was no hope of that. No one knew they were here or that this meeting was happening.

Grant drove into an abandoned docking area past a broken fence and over a rusted chain that was strewn across the concrete road. The irony was, if it wasn't for all the condemned warehouses and the towering cranes, they would probably be able to see the McCormack peninsula from here. Her former sanctuary was just a couple of miles away.

Heading toward a mildew covered, gray corrugated building, she read the word "Atlas" in flaking faded paint on the half sign left hanging above the massive entrance. Driving inside, she saw nothing but bare concrete, rusted pipes and stairways, and stripped down machinery, long since forgotten. The roofless structure hadn't endured well in the sea air. The windows had rusted and there was broken glass scattered between the weeds growing through the cracks in the structure.

The setting was apt, yet unexpected because enough money was being exchanged today that this could have been done at the Ritz. The point of the location was secrecy. A deal could be done here, property exchanged, and there would be no evidence that the incident had ever happened.

But the isolation that reassured Sutcliffe and Grant only concerned her. Grant maneuvered the vehicle so that it was inside, parallel to the entrance, facing a sidewall, and then he cut the engine. They were here. It was time. She tried to be discreet about wiping the sweat from her palms onto her knee-length skirt, but her nerves were making her shake.

She didn't notice anyone else. But their position meant they'd have their backs to the space when they climbed out of the vehicle. Being vulnerable and unaware like that increased her agitation.

Grant got out first, showing no fear, but she wished she had the Kindred in her ear or a camera on her necklace for them to keep an eye on proceedings. Before she had a chance to leave the van, another engine rumbled and in Grant's side mirror was the reflection of an identical van pulling up beside theirs. Jumping out before the newcomers had a chance to alight their vehicle, Zara hurried to catch up with Grant who was opening the back of their van.

In the hold was a single metallic case and a brown box, less than a meter cubed. "That's the device?" she asked him.

"Eight of them plus a control grid," he said, stopping the doors at right angles to where they had been.

"Eight," she said, having not considered the potential of selling multiple devices. "How did you have eight assembled so quickly?"

Grant grinned and slapped his hands together, invigorated by their progress. "Are you kidding? Sutcliffe wanted twenty of them originally. This is the last of the stock brought down from Quebec before the accident. Two of them are prototype units, but we won't tell him that," he said, leaning in to talk from the corner of his mouth like this was all one big joke. "Speed was more important to him than quantity. Bids were per unit. He requested the lesser number because he knew we could deliver fast."

So that was why his bid had been accepted. Grant made it seem like the deal wasn't about money. In truth, he'd just wanted the deal done and the cash in his account. Sutcliffe's flexibility provided him the opportunity for that. The other bidders would have ordered more units, thus requiring Grant to create another Winter Chill plant.

"Why didn't you sell a lesser number to all three bidders?"

"Exclusivity makes a deal more lucrative" he said and gave her shoulder a squeeze. "You know that."

How he could be treating this like any other business deal still eluded her. Her ears were beginning to ring as her consciousness slid out of reality. This couldn't be happening. She shouldn't be standing here at Grant's side. She should have blown the lid off the deal. But without evidence to show authorities, they would never have taken her seriously. And Brodie had taught her about the consequences of threatening to reveal a plot. If Grant hadn't killed her then Sutcliffe or one of the others would have.

"The viruses are in the case," Grant said and handed her their vehicle keys.

"Viruses," she murmured.

"Yeah, they should be refrigerated, so we should probably haul ass."

His jubilation had to be nervous energy. She couldn't believe that he was actually excited about what was going to take place here. The other engine stopped and Grant headed away from her in the direction of the second vehicle to greet Sutcliffe.

Alone, she stared into the almost empty van. This was a nondescript vehicle, which was much larger than they needed. The only reason she could decipher for using such a mode of transport was to divert future investigators. If Game Time was unleashed, the authorities would eventually trace the device back to here. Using an unmarked van with misleading dimensions might delay them in finding out the truth.

In that split second, Zara imagined the news stories, how they would start with an unusual outbreak of some disease and then the panic that would ensue. No one would know the truth until it was too late and Zara dreaded the potential of what lay ahead.

And eight devices! Eight. One could lead to so much needless death, and Grant was handing over eight. They could be positioned to poison cities, to wipe out civilizations of people who didn't subscribe to the bearer's ideologies.

"Your fair woman, Miss. Bandini!"

Sutcliffe's voice made her spin around. Grant and his buyer were moving into the void of the warehouse a dozen feet from where she was at the back of the van. They were drinking something and it took her a minute to realize it was champagne. Horrified that they could be celebrating, her mouth fell open, but when two stocky figures appeared around the shielding van door, she stumbled back and forgot about the alcohol.

Sutcliffe chuckled and came over to hand her a flute, then took her arm to lead her over to Grant's position. "You have nothing to fear. They are my men," Sutcliffe said and raised his glass. "To good friends and deals done."

Grant and Sutcliffe's glasses met and then touched hers before they sipped, but she wasn't in the mood to rejoice, so she didn't drink.

Sutcliffe sipped from his flute a second time. "I am sure you will get to know my men very well. This deal will be the first of many. I can feel it. We're going to do great work together cleansing our polluted world."

He wasn't talking about chemical pollution. He meant people and the word 'cleanse' made her nauseous. Sutcliffe's goons spent time examining the van door and the packages without touching anything and she wondered what they were expecting to find.

"What are they doing?" she asked, observing their scrutiny.

"A formality," Sutcliffe said, shaking an aloft hand in a flippant gesture. "They're confirming everything is in order and that nothing has been rigged."

Rigged for what? Neither she nor Grant were explosive experts and if the packages went up in smoke, she and Grant would go right along with them. Glancing at a sheathed knife on the hip of one lackey, she gasped and the condensation on her champagne flute made the chalice slip out of her fingers.

The delicate glass shattered on the dirty concrete. But before she could apologize or even look up from the mess, one of Sutcliffe's men staggered, bounced off the truck door, and collapsed onto the floor. The second man fell less than a second later and she was still gawping at their prone forms when Sutcliffe and Grant leaped away and ran to the shadows beneath a crumbling stairway.

"Zara," Grant hissed. She whirled around to see him cowering beside Sutcliffe who was on the ground wearing a grimace and clutching his leg.

It didn't click to her what had happened until she looked back at the men sprawled on the ground behind the van. A dark, wet stain began to seep onto the floor beneath them and she got it. They were dead. Someone had shot them. A sniper. A sharpshooter…

Spinning on the spot, she fixated upward to the empty space where the roof had once been and examined the buildings overlooking theirs.

Brodie was out there.

She couldn't see him—couldn't see anything out of the ordinary—but she didn't need to. He was there. Somehow, he knew where they were, he was watching, and he'd mistaken her mishap for a signal, for the signal.

Grant began to snap his fingers to get her attention and found more volume. "Zara! Get over here!" he insisted.

"A sniper!" Sutcliffe wailed, rocking and rubbing his leg. "You double-crossing, good for nothing—"

"No," Grant said. The party was over and his delight was replaced by fear and anger. "No, this wasn't us."

When their eyes locked, Zara knew he was thinking of his brother. But Grant's annoyance seeped away as it was overtaken by an expression of shock. There in the doorway was another person, who moved around Sutcliffe's van and into the open space of the warehouse with his hands up to show that he had no weapon. Though if Brodie was still on a nearby roof, this man didn't need a weapon.

"Art," Grant exhaled.

She remained in place, swinging in the wind between her faction's shelter and the van containing the weapon. No one was paying her any attention and she had no fear that Brodie would put a bullet in her. If he'd wanted to, she'd have gone down after Sutcliffe's men.

In a cool, soothing tone, Art spoke clearly, almost like a professional negotiator. "We're here to resolve this. We're here to tell you no deal will be done today," Art said, maintaining his focus on Grant.

"You keep out of this! It's nothing to do with you," Grant barked. "You put him up there, didn't you? This was your doing! You came to ruin this!"

Unruffled, Art didn't react to Grant's anger, which was why he'd have come to make this connection as opposed to Brodie. Art knew how to keep his cool. Brodie was too volatile to make first contact in this kind of fraught scenario.

"We came to make you see sense and we're family, boy. Someone suggested talk might get through to you. You're not alone. You're one of us… you don't have to do this. Whatever the problem is, we'll figure it out as a family."

"One of you?" Grant said in a voice so dark she might almost have mistaken him for Brodie. "You came to talk me down because he could never bring himself to talk to me. I'm not one of you, he'd never let that happen."

"What the hell is this?" Sutcliffe asked, still sniveling.

Sutcliffe hadn't been hit, as far as she'd seen anyway, but his tone suggested that he was in pain. There was no time for her to speculate about his injuries and no one answered Sutcliffe's question because another person materialized in the entrance, and the whole room went into suspended animation.

Her shock wasn't exclusive; Grant had to feel it too. This was the last person who she ever would have expected to show himself. It was Brodie, tall and merciless in his dark jeans and leather jacket. There was no weapon in his hand, and he didn't spare her or the men he'd killed a glance.

Without a flicker of emotion, he went to Art's side, and then moved a few steps further, stopping only when he was about equidistance from her in relation to Grant. She was right in the middle of the two brothers, but Grant was the sole aim of Brodie's focus.

"You're one dumb motherfucker, Saint," Brodie said in that husky snarl that her body immediately reacted to as though they were alone in his dark bedroom. "You think this shit was what you needed to do to get my attention?"

No one could mistake how mad he was, or how hard he was working to dampen and control the rage that radiated through him. The fury that vibrated his form could have seen them all dead. But he remained aloof and maintained his empty expression.

"Is that—"

"Can it, Sutcliffe," Brodie snapped when Albert Sutcliffe thought to talk. "This is a family matter."

"The Raven," Sutcliffe's said in a distant tone, making it clear that her once-upon-a-time-lover had a reputation that preceded him or previous business with the Brit.

"Yes, I suppose I should make the introductions," Grant said. "Zara this is my younger brother and my uncle. These are the men responsible for the destruction of our Quebec plant and the men working there. The men responsible for delaying our business, Albert."

Art might have looked at her but Brodie didn't. His laser precise focus stuck on Grant and Sutcliffe who were the principal threats in the room. She knew Brodie was working, but she wanted him to look at her so she could read, or at least try to read his intentions.

Was he here because it was her suggestion? Had their last couple of encounters been masks for his true feelings? Had he meant to protect her against getting involved with his darkness and way of life? Or was this him trying in a last ditch attempt to obstruct a deal that would otherwise force him to kill his own brother?

"If you do this, I'll have to act," Brodie said, offering no apology or explanation. This wasn't exactly what she'd meant by saying the brothers should talk. Making threats wouldn't soften Grant. It would make him push back, daring Brodie to follow through, which if he was pushed hard enough, he would.

"You're too late," Grant said, his voice full of triumph. "It's done, the device, the virus; it's all right there in the van. The money has been transferred. The deal is done."

"No, it's not," Brodie said. "Me and my crew are gonna drive that van right out of here. We've been waiting for this. You loaded it all up for the taking."

"No, I'm taking it out of there, Sutcliffe will load it into his van and then he'll be gone and you'll have failed."

Brodie began to move and when she glanced back, she saw that Grant was on a similar trajectory toward the van. Tightening her fist, jagged metal dug into her palm, reminding her that she had possession of the vehicle key.

So dashing forth, Zara made a beeline to get there first. Leaping over the dead men, she slammed the doors then turned her back on the vehicle while fumbling to find the lock button. Once she did, the lights flashed and she spread her arms out on the back doors she'd just locked.

Brodie and Grant had stopped less than eight feet from her, Grant to the left, Brodie to the right.

"Zar, what are you doing?" Grant asked. "Give me the

key and we'll load up Sutcliffe's truck. We don't need anyone's help. We'll do it ourselves. We're an amazing team."

After his address, she looked at Brodie with a heavy heart expecting a similar appeal. But as her breathing slowed and her soul screamed for avowal, he said nothing.

She'd run over here before considering how she wanted this situation to play out. Glancing from one brother to the other, she tried to think of a way out that would make them all happy. She wanted them to talk, to bond, to put their differences aside and move forward together. But as she examined them now, she was struck by their stark differences.

Brodie was aware, muscular, and lithe. Grant was shorter, polished, and less weathered. They had a different expression set on their features, which marked their different life experiences. The darkness made Brodie cynical, harsh, and angry. While Grant's privilege made him feel entitled, eminent, and optimistic.

"Give me the keys, Zara," Grant said with a sterner edge and raised a hand when he stepped toward her.

"You go one inch closer to her and I'll snap your neck on principle," Brodie said and his anger had become aggravated in a way that made her look twice at him.

Brodie pinned the evil eye on his brother for more than a few seconds, but eventually his attention drew around to her and he lifted his palm.

Grant glanced back and scoffed. "She's not going to give you the keys. She thinks that she's protecting me, she doesn't understand that you won't hurt me."

With his eyes locked on her, Brodie spoke to his brother. "She knows what I'm capable of. She watched me kill these men here, watched me kill that bastard's nephew too, and she knows priority one."

That the Kindred always watched each other's backs, she guessed that meant even if they were in a fight. But this was more than that, she wasn't one of them anymore at least she hadn't thought she was. Losing herself in Brodie's gaze, she begged for direction, for answers, for some kind of assurance.

"What are you talking about?" Grant griped. "She doesn't know your damn priorities. I don't know your damned priorities. Why don't you stay the hell out of what doesn't concern you!"

Brodie didn't respond to Grant's fit, he just moved forward until he was in line with his brother, though they remained eight feet apart.

"I'm right there with you, baby," Brodie murmured in the same tone he'd used in the earpiece the night of the Grand incident.

Taking a tiny sharp breath, she didn't exhale before she spoke. "How do I know that?" she whispered.

"You know it," Brodie soothed. "You were right about everything."

She wanted him to mean it, wanted him to want her, but she couldn't trust him in this perilous setup. "You're telling me that because it's what I want to hear," she said, more aware of his tactics now and less inclined to be gullible.

"Maybe I am," he said. "But how do you want this to end?"

She didn't want it to end with Sutcliffe getting the device, which was what Grant wanted. The Kindred were here to stop this, meaning she wasn't alone in her quest to subvert the deal anymore. Brodie could topple this. He'd already killed two men for the cause. He was more capable than she was and whatever the state of their personal relationship, he had the ability to achieve their united ends.

"Why do you think I'm here now?" he asked and the sound of his voice reminded her to breathe. "This is what you wanted."

Brodie could have shot Grant and Sutcliffe. If he'd wanted to get rid of her, he could have put a bullet in her as well. But he was here, talking to his brother, at her request, because she had told him he could break through to Grant. Brodie had chosen to do things her way rather than to take the easier option and kill all the players.

Exasperated, Grant was losing his cool. "What the hell is going on?" he demanded. "Give me the damn keys, Zara, now."

Brodie didn't ask for them but did elevate his hand further. She had to make a choice. Grant: her boss and constant. Or Brodie: her brooding ex with trust issues. Glancing her apology at Grant, she closed her eyes and tossed the key to Brodie. Betraying Grant broke her heart and his dismay was evident in his features, making her feel even more villainous.

"Atta girl," Brodie said and winked at her before he twisted and tossed the keys across the room to Art.

He took a step in her direction. A gunshot razed the air, forcing everyone into a crouch. Seeking out the shooter, they settled on Sutcliffe who was hobbling out of the shadows, dragging an injured leg as he hopped on the other. She couldn't see blood anywhere on him, but he could have injured his limb as he leaped to the floor out of Brodie's visual field.

Terrified about the possibilities now that a firearm was part of the equation, she returned to her state of panic. Seeking a way out, she noticed that while everyone fixated on Sutcliffe, Brodie was slowly moving, not toward the shooter as she might have expected him to, but toward her.

"This has been a setup," Sutcliffe exclaimed and fired off to the side again. "I want what I came for." Zara assumed Sutcliffe must have stashed the gun here before arriving or secreted it on his person because she hadn't seen it before.

Switching the gun between his hands, Sutcliffe kept it outstretched in their direction as he shuffled toward his van. Art crossed to get in his way and Sutcliffe swung the gun around to point it at the man in his path.

With Sutcliffe distracted, Grant took his chance to rush over to the back of the van beside her.

Brodie maintained his concentration on the action but was close enough to whisper over his shoulder. "Where's the Sig?" he asked.

Her thoughts pounced to the gun he had given her for protection. "In my purse, in the cab," she said, wincing against the growl he flashed back at her.

"Next lesson, readiness," he hissed.

"You brought a gun?" Grant asked, but she was given no chance to reply. "Where did you get a gun?"

"Shut up, Saint," Brodie snapped at his brother. "What

the fuck were you thinking bringing her here?"

It was nice that Brodie was being protective, but she wanted to point out that at least she'd brought a weapon. Grant was defenseless. Based upon that, she was more suited to this kind of gig than her boss was.

Grant's frown betrayed that he was definitely not pleased to have his brother passing judgment on him. "What's it to you? How do you two even know each other?"

"Biblically."

"Oh my God," she exhaled, rolling her eyes to the heavens, but couldn't deny it was the truth.

Brodie grabbed her arm and shoved her. "Get to the front, stay behind the wheels," he said, tussling her.

"No." Trying to push back, she put up poor resistance against his strength. "Beau—"

"No," he said, his eyes flared and he was already shaking his head. "This is not a fucking debate. Go."

She didn't want to, but glanced over to see that Sutcliffe was getting closer to Art. The standoff wouldn't last much longer. Slipping between the vans, she peeped out when Brodie moved in Art's direction. Grant came into the space with her, moving deeper into safety.

Sutcliffe was upon Art now, but Art didn't blink or move away. "Drop the gun and we'll let you go, Albert," Art said.

"I'm taking what's mine," Sutcliffe declared. "You can't stop me."

"You know I can," Art said, displaying nothing but ease. Brodie was edging closer, but his proximity was making Sutcliffe twitchy. "You don't want to get into it with me and mine."

"You stay back!" Sutcliffe called out and shook the gun at Brodie a couple of times before aiming at Art again. "You get any closer and I'll put a bullet in him!"

Brodie ceased and there was a tense pause. Zara sidestepped, trying to get a better view of what was going on. The triangle of men was locked in a stalemate. Art and Sutcliffe were only about a foot apart. Brodie was still at least ten feet away. Art's hands were up, Brodie was poised to move, and Albert Sutcliffe had no way out.

"Put down the gun and we'll let you go," Art said. "That's all you have to do."

"Give me the keys!" Sutcliffe insisted.

Brodie exhaled a laugh. "You think we're gonna let you do that? You'll have to shoot us all before you get out of here with that shipment."

Sutcliffe's scowl seemed to be considering his limited options. But his expression became panicked when Art swayed forward. Steadying his aim, Sutcliffe clenched his jaw and hopped on his good leg. He would never get the keys to the van carrying the device. Fighting his way through Art and Brodie was impossible given his injury.

Making a run for it wasn't an option either. There was no way he'd get between the two men and he would never be able to jump the vehicle anyway. It was on the inside, so he'd have to reverse through everyone and pass his own vehicle, which was currently blocking the way. That was a lot of variables for a man who might not even be able to drive at all given his infirmity.

"Think about it," Art said, still using his soft voice. "Be smart. You don't want to fight with us."

"You're right, I don't," Sutcliffe said, shambling back on his one functioning leg. He glanced around, probably considering the allegiances of those left alive. Brodie moved to the side, obstructing some of her view.

"Put the gun down," Art murmured.

But when Sutcliffe spoke again, he seemed to be talking to himself. "I only have one choice," Sutcliffe mumbled. "I need a clean getaway."

The gun popped again and the startling noise made her jump. But her fear became terror when the sound of a body hitting the concrete turned her to ice.

Brodie was still on his feet. Sutcliffe was limping away in the direction of his own van. She pounced forward to see Brodie rushing toward his uncle. Art. He was on the ground and didn't appear to be moving.

"I won't be taken down, you bastards!" Sutcliffe called out. "I'll be back for my money, McCormack!"

She didn't care about him. Her wide eyes were fixated on

Brodie who fell to his knees beside his bleeding uncle. Casting off her shock, she heaved in a breath, and ran across to Art's sprawled form.

Sutcliffe's van started and screeched backwards in a haphazard curve then belted off into the distance. No one hindered his getaway because Art's welfare had become their main concern. Brodie was in a crouch, ripping open his uncle's shirt to reveal a spurting wound on his chest that made her shriek.

"I got it, baby, don't worry," Brodie said to her, examining the wound as she collapsed onto her knees on Art's other side.

Brodie reached over to rip the sleeve off her top, and then pressed the balled fabric onto Art's wound. Hot orbs of moisture hung on her lashes, but she grabbed Art's hand and clutched it to her chest. She had never seen so much blood, but Brodie wasn't worried. If Brodie said he had this then she trusted that.

"Swift is on his way," Brodie said to Art, jerking off his own jacket to bundle it under Art's head. "We're gonna have you out of here in a minute."

"No," Art croaked.

Taking their joined hands out of her cleavage, Art pressed her palm down on the back of Brodie's hand, which was applying pressure to the wound.

"Brodie's right, you're going to be okay," she said, scooting closer to brush Art's hair away from his face while trying her best to smile.

Brodie wasn't even sweating. She was amazed by how together he was. "We'll do an occlusive and—"

"My lungs are shot," Art said and blood dribbled from the corner of his mouth. "There's nothing you can do, kid. This is my one day."

Opening her mouth, she felt the icicles curling around her hands and shoulders. Brodie wasn't worried, but Art, their mentor, he said… his one day. Zara knew what that meant. Brodie had told her that everyone was heading for their one day. Coming to such a conclusion might terrify most people, but Art didn't look scared. His focus stuck to Brodie's and the pure pride glowing from his expression made Zara's already sensitive sinus burn until the spheres of tears rolled over her lower lashes.

Patting their joined hands on his chest once, he lifted his other weak arm up to clasp Brodie's face. "You're my greatest achievement, kid," Art said. "Raising you means I leave this world a better place."

"Shut up, old man. You're not gonna die," Brodie said, batting his uncle's hand down from his face. He tried to turn away from the wound, but Art caught him and forced his hand to stay on hers on his chest.

"You've found your normal, kid. You've got a woman to love, who loves you back, don't be like me," Art said and when he coughed, blood erupted from his mouth.

Tuck appeared from somewhere and dropped down beside Brodie. Zara hadn't seen him arrive. Grief had thawed the ice consuming her and sent it streaming down her face from her eyes, blurring all her senses.

Art was slipping away, his eyelids were drooping, and the color was leaving his cooling skin. She wanted to do something. Wanted to make this better. Wanted someone to make Art better. "Brodie," she whimpered. "Fix this... can you fix this? Please, baby, just..." her sobbing inhale preceded her sucking her lips in around her teeth to silence her wailing.

Brodie wasn't working. Tuck slid the kit from his arm but took nothing from it. Art reached for Tuck's hand and he brought it onto hers and Brodie's over his wound. Blood seeped between all their fingers, dying them and bonding them in this tragic moment that left them all helpless.

Losing Art would devastate the troupe, but it was Art's insistence of pulling them all together that made her even more desperate to hold on to him. Her tears dripped from her chin onto their blood soaked skin. He was the glue that made the Kindred. In such a short time, he had such a profound impact on her. He'd looked after her, tutored her, protected her, and all the while kept the best interest of them all close to his heart.

"Look after each other, you three," Art said, his eyes drifting shut and his words slurring. "You're the Kindred, my legacy… watch… your… back." Each whispered word came slower until with a tiny last breath, his whole body went limp.

No one spoke.

No one moved.

Her crying continued in silence; her tears diluted the blood marring their clasping hands. Paused with their digits twined on the chest of the man who had brought them together. She wanted to call out, to wail, and beg him to come back, but this wasn't her grief. It was Brodie's. Uncertain as to how she should console him, she lifted her attention to his blank expression fixated on the lifeless body between them.

He just stared down at the prone man, like if he looked hard enough, somehow the truth would change. Gradually his brows became tense, they lowered, and the consuming darkness compressed around them all. Tuck was wearing the same concern that she felt, but he didn't venture forth.

Brodie broke the standstill. Removing his hand from Art's chest forced her and Tuck's release as well. Art's hand dropped to the concrete and she felt the need to pick it up again. Brodie swept aside his jacket, straightened out his uncle's form, and shifted onto his knees to begin chest compressions.

"It's no use," Tuck said, trying to pull Brodie's arm, but he carried on working.

"Breathe for him," Brodie said, bringing his eyes up to hers for only a second.

Torn between the inevitable end and Brodie's hope, she trembled for a moment. But she wasn't ready to let go yet, so tipping Art's head back, she held his nose and bowed to breathe for him. Tasting his blood made her chin quiver, but Brodie kept working, so she kept breathing.

After another two breaths, someone came in beside her and grabbed her shoulder to pull her back. Twisting to look up at her attacker, she saw it was Grant and he wasn't acting in malice. There were real tears in his eyes.

"He's gone," Grant whispered to her.

She glanced down to see no sign of life on Art's loose face. Brodie kept pumping his chest, but she leaned over and cupped her hand around his cheek.

"Beau, release," she murmured. Brodie stopped moving, but his hands stayed tense on Art's chest. After another second, his eyes came up to hers, and she shook her head, freeing more tears from her saturated eyes. "I'm so sorry."

Swiping her hand away from his face when she tried to reach out. Brodie surged to his feet and his hand moved to the back of his head. "Rave, we—"

Tuck was cut off by Brodie striding over Art to grab hold of Grant. "You goddamn, motherfucking..." Grabbing the back of his older brother's head, Brodie snatched Grant's throat with his other hand and began to squeeze.

"God, Rave, come on, man!" Tuck said, rushing over to try to break them apart. Grant choked and tried to hit out at Brodie, but his blows had no effect.

"Brodie," she called out, and hurried to his side. Tuck was trying brute force and it wasn't working. "Stop it!" Covering her hand with his, she dug her nails in deep and scratched the back of his hand.

He hissed and whipped around, looming over her with the rage he'd tried to vent on Grant. Unafraid, she finally got her hands to his cheeks to caress and soothe them. "I love you, beau," she whispered. "It's going to be okay. We'll figure it out... What would the chief tell you to do? Huh?"

Some of his anger ebbed, but his focus snapped downward to Art's stained corpse. Crossing to it with his hand in hers, he bent to retrieve the van key from the floor and pressed it into her palm before letting her go. Crouching again, he scooped his arms under Art and lifted his body from the floor. Without explanation, Brodie turned and carried him out of the warehouse.

Tuck grabbed her to pull her around to face him. "I gotta go with him," Tuck said, giving her a shake. "Tidy up here then return to base. Do you understand?"

Nodding, she struggled to regain her senses and glanced back to see that Grant was still here, coughing and clutching his throat. Tuck kissed her cheek then ran out of the warehouse in Brodie's wake.

She took a deep breath and ducked to pick up Brodie's leather jacket. She'd told her love to stay together, so she couldn't fall apart now. "I have to go," she murmured. Sapped and dazed, she attempted to pass Grant, but he snagged her arm.

He appeared vacant and his words were sluggish and wheezy, but she couldn't blame him for being numb. "You know him… you knew Brodie… for how long?" Grant asked.

They'd just watched a man die and witnessed what could only be the start of Brodie's unraveling. She didn't care about assuaging anyone's ego. "I don't have time to answer your questions," she said and tore her arm out of his hold.

He got into her path when she tried to pass him again. "We have to go after Sutcliffe," he said, spurred into desperation. "We have to give him the device. He'll kill us if—"

"Maybe you should've thought about his capabilities before getting into bed with him," she snapped and gave him a shove to move him aside.

Zara got two paces toward the van before Grant spoke again. "Did you take those considerations before getting into bed with my brother?"

His hoarse disapproval made her squirm. She stopped moving because beyond his anger, she deciphered hurt in his voice and Art would tell her to address, not ignore, the issue at hand. She couldn't deny her betrayal, not with everything that had just happened.

"No," she confessed. "I didn't know much about him at all before I got into bed with him. I didn't know he was your brother then."

"Would it have made a difference?"

"To me sleeping with him? Maybe at first," she said, turning a gradual inch at a time until she faced her boss. "I don't think it would've prevented me from falling in love with him though."

In his own exhale of disbelief, he shook his head and glowered at her. "You're in love with him? He's a… he's a monster."

Her anger made her frown and forget any thought of sparing Grant's feelings because she was overwhelmed by offense at his suggestion. "No, he's not. He takes on the responsibilities that men like you won't. He's been ruthless and at times harsh. But he sold his soul so that we could live and be safe… Don't ever forget that." There was no time to deconstruct her relationship with either of the McCormack men. "You can deal with the bodies of Sutcliffe's men, or you can call the cops and explain to them what you're doing here. You wanted to live the adventure and get your hands dirty. Now's your chance."

Brodie was in pain and Tuck had given her a task. Leaving Grant here would buy her some time. So jumping into the van, she drove away from the scene and headed for CI because before she took care of these devices, she had to make sure that no one could recreate the terror nearly sold on this day, the terror that had cost a much-loved man his life.

TWENTY-FIVE

WORKING AS FAST as she could, Zara felt the flames of urgency licking at her heels when she finally got back to McCormack Manor. Her fingerprint worked on the concealed security entrance revealing that she hadn't been as ousted as she thought.

Art's jeep was there with the keys in it, so she climbed in and started toward the house. Another vehicle on the edge of a clearing made her stop the jeep to get out and investigate. Through foliage and rocks, she came to a large open space with a sea view, which was protected on most sides by trees. She heard the sound of a shovel in dirt before she saw anything. The noise drew her attention right and there was Brodie, forty feet away shoveling dirt into a rectangular hole.

Tuck came out of the trees to her left and strode over to join her. "You came," he said. "You take care of everything?"

Concern for Brodie was her priority, but in a distant tone, she answered Tuck's question because the job was still important. Art didn't die for nothing; they had to make it their mission to ensure that.

"I removed the van from the scene and picked up all the plans and paperwork from CI before Grant could get back," she said. "One advantage of his fear of digital exposure is that we can be sure we have everything."

Tuck put a hand on her shoulder. "Sutcliffe won't go quietly. He's going to be a problem down the road."

In awe that Tuck was forward planning while Brodie was still doing manual labor, these men were still in combat mode. But she just wanted to get through this night before thinking about tomorrow. "We'll deal with it when it's more imminent," she sighed. "For now, there's nothing to sell and Grant has no schematics to commission any reproduction. We've bought ourselves some time at least."

"Good. Where is the device?"

She was still fixated on Brodie's shirtless form glistening in the low dusk sun as he worked to fill the hole. He stepped back to wipe a hand over his mouth and Zara noticed the side view of two headstones beyond Brodie's position.

"It's safe." Transfixed by the beauty and the sadness of the sight, her heart swelled for her love's toil. "How is he?" she asked, watching Brodie return to his shoveling.

Tuck exhaled and his arm sagged, causing his palm to skim down her back. "We all discussed our final arrangements, but you never think you'll need them, you know? Brodie's parents are buried there and Art wanted to be at his sister's side."

"Should we help?" Zara asked. The sight of the sole man sweating for his mentor, his father figure, his family, made her inflamed heart shatter as the tears welled in her eyes again.

"He wants to do it," Tuck said. "He told me to leave him… and he's almost done."

"How will we get through this?" she murmured, the weight of anguish dropped through her gut and she almost screamed for the torture Brodie was enduring.

When Tuck's fingers slipped in between hers, she forced herself to look away from Brodie. "Art told us to stick together," Tuck said. "We do that and we'll be fine… But Brodie… he's gonna need you and it might get rough."

Encouraged by Tuck's confidence, feigned as it may be, she fortified herself. "Rough I can handle," she said. "He's tried so hard to push me away."

"Falling for you freaked him out," Tuck said. "Art and I

talked about it. Rave's been like a bear with a sore head since you found out about Quebec. Art says he kept it secret because he knew he'd want to scare you away."

Brodie was a loner and love probably wasn't on his agenda. It hadn't been on hers, neither was a man as intense as Brodie. He was flawed, far more damaged than most other men were. But his demons didn't scare her. She would have to get used to him pushing her. In time, he would learn that he wasn't going to get rid of her, no matter how hard he tried to provoke her into leaving him.

"He failed," she murmured and noted how tired Tuck looked. This day had taken energy from him too. Art had been a rock. Without him, the Kindred would probably flounder for a while, but she was determined not to let it die. "Come here."

Stepping into him, she wrapped her arms around his neck and felt him slump as he exhaled into their hug. They would have to get used to leaning on each other now that they didn't have Art's guiding hand.

She and Tuck held onto each other for a while. When he drew back, he was looking in the direction of Art's grave. Zara turned and noticed Brodie was coming toward them. A few feet away, he brought the spade up and drove it down into the dirt. Crossing the final distance, he snatched the back of her neck with his dirty hand.

Dried blood and dirt covered his hands and arms, but she wasn't deterred. Zara edged nearer and rested her fingertips on the ridges of his abs. "Swift's gonna take you to your apartment," he said. "Pack your shit and bring it here. You're not to leave this house. You understand me?"

"I understand," she said and let him pull her head back so far that she lost her balance. He caught her weight with his hand on her neck and his forearm on her spine. With an open mouth, he tasted her tongue then separated their kiss.

"You're Kindred now," Brodie said and curled his fingers around her wrist. Examining her hand, he had to see that Art's blood was still crusted under her fingernails. But he brought her hand up and kissed her fingertips before transferring his focus onto Tuck. "You watch her and bring her back to me."

"You got it, Chief," Tuck said and after a brief silent exchange, Brodie passed him and marched through the trees toward the house.

"Chief," she murmured, recognizing Art's moniker. With him gone, Brodie would have to step up and take over the head role in the Kindred. He was Art's heir and rightful successor.

Tuck sighed. "Now he has to go inside and tell Bess and the others. He's gonna need time to get through this. You'll have to wait for answers about your relationship. I don't think he's capable of being rational or reasonable now," Tuck said. For now, she had all the answers she needed. Brodie needed her and her place was at his side. "I'll go and get my bike. We'll bring your essentials and get the rest when we can take a car out later."

Tuck walked away through the trees on the route Brodie had just used. When she was alone, she turned toward the graves. Zara walked over and read Brodie's parents headstones beside the fresh dirt.

Lowering to her knees, she exhaled. Opening her hands on the soil beneath her, she opened herself to what her future would be.

"I hear you," she whispered. "You didn't need to leave him to make your point. I do love him, and I know he plays games to test me. And I promise… I'll stay by his side and get him through this. I won't let him sabotage us. I'll abide by priority one because you were right. I'm Kindred now."

TO BE CONTINUED...

Thank you for reading this tale!
If you can, please take the time to review.

~

Ask your local library for more Scarlett Finn novels!

~

For all things Scarlett Finn
check out:

www.scarlettfinn.com

BOOK TWO

The assassin needs an ally... on the inside.

SWALLOW

Kindred Book Two

SCARLETT FINN

OUT NOW!

Made in United States
Troutdale, OR
03/07/2025